A FICKLE FORTUNE

BOOK SIX
THE HAPGOODS OF BRAMLEIGH

CHRISTINA DUDLEY

Cover design: Kathy Campbell, www.kathryncampbell.com

ISBN: 978-1-963408-05-8

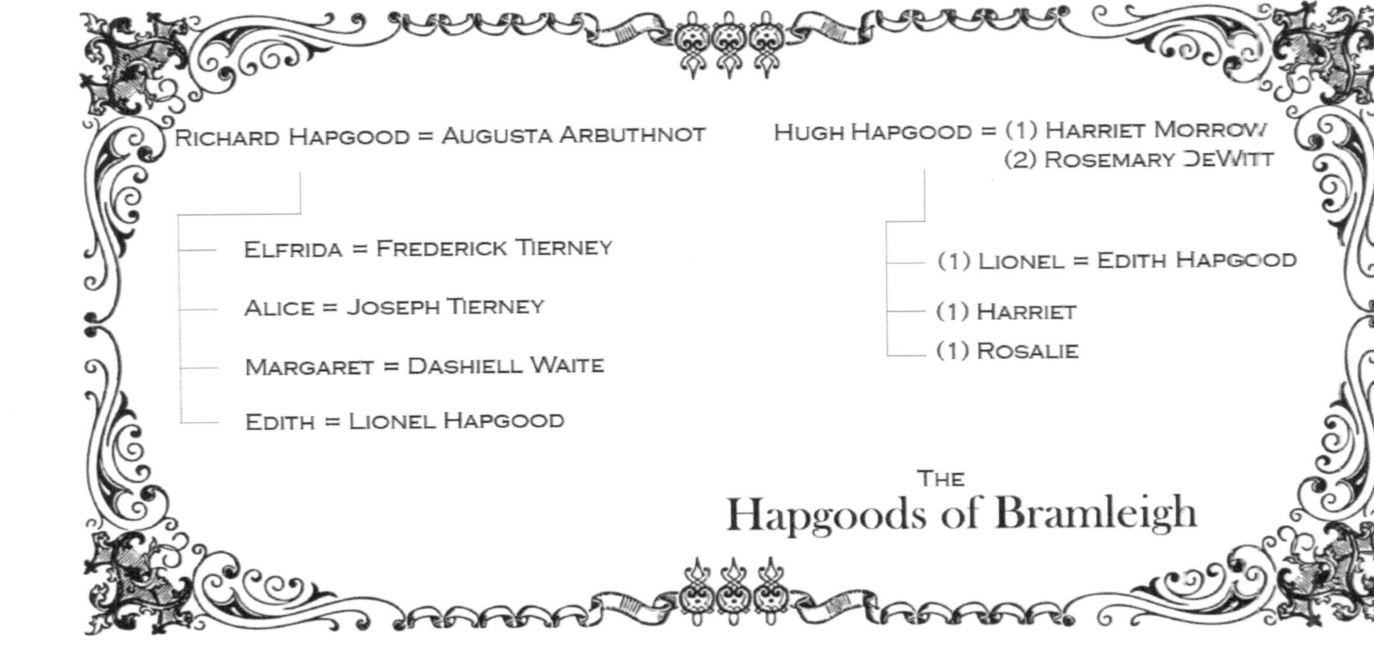

THE
Hapgoods of Bramleigh

CHAPTER ONE

As for learned tutors Noel and St. John,
’Tis common-room knowledge
That of bookish industry
They’re the coal and engine
Of famed Magdalen College.
—Edward Clinkett, *Unpublished Verses* (1814)

“Papa! Papa! Wait!” Eagerly, Harriet Hapgood dashed up behind her father outside the Angel Inn and seized his sleeve. “Did you not hear me calling? Look what I found in the bookshop!”

Laughing, she spun him around, only to nearly choke in surprise. “Why—you’re not Papa!”

To say the least of it. Harriet’s father Hugh Hapgood was in his middle forties, tall and lean and dark, with grey at the temples and quiet fondness for her in his eye. Whereas this man—

This man was young—perhaps in his early twenties. Yes, he was also tall and lean and wearing a parson-grey greatcoat (hence her mistake), but his beaver hat covered hair of a medium brown, and he had blue eyes. Blue eyes which held no quiet fondness for her, but rather surprise and umbrage.

Surprise she could understand, but the umbrage annoyed her and made her brusque. "Pardon me, sir. Quite obviously I would not have accosted you, had I not mistaken you for my father."

She realized later that perhaps telling a young man he resembled her middle-aged father was not likely to soften his heart, for his only response was a tightening of the lips and a jerk of a bow. "Of course. If you will excuse me..."

And then, without waiting to see if she *would* excuse him, he turned and marched into the Angel Inn.

"Well!" she exclaimed, placing indignant hands on her hips. "It was an honest mistake, and he needn't be rude about it."

"Who was that, Hetty?" asked her young sister Rosalie, just then catching up with her, a hand to her bonnet to keep it on.

"I don't know. All I can tell you is, he wasn't Papa, and he wasn't very pleased to be mistaken for him."

"Well, you did clutch at him," little Rosie pointed out. "You probably startled him. But what will we do now? He's gone into the inn, so we can't enter, because what if he is standing there? That would be very awkward."

Awkward indeed! Hetty frowned over this a moment, but then she gave Rosie a nudge. "You go and peek around. He didn't see *you,* in any event. If the coast is clear, let me know, and I will steal up to our room."

The operation worked as planned. Rosie darted in and returned a few moments later, nodding and beckoning. Stifling their giggles, the sisters raced inside and flew up the staircase.

"Heavens, girls," said their stepmother Rosemary when they tumbled into the room. "Here you are at last. It's nearly time for our dinner with Lionel and his friends. You must make yourselves presentable, quickly."

"Hetty grabbed at some young man outside," reported Rosie, earning an aggrieved groan and a pinch from her sister.

"I grabbed him by the *arm*. Because I thought it was Papa," Hetty explained once more, "and I wanted to show him the book I found."

"Very well, very well," said Rosemary, taking a brush to her younger stepdaughter's hair. "Showing your father the book may have to wait until after the dinner, though."

"Who will be there, Mama?" Rosie asked.

"It is hard to say—you know Lionel," replied their stepmother. "I suspect the Clinkett brothers, that friend of theirs Mr. Bailey, and perhaps a tutor or two."

The Hugh Hapgood family was in Oxford, having arrived the day before to deliver their oldest child Lionel for his final year at Magdalen College. Lionel left Somerset with great reluctance because he had recently become engaged to his third cousin Edith. And besides Edith, he would also dearly miss her father Squire Richard Hapgood and the countryside where the squire's estate of Bramleigh lay. Bramleigh, which the Hugh Hapgood branch of the family stood to inherit whenever the time should come. Lionel's parents Hugh and Rosemary suspected that, if Edith had not positively insisted Lionel finish his degree before they married, it would have been impossible for *them* to convince him. But fortunately Edith had plans of her own for the intervening time: she would go abroad with her Arbuthnot relations, studying art first in Rome and then in Paris.

Lionel was not the only one who would miss Edith; Hetty did not much look forward to the winter that lay ahead either, with her ten-year-old sister still in lessons and she herself with nothing on the horizon beyond occasional trips such as this one with her parents. But she was not the type of young lady who dwelt on misery ahead of time, allowing it to overshadow present pleasures. Tomorrow would have trouble enough of its own, as their vicar Mr. Benfield would say, and she meant to enjoy her time in Oxford, the evening's meal included. Hetty already knew the Clinkett brothers (nicknamed Clinker and Clunker by their schoolmates) and looked forward to meeting the third friend Mr. Justin Bailey. Any tutors who joined them at supper would likely be stiff and dull, but as they would surely sit beside her parents she need not bother about them.

For their party, the Hapgoods had reserved one of the larger sitting rooms in the hotel, with food to be brought over from the coffee room, and when Rosemary descended with her stepdaughters, the gentlemen were already gathered. Little Rosie hung back, daunted, but her timidity gave Hetty courage, and she strode in behind her stepmother with lifted chin.

"Mrs. Hapgood. Miss Hapgood. Miss Rosalie," murmured the young men, making their bows. Mrs. Hapgood was plain and pleasing, but at the young men's age it was Hetty who drew their attention. They saw a young lady of medium height and light figure with vivid reddish-blond hair, who might generally be deemed pretty. It was only a closer look that made the young men think she might also be somewhat intimidating, for her blue eyes were perhaps too direct and quick, and her expressive mouth (too wide to be fashionable) often seemed to be holding back amusement or pointed remarks.

For her part, Hetty picked out the weedy, brown-haired Clinkett twins right away, with their prominent eyes and Adam's apples. Clinker (James) gave her a mischievous wink in his usual fashion, and the poetic Clunker (Edward) had his habitual abstracted look. Her smile for them was genuine. The Clinkett brothers proved loyal friends to her brother in his difficulties several months earlier, and she would not forget it.

Mr. Justin Bailey was as short as his three friends were tall—Hetty's eyes came even with his forehead, but he gave her a friendly grin, not at all abashed, and she liked him at once. A relief, given that Lionel, in typical Lionel fashion, had not provided any details about Mr. Bailey, beyond saying, "as a cricket bowler, Bailiwick can't be beat." But even that gave Hetty to understand that Mr. Bailey would be athletic and therefore admirable in her brother's book. More difficult to interpret were Lionel's summaries of his classics and mathematics tutors. Of the former he only said, "Tumwell can be counted on to know a fellow can't always have his head in books," and of the latter—Lionel just shook his head slowly: "Rotherwood."

Hetty's own prejudices regarding academic fellows and clergymen were therefore left to supply guesses about the two gentlemen, and while she was satisfyingly accurate in Mr. Tumwell's case, she was almost entirely wrong in Mr. Rotherwood's.

Mr. Noel Tumwell was pale and slight, bespectacled and earnest, not unattractive with his fair golden hair, and he had a lovely speaking voice that Hetty thought would do well in a pulpit or declaiming speeches in Latin. ("A pocket Apollo with myopia," she wrote to her cousin Edith later.)

And Mr. St. John Rotherwood—well, Mr. Rotherwood turned out to be the very man she had clutched at in the High Street, and Hetty was hard put to hide her chagrin. Of *course* it would be him. Exactly her luck—wait till Edith heard this!

Mr. Rotherwood was, as she knew already, of her father's height and proportions, and Hetty would have called him handsome, had he not been peering so sternly at her, the corners of his mouth turned down. "You would think I was doing something unseemly, like barking at him or blowing my nose on my sleeve," she muttered. With his hat off, she noted his hair was not merely brown, but rather curling and shot with gold.

"He looks like the Bernini *David* Mr. Eldredge showed us a sketch of," whispered Rosie.

Hetty grinned because Rosie was exactly right. Their former drawing master had given the girls a thorough grounding in art history, and Mr. Rotherwood lacked only a sling and five smooth stones to pass for Bernini's young hero, having already the coiffure, the form, and the fearsome marble sternness.

Pressing a hand to her mouth to suppress her amusement, Hetty debated apologizing to the man again for seizing hold of him in the street. But when Mr. Rotherwood only looked away, giving no hint that he chose to remember the incident, she dismissed the idea. Very well—let them both pretend it never happened.

The dinner did not begin successfully. It was not the fault of the food. It was that the presence of their tutors muted the young men, leaving the burden of conversation with their elders. Hugh and his wife made dogged efforts to draw the tutors out, while the younger people kept what passed for respectful silence by concentrating their attention on the meal.

Mr. Tumwell was willing enough to speak and replied in his mellifluous tones that, no, he had not been a tutor long—perhaps a few years less than Rotherwood, "and I expect I will not be one for always," he added. "I am promised a living by an uncle in Hertford-shire, when the incumbent retires."

"Is the incumbent near retirement?" asked Rosemary politely.

"*Nemo enim est tam senex qui se annum non putet posse vivere*," Mr. Tumwell said with a smile. But seeing his listeners' blank faces, he turned to Clinker. "Mr. Clinkett, you would perhaps like to translate?"

"Er—" Clinker set his fork down and cleared his throat. "Could you repeat that, please, sir? Yes, well—uh —excuse me, sir—long vac forgetfulness, don't you know. '*Nemo*'—er—nobody. Nobody is—old enough? Old enough that he—uh—that he thinks he can't live another year?"

"Excellent, Mr. Clinkett," pronounced Tumwell, while the latter feigned collapsing in relief. "Cicero, putting words in the mouth of Cato the Elder."

Hetty cast the tiny tutor an admiring look. Imagine being so learned you were able to crack jests in Latin! "That's wonderful, Mr. Tumwell! How very apt. I do wish girls learned Latin. I should like to read some of the classics—read them in the original, I mean, though I very much enjoyed Pope's translation of *The Odyssey*."

"Oh, my dear!" cried her stepmother, who dearly believed in education, "I did not know. Surely Mr. Benfield would not object to taking you on, if you like. It would be a good activity for you this winter, with Lionel and Edith gone and Rosie at lessons all day with the new governess."

Hetty's face lit up. "May I, then, Mama?"

"Latin with Mr. Benfield!" protested Lionel. "Whatever for, Het?"

"Your sister loves to learn," his father said, somewhat severely. (Lionel was not known to share this love.)

"Well, I suppose," her brother conceded, "as something to do. Something to occupy her *voracious* mind."

"How disgusting you make it sound," Hetty observed. "It seems to me hardly fair that young men of our class often attend university, whether they want to or not, and whether they appreciate it or not, while young ladies who would very much like to..." She trailed off, remembering they were in company, after all, and she and Lionel could save their wrangling for when they were alone. Therefore she was as surprised as the rest of the gathering when Mr. Rotherwood spoke.

"If young ladies were permitted at university, Miss Hapgood, what else would you like to learn?"

"Oh!" Her color rose. "I suppose—everything and anything. The only subjects my governesses taught which did not interest me were sewing and embroidering. I didn't much like drawing, either, but only because I was so wretched at it."

"Did you enjoy arithmetic, then?" With his stony remoteness, Hetty thought it was like being questioned by an Oracle.

But there was no mistaking the sincerity of her reply. "I *love* mathematics. In fact—" she leaned forward to catch her father's eye at the far end of the table "—Papa, you will never guess what I found in the bookshop this afternoon. I meant to show you, but—" Her gaze flicked to Mr. Rotherwood, and she almost, almost thought she saw a glint of humor there, but it was gone (if it ever was) before she could decide. "—But we had to come to supper."

"You will have to show me later," Hugh said, knowing his wife thought they should turn the conversation back to their guests, but Bailiwick blurted, "What was it, Miss Hapgood? If you can say, in company."

"Certainly I can say. It was a copy of Wingate's *Arithmetic*. Eleventh edition, Papa, with additions and clarifications by Mr. John Kersey."

"So?" asked her brother. "You can't walk ten yards in Oxford without tripping over a pile of textbooks."

"But that wasn't all," she rejoined roundly, "although you ought to be more excited, seeing as you are reading mathematics. There was lots of writing in the margins that wasn't all calculations. They were little comments on the text. And then, on the endpapers were cunning little sketches! One of Sir Isaac Newton and one of Edmund Halley and others of people I hadn't heard of, but I am determined to learn more about each of them. Wait till I show Edith! She will love them. The sketches, I mean."

Whatever her listeners had been expecting, this was not it, and Hetty felt smug on seeing their interest. Even the marble Mr. Rotherwood appeared thoughtful. Or perhaps he always appeared thoughtful.

"Halley was the Savilian Professor of Geometry at Oxford in his time," he said, "before he became Astronomer Royal."

"Imagine!" cried Hetty.

"Did you show the sketches to the bookseller?" her stepmother asked.

"I did, Mama. But the clerk said Oxford students had been scribbling in books for centuries (though he admitted the sketches were very fine), and, if anything, it made the book less valuable for being defaced. So I bought it."

"For the mathematics or for the scribbles?" was Mr. Rotherwood's dry question.

"For both, naturally," Hetty answered brightly. "And for the history of it. The eleventh edition was printed in 1704. It said so on the frontispiece. So I may not be allowed to attend university, but now I can continue to study mathematics alongside a student from over a century ago and several famous mathematicians. Or, at least, the representations of famous mathematicians."

"Was there a name written in the book, Hetty?" Rosie asked.

"There was not. But there will be. For I intend to write on the inside cover in bold, black letters: Harriet Hapgood. Maybe in another hundred years someone will buy it again and think *I* was the one who wrote all the notes and drew the pictures."

Rosie shivered. "It's almost like finding and reading someone else's letters. Aunt Lavinia once said that reading other people's correspondence unauthorized was like rifling through their wardrobe when they were out of the room."

"Did she?" Hetty laughed. "What a disturbingly specific analogy. It almost rings of personal experience."

But she had held the stage long enough and turned deliberately back to Mr. Tumwell: "I fear we have gone very far astray from our original topic. You were saying your uncle's living is in Hertfordshire. Is that where your family hails from?"

He took her hint and made a speech of decent length until they could move on smoothly to Mr. Rotherwood, who was neither as chatty nor as forthcoming as the classics tutor. They learned only that Mr. Rotherwood did *not* come from a large family and had only a few relations scattered hither and yon, with whom he was not in contact, apart from his mother. "I was named to curry favor with a great uncle on my father's side," was the one enticing tidbit he shared. "Supposedly he was a traveler who once visited the isle of Patmos."

Seeing Rosie's puzzlement, her father said, "The apostle John wrote the book of Revelation while on Patmos."

"Then why are you not named John?" she asked shyly.

"I am." His sternness softened a measure, as he regarded the small, freckled girl. "My name is pronounced 'Sinjun,' but it is actually St. John. Saint John. Two distinct words."

"Ah. I am called Rosie, but my name is actually Rosalie. One word, though."

"Clunker is grateful for Mr. Rotherwood's truncated name, however," his twin Clinker spoke up, "for it led to one of his most successful verses, one that was pinned up in the JCR—junior common room—for a month."

"It's there still," said Lionel. "It just got covered up by handbills and records of bets and sporting scores."

"May we hear the verse, Clunker?" Hetty begged.

Clunker gulped. "It was—er—it was written for a particular audience."

"Just the clean bits, then," grinned Clinker.

"It isn't a matter of cleanness," Clunker retorted with a scowl. "It's just that—Mr. Tumwell and Mr. Rotherwood, I took the liberty of using your Christian names, rather than your family names."

Rotherwood said nothing, but Tumwell nodded agreeably. "I am glad to hear it, Mr. Clinkett. For little rhymes with Tumwell besides 'dumb-bell.' Please do not hesitate on my account."

With another glance at Rotherwood (which was not acknowledged), Clunker cleared his throat. "I will just give you the first bit about the tutors:

As for learned tutors Noel and St. John,
'Tis common-room knowledge
That of bookish industry
They're the coal and engine
Of famed Magdalen College."

"Rhyming 'St. John' with 'engine' is marvelous!" Hetty praised him.

"I thought at first of rhyming 'Rotherwood' with 'rather good,'" Clunker admitted, warming to the subject, "but then I would have to use 'Tumwell' instead of 'Noel,' and—well—"

"There you have the dumb-bell problem again," finished Tumwell placidly.

"If only you were the mathematics tutor, Mr. Tumwell," said Hetty. "Then he might have tried 'Tumwell works his sums well.'"

"That was quick of you," Clunker declared. "Maybe you should try your hand at poetry, Miss Hapgood."

"Did you think of any other rhymes for 'St. John,' Mr. Clinkett?" spoke up Rotherwood.

Clunker flushed. "Well—er—just imperfect ones."

"Such as...?"

"Such as—such as 'henchmen' and 'linch-pin.' But—but—I won't bore the company with those verses."

"I should like to see a copy of the full poem," Rotherwood said lightly, but everyone could hear the command in it.

"Certainly, sir," strangled Clunker, picturing himself gated for the entire Michaelmas term.

His friends must have arrived at the same conclusion, for they fell rather silent, leaving Hugh and Rosemary and Mr. Tumwell to carry the lion's share of the conversation for the remainder of the evening.

Chapter Two

Be happy in all the enjoyments
this dead season can afford.
—Anonymous, *The Triumphs of Fortitude* (1789)

Hetty was right to think their time in Oxford would be the highlight of the autumn for her. When they returned home to Patterton, the fun of telling her cousin Edith about their visit was quickly followed by the gloom of watching her prepare for her trip to Rome and Paris.

"To think," Hetty said, as she perched on Edith's bed and occasionally handed her things to be stuffed in her trunk, "you will see the *originals* of so many things Mr. Eldredge showed us! Not for you, charcoal and pencil sketches or engravings printed in the newspapers. You will see real, true Michelangelos and Leonardos and Raphaels—"

"I hope we can gain admittance to some of the private collections," interposed Edith, holding up a handful of paintbrushes and tossing aside the most worn. She was a slender girl, barely older than her cousin, with curling black hair and observant eyes. The two of them had shared lessons with governesses and seen each other nearly daily for the previous six years, and Hetty loved her scarcely less than Lionel did.

"Yes, but your uncle Alwyn can talk anyone into most anything," Hetty pointed out. "So I would be astonished if doors didn't fly open for you. And even if they don't, there is Rome itself to see! The churches and fountains and buildings and arches and ruins. We have seen Piranesi's prints, but you will see the city itself!"

Pausing in her activity, Edith came and sat down beside her, taking her hands. "Yes! Oh, Hetty—I am so very, very grateful for this opportunity, and for my aunt and uncle's generosity in taking me with them. That is, mostly my aunt's generosity, since Uncle Alwyn didn't bring a penny to their marriage. I will be sure to learn everything I can and draw everything I can and write down everything I can, to share it all with you and Lionel. And in return you must write to me everything that happens here. You know my mother and father are little better correspondents than your brother. If not for you, Hetty, I will know absolutely nothing the entire time I am gone."

Hetty promised again, adding, "Though I very much doubt there will be much to tell. 'Dear Edie: Got up in the morning. Weather: fair. Re-read two chapters of a novel about a young lady imprisoned in a castle. Went to bed early. Next day: ditto. Day after: ditto ditto. Yours faithfully, Harriet Hapgood.'"

Edith laughed and gave her a playful push. "Only you could make utter dullness entertaining. Well, I give you leave to make up whatever you like, as long as you do write to me. And, while it will be too expensive to send back many drawings, there is one sketch I will be certain to enclose: Bernini's *David*."

"Oh, do," urged Hetty. "Send two copies. Because I suspect Lionel and his friends would like to post one in the common room and see if anyone else notices the resemblance." She sprung up, making her best stern face and twisting into the sculpture's posture. "There! I sling a stone at you, Edward Clinkett, who dare to include me in a poem. And one at you, Lionel Hapgood, for being such a mediocre scholar. And another at you, Harriet Hapgood, for taking hold of my sleeve in the High Street without my express permission."

"How I wish I had been there to see," Edith said for the dozenth time. "This is what I mean—you bring everything to life, even humdrum little things. I will miss you dreadfully."

"Speaking of humdrum little things," the wicked Hetty answered, "I have had a letter from my cousin Caroline Sidney." Caroline was Hetty's cousin on her late mother's side, who a few short months earlier had thought herself engaged to marry Lionel, only to be disappointed by his attachment to Edith.

"She wrote to you?" breathed Edith. "Does this mean she has forgiven you all?"

"Not a bit of it. In fact, I would hazard she is still smarting about it." Hetty shrugged. "Aunt Lavinia is still angry, too, for she didn't even send greetings. But the Sidneys must forgive us, sooner or later. I think what finally compelled Caroline to take up a pen again is that she has something new to crow about. She is going to have that season in London her father promised. You know she abandoned the idea when she was 'engaged' to Lionel, but now that *you* are going to marry him, it has been taken up again. They will go up to Devonshire Street in November when Parliament opens and stay through the spring, she writes."

"I am glad for her," Edith said with decision. "I do not blame her at all for being in love with Lionel and only wish she might find someone a fraction as dear this winter. If only you might join her, Hetty! You could certainly help her with that, as you did me. Didn't Caroline invite you once?"

"She has invited me again," Hetty admitted.

"That's perfect! I really think you owe it to her to find a replacement for Lionel," Edith persisted. "After all, it was by your intrigues that she was compelled to give him up."

"He would have found a way to escape his engagement to her, some way or another. I just expedited matters," replied Hetty. "And I am not yet so forlorn that spending several months with Caroline tempts me."

"Not even a little?" wheedled Edith. "Why should the glittering world be deprived of your skills at dancing and conversation? And why should I be deprived of potentially more interesting letters?"

"But spending time with only Caroline for company is a high price to pay for such letters, Edie. Don't you recall? When she was in love with Lionel, she could not be brought to think or talk about anything or anyone else. It was so fearfully tedious!"

"Her chatter did give me a headache. But—well—I doubt she will talk of him anymore," Edith pointed out reasonably.

"True. But she will substitute something or someone equally dull." Throwing herself across Edith's bed, she added, "I will try to be interesting, even without Caroline and London. Perhaps I will write you a story inspired by the marginalia in my mathematics book."

"That would be charming," said Edith, who had of course been shown the copy of Wingate, that she might pronounce the sketches delightful. "It could be about a girl who buys an arithmetic textbook and falls in love with its former owner."

"Or falls in love with the picture of Edmund Halley," Hetty suggested, "and begins to haunt the Queen's College in hopes of encountering his ghost."

The girls fell to laughing again, before the housekeeper Macready marched in to announce Hal would be coming for Miss Edith's trunks within the hour.

"Yes, yes. Thank you, Macready," Edith said, springing to her feet and resuming her task. But she grinned at her cousin. "Well, whatever you do write, I will promise my best illustrations for it when I return. Now help me again, or I will forget to pack half of what I need."

A month passed. A month in which Hetty found herself writing to Edith a letter that sounded alarmingly like the one she had predicted. She rose in the morning. She breakfasted with her parents and Rosie. She rode with or walked Rosie to Bramleigh for her lessons. She returned to Patterton to read or to assist her stepmother in household tasks or to study a little mathematics on her own. She practiced the pianoforte for forty-five minutes. Twice a week she visited the vicar Mr. Benfield to learn some Latin, but these lessons were rather awkward because his two boarder pupils were more advanced than she, younger than she, and male. If she could possibly help it, she avoided sewing. She rode or walked back to Bramleigh to fetch Rosie. She ate with her family. She went to bed. The next day it began again.

"My dear," said Rosemary Hapgood to her husband one evening when they had retired, "have you noticed that Hetty is excessively bored?"

"I had not," Hugh replied. He was lying on the bed, propped on his elbow, watching Rosemary brush her hair. "She seems cheerful enough."

"Just because she does not mope about the house or snap at us does not mean she is not bored."

"Well, we expected she would miss Edith."

"And so she does. And it will be some months before Edith returns." Her eyes met his in the looking glass, and she spun on her little cushioned stool to face him directly. "I have been thinking,

Hugh. You know that the Sidneys invited Hetty to join them in London."

"Of course. And that Hetty showed little interest."

"That was when they first invited her. I think she would go now."

He chuckled, lying back and crossing his hands behind his head to contemplate the coved ceiling. There was a crack in the plaster like a raised eyebrow. "Are you trying to marry off our seventeen-year-old daughter?"

"Not at all. But here she is, a clever girl, buried in the country with no peers and few opportunities. I teach her housekeeping, and she does what I ask, but her heart is not in it, as Margaret's was. I tell you, Hugh, it is a waste of her!"

"And you think attending dinner parties and assemblies with her cousin—who is most definitely husband-hunting—would be a better use of her?"

Rosemary examined the back of the silver hairbrush Hugh had given her for a wedding present six years earlier. How much littler the children had been then! "Hetty has a good head on her shoulders," she resumed. "Even if her cousin Caroline is wild to catch a husband, that need not have anything to do with our girl. And watching the process would provide her a great deal of interest and amusement, I daresay."

"Suppose someone were to offer for her?"

Rosemary's brow furrowed in thought. "It is hard to imagine Hetty in love. What man would be half clever enough for her? And she has too good a head on her shoulders to fall for any London fop or to entangle herself with some fortune hunter. You might even tell

Lavinia that Hetty's portion will be smaller than Caroline's—that would soon make its way about. And it would both please Lavinia *and* ensure the gentlemen pursue Caroline instead of our Hetty."

"So it would. You are very persuasive, wife."

"May we tell her, then? That we would like her to join the Sidneys in town?"

"I think, Rosemary, we will leave it up to her. She is not shy in speaking her mind. But if she asks—when she asks, we will say yes. Now come to bed."

Some weeks after this parental conference, Hetty received another letter from Caroline Sidney.

16 Devonshire Street
London

17 November 1814
Dear Hetty,

I thank you for your last letter and wish you all the joy of learning more arithmetic and Latin, though I cannot understand why you would want to. Mama thought I did not read your letter aloud to her because I was hiding secrets, but when I did read it to her, she said now she understood, and I might keep future letters to myself, if they contained so little of interest.

For my own part, since I last wrote to you, I have been

to a musical play, a concert, a card party, and a ball! There is endless amusement here. For the concert I wore my ivory silk with the clocked hem and believe I attracted some notice, though I was so cross because I set my fan down beside me, and this girl sat right down upon it and cracked it! I had to forgive her, however, because she turned out to be a Lady Sylvia Stanley and an earl's daughter! She is quite beautiful and quite rich, and Mama says she is an acquaintance worth cultivating. Since you will not come to London (will you come to London?), I will make friends where I can, and a friendship with Lady Sylvia will at least open doors to me. She is sure to have Almack's vouchers and might possibly put a word in for me...?

To the play and the card party I wore my new gauze gown with the long sleeves and ribbon through the bodice, but I saved my favorite light blue sarsenet for the ball, and how glad I am that I did because I danced every dance, and some of my partners were even handsome.

I am home this morning because I hope one of the gentlemen might call, and in the afternoon I will go for an airing in Hyde Park with Lady Sylvia. She mentioned having trimmed a bonnet with white ribbon, so I am going to do the same to mine.

I will write again when I have time, but you mustn't expect much because we are very busy. Papa and Mama remind you that you are welcome to come, and Mama goes so far as to say she cannot understand why you will not oblige us in this instance, when we were so very good to you all in Lionel's predicament.

Your cousin,
Caroline

It came as a pleasant surprise to Hetty that Caroline would repeat her invitation. To do so, amidst such a whirlwind of activity, meant she must genuinely wish for her company. The question was, did Hetty wish for hers?

"Perhaps she has grown through suffering," Hetty told herself. "She was quite cast down when she learned Lionel did not love her, and now that she cannot have him, she must take note of other people's existence. This Lady Sylvia, for example."

It was not that Hetty yearned to talk about clothing or gentlemen or earl's daughters, but the rest of it sounded tempting enough. Now that things were so quiet.

Her life was so quiet.

Everything was so quiet.

Yes.

She would like to go to the theatre, the park, concerts, suppers, balls. Aunt Lavinia's presence would sap the experiences of a good deal of the fun, but some would still remain. And perhaps, when

Hetty tired of the social round, they might let her play tourist with her uncle Wellington. She had still never seen the British Museum at Montagu House, nor Westminster Abbey, nor the Tower. And she ought to see the Rubens ceiling in the Banqueting House for Edith's sake. Hetty knew better than to suppose her cousin Caroline would be interested in any of this—it had only been Lionel's presence that persuaded Caroline to visit St. Paul's, after all. But one never knew. Perhaps another one of Caroline's suitors might share Hetty's interest in history and Caroline would come along for his sake.

Yes.

She would go. If her parents let her.

"Of course you may," her stepmother told her at dinner, after a smile and a glance at Hetty's father. "As soon as we can have a few gowns made. It would be too much to ask Lavinia to take you to appointments with a modiste."

"The gowns would likely be more fashionable if they were made in town," Hugh pointed out, and it made Hetty giggle to see her grave father expressing such a thought.

"And more expensive," Hetty observed. "Oh, Papa—please don't make me go to dressmakers with Aunt Lavinia. I don't care a bit if I'm wearing last year's styles. Not to mention, it would add to the Sidneys' pleasure if they could tell me I am out of date."

That succeeded in making him smile. "Very well. You're very considerate to think of their pleasure. You will go up in the best that the Taunton dressmakers and milliners can contrive."

"Thank you, Papa."

Only Rosie looked woebegone. "Papa, Mama—may the rest of us visit sometime?"

"Certainly we will. We cannot go months and months without seeing our Hetty, or Lionel, for that matter. Have no fear."

The next day Hetty's dull letter was sent on its long journey to Rome, with the flourishing postscript that her next would come from London. In her excitement she even wrote to Lionel, saying, "I know you would a hundred times rather rusticate in Somerset than spend a fortnight under the Sidneys' roof in Devonshire Street again, but I assure you I am very glad of the chance. I even intend to discover hitherto-overlooked finer points in our relations and to dance with a duke or two (if I can manage, as Caroline says we have no vouchers for Almack's...*yet*. She is apparently hard at work trying to remedy this, however, by making up to some earl's daughter)."

And to the family's utter amazement, Lionel troubled himself to reply. Perhaps he was trying to inculcate a new habit, in order to write to Edith on her travels. "I don't know about dukes, Het," he scrawled, "but I suspect there will be one wealthy nabob who would not cut you. Be on the lookout, but don't go grabbing everyone in the street."

"What can he mean?" wondered Rosemary.

"It bears repeating," Hetty sighed, "that I grabbed Mr. Rotherwood the tutor because I thought he was *Papa*, not because I am in the habit of 'grabbing everyone in the street.'"

"Just the same," said little Rosie, looking up from her embroidery hoop, "do try, Hetty, to keep your hands to yourself."

Chapter Three

**Some are born great, some achieve greatness,
and some have greatness thrust upon 'em.
—Shakespeare, *Twelfth Night*, II.v.1166 (1601)**

St. John Rotherwood was not born a man of marble.

If anything, he was born playful and trusting, but his family circumstances quickly taught him the world was neither a playful nor a trustworthy place. One of his earliest memories formed the basis of this understanding: a trip taken with his pale, pretty mother to see his grandfather.

"What brings you back, Anne?" demanded the fearsome old man with his ramrod posture and voice of ice. Mother and son had been ushered into his presence in the library of a house larger than St. John had ever seen, full of heavy, solemn furniture and servants that crept about.

"It is good to see you, Father," St. John's mother said. When he did not respond, her breast heaved in a silent sigh. "I am sorry to say, my husband Mr. Rotherwood is very ill."

"And what is that to me?"

"Father, I know you never approved of my marriage—"

"To that hopeless dreamer? No, indeed. And I see his son resembles him thoroughly. No Holt to be seen in that boy. All Rotherwood. All rotten wood. Let us hope there is some Holt within, hidden away."

"Father, please—" St. John's mother pulled him behind her. If she had hoped the sight of the little boy would arouse affection and interest, she was mistaken.

"Fortunately for our family," continued Sir Gordon, "your older brother married good stock. That wife of his has borne him a strapping son."

"I am glad for him," Anne Rotherwood replied stiffly.

"As am I. He made wiser choices than you."

St. John felt his mother's hand tighten on his. She was trembling. He edged closer to her and leaned his curly brown head against her legs. Whether his touch gave her courage, or whether it merely resigned her to her task, when she spoke again, her voice was humble in a way he had not heard before.

"You are right, Father. Gordon made wiser choices. You will say again that I have made my bed, and I must lie in it, and I know this. I only ask that you might have mercy on the child." Releasing St. John's hand, she wound her own in his curls. "My husband has not been able to work—"

"Has he ever worked?" her father scoffed. "You mean to say, I gather, that you have run through his income and are now at the mercy of creditors."

"...Yes, sir."

"And you require rescue."

"...Yes, sir."

"You were haughty enough when you left. No patience then for a father's advice, and you waved your hand at the thought you might ever come to grief."

"I was mistaken, sir." She bit the words out as if her jaw hurt her.

Seeing her so thoroughly chastened, the old man took a long, satisfied breath and looked the boy over again. "What is your name?"

St. John's mother had instructed him not to speak to his grandfather unless addressed, so the boy glanced first at her before replying, "St. John Rotherwood, sir."

"Well, St. John—" (his grandfather drew out the name mockingly, "Sin...Jun...") "'The fathers have eaten sour grapes, and the children's teeth are set on edge,' as they say. You are not a Holt. You cannot enjoy all that a Holt may enjoy, but some arrangement can be made for your schooling." When his daughter burst into tears, he added. "I will pay the school directly. I would not trust your spendthrift husband with a farthing, Anne. St. John, you must learn what you can and prepare to work to support your mother. Do you think you can do it?"

He swallowed. "Yes, sir." He was only five and had not yet had schooling of any kind. But he already knew his alphabet and numbers and could make out some words in the few books left to his parents. (Most of these were unsold copies of his father's volume of poems, published at his own expense in earlier days.) St. John understood that his grandfather was making some great concession, for which his mother was both relieved and resentful, and he was vaguely aware of his own unhappiness. He did not like to see his pretty mother cry, and he had never heard her addressed in such a cold manner. Even St. John's father, who had been ill for as long as he could remember, spoke kindly to his wife.

Therefore, St. John's chin came up, and though he said, "Thank you, sir," there was no thanks in his eye, and he thought he would like to come back and kick this man when he was older and bigger.

But that moment never came.

St. John was sent to board at a school in a neighboring town, where he received a decent education accompanied by a decent amount of hardship. The other boys began by calling him "Charity" (for his status at the school) and "Rottenwood" (unwittingly taking a page from his grandfather's book) but ended in liking him, respecting his fists, his intellectual abilities, and his energy. St. John might not look like a Holt, but the Rotherwoods were a handsome breed, if not long-lived. St. John's father died before the boy's tenth birthday, bequeathing him a lifelong dread of falling ill. To avoid his father's fate, St. John pushed himself to his athletic limits: boxing, rowing, fencing, running, playing cricket.

Nor did he forget his grandfather's charge. He learned as much as he could, matriculated at Magdalen College, Oxford, when he was sixteen, and took a first in mathematics. He was soon elected a probationer and then a fellow, and he carefully sent half of his fellowship home to his mother. Three more years rolled on, and St. John had little expectation of change.

From time to time his mother would mention his more fortunate Holt relations in her letters, and the yearning and envy in her tone grew. One time it was that his grandfather's younger sister had died childless and passed her considerable fortune to her brother ("As if he needed more money," St. John's mother sniffed). On another occasion Anne noted that her brother's wife had come into an inheritance of her own from some distant cousin. ("Money attracts money," was her comment on that turn of events. And St. John thought ruefully to himself that the converse was also true: poverty attracted poverty.)

So while his Holt relations grew richer and richer through no efforts of their own, he and his mother faced a limitless vista of shifting as best they could for themselves. Anne's brother wrote once to her of possibly giving St. John a living, but when it came open, Gordon passed it to someone else with no explanation. Another time Anne showed St. John a brief letter containing the sentence, "I have encouraged my father to reinstate you in his will," but nothing more was ever said of that either, and the Rotherwoods had no way of knowing if Gordon followed through or forgot that as well.

It was not that misfortunes never befell the Holts: a year after the lost living, Gordon wrote to his sister to say his wife and new infant had died after a difficult lying-in, but almost before Anne could pity him, he announced that he had engaged himself to another woman and would marry her when his year of mourning was complete.

"This new woman is a wealthy widow, naturally," Anne told her son with a sigh. "As if Gordon needed another penny. I hope she will make a good stepmother to his son. How unfair life is. If only *you* might marry, St. John!"

To which he replied lightly, "That isn't likely, is it?"

"Perhaps one of the students will have a rich sister come to visit," she persisted, "and she will fall head over ears in love with you and will pursue you. You are a catch, you know—if money be no object."

"Are there times when money is not an object?" he teased.

And indeed, no rich sister visiting her brother had yet shown any interest in St. John Rotherwood, after learning the handsome young man was a penniless tutor with no prospects.

Why, the closest he had ever come to being pursued was when the sister of Lionel Hapgood took hold of him outside the Angel Inn, and even she had mistaken him for someone else. But St. John had been exhilarated that night, after he overcame his surprise. He so rarely talked to anyone of the female sex, and Hapgood's sister—what *was* her name again?—had proven not only clever but interesting. As vivid in personality as she had been in coloring. It would be a pleasant thing if life held more of such experiences.

But no, life would jog on. Michaelmas Term would turn to Hilary Term would turn to Trinity Term would turn to the long vacation, and then it would start over.

Even the first express that arrived from his mother just after term began did not alter his outlook.

St. John. Your grandfather Holt has died of stroke. I will be traveling to Dorset to offer what comfort I can. You had better wear a black armband. Do not expect any bequest from his will, as you know he considered his duty done in sponsoring your education, and I do not think your uncle succeeded in changing his mind. A.

St. John doubted his uncle even remembered to take the matter up with his father, so there was no disappointment when this turned out to be the case. The estate in Dorset and Sir Gordon Holt's fortune and baronetcy passed intact to his son, the new Sir Gordon. And term went on.

But the *second* express from his mother, only another fortnight onward, was nothing less than a bolt from the blue, striking the very foundations of his world.

My darling, I write in haste. I must go into Dorset again, for calamity has struck our Holt relations. So soon after the death of your grandfather, I now learn my brother Sir Gordon and his son have been killed in a hunting accident! All is confusion. I know no more at present, except that Gordon's second marriage had not yet taken place. I will write to you from Glennard when I have learned more. A.

What Anne Rotherwood did not mention in this hasty note was so obvious to both of them that it needed no mentioning. That is, with no heirs male from the Holts surviving, the baronetcy was now extinct. And because Anne's now-deceased brother Gordon had no living wife or children, what remained, specifically the estate of Glennard and St. John's grandfather's and uncle's vast fortunes, now devolved upon Anne herself, unless her brother's will specified otherwise. And why would it? A man so careless of the concerns of his nearest relations would be unlikely to bequeath all he had to the Church or to a faithful valet.

The Rotherwoods were penniless no more.

It was fortunate St. John had finished with his students for the day, for he likely would not have heard any knocks upon his door, so deep in thought was he. He spent a good long time staring blankly at nothing until the shadows stretched.

In his mind's eye he saw again the long drive to Glennard, beginning in bricked gateposts and culminating in a grand pile of a house, sunlight glancing off its many windows. It was probably not as enormous as he recalled. He had been very young at the time of the visit, when the world loomed larger. Nevertheless, Glennard could not possibly be smaller than the bedroom, office, and sitting room assigned him at the college, nor his mother's shabby lodgings in Avebury.

He tried but could not remember his grandfather's face—there was only an impression of height and age and coldness—and as for his uncle and cousin, he had never even met them, despite his uncle's passing flickers of interest in Anne and her son. The estrangement had been complete. From the day Anne had brought her son to Glennard to the time of her father's death, she had not set foot in Dorset, and now she was gone twice in the space of a month! What a revolution in circumstances!

A vengeful man might have rubbed his hands in glee as he pictured triumphing over the relations who had disdained him, but St. John was too dazed for that. Besides, any resentment he felt at the age of five was too faint to be revived at this late date. However little the Holts had regarded him, they had nevertheless paid for his education. Doubtless he and his mother would have ended in the workhouse without the allowance his grandfather made. But how the old man must be turning in his grave to have Glennard and the immense Holt fortune fall into the hands of the despised Rotherwoods!

And what would happen now? Would his mother take up residence at Glennard, and would she expect him to join her, leaving Oxford to live in a place he didn't know, among people he didn't know? He shuddered at the thought. Perhaps he could convince her to let it to tenants.

In the week that followed, no one at the college was any the wiser about Rotherwood's reversal of fortune. He met with students, he appeared in the senior common room, he ate his meals, he attended service. In short, he behaved as he had every other day he had been a fellow of Magdalen, although he thought he would snap with the suspense of it.

At last, at last, a letter came from his mother, by normal post.

Glennard, Dorset
10 November 1814

My dear son,
Forgive me for the delay in posting this letter, but there did not seem to be any purpose in writing until I had news to share.

In brief, the will is read and the lawyers have gone. Glennard is mine, as is my brother's fortune, which includes, of course, my late father's wealth. Or I should rather say that all of this is now ours. *When I think how half my life (and all of yours) has been spent in struggle and anxiety to keep the wolf from our door, it strains credulity. I still think I will wake to find myself in my cramped rooms at Avebury, wondering how I will buy enough coal for the winter. But no—here is the draft in my hand from the banker, for more money than we have seen in twenty years, and he assures me there will be another just like it every quarter.*

I hope you will forgive me, but I do not want to live at Glennard. The memories are too painful still. If you desire to live there, I would understand, but you must know I could not breathe under that roof. Instead, I would make me a willow cabin at your gate and call as often as I could bear to, my darling.

If you do not desire to live there, I will instruct the solicitor to find us a tenant until we decide what will be done with the place. I think it will be a simple enough matter—with the peace, many men who distinguished themselves in the war are returned and in search of fine homes. Perhaps when you marry you may reclaim it. But this is what I mean to say, St. John—I want to weep and clap for joy when I think that now you may do so—marry and have children. Nay, now every girl in the kingdom will set her cap for you, and not one of them will be more than you deserve. When I think how many years my brother's son had the world at his feet, while you had nothing! Now I am determined you will have everything you have lacked. For you are my sole heir and I am enclosing a draft for you. Everything I have always wanted to give you I must make up in arrears, my dear, dear son.

For the near future, I have taken a house in town at 28 North Audley Street. I beg you, if you can see your way to giving up your fellowship and your duties, do come join me. I think you had better, darling, because the gentlemen in Dorset were already lining up for me, and I expect news of our good fortune will not take long to reach London. I have no intention of doing anything foolish, for all my hopes and dreams are bound up in your future, but your company would make it much easier to keep fortune hunters at bay.

Your loving mother,
Anne

If any students had been peering through the second-floor windows of the New Building that frosty November evening, they would have seen the marble tutor's face crack into a grin. Still more inconceivable, they would have witnessed the man whooping, capering, tossing his cap. No longer would he be the linchpin holding the mathematical wheels to the axle-tree of Magdalen, as Edward Clinkett put it in his poem.

St. John Rotherwood was for London.

Chapter Four

Are my discourses dull? Barren my wit?
—Shakespeare, *The Comedy of Errors*, II.i.90 (c.1616)

Her new gowns made and her trunks packed, Hetty arrived with her father at the Bolt in Tun a fortnight later.

"A happier occasion, this," muttered Hugh, when they descended from the coach to the tumult of the innyard.

"Indeed," she agreed, remembering with a shiver their arrival at that same inn some months earlier, when her brother lay feverish and in danger of his life. "Although I am sorry not to have Edith with us this time."

Fog and smoke lay heavy over London, and she drew her cloak tighter about her, staying close to his side in the bustle of Fleet Street. A few heads turned to inspect the fresh, neat girl, who gave them back look for look. If she could not draw what she saw, as her cousin

Edith did, she could at least describe it in words. Through her letters home and to Edith, she could share this adventure with her family.

The Sidneys' house in Devonshire Street was as Hetty remembered: a short distance from the developing Regent's Park, four storeys in height, faced with cream stone and beribboned with railings and carved ornaments. It lay in a quieter, newer area of town, and the Hapgoods were surprised to see more than one carriage drawn up in front.

"Hetty! Uncle Hugh!" cried Caroline Sidney, rising to greet them when they were shown into the drawing room. She was a very pretty girl of average height, with a fine figure and golden hair, and Hetty thought that she seemed somewhat recovered from her ill-fated attachment to Lionel. It was not only her cheerful demeanor—it was also the presence of three gentlemen and another young lady, whose call the Hapgoods' arrival interrupted.

"Brother. Harriet," was Lavinia Sidney's more subdued welcome, but her smile was complacent as she gestured at the other guests. "We have company, you see. Allow me to introduce Lady Sylvia Stanley, Sir Keane Montridge, Mr. Charles Pickford, Mr. Philip Elwood. This is Mr. Hugh Hapgood and Miss Hapgood."

Hetty had to admit that, however much self-interest contributed to Caroline's admiration of her new friend Lady Sylvia, it had not led her to exaggerate. If anything, calling the earl's daughter "quite beautiful" failed to do her justice. Lady Sylvia was a vision. Brown-gold tresses artfully dressed, frankly enormous eyes of pansy blue, flushed cheeks and rosebud mouth, a figure of just the right height and proportions—Hetty positively stared at her and wished with all her might Edith could have seen her. Heavens! To unite in one individual such loveliness, rank and fortune struck Hetty as rather unfair to the rest of womankind. Only when she was able to tear her gaze from Lady Sylvia's face did she realize she could spend another half-hour admiring the cut and style of her clothing. My, my. Caroline wanted to be *friends* with this creature? To spend the season in such a person's shadow?

As for the gentleman, Sir Keane had his baronet's title to hug, but this was ranged against the disadvantages of age (he appeared older than Hetty's father) and a weak chin. Mr. Pickford was by far the handsomest, but as her aunt Lavinia merely fluttered her fingers his direction when making the introduction, Hetty surmised he must also be the least eligible. And Mr. Elwood fell somewhere in the middle, both in age and looks. No finger flutter for him, and Aunt Lavinia smiled his direction *almost* as warmly as she had Sir Keane's.

"Miss Hapgood is my late sister's daughter," spoke Lavinia to the visitors, "and we rejoice that she has agreed to spend a few months with us. I do not see my sister's family as often as I would like. They live in Somerset now, quite buried away."

Everyone murmured appropriate responses while Hugh grimaced at the veiled reproach.

"We must try to entice you to remain, Miss Hapgood," Mr. Elwood said politely. "Do you enjoy dancing and driving as much as your cousin?"

"I haven't ever driven," she admitted, "but I like dancing very well."

Hugh and Lavinia excused themselves after a few minutes, leaving the others to converse, and Hetty was soon sorry for her father's absence, for while he was not a talkative man, what he did utter was sensible and interesting.

"So you have come from Somerset," said Mr. Elwood, starting anew.

"Yes," she replied. "But I spent the early years of my life in Crawley, like Caroline."

"I see. Crawley. In Sussex."

This was a good start, Hetty thought. Basic geography of England. "Yes. In Sussex. Where do you hail from, Mr. Elwood?"

"Surrey. There have been Elwoods in Surrey since shortly after the Conquest."

"Fancy that."

"Have you ever been to Surrey, Miss Hapgood?"

"I have only passed through, on my way to Sussex. Lovely country."

"We are glad you've come," Sir Keane put in.

"I'm glad to be invited," Hetty answered politely. It surprised her a little that they were bothering with her, when Lady Sylvia was on hand. *But I suppose* every *man can't marry Lady Sylvia,* she thought. *They're probably wise to keep several irons in the fire.*

"You didn't tell us your cousin was so lovely, Miss Sidney," Mr. Pickford offered, examining Hetty through lowered lids in a manner she supposed was meant to indicate he was a dashing blade who left ladies' hearts in ribbons.

"What would be the use?" countered Caroline airily. "Hetty has already told me she isn't here to find a husband."

"Indeed! So say they all. But…supposing a husband finds her?"

Caroline tittered, and Lady Sylvia gave the slightest smile.

"Childwen, childwen," intoned Sir Keane. "Miss Hapgood, you must ignore them. You and I know there can be many weasons to come to London…"

Hetty darted a glance around the room to see if they were having a laugh at her expense, but no—they all gazed upon Sir Keane as if he had spoken in a completely usual way. Did the aged man really lisp as if he were just out of leading strings?

Very well. She would ignore the impediment too. "Indeed, sir. Although I have been to town twice before, there remain a great many things and places I have yet to see."

"You've been to town *two* times," marveled Sir Keane, drawing smiles. "So many as that? Indeed, then, two visits cannot begin to encompass the wonders of our capital. You speak twuly. I suppose you long to be pwesented at St. James?"

"Oh—not particularly. I haven't the right sort of thing to wear."

"Then you dweam of acquiwing vouchers to Almack's?"

"I already said Hetty isn't looking for a husband," Caroline interjected, a trifle cross at the mention of Almack's. Despite her hints, Lady Sylvia had not yet offered to speak to the patronesses for her.

"No, thank you," Hetty answered.

Sir Keane chuckled. "I see. No Mawwiage Mart for you, Miss Hapgood. But surely you plan on attending Lady Auwowa Wobillard's wout?"

"I—I beg your pardon?" asked Hetty.

"Don't tell me word of Lady Auwowa's wout has not weached Somerset!"

"I'm afraid it hasn't."

"We will be there," Caroline announced, to Hetty's relief. "Lady Aurora was at school with my grandmother Morrow and was kind enough to include us."

Ah. Au-ro-ra. "I am glad to hear it," Hetty said, with what sincerity she could muster. "I don't mind admitting that I've never been to a rout either. Anyone's rout."

"I don't like them," Lady Sylvia pronounced suddenly. "I won't go."

"Of course you will," Caroline urged. "Because everyone will be there. *Everyone.*"

This last must have held special significance for Lady Sylvia because the rose in her cheek deepened.

Good manners dictated that no one acknowledge this, and Mr. Elwood obligingly turned the subject. "I say, have you heard the latest about Collingford's horse…"

The gentlemen stayed another quarter-hour, and Hetty decided the entire visit would not furnish enough interest to fill a paragraph.

But when the footman showed them out, things picked up accordingly. Caroline swooped down upon Lady Sylvia and waved Hetty closer.

"Well, Hetty? What did you think of them?" her cousin demanded.

Hetty forced a neutral expression. "They seemed pleasant."

"Bah! You didn't like them. I could tell." Caroline turned to Lady Sylvia. "Hetty is very hard on people."

Hetty thought this was rough—she would have liked to make her own first impression, even if what her cousin said was true.

"I don't want to be hard on people!" she protested. "I don't mean to be. Caroline, if you like them, I will like them too. So there. Which one do you prefer? If one of them may have the good fortune to win you, I will certainly try to love him."

"One of *them*?" cried Caroline disdainfully. "I don't love any of them." Her voice tightening, she took Lady Sylvia's hand. "Why should I want any of them? I told you, Lady Sylvia, about my Broken Heart."

Lady Sylvia nodded. She knew about the Broken Heart.

"You mean Lionel, I suppose," Hetty said reluctantly.

"Of course I mean your brother. He was my first love. I only hope he won't be my last."

Hetty made a pained face. "I hope not either. At least you are only eighteen, and London must be full of gentlemen more interesting than my brother."

"He treated me very badly."

It was going to be a long winter if Hetty could not nip this in the bud. She took her cousin's other hand. "I cannot defend him, Caroline, except to say there were miscommunications and misunderstandings. But he is very happy with my cousin Edith and hopes you will be very happy as well."

With deliberation, Caroline removed her hand from Hetty's grasp. "I suspect you're happy about Lionel choosing Edith. I know you prefer her to me. Had it been Edith inviting you to London, she would not have had to ask three times."

"Oh, Caroline," said Hetty helplessly. "Don't be angry. I *did* want Lionel to marry Edith, but only because they have known each other so long and are so well-suited. That doesn't mean I don't want you to find someone who makes you supremely happy as well! And I am sorry it took me so long to make up my mind about coming. You know how it is—I am not as easy with other people as you are. Now, please—tell me about some of the other gentlemen you've met."

Lady Sylvia and Caroline exchanged glances, and the earl's daughter pinkened again.

"There is *one* gentleman," ventured Caroline. She and Lady Sylvia looked at each other again, as if to decide if Hetty should be let in on the secret. Lady Sylvia gave a tiny nod.

"There is *one* gentleman," Caroline began again, more boldly, "whom we haven't met, but whom every girl in London hopes to meet."

"Ooh! That's more like it," Hetty said in relief. "Do tell. Is he handsome like Mr. Pickford, yet wealthy and titled like Sir Keane?"

"They say he's handsomer and wealthier," said Caroline. "But not titled."

"A 'Mister,' then. Very well. I prefer misters myself. I don't see all the fuss."

"Though he's already been given a nickname by gossip," Caroline added eagerly. "The Marble Millionaire."

"The what?"

"The Marble Millionaire," she repeated.

"Why?" asked Hetty. "Did he make his million quarrying marble? Or sculpting Bank of England paperweights?"

"No, no," said her cousin impatiently. "The marble refers to his demeanor. They say he's quite stiff and heroic looking."

Lady Sylvia nodded. (Really, for all her beauty, the girl hardly spoke at all, and Hetty began to understand why the gentlemen had been willing to talk to Miss Sidney's country cousin.)

"And is he really worth a million pounds?" Hetty marveled. "I doubt even the Prince has as much in his exchequer."

Caroline gave a shrug. "Oh, likely not, though supposedly he—or rather, his mother—came into two enormous inheritances at once."

"I see. Some poetic license has been allowed," sighed Hetty. "'The stiff fellow with the rich mother' doesn't have quite the same sound, does it?"

The two girls frowned at her. She was not getting into the spirit of things, and Hetty felt herself in danger again. If she was going to spend several months as the Sidneys' guest, she must make a better effort to please. A *sustained* effort to please.

Perhaps Edith's suggestion was a good one. If Hetty had sundered Caroline from her First Love, then she really owed it to her to help her find a Second. It would make Caroline happy, and a happy Caroline would be more pleasant for everyone. Beyond that, it would go far in restoring Hetty to her aunt's favor, which would also make the winter more comfortable.

I'll do it, she thought. *If Caroline wants to meet this Marble Millionaire, I'll do what I can to bring it about. Not that it will do much good—I'm sure he'll take one look at Lady Sylvia, and marble will call to marble, and that will be the end of it.* Under ordinary circumstances, Hetty rather prided herself on her ability to invent successful schemes and arrange things to her own liking, but the competition provided by Lady Sylvia might prove too great to overcome. Nevertheless, the effort would be made. Such a goal would provide zest to her visit. She only hoped this person was a worthy fellow. If he turned out to be as much a booby as the three gentlemen callers, Lady Sylvia was welcome to him.

Feeling a satisfied glow spread through her, it was not very difficult for Hetty to smile and look eager. "In any event, I am excited to hear more of this man who is the talk of the town. Is everyone in love with him? Or is he already engaged to a duchess?"

She could tell from Caroline's raised eyebrow that her sudden interest was suspect, but the subject was too absorbing to resist. "He is not yet engaged, that we know of, and has only so far been seen once or twice at various places, and always in the company of his mother. But—yes—he has caused quite a flutter and we are all *dying* to be introduced when the opportunity arises. We hope he will be at Lady Aurora's rout," Caroline added. "She told Mama he and his mother were invited."

"And what is the name of this paragon of eligibility?"

"Rotherwood. His mother is Mrs. Anne Rotherwood, and he is Mr. St. John Rotherwood."

The two girls had the unexpected gratification of seeing Hetty thoroughly and sincerely astonished. Her eyes widened and she had to make several attempts to speak, but when she finally succeeded, their satisfaction proved fleeting. "But I know him! I know that man! I mean—I have met him. Been to dinner with him. It must be the same person, for it isn't a common name, is it?"

Lady Sylvia and Caroline were too nonplussed by this announcement to muster a reply straight away, and Hetty rushed on. "*This* is what Lionel meant! He said I would meet some wealthy nabob in London who wouldn't cut me." She laughed in delight. "Why—isn't it wonderful? Mr. Rotherwood was Lionel's mathematics tutor at Magdalen. Poor Lionel—he must have had to get a new tutor, but this is the first I've heard of it because Lionel never bothers to tell us anything. 'Marble Millionaire' indeed. The 'marble' part is certainly apt. I thought he looked made of marble myself! Because he was so stern. Fearfully stern. My sister Rosie hit the nail on the head when she said he looked like Bernini's *David*. What do you think?"

"You *know* Mr. Rotherwood?" Caroline asked, faint.

Hetty colored, then, just perceptibly. "Oh—I should not have stated it so decisively. It is absolutely true that we dined with him when we brought Lionel up in October. Had dinner with Mr. Rotherwood and another tutor Mr. Tumwell and some of Lionel's friends—but that's all. Just the one meal."

"But would he remember you, if he saw you again?" pressed her cousin.

Hetty's color deepened. "I suppose so." She didn't really want to tell them how she grabbed the man in the street. "I wouldn't presume upon it, though. I mean, I would hesitate to make an introduction for you. I myself would not—I won't be putting myself forward, in any case."

"Why ever not?" Caroline demanded, while Lady Sylvia almost frowned.

"Well—" Hetty held up her palms helplessly. "He's not...friendly, exactly. He's marble, remember? I would rather wait and see if *he* would like to continue the acquaintance."

Even as Caroline huffed in disgust at her lack of cooperation, Hetty remembered the plan she had just made to get Caroline the man she wanted. *But I didn't know it would be* Mr. Rotherwood *she wanted! I don't know if a man such as Mr. Rotherwood can be easily got!*

But their displeasure convinced her she had better make the effort, in any case, and she hastened to amend, "No, you are right. If Mr. Rotherwood knows so few people in town, perhaps he wouldn't mind if I presumed a little. Lionel didn't think he would, at any rate. He might not freeze me, for Lionel's sake. Therefore, I—will certainly be happy to make the introductions if need be and to do all I can."

She was rewarded with Lady Sylvia nearly smiling and Caroline putting an arm about her waist. "Dear Harriet, how helpful of you. Now you must tell us everything you know of him..."

Considering that Caroline used only to talk about Lionel when she was in love with him—Lionel this and Lionel that—talking about somebody else must be viewed as an improvement, Hetty decided. At least Mr. Rotherwood wasn't Hetty's brother. But she hoped when they saw the man they would have new material to discuss because Caroline managed to wring an entire hour of questions and speculation out of the very, very little Hetty knew of him.

She was plied for a complete and minute description (for which Hetty substituted a complete and minute description of Bernini's *David* because, frankly, Mr. Rotherwood had grown blurry in her memory), as well as a thorough account of everything the tutor said at the dinner, which wasn't very much.

It was all rather exhausting, and Hetty briefly considered asking her father to take her back with him to Somerset. Considered and rejected the idea. Because, however trying it would be to marry Caroline off, at least it was something to do.

Yes, she told herself again as she went to sleep that night, she would stay. Stay and behave herself. Because how hard could that possibly be?

CHAPTER FIVE

I am in name and fame with the very best.
—Shakespeare, *Henry IV, Part II*, II.iv.1321 (c.1598)

By the time St. John Rotherwood arrived in London, he was a famous man. Not by sight, of course, for few outside Oxford knew what he looked like, but what he looked like hardly mattered.

"Half London dreads your arrival," his mother announced when they were closeted alone in North Audley Street, "and the other half wants to marry you."

She was richly dressed in blue-black silk, her fading blonde hair ornamented by a matching feathered head-dress, and this unexpected transformation struck him more than her words. Seeing his expression, she pirouetted before him. "My family may have cast us off decades ago, but I have affected some level of mourning. Though I am not calling it mourning. It's more of a...becoming solemnity."

"It is not the dark colors which surprise me," he replied gravely. "You are more...dazzling than I am used to."

"So I am," she laughed. "We are wealthy now. Why should I not be allowed to enjoy it, after so very many years of deprivation? But the dark colors serve a defensive purpose as well, St. John. For I am the most wanted woman in England. Do you know a man as young as thirty proposed to pay his addresses to me already? And another as old as seventy?"

"And what did you say to them?"

She pouted. "If you have to ask, I ought to punish you by saying I am to be married next week."

"Would you like to marry again, Mother?"

"Not to any of the men likely to ask me now. If one would have approached me when I was the aging Cinderella of Avebury, I would have been more inclined to listen. Though I confess the attention is flattering, if insincere."

"If you are already so hounded, I can see why you are happy I've come."

"Exactly. And this is why half of London is sorry you've come. You will be my companion and guardian in society, I hope. There are already bets laid, I hear, in several clubs, as to when and to whom I will give in."

St. John absorbed this in silence, absently fingering the black armband around his own sleeve.

"It's a proper mathematical problem," his mother continued. "One you would enjoy. For the odds change, of course, depending on if you or I marry first."

"Are they also betting on me, then?" he asked quietly.

"They are. You see, if I marry first, the odds of whom you may marry plummet, for fear that all my money will be absorbed by my new husband and any family he might have. If you marry first, however, the gamblers predict I will make a large settlement upon you, and then my own chances at remarriage dwindle accordingly."

This drew a smile. "Does no one think we might *both* marry well? There is a great deal of money, after all. Enough for ten families to live comfortably, much less two."

"Ah, St. John, ten modest families might live comfortably—twenty, even—but so few people are modest in town, it seems. Our new fortune in this environment would likely only be enough to get two or three of the worst debtors back on their feet." Smiling, she reached for him and patted his sleeve. "To your question—no. No one seems to think we might both marry well. There are probably better odds that we will both marry ill. So many fortune hunters about, you know, of both sexes. Ones who have dug themselves into bottomless financial pits. They cannot help but hope we will rescue them from their own profligacy. I am taken to be an innocent fresh from the provinces, and *you*—well, you are thought likely to have as little knowledge of the world as a monk. The Rotherwoods: a country widow and her academic fellow of a son! We are ripe to be taken advantage of."

His aloof aspect gave way to a surprisingly boyish grin. "If we are so vulnerable, Mama, we must provide what protection we can for each other. What sorts of society dangers do you propose to lead us into?"

"Oh, anything and everything! Dinner parties, concerts, plays. And I have already decided we will present our united front for the first time at Lady Aurora Robillard's rout—if all London wants to stare at us and try to win the ring, we should show ourselves to as many as possible at one time, thus to give everyone a fair start."

Rising, she compelled him to his feet, and put her arm through his. "In the meantime, let me show you the house and your rooms."

"You have found a dazzling new setting for your dazzling new self," he said, as she led him into the passage. "Who has arranged all this?"

Anne waved an airy hand. "Oh, my late brother's solicitor gave me the name of an agent in town. A Mr. Pinckney. Mr. Pinckney found this house. Mr. Pinckney hired the servants. Mr. Pinckney arranged where I will bank."

"What a helpful man."

She made a face. "Helpful? I suppose so. One might also call him officious. High-handed. He seems to think I will squander everything and make a fool of myself, if not for his good advice. It is Mr. Pinckney who told me of the betting books and the fortune hunters, and it is Mr. Pinckney who implied I was an innocent who must be protected. I think he intends to *supervise* me."

"Shall he supervise me as well?" asked St. John, when he had seen the dining room, the breakfast room, the morning room, the parlor, and the library.

"He will certainly take the measure of you," his mother answered, leading the way to the second floor. "He asked that you might be present the next time he comes, which will be tomorrow noon. Mr.

Pinckney insists on calling weekly." She pressed a fond hand to her son's cheek. "But look at me rattle on. You must be tired from your journey and all the change and uncertainty of the last few weeks. Let me show you your rooms."

As promised, the solicitor Mr. Pinckney was announced promptly at midday. The Rotherwoods had finished their breakfast, and St. John spent a satisfying morning arranging the library for his own use, his books neatly alphabetized on the shelves and his writing materials spread on the walnut desk. Not that he had anyone to write to, really. His Oxford colleagues were naturally amazed and disturbed by their fellow tutor's apotheosis into one of England's most eligible bachelors, and they grew reserved around him. Not an approachable man to begin with, by the time of his departure, St. John had begun to avoid the senior common room. Only some of his students continued to treat him as they always had—students like Lionel Hapgood and James Clinkett. But he supposed that was because they were reasonably well off themselves, and his newfound riches neither allured nor daunted them.

From his mother's comments, St. John expected to find the agent a desiccated, aged, scolding sort of man, so Mr. Pinckney came as a surprise. For one, he was in the prime of life, with an upright figure and intelligent expression. For another, he neither condescended nor flattered, merely making his bows and saying, "I am pleased to make your acquaintance."

"Thank you for all the preparations you made here in town," St. John responded, indicating a seat.

This met with a wry nod. "It is in my best interests, naturally, to manage the Rotherwood account well."

"Mr. Pinckney tells me we will also have solicitors clamoring for our business, St. John," put in Mrs. Rotherwood with a mischievous smile. "Therefore he must remain on the *qui vive* if he hopes to keep us."

"Just as you must, madam," he countered, unperturbed. "For no fortune is so vast that it cannot be lost, and if yours is not carefully shepherded, you will find that suitors of both the business and the marital variety will vanish in a twinkling." He balanced his hat carefully upon his knees and observed St. John with candor. "Mrs. Rotherwood has told me plainly that she means to make a splash this winter. May I ask what you hope for yourself, Mr. Rotherwood?"

It was a matter St. John had given much thought to over the past several weeks. A man more used to wealth, rank and privilege might have resented the solicitor's question as impertinence, but resentment did not occur to one so recently penniless and future-less.

Rising, he went to lean over the fireplace, resting an elbow on the mantel and taking up the poker to jab at the embers.

"Mr. Pinckney, I believe you know I have been an academic fellow, a mathematics tutor at Magdalen College. I never expected anything of this sort to happen, and, to be frank, I envisioned life going on much as it had to this point. I saw myself quiet, single, living in my chambers, and sharing my meager fellowship with my mother to the end of my days."

"And now, sir?"

St. John replaced the poker and turned to meet the man's gaze. "And now I suppose I would like to explore the greater possibilities open to me."

"You mean to say you would like to explore the life of a man of fashion?" prompted Mr. Pinckney, one eyebrow arching.

"Yes."

"And all that that entails?"

Mrs. Rotherwood leapt in here, rapping her embroidery hoop against her other palm as if it were a tambourine. "Yes, Mr. Pinckney! St. John must have everything his heart desires. Everything a young man of fashion should have."

"Clothing, horses, vehicles, club memberships,...gambling debts?"

"Everything!" insisted St. John's mother, with another rap of the hoop. "And why should he not?" Turning to her son, she added, "You must not let Mr. Pinckney overawe you, St. John."

St. John's boyish grin flashed again and was gone. "Thank you, madam. But nor must I let *you* dictate what I might require. For starters, Mr. Pinckney, I think we might dispense with the gambling debts. Having both studied and taught mathematics, I am well aware that gamblers do not face favorable odds. Though I wouldn't decline a game of whist. No house, you know."

"*You* are wealthy enough to gamble for amusement, not for gain," protested Mrs. Rotherwood, who now took to pointing her needle at her son for emphasis.

"Madam, I could find no amusement in playing losing odds."

"You might *open* a gambling club, then," she insisted. "A Brooks's or a Watier's. Then you would *be* the house, and the odds would favor you."

"You seem determined I pursue a career of dissipation."

"I admit it would make me happy," she admitted, "for a little while. I want you to have everything my brother Gordon's son would have had. Don't you understand, St. John? I want everyone to envy you. I want you to *spend*."

"You needn't fear—I am perfectly happy to spend money on other things. Just not gambling." He thought he caught a glimpse of approval in the solicitor's eye, but it vanished into professional blankness soon enough. "For instance, I will indeed need new clothing, Mr. Pinckney. But no vehicle or horse of my own, I think. My mother and I can share the Holt coach and hire at the stable. And never mind the club memberships for now."

"Oh, St. John," sighed his mother, disappointed in his moderation.

Mr. Pinckney nodded thoughtfully, however. "Mr. Rotherwood, I am aware that, of the quarterly draft your mother received, she made over a significant portion to you. Will that be sufficient to cover your tailoring needs, or will you need more?"

"I should be quite the beau if it were *not* sufficient," observed St. John, bemused. Leaving the fireplace, he wandered to the window to peer down into North Audley Street. A maid was beating out a carpet on the stoop opposite. "No. It will suffice. Mr. Pinckney, you may be relieved to learn that, apart from squiring my mother about and attending the theatre and some lectures, I have no other ambitions at present. Or none that will require additional outlays."

The solicitor ventured a measuring look at Anne Rotherwood. "Madam, I would like to speak practically to your son now about...other things a fashionable man about town might encounter."

"Have you not already?" she returned. She pulled her stitch through and cocked her head to study it. "When you brought up gambling and horses and such? But I suppose this is your stiff, lawyerly way of saying you would like to talk to him about the expenses of debauchery."

He bowed at this, not the least bit embarrassed by her candor. "Mrs. Rotherwood, as your son's allowance comes from you, he may wish to be made aware of any—boundaries—you place around his expenses."

"I place no boundaries," she declared.

St. John gave a silent chuckle and turned from the window. "You don't mind then, if I drink myself into the gutter, or set up an establishment for a mistress?"

She twitched at this. "Well, of course I would rather you did not, St. John, but I cannot help wanting to give you as much latitude as possible. You, who have never, to this point, been able to indulge yourself."

"You see how it is with her, Mr. Pinckney?" asked St. John.

"I do," replied the solicitor. "And permit me to say, Mr. Rotherwood, it might have been a stroke of fortune that you *had* no fortune, when your character was being formed."

"Oh, well," she retorted, "if you two are going to band against me! However, I am not as hopeless a mother as you think, Mr. Pinckney. The very reason I dictate no boundaries to St. John is that I know he can be trusted. Trusted not to turn ne'er-do-well, nor to squander our money on vanities or speculation, nor to take up with swindlers or expensive opera dancers."

"How can you be so certain?" murmured St. John. "Perhaps I have only lacked the means to misbehave."

"Perhaps," conceded Anne. "But perhaps not. This is the only way we can determine. I suppose if you begin to do all those things Mr. Pinckney fears, he and I will revisit this discussion. But until then, I mean to give you your head."

Mr. Pinckney held up his palms. "Very well, then. Mr. Rotherwood, I suspect many young men in London will think you the most fortunate person they know. And if you cannot think of ways to spend your money, your new acquaintances will be glad to assist you. As your mother's solicitor, I have no power beyond her commands, but I cannot help offering one piece of advice: that being so moderate yourself, you would do well to avoid extravagant companions. They may not ask for loans outright, but a common tactic is to request that you co-sign for their debts, promising you that they will repay you shortly."

"I thank you for the warning," answered St. John. "Again, as a mathematician, I am well aware how interest compounds and have no desire to place myself at a moneylender's mercy. I will take care."

"You see?" demanded Mrs. Rotherwood. "St. John is too clever for all that. No—the chink in his armor will be a girl," she sighed.

"He has had no opportunity to fall in love as yet, and I only hope he will select an appropriate bride. I did not marry wisely, St. John, but I hope you might."

"Although we were not rich, Mother," he answered, "I hope you never regretted marrying my father."

"Mm," was her noncommittal response. "Let me just say I was not as *prudent* as I might have been, when I was young. As I trust you will be. You see, it is only by choosing someone of equal wealth and rank that you can be certain she loves you for yourself. A poorer woman will want your money, and a lowlier woman will covet your station."

His only reply was a bow, not wishing to discuss his marriage prospects or lack of experience in front of their man of business. But his mother went on. "I think you will have your choice, and I also think, with a mother's pride, that you are the equal of any girl in the kingdom. Why, a duke's daughter is not too good for you."

"By all means, let it be a duke's daughter," observed Mr. Pinckney mildly. "Only let the dukedom be not already mortgaged to the hilt and his grace fled abroad."

Chapter Six

There is a squeeze, a fuss, a drum, a rout,
and lastly a hurricane, when the whole house is full
from top to bottom.
—A. L. Barbauld, *Letter*, 20 January (1779)

"Is he tall?" Caroline asked, fidgeting with her gloves and fan. "Will we be able to see him over the heads of other guests?"

The Sidney carriage was making its slow progress through Mayfair, joining the crush of other vehicles headed for the Robillard rout.

There was no need to ask her cousin to whom she referred. Hetty mentally replayed the scene in the High Street of Oxford and answered, "He is a deal taller than I am. Perhaps near to Lionel in height." And such was Caroline's excitement that she did not bother to wince or throw Hetty a reproachful glance for mentioning her

Lost Love. The same could not be said for Hetty's aunt Lavinia, whose bosom swelled in remembered indignation.

Hetty estimated it took an hour to go the ten or so streets to Portman Square, but her sincere suggestion that they could reach their destination more quickly if they descended and went on foot met with a laugh from Caroline and more grimacing from Aunt Lavinia. *Behave yourself, Harriet Hapgood.*

Caroline was nothing short of glorious that evening. Her golden hair was piled atop her head and curled, and the gold-embroidered overskirt of her spotless white gown glinted and flashed when she moved. Hetty, on the other hand, had chosen a muted ivory mull that would almost have been plain, if not for the pattern of green leaves woven along its neckline, sleeves, and hem. If she was going to help Caroline get a husband, she intended to do the thing properly and fade into the background, as much as a fairly pretty girl with red-blonde hair could. Not that she need worry, she supposed, for Lady Sylvia was sure to eclipse every other girl present.

She had given much thought as to how she would approach Mr. Rotherwood, whenever she should see him, and had formed one plan for if he acknowledged her and another for if he didn't. Although he was a stiff, unapproachable man, Hetty had a deep fund of confidence, born of a lifetime of success interfering in the lives of her immediate family. She could crack that marble, given the chance. Just see if she couldn't! But whether she could make him prefer Caroline to Lady Sylvia was another matter. In the end, it would be easier altogether if another eligible gentleman were to catch her cousin's eye. A second-place finisher who tried and failed to woo Lady Sylvia. Ordinary men were likely to be child's play in comparison to a man who'd taken a first in mathematics.

The Robillard home glowed like a house afire, so many were the torches and candles illuminating every window of its four storeys. Music and the hum of voices spilled from the open double doors, and Hetty had never seen so many elegant people. When the footman opened the coach door and unfolded the steps, Caroline clutched her hand, giving a squeal of delight, and Hetty grinned at her.

"Girls, girls," Lavinia Sidney admonished as she was handed out.

"How beautiful everyone looks," Hetty exclaimed. "Even the people who aren't beautiful!"

"That doesn't make any sense at all," answered Caroline.

Hetty didn't bother to explain, only gathering her skirts in hand and following her aunt and cousin up the front steps. The moment they passed inside, the close-crammed throng enveloped them in a blanket of warmth, making her glad of her fan. Plying it vigorously, she looked about her.

"He's here," she uttered, at the same moment that Caroline hissed, "Is that him?"

Indeed, St. John Rotherwood was not hard to find, as he stood at the top of the staircase with nearly every eye fastened on him. He was just as Hetty remembered: tall, heroic, curling brown hair, marble attitude. On his arm hung an older woman in dark blue silk, whom Hetty supposed was his mother.

Those nearest the favored pair were smiling and bowing, scraping and simpering, to Hetty's mind. An assortment of older gentleman, bustling mamas, and eager debutantes. Hetty gave especial attention to the debutantes and was heartened to see none of them were as pretty as Caroline. Lady Sylvia would be more than enough to contend with.

Would Mr. Rotherwood be the sort of man who looked beyond the surface, drawn to the quality of woman within? If he were satisfied with surfaces, Lady Sylvia must win. If he wanted more, Hetty could not guess whether Caroline or the earl's daughter might have the preference. Who knew what, if anything, Lady Sylvia's monosyllabism hid? And, as for Caroline, Hetty was hard put to specify what exactly was within her. After all, when her cousin thought herself in love with Lionel, he absorbed her entirely, and she could hardly be brought to think about or discuss anything or anyone else. Therefore, if Caroline began to think herself in love with Mr. Rotherwood, would he swell to fill that same vacuum? And if he did, would he view this as a good thing? He might, if he were a vain man. (And Hetty had to admit he had some cause for vanity, especially now that such beautifully tailored clothing hugged his sculptural person.) For a vain man, a young lady who reflected admiration at him from all sides like a hall of mirrors would be a dream come true.

"We must make our way up the stairs," Caroline urged.

"Absolutely everyone here is trying to do the same thing," Hetty pointed out. "Suppose we were to hang back and wait until the others have had a go at him?"

"Then we would never meet him at all," her cousin retorted. "For it isn't as if everyone will be introduced and then *walk away*. They're certain to hang about, and then the crush will only get worse and worse. I see Lady Sylvia is nearly to him and will anticipate us. Come on!"

With a sigh and a shrug, Hetty lined up behind her cousin as Mrs. Sidney began pushing. The plans she had formed would likely require revision, since Hetty had not envisioned straggling into his orbit, rumpled and perspiring. And doing so after he had already been introduced to the flawless Lady Sylvia. Estimating that climbing the staircase would take at least a quarter-hour, she set herself to observe the other guests.

Ironically, St. John Rotherwood noticed Miss Hapgood in the seething mob below precisely because hers was the only face not swiveled his direction. Instead he glimpsed a bright spot of reddish gold, which turned out to be a very nice head of hair, gathered simply in smooth twists and adorned with a half-circlet of leaves. With hair like that, he was sure the face would disappoint, but since the face did not turn, he could not be certain. For whatever reason—perhaps because the red-headed young lady was the only one not fawning upon him or preparing to fawn upon him—she piqued his interest.

Lady Aurora Robillard's voice recalled him. "...Present the Earl and Countess Stanley and their daughter, Lady Sylvia."

Glancing back, he found himself nearly eye to eye with the most beautiful woman he had ever seen in his life—where had she sprung from?—and he hastily met her curtsey with a bow, the red-haired young lady forgotten.

"Lord Stanley, Lady Stanley, Lady Sylvia," purred Mrs. Rotherwood, her grip on St. John's arm tightening. He knew even without looking at her that his mother was beside herself. An earl and an earl's daughter were not a duke and a duke's daughter, of course, but dukes and dukes' daughters were so rare as to be almost mythical, whereas the Stanleys were most concretely *there* and smiling upon them. At least, the earl and countess were smiling upon them. Lady Sylvia was nearly smiling. The corners of her perfect mouth *almost* lifted.

Flanked by her short, round, dumplings of parents, the glorious Lady Sylvia struck St. John as something of a changeling child, and he was not the first person to think so. For her parents looked no more capable of producing such a creature than they could a pumpkin or a canary.

Anne Rotherwood was vibrating with excitement. Her mind, at least, was made up. Beautiful, well-born, well-bred, rich, statuesque—was not this girl the very perfect one to partner her son through life? Would such a match not make up for all that he had lacked heretofore? Why, had her brother's son lived, Anne would have defied him to produce such a wife. And how well she and St. John looked together!

Now, St. John was not given to contrariness—he would never refuse to countenance an earl's daughter simply because his mother favored her. But to be presented with an earl's daughter such as Lady Sylvia Stanley made him think that, in pleasing his mother, he might please himself as well. Was matchmaking truly this easy?

But how exactly did one go about courting a Lady Sylvia? He had no experience addressing earls' daughters and found himself at a loss. Earls' sons were no trouble at all—Magdalen had been littered with "Honorables"—but a daughter...

For her part, Lady Sylvia did not seem inclined to help him. Unlike the other young ladies he had been introduced to this evening, she did not duck her chin and watch him through her lashes. She did not giggle or rap him with her fan. She did not make any remark along the lines of, "Oh, Mr. Rotherwood, I hope you are fond of dancing," or "I hope we will be seeing plenty of you this season. Will you be at So-and-So's such-and-such?" or even, "My! Isn't it hot in here?" In fact, she made no remark whatsoever. She merely stood there, beautiful and silent. The corners of her perfect mouth ceased to *almost* lift, and that was all.

Mrs. Rotherwood glanced at each of them in turn and hastily took charge. "What a pleasure to meet you all. St. John and I hope we will see much of you this season. My—how warm it is in here! I daresay we might make our way to an open window."

"Splendid," said Lady Stanley serenely, and St. John observed that there would be no obstacles to any match thrown up by Lady Sylvia's parents either. Knowing almost nothing of him, he had passed muster. In fact, the mothers all but shook hands with each other. He felt his own press his arm to urge him into motion, but before he could do more than determine on a route through the throng, a voice called, "My dear Lady Sylvia! Lord and Lady Stanley—here is my Caroline."

Compressing herself into the smallest possible space, Lavinia Sidney managed to tug her daughter up the last step into the orbit of the Stanleys. "Oh—pardon me. Good evening," she added, as if she hadn't noticed the Rotherwoods until that moment.

Both Lady Stanley and Mrs. Rotherwood would have resented this intrusion, except that it had the happy consequence of inducing Lady Sylvia to speak!

"Mrs. Sidney, Caroline, this is Mrs. Rotherwood and her son Mr. Rotherwood. Mrs. and Mr. Rotherwood, this is Mrs. Sidney and Miss Sidney." As if this bounty of words were not gift enough, she caught sight of Hetty behind her friend and added, "And Miss Sidney's cousin, Miss Hapgood."

Miss Hapgood! The name gave St. John a little jolt, as he put it instantly together with the flash of red-gold hair seen a few minutes earlier. He made his bows automatically, but when he straightened he looked straight over Miss Sidney's head for confirmation.

Yes. It was she. Lionel Hapgood's sister—the one who had accosted him in the High Street and proven interesting at dinner. Of course, one evening's acquaintance hardly counted for much, but surrounded as he was by complete strangers, it felt weightier than he expected. He was—*yes*—he was glad to see her again.

He was surprised, therefore, to find her face devoid of recognition. She merely smiled pleasantly (and vacantly) at his left shoulder and did not even attempt to climb the top step to stand beside them all. Did she not remember him? How could she not? But—well—he could hardly trumpet an acquaintance with a young lady if she did not wish to acknowledge it, and the greeting on his lips died there.

"We were just going to make our way to a window," Mrs. Rotherwood said, looking none too pleased that the interlopers were joining what might have been a tête-à-tête between Lady Sylvia and her son. At least St. John offered his arm to Lady Sylvia, and she laid two fingers upon it. But close on her other side was that Miss Sidney, determined to come along, and Lady Sylvia made no protest.

The Progress to the Window was the jewel in the crown of Lady Aurora Robillard's rout, for it monopolized the attention of all, uniting the two people whom everyone was most interested in seeing, and generating the most discussion the following day. How could it be otherwise? If the most eligible bachelor of the season were to carry off the most eligible debutante, that meant every other candidate—rich or poor, attractive or hideous, sprung from ancient lineage or mushroom of recent growth—must rearrange and scramble into the next best match possible. The party was thus the object of both admiration and disgust.

Trailing in their wake, Hetty fell in the disgusted camp. Mr. Rotherwood's sudden and obvious admiration for the earl's daughter had not escaped her notice as she labored up the stairs, and she saw all her initial plans to put her cousin forth spoiled.

Just like that.

She had thought more highly of his intellect than it deserved, Hetty decided, for he gave every appearance of having been blown down like a house of cards at this first sight of a pretty face. So much for his first in mathematics!

Having come to this conclusion, she mutinously refused to meet his eyes when introduced. Honestly, if Lady Sylvia were to carry off the prize without even lifting a finger—and before he could even *meet* Caroline, what chance did her cousin have? What chance had any schemes Hetty might devise?

The crowd which pressed upon them formerly now parted to make way, as if Mr. Rotherwood and Lady Sylvia were the king and queen or Moses and the Israelites. Caroline, for her part, looked elated, so proud to be included that she did not realize she had already lost. How Lady Sylvia felt, on the other hand, Hetty could not determine, for her expression remained impassive as ever.

When the open window was gained, Lady Sylvia and Mr. Rotherwood were given the places of honor, on either side of the raised sash, with the others fanning out in a semicircle between them. Hetty found herself wedged between her cousin and aunt, and Aunt Lavinia seemed to resent even the small space allotted her niece, for she encroached inch by inch until Hetty gave up and switched positions with her.

It was just as well. Then she might observe to her heart's content and determine if there was any chance for Caroline. Her natural optimism began to return in those few minutes. All right, then. Superior beauty won the first battle—it did not necessarily follow that it would win the war. Besides—had it been anything more than Hetty anticipated?

Between the buzz of a hundred voices and the musicians scraping away in a nearby alcove, Hetty was not expected to contribute more than smiles and nods to the conversation—even if anyone wanted to hear from her in the first place—so she must get to work. Such persevering conversation as there was, in any event, was dull enough that her mind might have wandered without the task set before her. Therefore she tried to listen as if her life depended on it. Like a tennis ball batted back and forth, remarks were made on the crush of guests, other crushes experienced, the Robillard home, other homes, the weather, the music, wondering about refreshments, refreshments served elsewhere, whether routs were to be preferred to balls or dinners, and so on.

Mr. Rotherwood contributed little to this and Lady Sylvia nothing at all, though she nodded once or twice and almost smiled one additional time. Hetty did not waste time trying to judge whether the earl's daughter was smitten yet. She hardly cared if she was. Her mission did not involve Lady Sylvia. Besides, the Lady Sylvias of the world had so many advantages over other girls that concern need not be wasted on them.

Instead Hetty studied Mr. Rotherwood, her gaze lingering on his lofty brow and curling hair. Even staring at Lady Sylvia did not soften his sternness, though the corners of his own mouth lifted infinitesimally whenever that lady's so much as twitched. He glanced once or twice at Caroline as well, mostly because Caroline interjected with a "Yes, Indeed!" once and a "You don't say!" another time.

Hetty frowned. Very well, then. If it turned out Mr. Marble preferred a young lady as silent and statue-like as himself, Hetty would have to advise Caroline to hold her tongue in his presence. Stop all that laughing and interjecting. Affect a remote, mysterious air.

Unconsciously she straightened, adopting a remote, mysterious air herself, as if to model it for her cousin. Throwing her shoulders back, she gazed without expression at the fringe of the window draperies and imagined what it would be like to look, as Lady Sylvia did, like Flora in Botticelli's *Primavera*. She wondered if Edith had seen any of Botticelli's paintings yet. Or what Edith was doing at that precise moment. Sleeping, most likely.

Just then, St. John happened to glance at Miss Hapgood again. The dullness of the conversation had him fighting off the urge to fidget. He had tried without success to catch Lady Sylvia's eye, thinking that, if she shared his ennui, they might exchange an understanding smile. But it was not to be. Lady Sylvia never looked his way when he looked hers, and her thoughts remained her own. Her friend Miss Sidney was glad enough to meet his gaze, but that young lady was eagerness itself—plainly she could think of no place she would rather be than right *here* in this hot, stuffy, overcrowded, loud room, trading commonplaces. Well, then. And what of Miss Hapgood? She might somehow have forgotten him, but at least he knew she was capable of being interesting.

The girl was staring distantly again, and this time it irked him. If there was to be no acknowledgement of their former meeting, they must begin anew.

He addressed her abruptly. "Do you share that opinion, Miss Hapgood?"

Hearing her name, Hetty started, and her affected air vanished. "Oh—forgive me, Mr.—Rotherwood. I was not attending. To what opinion do you refer?"

Ah-ha! thought St. John. So she found this tiresome as well.

Beside her, her aunt clucked disapprovingly, and even Caroline's voice had an aggrieved note. "*Hetty*, we were speaking of whether there would be another frost fair this winter."

"Oh. Who can possibly say?" Hetty replied, annoyed in her turn. "It was a cold summer, I suppose, but that means nothing. It's certainly hot enough in here." Her aunt lay firm fingers on her gloved forearm and Hetty shut up.

"You are right in saying we cannot predict a winter's weather based on the summer which preceded it," rejoined Mr. Rotherwood, perking up. "But Benjamin Franklin once tracked the path of a storm by recording the visibility of a lunar eclipse at various points." He gestured with his fingers in the air, as if marking sections of the sky. "He postulated therefore that, if a time comes when information can be shared faster than a storm can travel, some level of weather prediction will become possible."

Mrs. Sidney gave an uncomfortable titter. "Benjamin Franklin? Dear me."

"That's clever," said Hetty, forgetting herself again. "But the information would have to travel very fast indeed. And it would not then be a 'prediction,' so to speak, but rather a—a notification."

"True," agreed St. John, with a little bow. "Miss Hapgood is precise in her definitions."

"As you ought to be," she returned, "being a mathematician."

"A *former* mathematician," spoke up Mrs. Rotherwood, regarding this pert Miss Hapgood beadily. "Now my St. John is a man of leisure."

"A man of leisure—what a pleasure," Hetty rhymed irrepressibly, half to herself. "Clunker would like that one."

Then the mothers present did round on her, united in their desire to silence her and put their daughters forward. Aunt Lavinia positively pinched her, and Mrs. Rotherwood began plying her fan like the beginnings of a hurricane, saying loudly, "Whatever the weather, St. John and I will be quite cozy in North Audley Street. You must call on us, Lady Sylvia, Lady Stanley..." (for the rest of them she waved a vague hand). "And if the Thames does not freeze this winter, surely the Serpentine will. Do you skate, Lady Sylvia?"

Addressed directly, Lady Sylvia was forced to utter, "I do not." Upon which Caroline leapt in to say how easy it was and how Lady Sylvia simply must try it; Mrs. Rotherwood then boasted about her son's skating prowess; and the Stanleys were forced to express how they had longed for Lady Sylvia to learn, and how her health had not permitted as a child, though she was the picture of health now; and so on and so forth.

Hetty knew better than to speak again, even if there were anything worth saying. Mr. Rotherwood, too, contributed no more than the minimum, and the party disbanded shortly afterward to mingle with others.

The Stanleys carried off their triumphant daughter to be displayed to other worthies they could discover, while the hostess Lady Aurora descended on the Rotherwoods and pinioned them to her side. There followed a parade of middle-aged fortune-hunting men and giggling, twitchy debutantes before them, and St. John wondered if this was what generals experienced when reviewing troops before what would surely be a crushing defeat. For his initial elation on meeting Lady Sylvia was already fading, blunted by her rock-like silence.

He should not give up so easily, he knew. Perhaps she was the sort of person who preferred smaller gatherings. Like he did, as it happened. He had not known that about himself, having never been in a gathering of this size before. Or any gathering where he was the focus of attention.

He would try again with Lady Sylvia on the morrow, he decided. Make a proper effort. All he knew now was that he never wanted to go to another rout again.

Faces began to blur. Names flitted in and out of his head. Something odd was happening, where he seemed only able to notice everyone's teeth. Perfect, pearly teeth. Missing teeth. Long, horsey teeth. Glinting teeth. Crooked teeth. One blackened tooth that would need to be pulled.

He ground his own set together. From time to time his gaze wandered over the heads of the throng. He was not looking for anyone in particular, but it was not hard to pick out Lady Sylvia wordlessly holding court or a bright head of red-gold hair that hove into view on occasion. "A man of leisure—what a pleasure," he muttered.

When he had had enough and persuaded his mother to go, he called for the carriage, but in descending to the ground floor he unexpectedly found Miss Hapgood there as well. She was seated on a bench, her leaf-crowned head tilted back against the wall and her eyes closed. A maid knelt beside her, repairing some damage to her hem.

"Thank you, and please take all the time you like," Miss Hapgood sighed. "I wouldn't mind just sitting here until my family is ready to leave. I'm so sleepy that I'm sure this bench would feel like a cloud, if only I could recline upon it."

He was in motion before he was aware, stepping away from the footman who held his cloak. "Good evening again, Miss Hapgood."

Her eyes popped open and she hurriedly sat up straight. "Why—good evening again, Mr. Rotherwood."

"You seem to have come to some injury." He nodded at the maid, who gawped up at this apparition.

"It is nothing. Sir Keane stepped on my hem and tore it."

He hesitated, but then said, "You have a pattern of violent interactions with people, then."

She looked at him sharply and decided that—would wonders never cease?—the man was teasing her. The stern Mr. Rotherwood, making a joke! Clearly they were dropping the pretense of not knowing each other.

"Can you draw such a conclusion, sir," she countered, "with only two meager points of data?"

The corner of his mouth twisted. "Perhaps your Wingate's *Arithmetic* did not treat with geometry. If it did, you would know it only requires two points to draw a line between them. And with a line, if one adds time as a third factor, one has a trajectory."

"Hm. My copy of Wingate did *not* cover geometry, Mr. Rotherwood. Therefore I grant you your conclusion: I must have violent interactions with people." After a moment she added, "You need not fear—I would never mistake you for my father now, nor dare to lay hold of you. For you have become very grand."

He spread his hands out, palms up, not knowing how to respond to this.

"I did not know whether to presume on our slight acquaintance," Hetty explained in a rush, seeing Mr. Rotherwood's mother approaching behind him. "I should perhaps not have mentioned you being a mathematician. Lionel hinted at your great good fortune, and I congratulate you. I wish you very well."

His lips parted to reply, but before he could, he felt his mother beside him and heard her say, "Miss Haywood, is it not?"

From her bench Hetty made an awkward half-bow, not wanting to stand and rip her dress from the maid's needle. "Hapgood, madam. It is Miss Hapgood. I hope you had a pleasant time."

"Very," she answered with a cool smile. "Are you and your cousin good friends of Lady Sylvia?"

Which answer would help or hinder Caroline's cause? Hetty weighed her options and said, "I believe Caroline and Lady Sylvia are fond of each other. For my part, I am only lately arrived in town, but I hope to know Lady Sylvia better soon."

"Miss Hapgood is the sister of one of my former pupils," Mr. Rotherwood told his mother.

Her mouth compressed. "Ah. I see. That was how she knew of your previous life, St. John." When her eyes returned to Hetty, Hetty felt ice run down her spine. "Well, Miss Hapgood, those days have gone now. Good evening to you."

She turned and the Rotherwoods walked away.

Hetty gave a silent whistle and raised her eyebrows at the maid, who gave a sympathetic smile before snapping off the thread and pronouncing her fixed.

How lucky it is, that I am not trying to win Mr. Rotherwood for myself, she thought, as she examined her gown and smiled her thanks. His mother clearly did not appreciate Hetty mentioning her son's humble history, and Hetty could only hope the woman's dislike would not extend to Caroline. If it did, that might make a difficult task nigh impossible.

CHAPTER SEVEN

I like thy counsel; well hast thou advised:
And that thou mayst perceive how well I like it,
The execution of it shall make known.
—Shakespeare, *Two Gentlemen of Verona*, I.iii.337
(c.1592)

Dressed and breakfasted, Hetty could wait no longer. Tossing aside the guidebook she had been reading, she cracked Caroline's door and peeped in.

"I'm awake," grumbled her cousin, "so you needn't creep about. What time is it?"

"Eleven."

"Eleven?" She sat bolt upright, her golden hair a bumpy nimbus of curl rags and loosened strands. "Why didn't you wake me sooner?

Lady Sylvia once called on me earlier than I expected, and I had to dash to make myself presentable."

"What's the worry? She isn't here now."

Caroline was already out of bed and splashing water on her face. "Call my maid! Do you think Mr. Rotherwood is an early riser? Suppose he goes to call on Lady Sylvia, and *we are not there?*"

Hetty's brows rose. "I haven't the least idea what time Mr. Rotherwood rises, though I suppose after so many years at Oxford, he would more likely rise early than late. Does this mean you approve of him?"

Reddy rushed in, and Caroline did not respond for some minutes, as maid and mistress dealt with wardrobe and undergarment issues. Hetty flapped the bedclothes back across the mattress that she might sit atop it, smiling to watch her cousin's morning transformation.

When Caroline was clothed in a charming blue frock that matched her eyes, she seated herself at her dressing table, and Reddy began nimbly to unravel the rag strips and bring order to her mistress' resulting spirals.

"Meeting Mr. Rotherwood sent shivers all up and down me!" resumed Caroline. She made a dismayed face in the looking glass, liked it, and made it again from another angle. "He was even handsomer than gossip put about, but they were quite right to call him marble. So unapproachable! I could not tell what he was thinking. He seemed remote as Olympus, and I was a mere mortal far below, hoping I would not be blasted."

Hetty thought it boded well for her cousin that she could at least express herself in interesting ways. Would Lady Sylvia have been able to come up with such an analogy? But her good feelings were dispelled when Caroline added, "And so much for your supposed acquaintance with him—he did not even look twice at you when you were introduced."

Riled, Hetty retorted, "Zeus did speak to me eventually, I will point out."

Caroline scoffed. "Yes, but you had to resort to calling him a mathematician, as if to remind him that he had met you before."

"Resort"? For a moment, Hetty debated telling her smug cousin that Mr. Rotherwood had spoken to her again, later that evening, and hadn't seemed at all inclined to duck the acquaintance, but what would be the use of that?

She let her cousin's assumption stand. There were more pressing matters to discuss.

"But you did like him?" Hetty asked. "Mr. Rotherwood."

Caroline gave her reflection a coy smile. "Certainly well enough that I would like to know him better."

"Mm. And Lady Sylvia? Could you tell if she liked him?"

"Why do you ask?"

"Er—only that he looked at her so admiringly when he met her."

"Everyone looks at her like that," her cousin snapped. "It needn't mean anything particular on his part." Despite this show of bravery, however, her brow knit. "In any event, that is why we must hasten over there, to the Stanleys'. Because if he calls, I want to be there."

Hetty nodded, but Caroline wasn't looking at her.

"Are you nearly finished?" Her cousin snapped at Reddy.

"Can I help it if your hair's in such a tangle?" was the maid's imperturbable response.

"Mama warned me that cultivating Lady Sylvia's friendship would be a double-edged sword," continued Caroline. "She said she would elevate me socially, but she would also be the gentlemen's first choice."

Whatever her aunt's flaws, Hetty didn't doubt her intelligence. She answered lightly, "Fortunately, Lady Sylvia can only marry one person. So if you can manage not to desire the same gentleman, I think her friendship will ultimately improve your chances of marrying well."

Spinning on her dainty padded stool, Caroline twitched out of her maid's hands. "But that's just it! I think she fancies him—Mr. Rotherwood, that is. Fancies him—nay!—she was head over ears!"

Hetty stared. "Are you in earnest? I see you are. But—how could you tell? I know I don't know her as well as you do, but to my mind she didn't give the least indication."

"She's an earl's daughter, Hetty," said Caroline, as if that made everything clear. "Do you expect her to throw herself at his feet? I know you've been positively buried in the provinces, but I can tell you that she would catch him if she can. Why, she blushed twice and almost smiled at him. And then, when we were taking leave of each other, she squeezed my hand significantly."

"Well—if that's all," laughed Hetty. "If a gentleman stood near me for half an hour, saying absolutely nothing, and only turning colors once or twice, I would think it dyspepsia, sooner than love. But I'm sure you know what you're about. It's too bad, though. If

Lady Sylvia chooses him, and he chooses her, that will be the end of it. Did you like anybody else you met last night?"

"You think I don't stand a chance against her," Caroline fired up. "I know I haven't her rank, but my portion is at least as good."

"He doesn't need money," Hetty pointed out.

"So? Who doesn't like more money?" Caroline slapped her palm on the dressing table. "You must be jealous. Or envious. Because my portion is larger than yours and I'm—I'm prettier."

"How did *I* enter into this discussion?" demanded Hetty.

"You say you don't want a husband, but it's just your boastfulness. Every girl wants a husband."

"My 'boastfulness'?" Hetty's bosom swelled, and she felt her own palm itching to slap something. Something with golden curls and blue eyes. "I didn't say I *never* wanted a husband—I just said I wasn't seeking one now, so you and Lady Sylvia may keep your precious Mr. Rotherwood."

"Fine. We will!"

"Fine!"

Ooh, she was glad she had helped her brother escape his engagement to this spoiled creature! Yes, glad. Ever so glad that Lionel was going to marry Edith, and not Caroline.

But the thought of Edith acted like a cool hand on her arm, and Hetty found herself struggling to choke down her ire.

Come, now. She had never known Caroline to be cruel before. Blind to others, perhaps. Thoughtless. But not cruel. Edith would surely say Caroline's spite was a result of her disappointment in love, whether Caroline knew it or not.

Get her a husband, Hetty reminded herself. *Get her a husband, and she'll be cheerful enough.*

"You *are* prettier than I," she ground out. "And your portion is larger. But it does not follow that I am therefore jealous. I have been honest enough with you. I told you I wasn't seeking a husband while I stay here, and, to prove my good faith, I am determined to help you make a good match. I only mean to say that, if both you and Lady Sylvia decide you want Mr. Rotherwood, we will have our work cut out for us. I am not saying it cannot be done."

These concessions on Hetty's part mollified her cousin. "You mean that, Hetty? You would help me?"

"Yes."

The beginnings of a smile appeared. "Well, I would like that. I suspect—I suspect you are cleverer than I." (This reluctant praise did much to soothe Hetty's ruffled feathers.) "And that Mr. Rotherwood must be clever too, if he was a mathematics tutor. But I can't think what help you can provide, since he hardly recognized you."

"It was enough," said Hetty. She was recovering—starting to see the humor in the situation. "I may not be as pretty or as rich as you or Lady Sylvia, but that doesn't mean I can't be a good observer of Mr. Rotherwood, and I tell you, when we were all standing around at the window, the only time he didn't look half asleep was when he was talking about Benjamin Franklin. I think you could *interest* him more than Lady Sylvia, if you put your mind to it, since she hardly speaks at all."

"By talking about Benjamin Franklin?"

Caroline's alarm made her cousin laugh. "No—not Benjamin Franklin per se, but by talking. About subjects which might appeal to him."

"But what would those be?"

Hetty frowned, running through what had been discussed at the Oxford supper and when her dress was being repaired at the rout. "Oh...I suppose mathematics or education or astronomy or—" she broke off at Caroline's dawning horror. "Well, never mind that for now. You might just start with the man himself. Ask him questions. Perhaps he likes to talk about sport. Lionel always does. Yes. And everyone likes to talk about himself, in any event, so why should Mr. Rotherwood be an exception? Ask him about himself. Just *speak*, and you will have the advantage over Lady Sylvia."

Caroline shivered. "I might be afraid to speak. You make it sound so hard, and he is so forbidding."

"Nonsense. You never had any trouble at all talking to my brother and asking him a thousand questions."

"But Lionel was easy to talk to, and Mr. Rotherwood—"

"Mr. Rotherwood is stiff and aloof," Hetty finished for her. "But it can be done. Trust me. You must make the effort."

The girls arrived in Cavendish Square, where the white-and-brick Stanley home anchored the northeast corner. It had been Hetty's idea to walk on the chilly morning, both for exercise and also to arrive without warning. "We can then see if Lady Sylvia has other callers. We might even walk right past, if it is only the three mutton-heads."

Caroline frowned at this vulgar denomination for Sir Keane, Mr. Pickford and Mr. Elwood, but she raised no objection. And when no carriage at all stood outside Number 9, she exclaimed, "We have beat Mr. Rotherwood here! Come, Hetty."

Her surmise proved wrong, however, for when the butler admitted them to the drawing room, they found the man already standing among the Stanleys. He had only just arrived himself, and Lady Sylvia had yet to do more than curtsey to him. Clothed in a bottle-green frock coat, snowy linen, and tan breeches, he was even more immaculate and imposing by day, and Hetty suspected the rivals would only want him the more.

"Girls," Lady Stanley greeted them, with a smile that did not reach her eyes. "Did you walk? How unexpected, on such a frosty morning."

"I found the cold bracing, myself," said Mr. Rotherwood, bowing to them.

"Yes, you would," Lady Stanley answered him. "A strong young man with a robust constitution. But young ladies often hesitate to walk abroad in cold weather. It's too likely to give them red noses and bleary eyes."

Dismayed, Caroline could not help but dart a glance at the mirror over the mantel, to see if her nose was truly red and her eyes bleary, but Hetty gripped her arm a little more tightly and compelled her toward the sofa opposite where Lady Sylvia sat enthroned in a gilded Louis Seize chair.

It was only good manners to let the earl's daughter begin the conversation, since this was her home, and she did so after another minute.

"Last night was very pleasant," she said.

Unbeknownst to Lady Sylvia, St. John had come this morning to settle something in his mind. He was an efficient man; if this young lady were to charm him and he her, he intended it to happen as soon as possible. And if they could not manage it, let them both close that door and be satisfied. With this end in mind, the arrival of Lady Sylvia's friends must not distract him, although he could not help but notice that Miss Hapgood was back to gazing anywhere but at him. Odd creature!

With a wrench, he returned to his task, only to find himself wordless. How would he get past Lady Sylvia's reticence, when he himself was so unpracticed in the social graces? It had not been difficult to address Miss Hapgood the night before, he remembered. But how had he gone about it? He had merely greeted her—that was it—and then a joke had come. But that was different. Miss Hapgood was different. Because he had met her at Oxford, she was somehow of his world. Or—his former world.

He should try to joke with Lady Sylvia in the same manner. See if a laugh would help her unbend. He would like a wife with a sense of humor.

No joke came to mind.

Instead he heard himself say vapidly, "It was indeed pleasant. What did you most enjoy, Lady Sylvia?"

She colored and her hands flexed fitfully. Lady Stanley did not appear at all oppressed by her daughter's reserve, and Lord Stanley even took up the newspaper. St. John could only suppose they did not think any exertion required on their part. If a young lady was blessed with their daughter's face, fortune, and place in the world, men would clamor for her, even if she had no more personality or conversation than a seat cushion.

His marble brow hardened. Well, they would find they were mistaken. Here was one young man who had no desire to woo a seat cushion, even a pretty one stuffed with banknotes. He could understand shyness, being shy himself, but he would also be grateful if she would meet him halfway. Perhaps because he had been a tutor so many years, St. John could not help but recall that even the most unprepared or indifferent student knew to gabble and make excuses, out of an awareness he was wasting his tutor's time.

In the silence, Caroline ventured to elbow her cousin, but Hetty gave an infinitesimal shake of the head. She was not to speak yet, even if the silence stretched. If they gave Lady Sylvia enough rope, with some luck she might hang herself.

Lady Sylvia must indeed have sensed the possibility of failure because, after turning red and then white again, she blurted, "What—did *you* most enjoy about the evening, Mr. Rotherwood?"

His mouth twitched and the joke came. "I'd have to say...its conclusion." This reply drew a giggle from Hetty, which she smothered as soon as she could, covering it with a throat-clearing and a thump on her chest. He glanced at her, but she immediately began to pick at a thread in the sofa upholstery.

Lady Sylvia tilted her head in beautiful puzzlement over his reply, while Caroline's mouth popped open, and Lady Stanley's eyes threw sparks.

"It was indeed a crush," Lady Stanley conceded, after a pause. She might look like a dumpling, but Hetty could see wheels turning as she regarded her daughter's would-be suitor.

More silence. Hetty thought this might be the longest quarter-hour of her life. But she and Caroline would never depart before their quarry.

St. John was inwardly berating himself. It was rude of him to mock something they must have enjoyed, even if he hated it. Perspiration threatened to break out on his forehead, and he was swamped by a sudden, inexplicable longing for his cramped, solitary chambers at Oxford.

Peace.

Quiet.

Solitude.

No social pitfalls.

Slowly, imperceptibly, Hetty's foot inched over and pressed against her cousin's.

"Mr. Rotherwood!" bleated Caroline. "What do you like, if you don't like crowds?"

St. John started, but then his broad shoulders relaxed visibly, to have someone else step into the breach. In his relief, he cast a soft look on his rescuer that not a person in the room missed. "This is my first season in town, as you probably know. My first time, even. That rout—I fear I am not very good conversing with strangers, but

I hope to improve. Sad to say, if I were left to my own devices, I would probably prefer to spend my time attending lectures at the Royal Society or seeing the sights."

"But we *love* the sights, don't we, Hetty?" cried Caroline, beaming upon her cousin in elation. She had got the most words out of him yet! "And have seen so few of them, really. St. Paul's, I mean, and Regent's Park because we live near it. But we should like to see so many more! Which ones would you like to see, Mr. Rotherwood?"

Not noticing the Stanleys' exchanged glances or the countess's indrawn breath, St. John answered, "Oh, everything. I know it makes me sound like a bumpkin, but I'm not particular. The Tower, the Abbey, the museum at Montagu House. St. Paul's, of course."

"St. Paul's is marvelous," pronounced Caroline, conveniently forgetting how she had protested being taken there, had complained about the art, and had to be coaxed to climb to the gallery. "So very big. And the paintings of the life of the apostle—!"

St. John was now smiling, his features thawed into flesh and blood, and it very much became him. He sat forward eagerly. "Perhaps we might play tourist together one afternoon? All of us?" He included Lady Sylvia in his glance.

The slightest shadow crossed her fair countenance, and it only deepened when Caroline urged, "Oh, let's, Lady Sylvia! When Hetty and I and—my other cousin—went to St. Paul's, we took a hackney coach, and it was such an adventure."

Lady Stanley visibly shuddered. "Nonsense, we can't have you all jolting across town in a hired coach. We can call for the carriage and you young people may go where you like. Sylvia, what do you say to this?"

"Yes, Lady Sylvia," her friend pressed, "you will decide where we go first, and when, although I hope it may be soon."

Hetty would have bet a golden guinea Lady Sylvia thought Doomsday soon enough to see any of the places mentioned, but she was cornered. "Perhaps tomorrow," she murmured, with a questioning look at Mr. Rotherwood. "If it suits you all. There. I have chosen the time. Mr. Rotherwood must name the destination."

To please only himself, St. John would have chosen the British Museum, but he doubted the young ladies would enjoy peering at coins and seeds, mathematical instruments and fossils. An inquisitive sort like Miss Hapgood, who loved learning, might, but—

"With the benefit of a carriage, perhaps we should visit the sight farthest away," he suggested. "What do you say to the Tower?"

Caroline clapped her hands and bounced, as if she had longed for just such a visit. "Delightful! Oh, Mr. Rotherwood, you are quite learned and will have much to tell us, I am sure."

"Well, if his knowledge fails us, I always have my Bowles' guide to hand," said Hetty dryly.

Caroline rolled her eyes and favored Mr. Rotherwood with a droll smile. "My cousin and her Bowles guide! I promise I will not let her read to us above half a page. Do tell us, Mr. Rotherwood, which animal do you most want to see in the menagerie?"

Half an hour later, St. John emerged again into Cavendish Square, setting his steps for home and feeling like an orange squeezed dry. For something had happened in the Stanleys' drawing room he could not put his finger on. But whatever it was, it unstopped Miss Sidney, as if she were a bottle of *sal volatile*, and drove the earlier silence quite away. She proved a potent conversationalist. Or inquisitor. She had wrung from him his favorite animal. Favorite king. Favorite prisoner of the Tower. She had learned what he had loved about Oxford and compared it with her own list. She pried from him what must have been a dull story about punting on the Isis.

"In another five minutes, she would have known my birth weight and mother's middle name," he muttered.

Several times he tried to turn the subject from himself, only to have her bring it back, like a terrier with a stick. Several more times he tried to include Lady Sylvia and Miss Hapgood in the conversation, but neither one helped him. Lady Sylvia remained beautiful and remote; Miss Hapgood merely smiled in her most vacant and maddening manner.

Very well.

Lady Aurora's rout and this morning's call taught him something, at least. They had given St. John a revelation, as it were. To wit: he did not like attention focused on him. He did not like being the cynosure of all eyes and the name on every tongue.

A rather unfortunate discovery, given his new position in life.

His lips curled as he trudged along Wigmore Street.

Could mathematical proofs be applied to life? Perhaps a proof by contraposition: if p, then q, to be confirmed by if *not p*, then *not q*. *If* to be wealthy and eligible was to be uncomfortable, could it be shown that, to be not wealthy and not eligible was to be comfortable?

It fell apart, he supposed. For being poor and overlooked as a mathematics tutor had its share of discomfort. Which meant it must be possible in some cases to be wealthy and eligible and comfortable.

Why was the thought so tempting, then, to retreat to his chambers at Magdalen and to tell his mother she might keep it all herself—the money, London, the fashionable life?

Chapter Eight

Strangers should be cautious not to approach too near the dens, and avoid every attempt to play with them.
— John Feltham, *The Picture of London for 1813* (1813)

By the time their little touring party arrived at the principal entrance to the Tower of London, they had doubled in number, and Hetty thought all enjoyment of the visit would be lost in forwarding her cousin's aims and keeping at bay the interlopers. For the three mutton-heads, Sir Keane, Mr. Pickford, and Mr. Elwood, called in Devonshire Street shortly after the girls returned from the Stanleys', and no sooner did they hear of the planned outing than they insisted in their various ways that visiting the Tower had always been their heart's desire.

"They are most definitely 'after' you," Hetty grimaced, when the gentlemen took their leave. "And next time we must keep our plans as secret as possible, to avoid their company in future."

"I rather like their attention," was her cousin's ingenuous reply. "And if they join us, Mr. Rotherwood will see that he is not the only prize to be won."

"Only the largest and most glittering," grumbled Hetty. "What prize would be threatened by such rusty ha'pennies?" (She had been vexed by Mr. Pickford winking his eyes at her in what he assumed was a lady-killer fashion.)

It did not add to Hetty's pleasure that so large a party could not possibly be made to wake up and organize themselves in time to witness the Tower's opening ceremony. She had wanted to see the yeoman porter pass and repass the keys, while the guards waited with rested firelocks, but it was not to be. When their company reached the place, so many hours later, the double gates were long open and the wharf and ladies' line milling with London's everlasting crowds. To make matters worse, somehow Mr. Pickford had attached himself to her and insisted on describing (inaccurately) all that she was seeing and had already read about in her guidebook.

"I believe Henry V was responsible for enlarging and refurbishing that central tower, called the White Tower," he told her, pointing with his walking stick as they strolled.

"Oh, do you not think it happened much sooner?" she suggested, "Perhaps under an earlier Henry?"

"No, no. I'm certain it was Henry V," Mr. Pickford assured her. "A war-like king, you know. War-like kings love rebuilding fortresses.

It was in the White Tower that the Princes were kept—the ones murdered by their uncle."

"Indeed Mr. Pickford, I think they were reputed to be held in the Bloody Tower," returned Hetty. "For which reason it was called the Bloody Tower."

He gave a deprecating chuckle. "A common misapprehension, Miss Hapgood. But the Bloody Tower is called the Bloody Tower because Sir Walter Raleigh was imprisoned there."

Hetty gave up.

"Shall we see the menagerie first?" asked Caroline, glowing up at Mr. Rotherwood, on whose arm she hung. Sir Keane had claimed Lady Sylvia, by virtue of his rank, leaving Hetty to wonder if Caroline welcomed the three mutton-heads' presence for that very reason. If she did, Hetty gave her credit, for that thought had not occurred to her. After Caroline and Lady Sylvia paired off, she herself had stood uncertainly, hoping Mr. Elwood would crook his elbow at her, he being the lesser of two evils. But Mr. Pickford had been too much for him, and Mr. Elwood drifted behind the rest, forgotten and disgruntled.

No objections were raised to Caroline's suggestion, and they rang the bell for the keeper and paid over their shillings.

Truth be told, Hetty was not terribly brave when it came to large animals. She could countenance her brother's mare Mannerly, and one could not live in rural Somerset without frequent encounters with sheep and the occasional cow or deer, but she always gave such creatures a wide, wide berth. On this day, confronted with so many lions and other large cats, she could not help but tighten her grip on Mr. Pickford and hang back.

Mr. Pickford naturally interpreted these actions as attempts at coquetry, and he favored her with a heavy-lidded smile. "Never fear, Miss Hapgood. In addition to being spacious and clean, these new enclosures are quite safe, if one does not draw too near the gratings. Why, I remember coming as a young lad, when there were still monkeys here, in a special room. Yes, you might well shiver. One of them attacked and injured a boy, and the monkeys were subsequently removed, by order of his majesty."

This did not comfort her, but she pressed her lips together and soldiered on, as the keeper led them from den to den. He had much to say of interest about each cat and its history, and after a time Hetty began to relax enough to listen. This reprieve only lasted, however, until they had gone halfway round and reached the den of the Moroccan lionesses. There, a mischievous boy took to poking a stick through the iron grating of the enclosure, rattling it back and forth. One of the lionesses took offense at this teasing, and she flew at the grating to swipe it with a heavy paw while sounding a fierce, rumbling growl, to a chorus of gasps from her onlookers.

With both arms, Hetty seized Mr. Pickford around his middle before she knew what she was about, just as both Caroline and Lady Sylvia screamed, Caroline nearly climbing Mr. Rotherwood like a tree.

"Miss Hapgood, Miss Hapgood," the handsome Mr. Pickford laughed in her ear. And then, before the flustered Hetty could detach herself, he reciprocated with a squeeze of his own. Furious at this liberty, as well as by his (plausible) interpretation of her actions, she refused to take his arm again. Instead she muttered unintelligible and insincere thanks, removing to Caroline's other side. She would have to trust that any more rampaging animals would be forced to eat Mr. Rotherwood before they could reach the girls.

"How frightening!" Caroline was gasping. "Oh, Mr. Rotherwood, did your heart not leap within you?"

"It might have—had your vise-like grip not restrained it," he said dryly, smoothing the sleeves of his parson-grey greatcoat where she had wrinkled them.

"We had better move on," Mr. Elwood proposed, a little bitter to be the only gentleman who had not been clutched at by a pretty young lady. He noted that even aged Sir Keane had been gripped by Lady Sylvia, though he was old and feeble enough for it to have snapped him in two! "A visit to the armories or the Jewel House might be less alarming for the ladies."

"But I should like to see the black leopard!" protested Caroline. "Wouldn't you, Lady Sylvia?"

Lady Sylvia was not inclined to be helpful, having been steadily lisped at by Sir Keane and still smarting over Caroline's hold on Mr. Rotherwood. She merely shrugged.

To Hetty's surprise, Mr. Rotherwood turned to her. "You must cast the deciding vote, then, Miss Hapgood. Would you like to see the black leopard, or have you had scares enough for the day?"

She knew what to answer, without Caroline giving her a pointed look. "We had better see the leopard. And the remaining creatures, for that matter. We have paid our shilling, after all."

"Though we've already got our money's worth, haven't we?" drawled Mr. Pickford, springing up like a jack-in-the-box at her elbow.

Hetty ignored him and his impudence, trailing after her cousin as the keeper directed them onward. On one thing she was determined: even if a lion overleapt the grating to maul her, she was not going to touch Mr. Pickford again. The thought made her mouth twitch unexpectedly, however. Had Lionel not warned her in his letter, "Don't go grabbing everyone in the street"? Better advice than she had realized! If her brother had been there, he would have teased her without mercy.

No martyrdom was required of her, thankfully, for the rest of the menagerie tour was so uneventful that even Caroline could think of no reason to fling herself at Mr. Rotherwood again, and the group proceeded into the inner court to the Jewel House, where another shilling apiece gained them entrance.

Such was the magnificence of the items on display within that the young people forgot their individual agendas, Caroline and Lady Sylvia even releasing their would-be suitors to press forward for a better view of the imperial crown, rich with purple velvet, ermine, and jewels.

"It must be very heavy," Lady Sylvia was moved to say, and so beautiful was she that the keeper of the regalia gulped, lost his place in his rote speech, and had to begin again. But then he thrust out a proud chest and regaled the tourists with every last detail he could remember about the history and provenance of the crown, orb, sceptre, and rods, all the while glancing at the earl's daughter every third word. Hetty thought with amusement that, had Lady Sylvia only asked, he might have let her try everything on.

"You find it a source of levity, the attempted robbery by Colonel Blood of our nation's treasures?"

Hetty jumped, finding Mr. Rotherwood at her shoulder, looking his sternest and most tutorial.

"No, indeed, I—" she broke off, catching a gleam in his eyes in the darkened room. "Ah. You are teasing. No, Mr. Rotherwood—I was simply thinking that, if one of Colonel Blood's accomplices had looked anything like Lady Sylvia, they would not have needed to knock down the keeper of the regalia with a mallet. She might simply have asked nicely for the items, and I'm sure Mr. Talbot Edwards would have wrapped them up in velvet and handed them over. Only look how this keeper is eating out of her hand."

"I think you may be right. Do you think men more susceptible to beauty than women?"

He certainly had been, a few days earlier, she thought. But she pretended to consider. "I don't know. I suppose both sexes respond to beauty. But while men will admire and love in response to female beauty, women's admiration will always be mixed with envy and perhaps a little self-criticism."

The keeper of the regalia motioned for the group to follow him on toward St. Edward's staff, but Hetty and Mr. Rotherwood lingered in the back of the group.

"Do you speak from experience, Miss Hapgood—if one may ask so personal a question?" His voice was pitched low for her ears alone.

"Of course I do," she answered frankly. "I am a woman, therefore I will admire superior beauty while at the same time feeling a twinge of envy and saying a few hard things to myself for falling short."

The gleam in his eye returned. "What hard things could you have to say?"

Belatedly she remembered herself. The man did have a way of drawing her out! *This will never do, Harriet Hapgood. If you succeed in withdrawing his attention from the peerless Lady Sylvia, you must direct it where it will be fruitful!*

"Never mind me," she murmured hastily. "We do not know each other well enough for you to ask me such a question." Indeed—she could feel her cheeks warm and was glad she could train her gaze on the treasures of the Jewel House. "But only see how you gentlemen buzz around Lady Sylvia like honeybees to a blossom," Hetty continued. "Why—why you are all hard put to notice any other young lady—even so lovely a one as my cousin Miss Sidney."

He thought about this, his hands clasped behind his back and his brow more Bernini's *David* than ever. "Mr. Pickford seemed content to buzz around *you*, Miss Hapgood."

Her surprise at this observation was quickly hidden, for they were moving again, being led to stand before the unpointed Sword of Mercy.

"Oh—well—I suppose he had no choice," she replied. "Lady Sylvia and Miss Sidney were claimed."

"You think no one might happen to prefer you to Lady Sylvia or Miss Sidney?"

Why on earth must he insist on talking about her? She did not look at him, but she was frowning. "No man with sense would," she declared. "It's not just a matter of beauty, though there they already hold the advantage. There is also the matter of wealth and rank."

He nodded sagely. She sounded like his mother. "Yes. I understand perfectly. Therefore, young ladies such as yourself, who are only middling in looks and wealth and rank, must *seize* what opportunities present themselves."

As if the word "seize" were a password, the door to Hetty's self-command swung open, and she whirled on him, her blue eyes flashing in the dimness. Had it been an innocent choice of words on his part?

"'Seize'?" she whispered. "Contrary to appearances, sir, I am not in the habit of seizing people."

Mr. Rotherwood made a clicking sound with his tongue. "Alas. What did I teach you at the rout? About two points making a line, and this line having a trajectory? I distinctly saw you *seize* Mr. Pickford in the menagerie."

Before Hetty could summon a response, the keeper of the regalia beckoned his listeners once more, and the group shuffled onward again, this time toward the crown of state. "When he appears in Parliament, his majesty shines forth," the keeper recited, arm uplifted, inviting them to imagine the scene. "... Pearl of unmatched fineness...priceless ruby...emerald fully seven inches round..."

"I happened to be startled," Hetty hissed, when the others were sufficiently engrossed again. (Caroline was leaning so far forward that she appeared in danger of touching the crown of state with her nose.) "Grabbing Mr. Pickford was an *involuntary* reaction. Had he been a post or a tree or the king himself, I would have done the same."

From the corner of her eye she glimpsed Mr. Rotherwood's shoulders shaking, and one sharp look revealed to her that the man was laughing. *Laughing!* Silently, giving no other sign than a compression of his mouth.

"What is so funny?" she demanded, *sotto voce*.

"You," he said simply. "I call you 'middling' in looks, yet you are only angry with me for accusing you of laying hands on Pickford."

"Oh." She was nonplussed for a second but then gave a little shrug. "I do not object to truths, Mr. Rotherwood, even if they be home ones. Only falsehoods."

"But what if you have things the wrong way 'round?" he rejoined. "What if the falsehood lay in the premise, rather than the conclusion?"

She was not a slow girl by any means. In fact, Hetty's last governess Miss Blenkensop (now Mrs. Eldredge) had been wont to call her clever. But she could not make sense now of his speech. Was Mr. Rotherwood telling her he did not think her "middling" in looks? That he thought her rather prettier than otherwise? But why should he say so? Was he teasing her? *Flirting* with her? He did not strike her as a flirtatious man, and yet, five minutes ago, she would not have thought him a teasing man either.

Caroline, she reminded herself. *I don't know what he is about, but we must get back to the matter at hand. Which is Caroline.*

And yet, she could feel her heart thumping in a disorienting, not wholly unpleasant manner. Oh, dear. What could it mean? Supposing she herself were to begin to like Mr. Rotherwood, the man every other girl in London already liked or was disposed to like?

Supposing she had already begun?

Hetty took hold of herself by the elbows. She remembered a time her stepmother had been teaching her cousin Margaret to brew beer. Margaret's first batch ended in several exploded bottles which made the outbuilding reek for months. Hetty thought she knew now how those bottles felt, just before they burst. Trembly. Full of fizz. Excited.

He is a stiff, marble man, she tried to remind herself. But she already knew, from their few interactions, that he was neither as stiff nor as marble as she first imagined.

But he was still the most eligible young man in London. The richest. The handsomest (Hetty now admitted). The most learned (not that that mattered to anyone but herself).

Even if she were to forget herself and her assurance to Caroline so far as to dream of him, that did not put him within reach. And she was *not* the sort of girl who forgot herself or her assurances to others.

Or she had not been heretofore. How dreadful! Should her first brush with attraction immediately render her unrecognizable to herself? Should it instantly transform her into someone she had rather not be? Someone who forgot her promises to others in the face of her own interests?

And what could Mr. Rotherwood be thinking? Why should he talk to her in the first place?

She hit very near the truth when she thought, *Perhaps because he first met me in Oxford, as Lionel's sister, I seem already a comfortable person to speak with. He did not speak comfortably with me then, goodness knows, so it might be that he is shy. Shy and unused to these situations.* Which meant he would grow more comfortable and talkative with Caroline and Lady Sylvia and potentially countless other young ladies, as they too became more familiar. Therefore, she must not place too much weight on these moments, these words.

She must not now let this little...effervescence...inside her grow, lest it become something dangerous. Something that would burst her like Margaret's beer bottles and possibly injure those around her.

It would be best not to engage further, Hetty decided. Whether he were teasing or flirting, he must practice upon someone else, never mind that she would like to go on and on hearing him.

All this passed through her mind in the space of a moment. Then she released her elbows. Throwing him a half glance that did not quite meet his eyes, she smiled and said, "We are missing what the keeper has to say, and I did want especially to see the items that belonged to Queen Mary. If you will excuse me..."

With that she slipped away, squeezing through the other listeners to join her cousin.

CHAPTER NINE

Elusive of the bridal day, she gives
Fond hopes to all, and all with hopes deceives.
— Pope, *The Odyssey by Homer* (1725)

St. John returned to North Audley Street to find the drawing room cluttered by four gentlemen, ranging in age from eighty to little older than himself. The most advanced in years was at the most pains to appear hale, standing with hunched jauntiness by the fireplace. The two middle-aged ones, one bald and one not, sat in armchairs flanking his mother; while the youngest, trying his best not to look foolish, perched on a chair before her writing desk. Like a bloom in this garden of suitors his mother sat among them, clothed in her blue-black and embroidering steadily.

"My dear boy," she greeted him, her face alight with affection and ironic amusement, "how was your outing? St. John has been to the

Tower with some friends." Turning to the man at her desk she added mischievously, "Perhaps you might know some of them. For they are nearer your age, I suspect."

He went an uneven red and coughed and blurted, "I don't know what you mean, madam! You speak of age to me? Why, age—age is all in the—the perception of it."

"Well," she replied evenly, "St. John's friends are perceived to be young in the ordinary sense—meaning, they have not accumulated as many years as I." Rising and waiting for her swains to rise in turn, she said, "St. John, may I introduce Mr. Winston"—the old man by the fire— "Lord Camberwell"—bald— "Mr. Fletchley"—not bald— "and Mr. Quint"—foolish youth. "Gentlemen, my son Mr. Rotherwood."

They all bowed, none of them (including St. John) appearing well pleased to meet the other.

"So you've been to the Tower," said Mr. Winston, striving for an avuncular tone. "It has been quite a while since I have visited. Did you see the monkeys?"

"We saw the menagerie, but I hear the monkeys were removed some years ago."

"Wouldn't be surprised. One of them tore the leg of a little boy, begging your pardon, madam."

"That would have been frightening for the young ladies of St. John's acquaintance," murmured Anne. "How many young ladies were in your party this afternoon?"

"Just three: Lady Sylvia Stanley, Miss Sidney and her cousin Miss Hapgood."

"Such lovely creatures," Anne said to the room at large. "You gentlemen are remiss in letting my St. John steal a march on you, while you pay charity calls on old ladies."

This reference to herself met with a swell of protests from the visitors, and was followed by declarations of her winsomeness, disparaging comparisons of vapid youth with graceful experience, and so on, which mother and son heard out with solemn faces. But soon enough Anne grew impatient to talk to St. John alone. She rose once more, declaring, "I must rest now. St. John and I will be attending a musical performance tonight, and I would hate to yawn my way through it. I wish you all good afternoon."

When they were gone, however, she threw herself into a Hepplewhite chair, laughing. "Oh! How relieved I was when you returned! Remind me to invent a secret code for the servants: if I ring the bell short-short-long, that means they must burst into the room, as soon as ever they can, and announce I am needed at once because somebody is dying, or something has caught fire, or an express has come from the Archbishop of Canterbury."

He chuckled, stretching on the brocade chaise longue and crossing his booted legs. "You treat them all poorly enough. Are you certain they are all deserving of it?"

"Mr. Pinckney my solicitor takes pains to write little reports on any gentleman who shows me undue attention. For example, out of those four whom you just met, the man old enough to be my father is in the best condition financially—in fact, he might feel genuine esteem for me, only I wish he would direct his courtesies to someone closer in age to himself. I have no desire to escape poverty only to play nursemaid for my remaining years. But Mr. Pinckney gives ancient Mr. Winston his grudging approval. He is less approving of Lord Camberwell and Mr. Fletchley. The lord apparently has both a heavily-mortgaged estate and a mistress with children. Mr. Fletchley is not guilty of keeping a mistress, but Mr. Pinckney says he frequents the gaming tables and is not always in command of himself. His fortune has borne it thus far, but he may be down to his last half-crowns unless luck favors him soon. But altogether, the most reprehensible in my solicitor's opinion is the silly young Mr. Quint. As if I would take seriously that a man his age—little older than you, St. John—should prefer me to every young lady in the kingdom! I will do, for a woman of fifty, but I do not flatter myself that my charms can make someone overlook a difference of five-and-twenty years. And Mr. Pinckney confirms that Mr. Quint is in a great deal of trouble. If he cannot bring some wealthy woman to the point—and quickly—he will have to flee abroad to escape debtor's prison!"

"He should try for Lady Sylvia," suggested St. John.

His mother sniffed. "He hasn't a chance with a Lady Sylvia. Do you think the Stanleys would let a penniless fortune hunter of his stamp within twenty feet of her? Why, if he had any sense at all, he would not make himself ridiculous to me, but would instead pursue someone of, say, Miss Hapgood's position: pretty enough, a healthy portion attached to her, and no parent hovering about to shoo him away."

She spoke this in perfect innocence, but St. John's reaction surprised them both. He sat up abruptly. "*I* should shoo him away, if he dared to bother her."

Anne blinked at him. "Well—to be sure," she said. "She is the sister, after all, of one of your former students. I am not surprised you feel—protective of her interests."

"So I do," he answered, thoughtful.

"Hmm." Brightly, she reached for her embroidery hoop and made a show of scrutinizing her progress. "Tell me—was Lady Sylvia in looks today?"

"Of course. She is a beautiful girl."

"She certainly is. Beautiful and well-mannered."

He chuckled. "As she rarely opens her mouth, she has few opportunities for rudeness."

"Oh, St. John—did she not speak more today?"

He shrugged. "Not particularly."

His mother's bosom heaved in smothered vexation. "She is shy, I suppose."

"I think she might be, but who is to say?"

"Perhaps we might have the Stanleys to supper. Some young ladies do better with fewer people about." She gave him a sly glance but was forced to withdraw it hastily when he caught it.

"Mama—I know you would like me to like Lady Sylvia."

"Nonsense! Of course I can't help thinking of her, since I would love you to have a rich, beautiful wife you can be proud of."

"I know. It is written all over you. But I hope you will allow me the luxury of falling in love with her before she is forced down my throat."

"'Forced down your throat'! Indeed! St. John, I beg you will not accuse me of such things," his mother protested, pulling her thread too tight in her distress. "I force nothing and no one."

"Then we will both be happy."

"But do you think, if she were to cease being shy and silent, you might possibly come to like her?" she coaxed. "That you'll 'look to like, if looking liking move'?"

"I can't say," was his unsatisfactory reply.

Anne pressed her lips together and squinted at her needlework, a fanciful partridge against a background of flowers and pears. She knew her son to be dutiful. As she had told Mr. Pinckney, St. John had never given her cause for anxiety. From his days as a young schoolboy he had been diligent and quiet—there had been no bad reports, no letters from the headmaster. And at Oxford he had remitted half his fellowship to her faithfully, term after term. She knew he would heed her counsel as much as he could, both from habit and from character. And would it not be right for her to insist on Lady Sylvia—just a little? After all, this was so new to him. Everything. Where she had once been Miss Holt of Glennard, daughter to a baronet, St. John had only ever known poverty and anonymity. He needed her guidance.

Yes.

He must be made to give Lady Sylvia every chance.

Carefully, she drew a long stitch through the muslin along the edge of a flower petal. Perhaps the girl shone brightest when dancing, and that should be attempted before an intimate supper. If the Stanleys came to North Audley Street for an intimate supper and *still* the chit said nothing, that might be the death knell of Anne's hopes.

She lifted her head and smiled at him. "I did not tell you my other piece of news, St. John. While you were out, a note came to me from Lady Aurora. She is very good friends with Lady Cowper, you know. Lady Cowper—one of the patronesses of Almack's. Lady Cowper told Lady Aurora that she would be pleased to issue us vouchers, if we would like. It's a signal honor, St. John. I am sure the Stanleys will be in attendance, as well as the very best of the season's young ladies."

St. John was fiddling with his cuff, his face expressionless.

"I—I know you did not enjoy Lady Aurora's rout," his mother began again, her tone the slightest bit wheedling. "So many people and such a crush and such noise..."

"I do not suppose I will ever attend another," he replied.

"But an assembly will be a much more organized sort of thing," she persisted. "You need only ask a few girls to dance, and, if they are not easy to converse with, there is always the dancing to distract."

"Would—Miss Sidney and Miss Hapgood be there?" he asked, after a hesitation.

Anne felt the first faint stirrings of alarm. Miss Hapgood again! Why should St. John ask after her?

"Why, who can say?" She gave a light laugh, to hide her racing thoughts. Maybe it was all nothing—he asked after Miss Sidney as well—having seen the three young ladies at the rout and the Tower, he naturally thought of all of them together. To her mind, Miss Sidney and Miss Hapgood were just two more butterflies fluttering around her son—pretty but indistinct. However, if it would add to her son's pleasure for the insignificant butterflies to be present, she should use this to her advantage. "They very well may be. There is only one way to be certain…"

He nodded. "Of course." Rising, he paced the length of the room in slow strides, his face at its most reserved. "Very well. Like a prize bull at a fair, I am ready to be displayed again."

"What a dreadful analogy, my dear. Bulls aren't known for their graceful dancing, I daresay. Nor their conversation." Laying aside her embroidery, she joined him, threading her arm through his and resting her cheek against his sleeve. "Thank you, St. John. I will confess to you now that I am dying of curiosity to see Almack's and would very much like to dance myself, if anyone will ask me, old lady that I am."

This brought a smile. "You might have led with that, you know. Although if you continue to add to your string of conquests, I will be hard pressed to dismiss them all. Getting rid of Penelope's suitors in *The Odyssey* required the combined efforts of a husband *and* a son, if I remember aright."

"Ha." She tapped him with a chiding finger. "If it gets that bad, I am sure we can call upon the services of Mr. Pinckney."

The Rotherwoods arrived at Almack's Assembly Rooms in King Street on late Wednesday evening, coveted vouchers in hand. Anne, eager to make the way smooth for her son and accompanied by Lady Aurora, had made the requisite call earlier in the week to gain the patronesses' official approval, and she could only hope and pray the effort would be rewarded.

Their appearance on this night was also under Lady Aurora's aegis. Having so lately hosted her successful rout, there was no one better than she to perform introductions. It would be like having their own personal patroness.

To Anne's delight, they no sooner entered the spacious ballroom, warm and slightly shabby, but glittering with crystal chandeliers, mirrors and gilt, than she spied Lady Sylvia taking hands with her partner to go up the middle. It was a sign, she was certain. How else could she have picked her out so quickly, among so many?

Turning to St. John, she found his eyes surveying the hundreds of guests, but if he saw Lady Sylvia, he gave no sign. Instead, she saw the set of his jaw and the stiff precision of his bows when introduced. She heard the remote politeness in his voice when he spoke.

She was soon whirled away herself, as popular as any of the young beauties there, by virtue of her immense fortune. But while she added absently to her string of swains, she kept one eye always on St. John. And was frustrated.

Like the ghost of Hamlet's father, doomed for a certain term to walk the night, St. John danced every dance. Lady Sylvia was the most beautiful of his partners, but Anne could see that other young ladies had more life in them, and all spoke more. If only he would smile! If only his stony aspect would soften into flesh and blood! If only he would ask Lady Sylvia or, indeed, any other young lady present for a second dance. Then Anne might congratulate herself and call the evening a success.

But he did none of those things.

Because every atom of her hoped his woodenness had nothing to do with the fact that Miss Sidney and Miss Hapgood were *not* present, she would have been much grieved to learn that it did.

The ballroom was large, but it was nonetheless possible to glimpse every person present, unless someone escaped to one of the card rooms. It was natural for St. John to look about him when he entered through the Ionic doorcase with its elegant pediment. It was natural for him to look about as he bowed through every introduction and asked girl after girl to dance. It was natural for him to look about as he moved through the figures precisely and correctly.

But in all this looking about he never once saw Miss Hapgood, and it was only when he had danced and conversed and fetched lemonade and escorted any number of young ladies hither and yon to this or that chaperone, that he finally admitted to himself that it was Miss Hapgood he sought.

And because she was nowhere to be found, everything felt flat.

It was not that she was the prettiest girl of his acquaintance—Lady Sylvia carried off that palm from the first. Nor the most stylish—Lady Sylvia again. He had no idea if she was a graceful dancer or if she had any accomplishments besides her unusual interest in mathematics. He only knew that he enjoyed talking to her. He enjoyed the ease of her company.

If Miss Hapgood had been there, he would have asked her to dance for the sheer pleasure of trading thoughts and opinions and jokes. Miss Hapgood would not say, as Miss Prentice did, "A mathematics don! How alarming. To save my life I couldn't tell you how many pennies are in a shilling!" Miss Hapgood would not giggle or blush at him or answer his lame attempts at conversation with a "how right you are!" or a rap of the fan. He had seen her enough times to find his cursed stiffness and awkwardness were forgotten when he talked to her. When they spoke apart from others.

He had been disappointed at the Tower when she ended their quiet talk and returned to her cousin's side. That same cousin then claimed his arm again, when the glitter of the Crown Jewels faded away, and chattered at him so indefatigably that Miss Hapgood could not have got a word in if she wanted to. Not that she seemed to want to. She retreated again under that mysterious, intermittent vacant air, as if she imagined herself becoming invisible. Whatever brought it on, St. John wished he could learn the trick of it. For everywhere he went now, he attracted stares. Stares ranging from open admiration to flirtation to awe.

At Almack's the intensity of these stares increased. It was known as the Marriage Mart, after all, so he could not blame the young ladies and their mothers for doing what they could to charm him. His dance with Lady Sylvia would have come as a relief, she was so silent and serene, except that he felt those eyes, eyes, eyes upon him. And he heard the swell of talk when he led her to the floor. He saw the leaning in and the whispers behind fans.

Most of all, he saw his mother's head turn from far down the line, and he could not mistake the shine of her smile.

And so he retreated in his own fashion. He might not be able to become invisible, but he had mastered the art of turning to stone. Hard, impenetrable, cool, remote.

The Marble Millionaire indeed.

Chapter Ten

I have given suck, and know
How tender 'tis to love the babe that milks me:
I would, while it was smiling in my face,
Have pluck'd my nipple from his boneless gums,
And dash'd the brains out, had I so sworn as you
Have done to this.
— Shakespeare, *Macbeth,* I.vii.533 (c.1606)

"It's hateful," said Caroline Sidney. Her arm through her cousin's, they were walking in Regent's Park. "I cannot understand why she would not help me."

Hetty smothered a yawn. This was not their first time canvassing the topic. "Perhaps it's me," she offered. "It could be that Lady Sylvia once thought of using her position and influence to secure you vouchers to Almack's, only to have me arrive! And then she feared it would be altogether too much to ask of Lady Jersey to admit not just one new friend but *two* young ladies whom no one has heard of."

Caroline scowled at the workers in the distance, busy with the construction of one of the villas. "Then she might have said so. I would have told her she needn't trouble herself or Lady Jersey over *you*. It isn't as if *you* want a husband."

"Well, of course she didn't say so because Lady Sylvia never does say anything," said Hetty reasonably. "Unless you ask her a question point blank. Did you ask her the question point blank?"

Here her cousin turned and dropped her arm. "What—ask her, 'Pardon me, Lady Sylvia, but have you asked Lady Jersey yet if she will admit me?'"

"In so many words."

"Of course I didn't! How could I?" Caroline protested. "How ridiculous you are. But—she should have known without my saying so! I spoke of the place often enough."

"Yes," answered Hetty, pulling on her arm to get them moving again. "But her silence can be a weapon, you know. If she doesn't speak, all the onus is on you. And if you do not dare raise the subject, she is spared the trouble of dealing with it. It's rather clever of her."

Caroline was silent for a time, continuing to frown and dawdle. Finally she said, "I suppose she wants him for herself."

There was no need to ask to whom her companion referred. "Yes, you said she liked him. It would only be natural to set her own interests before yours."

"Why do you defend her?" Caroline demanded, stomping her little foot.

"I'm not defending her. I am only telling you the facts. If the situation were reversed, you would do exactly the same to her."

Tossing her head, Caroline refused to concede this, instead striking out in a new direction. "I'm certain he asked her to dance at Almack's. Probably more than once. Which meant she had him nearly to herself for—oh—so much time. You don't suppose he might have offered already, do you?"

Hetty scoffed. "No. I don't think so. He does not seem an impulsive man. And offering for Lady Sylvia after one rout, one call, one visit to the Tower, and two dances at Almack's sounds very impulsive."

"You consider yourself an expert on Mr. Rotherwood, then? I saw you trying to stand next to him in the Jewel Room."

"Not an expert, no," Hetty rejoined crossly. "And I did not try to stand next to him. I simply happened to stand next to him."

"Did he talk to you?"

Hetty's hesitation was brief, but not so brief that it escaped her cousin's notice.

"He did!" Caroline cried. "He talked to you. I was on his arm nearly the entire time, and I don't suppose he said twenty words to me altogether."

"Perhaps he was waiting for an opening?" ventured Hetty. The two girls had reached the bridge where Edith had sketched Lionel and Caroline that summer, and Hetty's heart sank when Caroline halted to lean against the railing. Caroline was surely going to think about Lionel, and then she was going to think about how Hetty had interfered.

It was like magic, really. If there were indeed a frost fair, Hetty thought, she would set up a stall on the frozen Thames and offer to read people's minds. Because Caroline said, "He isn't like Lionel. No one is. I had a better chance with your brother. If only you hadn't—well."

"Yes, well." Hetty swallowed a sigh. What more was there to say about it, honestly? Moaning about it wasn't going to make Lionel jilt Edith and marry Caroline.

Her cousin hung over the railing to watch a pair of swans slip under the bridge. Then she straightened and gripped it with both hands, her little jaw set. "You told me I must make the effort to talk to Mr. Rotherwood, and I have, but I don't think it is working—"

"You can hardly determine, Caroline, based on one afternoon at the Tower—"

"I mean, why should he talk to you," she went on, ignoring Hetty's interjection, "when you aren't even *trying* to attract his notice, and then not talk to me, when I *am* trying? Unless you *are* trying, Hetty."

This last was said in an accusing tone, and Hetty felt herself on the defensive. "I assure you. I am not seeking him out or trying to attract his notice. I don't know why he opens his mouth when he does and refuses to open it at other times." She felt her pulse speeding. With what? With awareness? Guilt? Was she lying?

"But are you genuinely trying to help me, as you did Edith? When he talked to you at the Tower, did you mention me?"

"Yes!" Of that she was certain. She had tried to mention her cousin. "Look here, Caroline. It is unfortunate that he hadn't much to say to you at the Tower. And it is unfortunate that Lady Sylvia did not procure you vouchers for Almack's. But I am guessing she did not have any more luck getting the man to talk than you did, so there is no harm done—unless dancing is the way to his heart. Which, I don't see how it could be, because what use had an Oxford fellow for dancing? But, yes, I am genuinely trying to help you."

"Then why don't you have a plan, as you did for Edith? What am I to do next?"

"For pity's sake! We can hardly tie the man to a chair until he loves you," Hetty protested. "We must simply take full advantage of your next opportunity. Did your mama not mention some musical evening next week? Perhaps he will be there. And, if he is, I will stay by your side as much as possible, so that, if he wants to make comfortable conversation with me, as the sister of a former pupil—nothing more—he will be forced to make conversation with you as well. Remember—if you ask him questions, he cannot avoid answering them. He answered many of your questions when we were at the Stanleys'. My advice to you would be to think of more of them which require long answers. And—and show a little curiosity about the greater world."

"What do you mean?" Her Wedgwood-blue eyes were lost.

Hetty tried not to grimace. "Remember Benjamin Franklin? We talked about this. Perhaps you could say that we are planning to attend the Royal Society talk next week, and will he be there? We must remember to find out who the speaker is."

"Royal Society talk!" Caroline groaned. "I do not believe I can say such a thing in a credible manner."

"Hmm." Hetty snapped her fingers, her face lighting. "All right then—ask him if *he* has attended any lecture there yet or if he plans to in future. And then ask him a dozen questions about it. I'm sure it will be on some arcane subject, so it will be plausible enough that you need clarification."

Grimly, Caroline nodded. "This promises to be worse than lessons with my governess. You will help me prepare, won't you, Hetty?"

"Most assuredly!" As ever, the thought of studying and adding to her knowledge filled her with eagerness. "Let's go now to Booth's in Portland Place. They might have a book or two that will prove helpful. Maybe something mathematical or scientific."

This elicited another groan. "If they do, you must look at them and write to me a little summary and a question or two. Because I would rather choose some new novels."

Poor Caroline did not have as much time as she might have liked to prepare for her next encounter with Mr. Rotherwood, however, because they saw him and his mother the very next evening at the Theatre Royal in Drury Lane for a performance of *Macbeth*.

To Caroline's disappointment, her father had been unable to secure the front row of a box, and they found themselves buried four rows back.

"It's better this way," Hetty told her. "For then we may look around without being seen ourselves."

And the first people they saw were the Stanleys in a private box, Lady Sylvia at the forefront, like a figurehead on a ship, Hetty thought. The earl's daughter was her usual solemn self and made quiet conversation with her parents; if she scanned the audience to see who else was in attendance or who was staring at her (almost everyone), she did it so slyly that Hetty couldn't catch her.

"That's a new dress," said Caroline with a sigh. "She looks quite lovely. Of course, she might wear a bag and look just as well."

"You look lovely too," answered Hetty automatically. But it was true. In a gown of silver-blue with white trim, Caroline did not exactly blend with the carpet.

"Do you suppose we should visit her box during the interval, or stay away, since she did not call or send a note yesterday?"

"I think it would look odd if we stayed away. Besides, don't you want to know what happened at Almack's, if anything?"

But Caroline's only reply was a soft gasp. Following her gaze, Hetty saw the Rotherwoods, mother and son, taking their seats in the box directly above the Stanleys'. Both girls shrunk back into the shadows, even as clashing and rushing sounds filled the theatre, heralding the beginning of the play and the entrance of the three witches.

All of the Hapgood girls had been thoroughly inculcated in love of Shakespeare by their governesses, and Hetty was chagrinned to divide her attention from the stage. Especially because Mr. Kean thrilled as the tragic thane. The actor was not a tall man, as she imagined Macbeth should be—was it not slightly ridiculous to be murdered by a short man?—but his electric presence soon made her forget his stature. In fact, she soon also forgot to check periodically on Mr. Rotherwood and Lady Sylvia and even forgot Caroline sitting beside her. All her attention was for the vital actor as he strode the boards.

Therefore, when the banquet scene ended in a swell of music and the interval followed, Hetty woke as if from a dream. The box in which they sat was soon in a bustle as those around them rose to move about, and Caroline was tugging on her hand. "Shall we go? Do you still think we should visit Lady Sylvia, or should we venture to the Rotherwoods' box? I could hardly attend a word, I was so torn, trying to decide."

Hetty shook herself. "Yes. Yes, we should go. We will greet the Stanleys. It would be too awkward to seek the Rotherwoods." Her uncle Wellington kindly offered an arm to each girl, and the family made its slow progress through the milling crowd to the opposite side of the theatre.

The Stanley box was full of visitors by the time they reached it. Hetty recognized only Sir Keane, who bowed to her and said, "Marvelous pwoduction, is it not, Miss Hapgood? That banquet scene was worthy of a woyal festivity. But I confess I pweferred Kean as Wichard the Third."

"You are so fortunate to have seen him perform in other plays," she answered, "for I think he's wondrous."

Caroline was pulling on her, and they went to stand beside Lady Sylvia, who gazed at them serenely as she fanned herself.

"Good evening," said Caroline abruptly. "Your dress is beautiful."

"Thank you."

"How do you like the play, Lady Sylvia?" asked Hetty.

"Very nice. I like the costumes."

This was a topic which broke the ice nicely. Waxing enthusiastic, Caroline began to list every detail of Lady Macbeth's gown which caught her eye, to which Lady Sylvia nodded and almost smiled. And then she did smile and raised her gloved fingers.

"Mr. Rotherwood. Good evening."

The girls turned to discover he too had entered the box to stand solemnly, his hat in his hands. Mrs. Rotherwood and Lady Stanley were close together behind him, greeting each other and wreathed in smiles, but Hetty couldn't hear what they said over the sudden thumping of her heart. He really oughtn't to creep up on people like that! It was like turning around to find someone had built a two-storey brick wall behind you when you weren't looking.

Curtseying in response to his bow, she made a pretense of re-arranging a curl on her head, that she might raise an eyebrow at Caroline unseen. *Now, girl!*

"Mr. Rotherwood," Caroline responded, "how—how are you enjoying the play?"

"My enjoyment of it exceeds my ability to express, Miss Sidney." Unseen by Hetty (because she was looking past his shoulder), his stern face softened considerably. "And you—all of you? How are you liking it?"

"I love it!" glowed Caroline. "The scenery and the costumes and the music. Glorious." She pressed her elbow lightly against Hetty's, as if to say, *See? We have found something in common!*

Not to be outdone, Lady Sylvia roused herself to say, "Yes."

"And you, Miss Hapgood?" he prompted. "What is your opinion?"

With an effort, Hetty stuffed down everything she would like to say and instead murmured, "Exactly what Caroline said. Glorious."

"But have you young ladies nothing to say about the celebrated Mr. Kean?" he persisted. "I had never heard the line delivered like that—when Lady Macbeth asked when King Duncan would be leaving, and Kean said, 'Tomorrow as he...purposes.' It was all in the pause he took. You could see the murder was already in his mind."

Both Caroline and Lady Sylvia frowned faintly, trying to remember the moment referred to, and Hetty was speaking before she could help herself. "Yes! Before I always thought it was Lady Macbeth egging him on—with Macbeth being little more than a—a henpecked husband. But Mr. Kean plays him as an equal partner to his wife. An equal schemer, and thus equally guilty."

"It makes a difference to the tragedy, does it not?" Mr. Rotherwood asked. "Is he a noble character who degenerates into a pitiful one, or is he a wicked man who only requires opportunity?"

"Or it could be that he is no more wicked than the rest of us," Hetty offered, "but the tragedy lies in his circumstances: that he is put in a position of power, and the opportunity arouses wickedness which might otherwise have lain perfectly dormant."

"Do you think? Do you think wickedness can ever lie 'perfectly dormant'? Will it not always seek a path—an opportunity, like quicksilver?"

"Ordinary levels of human wickedness might lie dormant enough, left to themselves," she insisted. "Otherwise, wouldn't we all be murderers and thieves? No—the tragedy for Kean's Macbeth is in his circumstances. Had the witches never encouraged his ambition, or had he been married to a woman who recoiled from the thought of murder herself and begged him not to commit any crime, he might have gone through life a contented thane and been thought reasonably virtuous."

Mr. Rotherwood smiled—actually *smiled*—at this. "You are persuasive, Miss Hapgood. I suppose we gentlemen, in order to be saved from our dormant wickedness, must resist those who stoke our ambitions, and we must also choose our spouses wisely."

"That will do for the gentlemen," she returned, "but ladies have their dormant wickedness as well, as Lady Macbeth shows. Did not her circumstances equally serve to unleash her wickedness? Shakespeare gives no hint that she was anything beyond an ordinary wife and mother before the events of the play. She might speak of dashing her baby's brains out, but she never did such a thing in fact. No—it is the accumulation of tragic circumstances. They all combine perfectly to elicit the worst behavior from both husband and wife."

"Hetty, do stop!" entreated her cousin, with a brittle laugh. "Such talk—dashing babies' brains out, indeed—" She gave Mr. Rotherwood an apologetic smile, even as she pinched the flesh of Hetty's arm right above her glove, causing Hetty to hiccup in surprise.

In her turn, Lady Sylvia was moved to rise. She snapped her fan shut. "I think the play begins again soon, and it will take some time to regain your seats."

The dismissal was clear, and Caroline and Hetty could only take their leave, Mr. Rotherwood bowing them out.

This time when Mr. Sidney escorted them back across the theatre house, Caroline took hold of Hetty's other side, that she might hiss in her ear, "What have you done? You inserted yourself *again*, instead of helping put me forward! And I was doing so well. I am very angry with you, Hetty. Very angry. You promised me. If I had made such a promise to you, you would not find me forgetting myself in such a manner. You speak of wickedness—you should look to your own!"

And Hetty was indeed chastened. Caroline was entirely justified in berating her. Instead of helping her cousin, as she had promised, she had been caught up in the excitement of discussing the play. She should feel very, very guilty.

And she did, for all of five minutes.

That is, until the heavy stage curtain rolled open again and the show went on.

Chapter Eleven

**The moste hygh & moste profytable
science...is selfe knowledge.
— R. Whitford, *A Dialogue Bytwene Curate &
Parochiane* (1537)**

St. John had difficulty falling asleep after their attendance at the theatre. Not only because of the sublimity of the play, though it held him spellbound. No—his restlessness stemmed from a realization. He realized that his enjoyment of *Macbeth* heightened when he had someone stimulating to discuss it with. His interchange with Miss Hapgood had been all too brief. He wanted to continue it.

He had not known her party was present until the interval, when he and his mother entered the Stanleys' box. "We must go down and see them," Mrs. Rotherwood insisted. "I told Lady Stanley we would." Seeing his fleeting expression, she prodded him playfully.

"The play will give you a natural subject for conversation. Even shy Lady Sylvia must have an opinion on it."

For his part, St. John was beginning to suspect Lady Sylvia's reticence did not stem altogether from shyness. She had surprised him at Almack's by volunteering three separate comments during their twenty-five-minute dance: one regarding the tune being played (she liked it); one to express a preference for the refreshments at private balls; and one to say the room was quite warm, considering the temperature out of doors. Granted, it was almost impossible to scintillate in a ballroom. The intermittent nature of the conversation, the exertion, the music, the other conversations taking place around one all conspired to keep the talk at a surface level. More power was granted the eyes to meet and duck away, the hands to touch and thrill. But in the absence of these physical allurements, words must serve or not serve. And Lady Sylvia's did not serve. To be fair, he doubted any of the young ladies he partnered at Almack's found much to admire in either his own dancing or his conversation—the former was correct but rather wooden, and the latter nearly nonexistent.

But if his mother continued to hope Lady Sylvia would yet transform into a wit, there was no need to quibble about it in the moment, and he escorted her down the staircase to rap upon the door. The Rotherwoods were not the only ones paying court. The fullness of the Stanleys' box forced them to wait in the doorway until someone should pass out, but in looking over the little clutch of heads within, a flash of bright hair drew his eye directly, and he was aware of a corresponding lift in his spirits.

Ah, he thought. *I might indeed be in danger.*

What else could he conclude, if he should be disappointed by her absence at Almack's and delighted by her presence here?

But then, was Miss Hapgood so very dangerous a danger? She might not be a peer's daughter, but she was at least the daughter of a gentleman. Moreover, he was acquainted with her family and found them agreeable people. If she was not lavishly wealthy, neither was she poor. And if she was not the most beautiful girl in London, she was by no means lacking in attractions. And fully on the credit side of the balance sheet, she interested him—her demeanor, her conversation—which was more than could be said for Lady Sylvia or the talkative Miss Sidney.

Certainly there was enough to Miss Hapgood that he need not shrink from seeking to know her better. Why should he think her dangerous, then?

The answer lay in his mother's face, as she regarded the earl and countess and their beautiful daughter. The baronet's daughter in her had come to the fore, after having been denied and suppressed for decades, and its return was not to be gainsaid. Anne Rotherwood was ambitious again, for herself and for her son, and she was no longer the impulsive young woman who thought the world well lost for love.

Trusting that his mother would think he went to do his duty by Lady Sylvia, however, St. John thought himself safe in approaching the three young ladies. And he had indeed done his duty. When Miss Sidney accosted him, St. John widened the conversation to include Lady Sylvia and Miss Hapgood. Could he help it if he and Miss

Hapgood then forgot themselves in their enthusiasm for Kean's performance? The young lady had a peculiar habit of not looking his way whenever she first saw him, and it had become a game to make her do so. A game with a rich reward, for, when he succeeded, her blue eyes would flash upon him like a sunrise. The brightness of her hair mirrored the brightness of her aspect as words bubbled to her lips. Thoughtful, insightful words—words which reflected her intelligence and humor and curiosity about the world. St. John could not help but think that, even if words began to spill unchecked from Lady Sylvia, as they did from Miss Sidney, they would probably not be any more interesting to him than those of Miss Sidney. Miss Sidney offered *quantity* of conversation, Miss Hapgood *quality*, and Lady Sylvia possibly neither.

Rolling over in his bed, he punched his pillow to plump it.

He would call in Devonshire Street, St. John resolved, as drowsiness finally crept over him. He need not inform his mother, at this point. It would only cause her premature anxiety. After all, Miss Hapgood might prove less engaging, the more one knew her. Did not most people, after all, himself included?

His last thought, as he dropped to sleep was, *I wonder if Miss Hapgood ever thinks of me.*

A walk of approximately a mile through neat and relatively well-kept Mayfair would lead a midnight stroller from the Rotherwood home in North Audley Street along wide Oxford and Portland Streets to the Sidney home in Devonshire Street, where Hetty Hapgood sat at the writing table in her bed chamber and did indeed think of Mr. Rotherwood.

Her hair was braided in a neat crown and her knees were tucked up under her nightdress as she brushed the end of her quill against her cheek. A half-finished letter to Edith lay before her.

...Heaven knows when I will ever hear from you. I have addressed my letters to the Poste Restante in Rome but have received no word from you, so I have no idea if they even reached their destination or if <u>you</u> have reached your destination! In any event, I must write to you, even if my previous missives have tumbled out of a mailbag into an Alpine crevasse, or <u>you</u> have tumbled out of your coach into that same, treacherous crevasse. Because Edie—I have already got myself in a scrape! You will shake your head when (if) you read this. I can even hear you sighing, "Oh, Hetty."

Because you counseled me to redeem myself in Caroline's eyes by helping her find someone to love as she loved Lionel, and I assure you I was perfectly willing, especially since she and Aunt Lavinia were somewhat cold and reproachful to me when I arrived in London. The good news was that I found Caroline full ready to fall in love again. The bad news was that, who should she set her heart upon except the very man every debutante in London wants? Very well, I thought, it will be a challenge, and I love a challenge. This man was reputed to be young, handsome, and rich as Croesus—and he is indeed all those things, Edith. For you will never credit it—the gentleman who has set the town on its ear is our very own Bernini's David! Yes! It is Mr. St. John Rotherwood, Lionel's former tutor! My astonishment when I heard this will beggar even your imagination, Edith.

Now I hear you asking, "Is this the scrape you refer to, Hetty? That Caroline has set her sights so high you cannot meet the challenge?" In a word: no. The abundance of competition would not necessarily have signaled defeat for my cousin (though among the competitors is her new "friend" Lady Sylvia, a beautiful earl's daughter who is rich, to boot).

No, Edith—

Here the scratch of Hetty's pen paused. She groaned, resting her forehead in her hand. To continue—even in a letter, and even to her beloved cousin and soon-to-be sister—was difficult. Embarrassing. But to herself she had always striven to be baldly honest. Nay—her family would have said that Hetty was apt to be too honest about everything, no matter the discomfort it might cause others! This predicament in which she found herself, she supposed, was repayment in kind.

She resumed.

...I am in a scrape because I think I have begun to like Mr. Rotherwood myself. Yes! I! I, who have never particularly cared one way or another for any young man. And it is not his handsomeness (though I like it better and better), nor his stiffness—which borders on pomposity—nor his ridiculous wealth. It is that I would like to sit and talk to him for a hundred years, Edie. And to admit such a thing only proves I have lost my mind because I don't believe he and I have conversed for even an hour, taken altogether. (I do not count the dinner in Oxford, for the talk around that table was general.)

It does not matter, of course. I do not dream that I alone of every young lady in London may charm him, even if I forgot myself enough to try for it. Nor am I really thinking of marriage, I promise, Edith. It is just that, those times I have been in Mr. Rotherwood's company, I have been interested. I have been entertained. I have been myself, even when I have tried not to be. And I <u>have</u> tried not to be, for the Sidneys' sake.

You will ask if Mr. Rotherwood shares my enjoyment, but I will only go so far as to say I think he prefers talking to me over Caroline. No—that is not the entire truth. I have got him to laugh, Edie, which is no mean feat. But I must not place too much weight on that. I must not.

But here is my dilemma, dear Edith: while Mr. Rotherwood has no thoughts of me, I am certain, I am equally certain he has no thoughts of Caroline. And likely will not, for they are chalk and cheese. If he were to settle on a young lady so incompatible, would he not rather choose Lady Sylvia over her? Cheese is cheese, but Lady S would be a creamy Double Gloucester, where Caroline is merely a good Cheshire. (Oh, Edith, you see how chalky I am?) Therefore, if there is no hope of Caroline winning Mr. Rotherwood, and if knowing him better might begin to make me unhappy, we should forget all about him, should we not? We should avoid him, if possible. And it should indeed be possible, for he moves in higher circles than we, generally, and Caroline's fondness for Lady Sylvia begins to wane.

Yes. Thank you, dear heart. You see how taking up pen to write to you is enough to put my thoughts in order? We will avoid Mr. Rotherwood, and I will do my best to direct my cousin to more come-at-able young men. Come-at-able and compatible—how Clunker would delight in that rhyme!

Good night, good night. I will continue this later. But if I do not at least attempt to sleep now, I will have dark

circles under my eyes tomorrow, and Aunt Lavinia will
be sure to remark on them.

The first test of Hetty's hard-won resolution came at breakfast. Caroline looked up from buttering her toast at her cousin in the window seat. "What is that you're reading?"

Happy to see her cousin was once again speaking to her, Hetty replied, "The compilation of Royal Society lectures we got at Booth's."

"Perfect. Tell me something you've learned, so that I may try it upon Mr. Rotherwood."

That made Hetty squirm. "Oh—I don't know about that particular scheme after all. I begin to think it was not one of my better ones."

"Oh?" a chill returned to Caroline's voice.

"I mean to say, supposing you tried one of these subjects on him and got him to talk—would you not find it dull?" Hetty continued hastily. "Wouldn't you rather talk to a gentleman who doesn't require study to converse with?"

Caroline's brows drew together swiftly. "It is just as I suspected! You don't intend to help me after all."

"I do, I do," insisted Hetty, setting aside her book. "I just wonder if you wouldn't be happier with someone more *like* you. You know—someone who likes society and routs and the scenery and costumes of a play..."

With a clatter, Caroline let fall the butter knife and pushed her plate away. "You are as bad as Lady Sylvia, Harriet Hapgood," she uttered. "You pretend friendship, but all along you have your own ideas."

"Listen to me," Hetty commanded her cousin's mutinous back. "I am not pretending friendship. I am saying I do not know if a man like Mr. Rotherwood could make you happy."

"And you say this because you think you already know him so well?"

Hetty could feel her temperature rising. Springing from the window seat, she circled the table to confront Caroline directly. "I most assuredly do not claim to know Mr. Rotherwood well. But I do believe the little I know of him is enough to persuade me that both he and you could find more suitable partners."

To Hetty's alarm, instead of mustering a retort, Caroline's pretty face collapsed, and her blue eyes filled. "Oh! Oh," she gasped. "I suppose I'm not clever enough."

As Hetty would later write to Edith, she might have withstood any other response from her cousin: disbelief, scorn, suspicion. But to have Caroline give way so quickly and completely, to see her criticize herself as wanting, made Hetty suddenly, contrarily, want to buoy her up.

"Don't, Caro—don't," she soothed, patting her cousin's trembling shoulder. "You are as intelligent as every other girl we've met here so far. You mustn't disparage yourself thus."

"Do—do you truly think so?" sniffled Caroline, looking up at her hopefully.

Before Hetty could reply, the door opened and the maid Reddy appeared. "Mr. Rotherwood come to call," she announced. "If you be in, I'll show him to the morning room."

Hetty and Caroline gawped at each other in dismay, Caroline thinking of how dreadful she must look, and Hetty thinking this was hardly a good beginning to avoiding the man! But there was nothing to be done about that now, and Caroline gave Reddy a panicked nod, even as she turned to her cousin for assistance. Seizing a napkin, Hetty dabbed away Caroline's tears and ordered her to blow her nose.

"And take this," she urged, thrusting the book of Royal Society proceedings at her. "Put your finger in it—anywhere—as if you have been reading it. When the opportunity arises, just look at the page and ask him what one of the words means."

"You will help me, won't you, Hetty?" Caroline pleaded. "You won't try to put yourself forward again?"

"Yes, yes, I will help you," she agreed. "And I never meant to put myself forward, but this time I will make an extra effort to guard against it. Now, come."

Chapter Twelve

...Your own family, begin with that; do, pray, give me a little history of your own family?
— Fanny Burney, *Camilla: Or, A Picture of Youth* (1796)

St. John did not fool himself that he would get to see Miss Hapgood alone if he called in Devonshire Street, but he had hoped to do better than to have the entire Sidney family present. Mr. Wellington Sidney only made his bow, to be sure, before attempting to excuse himself, but his wife favored him with a particular look and tightness of the lips, and he resignedly took a seat.

Both Mrs. Sidney and Miss Hapgood took up light needlework, while Miss Sidney perched on the edge of her armchair, clutching a book, one finger slipped between the pages to hold her place.

Judging by how rigidly she held it, she must have been sorry to be interrupted.

"I hope you all find yourselves well this morning," he began, addressing Mrs. Sidney, though he had noted in a glance that Miss Hapgood appeared rather wan. Not that she had looked at him. Clearly this was to be another occasion in which she found his left shoulder a source of fascination if she turned his way at all.

"We are indeed," Lavinia replied. "Though I was out of sorts yesterday, for which reason I was compelled to miss the play."

"I am glad you have recovered," said St. John politely. There was a pause. He wanted to plunge into discussing the conclusion of the play with Miss Hapgood but didn't know how to go about it. With her stitching busily and the others present, he did not feel he could single her out.

"Caroline tells me it was a sumptuous production," Lavinia went on. (Caroline had also shared with her mother how Hetty monopolized the discussion during the interval, and the aunt was not feeling too kindly toward her niece.)

"Indeed," he agreed. "Magnificent. But, as I was saying to Miss Hapgood last night, the true revelation for me was Mr. Kean's performance."

The mention of her name did not succeed in drawing a glance, and St. John masked a twinge of amusement. It must mean something, surely, that the girl was so *pointed* in refusing to be drawn. He was not vain enough to imagine love overwhelmed her, but there was some mystery here to be plumbed.

He would go for the direct address. "What was your final verdict, Miss Hapgood? Did Macbeth, as Kean interpreted him, deserve our pity or our censure?"

Hetty swallowed. She could feel her aunt's displeasure and saw Caroline's stillness from the corner of her eye. *Just answer and be done.* She held her sewing up as if to inspect the line of uneven, lumpy stitches she had just put in. "Surely some of both," she murmured.

"Yes, but the proportions?" he persisted. "Would you say half pity and half censure? Or 40% pity and 60% censure, or what?"

"What—do you think, Caroline?" Hetty asked desperately.

"Half," squawked her cousin. "Half of each. That is, either. Or—or both. Fascinating. Utterly fascinating. What a treat."

Seeing his puzzlement, Caroline glanced at her cousin for assistance. But Hetty was equally uncomfortable and didn't look up from her sewing.

Flustered, Caroline clutched at the other part of Hetty's plan. Flinging open the book she held, she slid a finger down the page, stopping at random. "Ahem. I say, Mr. Rotherwood—how glad I am you've come. Because I was hoping to—ask you about—about—about the—transverse axis of any—er—c-conic hyperbola."

"Indeed?" He blinked at her, his confusion deepening.

She gripped the book so tightly Hetty thought the spine might give way. "Yes."

"Uh...well, then. What...about it?"

He might as well have asked her in Greek what color waistcoat the man in the moon wore. Poor Caroline looked at the page again, her throat working. "Would you—would you call it...2?" she peeped.

"The...transverse axis?"

"Yes. The transverse axis of—of any comic—I mean *conic* hyperbole—hyperbola. Would you call it... the number 2?"

He waited, but it seemed no further clarification was forthcoming. "Do you mean, would I label it with the number '2'?"

"Yes!" she seized on this. "That is what I meant to say. Would you label it with the number '2'?"

Knowing this hypothetical transverse axis might be labeled anything she pleased, he could not help throwing Miss Hapgood a perplexed glance (which she did not receive).

"Um..." he hazarded at last, "I don't see why not."

"Ah, thank you." Caroline beamed at him, clapping the book shut once more. "I was so puzzled by that."

With difficulty, Hetty refrained from screaming into her sewing. Why on earth had she told Caroline to pick something out of the *Philosophical Transactions of the Royal Society*, and how had Caroline's luck been so bad that she chose a mathematics article? And the poor, poor girl thought the venture a success!

Lavinia Sidney took charge once more of the conversation. "How are you and Mrs. Rotherwood liking town so far? It must be very different from your estate in Dorset. It *is* in Dorset, is it not?"

It was always a jolt to hear Glennard referred to as "their estate," but St. John fumbled a reply. "Very well, thank you. Yes, the estate, Glennard, is in Dorset. Near Shaftesbury. But I must confess, madam, that I have not set foot on the place since I was a stripling of five."

"Oh? Indeed," she breathed, clearly yearning to ask for more details but held back by propriety. There was only so much information in circulation about the Rotherwoods, most of it having to do with the enormity of their inheritance.

Had Miss Hapgood not been present, St. John likely would have left Mrs. Sidney to stew in her curiosity, but there is ever, when even the slightest affection is involved, the desire to know and be known. Therefore he found himself rehearsing the Rotherwoods' painful history for these near strangers. And while he addressed himself to Mrs. Sidney, his words were for her niece.

"Yes, madam, I regret to say I only saw Glennard and my grandfather, Sir Gordon Holt, the one time, when I was five years old. You see, my grandfather was a proud man. Proud of his lineage and good fortune. Until my mother married, she was the apple of his eye. Her own mother, my grandmother Lady Holt, had died shortly after the birth of my uncle, and so my mother had been her father's companion and the hostess of Glennard as soon as she was out of the schoolroom."

"Oh, dear," said Mrs. Sidney. She made no pretense of sewing now, and Hetty's stitches grew slower and still more careless. "Was it then your mother's marriage that—that—"

"That estranged them?" he supplied. "Yes, I am sorry to say. My father was a third son and a curate and an aspiring poet. Even one of these unfortunate characteristics might have been enough to earn my grandfather's disapprobation, but—in combination—well..."

"How very, very sad!" cried Caroline, and though Hetty succeeded in suppressing her own echo of this, she could not help but give the tiniest nod of agreement, and St. John saw it.

"It did not seem sad to me, as a young child," he returned stoutly. "If we...struggled...I had no awareness of it because I knew no other life. It was only when I met my grandfather that I began to realize my mother suffered. It was not that she regretted her choice—'regret' would be too strong a word, for she and my father loved each other—but certainly poverty entails suffering. There were times—well—there were times."

Caroline Sidney was not hard of heart. Her eyes filled at this allusion to woe, and even Hetty (who did have rather a hard heart, to be perfectly honest) felt her throat constrict. She had a thousand questions she would like to ask, moreover, and the unnatural practice of keeping her mouth shut and her thoughts to herself was proving more difficult than she would have imagined. *Let Caroline pose the questions, then. It will demonstrate her kindness* and *satisfy my desire to know more.*

Shifting her seat slightly, Hetty took a magnificently long stitch that required her to raise her elbow high enough to jab her cousin.

"Did your grandfather not pity you and your mother when he saw you?" Caroline asked obligingly. Drawing a handkerchief from her sleeve, she dabbed her china-blue eyes in an affecting, yet not at all affected, way.

"He did, in his way." St. John was a just man, and he had not intended to reduce his listeners to tears. "Please—you mustn't distress yourself about it. Sir Gordon provided for my education, and, though I was young, he instilled in me the knowledge of my duty to my mother. I learned from him that I must make whatever I could of myself through my schooling, that I might care for her and support her as far as I was able. After my father's untimely death, my mother and I had only each other. We still have. So you see, my grandfather gave me not only an education but, far more importantly, he gave me the closeness my mother and I share."

Such a picture of the Rotherwoods led to more dabbing of eyes, Lavinia Sidney joining in the activity, while Hetty was left to bite her lip and absorb the story as impassively as she could. She was grateful for her quiet uncle speaking up, therefore, to say, "Your words do you credit, Mr. Rotherwood."

St. John gave a rueful smile. Delightful. Now he had made both Sidney ladies cry and forced compliments from the father. Had Miss Hapgood nothing at all to contribute? Or did she—perish the thought—think he had told his story for effect? Perhaps she was now inwardly denigrating him as self-pitying and tied to his mother's apron strings. But who could tell? The girl continued to sew away at the shapeless heap in her lap which might have been anything from a fieldworker's shift to a parachute.

He strove for a lighter tone. "Of course, my mother no longer has need of my financial support, so thank heaven for affection, or all my use to her would be lost." He hoped the Sidney ladies would smile at this, and the conversation could move on, but instead both Mrs. and Miss Sidney took him literally.

"Oh, no, Mr. Rotherwood!" cried Miss Sidney. "That could never be."

And "I am sure nothing could unseat you from her heart," was Mrs. Sidney's response, as she held up a hand as if she wished she could comfort him from this fear.

"Thank you."

It might have been her imagination, but Hetty thought she detected a note of chagrin. In any case, he seemed to have done speaking about himself because he pointedly said, "Now, please, tell me something of your own family. I have more than enough of talking about myself."

Hetty observed her aunt swelling with complacence, and, indeed, if the servants happened to be listening, they would be justified in thinking they overheard preliminary negotiations, so to speak. She wondered if Mr. Rotherwood had any notion he was giving her aunt and cousin hope!

Lavinia glanced at her husband, who bore her look with his usual submission, and though she wanted to be in charge of telling the family history, she was simultaneously vexed with him for not wanting to do it himself. Did he think daughters married themselves?

Laying aside her sewing, she folded her hands in her lap. "Ah, Mr. Rotherwood, the Sidneys—my husband's family—have been in Sussex for quite some time. Mr. Sidney's father has a charming estate near Horsham, where Mr. Sidney's widowed sister keeps house for him. As my Caroline here is the only Sidney grandchild, you may imagine in what esteem she is held. I myself was born a Morrow of the Hampshire Morrows. Sadly, my own parents and indeed my only sister died some years ago. You will understand therefore why I cling to what family relations remain. My late sister's children, that is." She accompanied this last with a vague wave Hetty's direction.

"Yes." St. John straightened, determined to make use of this opening. "You are probably aware I was Lionel Hapgood's mathematics tutor at Magdalen until the recent upheavals in my life. In Oxford I had the good fortune to make the acquaintance of Lionel's immediate family. I hope they are all well, Miss Hapgood?"

Wincing at the beady gaze her aunt turned on her, Hetty replied briefly, "All well, thank you."

"Ah? Does that include Lionel? Have you heard from him?" The man didn't look the least bit marble then, as a grin flashed and he leaned forward. "Does he like his new tutor? I will try not to be jealous if he does."

Hetty fidgeted. Good heavens. Was the man unable to read her attitude? Did he not guess that she would rather not be spoken to, and that the others in the room (excepting her uncle, who appeared neutral) would also rather she not be spoken to?

But she could hardly *not* answer him—it would be impolite and even odd.

"Hmm." She smiled at his kneecap. "Perhaps you will not be surprised to learn Lionel is not the most dependable correspondent. In fact, I have not heard from him since my arrival in town. Though I am equally guilty because nor have I written him. Suffice to say, I have no *bad* news from any quarters; thus the new tutor must be passable. As my stepmother likes to say, *nulla nuova, buona nuova*."

"And what does that mean?" he prompted. "I read mathematics, you recall—not Italian."

Hetty colored, crossing her fingers underneath her sewing that Aunt Lavinia wouldn't think she was showing off. "No news is good news."

"Ah. Thank you. Did your stepmother teach you Italian, Miss Hapgood?"

"Governess," was her terse reply. "My governess did." She felt perspiration break out beneath her arms. The man regarded her genially as if they had all the time in the world for a nice, comfortable coze, and how she would have enjoyed that, under vastly different circumstances!

"My brother-in-law was quite heartbroken when he lost my sister," interjected Lavinia ruthlessly. "How glad we were when he found a stepmother for the children. They were quite young at the time."

Mr. Rotherwood threw Hetty a sympathetic look. "I think it must be difficult at any age to lose a parent. I hope—that is, the second Mrs. Hapgood seems a pleasant person."

"She is a jewel," said Hetty simply. All the dread in the world of her aunt could not keep her from saying so. "Do you—hope your own mother might remarry?"

"Hetty, dear—what an impossibly prying question! Never mind, Mr. Rotherwood, and please excuse my niece. These provincialisms!"

"I don't mind the question, in this company," he assured her. "Miss Hapgood asks me as one bereaved child to another. And my answer must be: it depends naturally on whom she might choose. Were my mother to choose 'a jewel' as Mr. Hapgood has, I could have no objection. She has had her share of unhappiness in life, and I would rejoice to see her well-settled."

He turned then, to everyone's surprise and pleasure, to address Caroline, adding drolly, "And as one only child to another, I think Miss Sidney will understand when I say it is not always comfortable to be the only egg in the basket. There is no one else over whom to distribute the weight of the hen."

Caroline giggled at this, not entirely understanding him but pleased to be included. On the other hand, her mother understood all too well and appeared indignant to be compared to an egg-smothering hen. And when Mr. Rotherwood proceeded to speak to her niece again, she actually huffed.

"What would you say, Miss Hapgood," he asked, "is the weight of your parents' concerns equally distributed over their three eggs?"

This picture made her laugh in spite of herself. "Oh, no. Not at all. I would say Lionel and I bear most of it, and Rosie is a tiny hummingbird egg because she is no trouble at all. At least, not at her age."

"I know your brother well enough to understand how he might try his parents at times, but *you*, Miss Hapgood? What trouble could you possibly be?"

"You cannot expect me to answer such a question, sir."

Even if he expected her to, however, he was robbed of the opportunity by Mr. and Mrs. Sidney rising abruptly.

"Oh, my dear," Mrs. Sidney said to her husband, "are you headed to your club now?"

"I am," he replied, having been sharply elbowed a second earlier. "Mr. Rotherwood, we thank you for your visit today."

Such a hint was too pointed to ignore, and St. John was forced to his own feet and found himself making his bows. But as he took his leave, he paused at the by-table where Caroline had laid the *Philosophical Transactions*. Taking it up, he opened it, bemused.

"A little light reading for you, Miss Sidney?"

Her reply was a titter and a telltale blush, and his gaze traveled to her cousin. "I would have thought this of more interest to someone like you, Miss Hapgood. A young lady who reads Wingate for amusement, after all."

"Oh, no," Hetty lied breezily. "I could make neither head nor tail of a book like that, but Caroline wants to attend one of the lectures at the Royal Society, so we got that at Booth's."

His eyebrow arched in the faintest skepticism. "A lecture, Miss Sidney? I hear Sir Humphry Davy will be speaking this Thursday..."

"But there is a ball that night!" protested Caroline. "I would never miss that, not for any old lecture in the world."

"Just so," said Mr. Rotherwood. With another bow he followed Mr. and Mrs. Sidney from the room, but not before his eyes flicked one last time toward Hetty, catching her off guard.

She could not be certain, but she almost thought he winked.

Chapter Thirteen

A trusty villain, sir, that very oft,
When I am dull with care and melancholy,
Lightens my humour with his merry jests.
— Shakespeare, *The Comedy of Errors,* I.ii.182
(c.1594)

"Did you see that?" Caroline pounced on her after Mr. Rotherwood was gone. "He spoke to me! And he answered my mathematics question. And made a little joke with me. Oh, Hetty!" She flung her arms around her cousin and hugged her joyfully. "Thank you! I could see that, yes, he would talk to you a little, but just because he did already know you and Lionel, not because he prefers you."

Hetty made an indeterminate sound in her throat and returned Caroline's embrace, being careful not to meet her aunt's eyes. She suspected Aunt Lavinia felt differently about how matters stood, but Hetty couldn't help that. She had done her best to keep quiet, and it was not her fault he would ask her questions. And it was so hard to repress every instinct she felt to enjoy the man's company! And she *did* enjoy his company, she was sorry to say. She was, in fact, beginning to think she expressed herself too mildly in her letter to Edith.

Releasing her, Caroline began to whirl around the room, humming. "He called on me. Even after having been at Almack's and knowing we were not there, he still called! And now that he knows I will be at the Finlays' ball on Thursday, he will surely go there, rather than to the Royal Society to hear some dull old lecture, don't you think?"

"I imagine he could do both in one evening."

Caroline's face fell as she halted before the gilt-framed mirror above the mantel. "Oh, dear—you don't suppose we have to go then, do you? I'm sure I don't want to at all, and then I would not have enough time to get ready."

"No, I don't think we need go," Hetty reassured her. "It would hardly help your cause for you to fall asleep because you are so frightfully bored."

"Exactly," her cousin agreed. "Mama, may Hetty and I go shopping now? There are a few little things I will need..."

Some hours later, two exhausted girls and the maid Reddy returned, laden with parcels. Even Hetty, who had not thought to buy anything, succumbed to the temptations of Oxford and Bond Streets, choosing little gifts for her family and a new flowered shawl.

But she forgot both her purchases and her fatigue when she saw a letter addressed to Miss H. Hapgood in the salver by the entrance!

Caroline, thankfully, only yawned when she saw it came from Hetty's parents, leaving Hetty free to seek her room and solitude.

Upon tearing it open, she found her stepmother's note enclosed two others, including a letter from Edith! It was addressed from Nice and already weeks old, and Hetty lost herself for a half hour reading and re-reading her cousin's account of their slow progress through France. "I am happy to report," wrote Edith, "that my uncle and aunt are cheerful companions, and my aunt's liberality makes for a smooth journey and secures the goodwill of those we encounter. After reading Mr. Smollett's *Travels through France and Italy*, I did fear it would be all bad food and swindlers, but it is not so."

Edith being Edith, she interspersed several little sketches: the *berline* they hired, with its dashing *voiturier*; a fine lady seen in the Tuileries in Paris; the Avignon *auberge* with innkeeper. "We flew through Paris, as we mean to spend more time there on our return, and, indeed, with the coming of winter, all travelers seem in headlong flight for the warmer climes of Italy. Hetty, I do believe one thing Mr. Smollett wrote was true: at this time of year, there are as many English invalids abroad as tourists! I wonder that any still remain in England. Do you suppose the streets of Bath are empty? I have been filling a book with delightful sketches of the people we see, but no face can be as beloved as those I have left behind."

Reading her letter made Hetty miss her dreadfully, especially since she and her Sidney relations did not seem to rub along as well.

With a sigh, she folded the pages together again and set them aside to examine her stepmother's second enclosure.

To her surprise, this one was from Lionel, of all people. It was as if telling Mr. Rotherwood that Lionel never wrote worked as a charm to make him write. And it was hard to say whether its roundabout delivery or the fact of the letter itself was more unexpected, but she was delighted in any case.

> *Het,*
>
> *I'm sure you won't have to rack your brain too hard to figure out why I didn't write to you directly. Am I still in my aunt's and cousin's black book?*
>
> *By the time you get this, the Clinketts, Bailiwick and I will be in town because we are coming up for the five weeks between terms. We've taken lodgings in Cleveland Street off Fitzroy Square. It's not far from you, but if you can possibly manage to keep your mouth shut, I'd rather the Sidneys knew nothing of it. We don't plan on gadding about with the swells as they do, in any event, so with a little care our paths need not cross. But if you, my fine sis, grow tired of the butterfly life, send word.*
>
> *Speaking of swells, Clinker has got the idea in his head that we should pose as footpads and give old Rotherwood a scare one night, but I told him I've had enough*

doings with the London constabulary to last a lifetime.
Not to mention, Edith would murder me if she heard.

L

Edith would undoubtedly murder Lionel if he got himself arrested again, after the trouble she took to rescue him, but Hetty felt a sudden longing for her brother. He was here? And not more than a ten-minute walk from her? What fun it sounded, to escape the confines of Devonshire Street, her aunt's frowns, and Caroline's demands! Ah, if only she were a boy—she could roam about town with Lionel and his friends and forget about tiresome things like husband-hunting and behaving oneself. The Sidneys could fend for themselves and not have her to blame if they did not meet with success.

But if she could not be a boy, she could see her brother in any case, she decided, entirely forgetting her fatigue and taking up pen to reply. Caroline had announced her intention of napping that afternoon. It only remained to enlist some maid to accompany her—

An hour later, Hetty stood in Booth's Circulating Library in Duke Street, Portland Place, perusing the offerings, having left the maid Trilby waiting outside. It had been simple enough, telling Caroline she was going to return the *Philosophical Transactions* and choose something less technical, and did she care to come along? "Heavens, no," replied her cousin, patting away a yawn. "I doubt any book could make such subjects intelligible, much less *interesting*, and I still have novels enough. You go, by all means."

Hiding her glee, Hetty obeyed.

Trilby's company would be the perfect blind for any escapades, as the maid was new to the household and frequently scolded by the housekeeper for her dreamy nature and forgetfulness. Moreover, Trilby was cursed with a stammer and rarely spoke if she could avoid it. Lavinia Sidney assigned the unpromising maid to her niece, assuming rightly that Hetty would mind the servant's incompetence the least. Once, shortly after Hetty's arrival in London, Trilby's mind wandered while she was ironing the young lady's frock, resulting in a scorched patch, but Miss Hapgood only sighed and said, "Well, I suppose I can pin my tucker over it." Trilby answered, "I'll-I'll s-s-sew it—on—for you, m-miss," which she did with uncharacteristic alacrity and characteristic skill. The fact that Miss Hapgood did not go telling tales to her aunt or the housekeeper was enough to earn the maid's gratitude, and they managed quite well with each other thereafter. Nevertheless, Hetty saw no need on this occasion to explain that she was going to Booth's in the hope of meeting her brother. Least said, soonest mended.

She was studying an engraving of a sailboat when she heard a voice behind her: "Shall I wrap it up for you, miss?"

"No, thank you, I—Lionel!" she cried, when she turned, and she couldn't help rushing at him, though he disentangled himself quickly enough.

"Whoa there, Het. What'd I tell you about grabbing people?"

"I don't care," she laughed, still holding onto the sleeve of his greatcoat. "I'm so glad to see you. Are the others here too?"

"I only had to say 'circulating library' before Clunker adhered to me," he answered, nodding in the direction of his friend, who stood with his nose in a book. "But Clinker and Bailey went to see about tickets to the Argyll Rooms."

"The Argyll Rooms? Whatever for? You told me you wouldn't be 'gadding about with the swells.'"

"Not generally, no, but we heard there's to be a masquerade ball, and that sounded jolly fun. It's not gadding about with the swells if the swells don't know you're there. You should come."

"Ha!" scoffed Hetty. "As if Aunt Lavinia would ever, ever approve of such a thing. Besides, I thought you don't want to run into the Sidneys. Even in a disguise they might recognize you."

"If they did, that only meant the disguise wasn't worth a fig." He shook his head with mocking regret. "Too bad you won't come. It's not like you, Hetty, to let our aunt cow you."

"Who says I'm cowed?" she countered, her color rising. "I'll ask her, then. Or, better yet, I'll tell Caroline about it. She would die to go to a masquerade, I'll warrant, and maybe she could wear her mother down."

"And if she can't?"

"Then—then—I'll go anyway," she declared. "Who would be any the wiser? You're not the only one who can disguise himself. But you had better stick by me. I imagine if Aunt Lavinia disapproves, there must be *something* objectionable going on there."

Lionel had already lost interest in his aunt's primness, however. "Never mind all that for now—have you heard from Edith? I've only had one sorry letter from her this entire time."

"And you've written her dozens, I suppose," his sister rallied him. But she drew Edith's letter from her pocket and held it out.

Lionel had the grace to look sheepish. "Well, one—just the one letter. But it's not like I have anything to write about. Just school school school and the same old people." He smiled at the letter in his hands as if it were Edith himself and then tucked it away.

"I want that back, you know," Hetty insisted. "Well, what about your new mathematics tutor? He's not 'the same old people,' and I bet Edie wants to hear about him. Do you like him as well as you did Mr. Rotherwood?"

Lionel shrugged. "He'll do. Truth be told, I miss old St. John the engine. Have you seen him yet? Or has he become altogether too grand and lofty?"

"He's grand all right. All London is falling over itself to pay court to him and his wealthy mother. And as for loftiness, he was lofty in Oxford, so he's most certainly lofty here. But I think that's because of his looks and because he doesn't talk very much in company."

Her brother put down the copy of *Waverley* he had been examining and eyed her. "My, my. Sounds like you're quite the expert on the man."

With a frown she took up the volume he had discarded so she wouldn't have to look at him. "I've seen him several times, yes. And spoken with him on most of those occasions, to my aunt's and cousin's annoyance. But he acknowledged that we knew each other from before, and I could hardly refuse the acquaintance, could I?"

"Not a bit of it. But why should it bother the Sidneys if you speak with him?"

Hetty flipped the pages in a blur, grinning. "This will hurt your vanity, brother, but I think your dear old tutor has supplanted you in Caroline's affections."

Lionel gave a bark of a laugh that caused heads to turn, and Hetty shushed him, giving the back of his hand a pinch. He only shook her off, before drawing her arm through his and leading her to a less populated corner. "Caroline and Rotherwood! Now that would be an odd pairing. I'm not certain she could work out what two and two make, while he—"

"Is a thinking man. Yes," finished Hetty. "But here is the thing, Lionel: you know how the Sidneys had been resentful of what they saw as my interference between you and Caroline. Well, when I arrived in London, to make it up to her, I thought I would help her find someone else to love—more successfully, you know—and I'm afraid I shared that idea with her. Little did I know she already had it in her head that she wanted your old tutor! She hadn't even seen the man—she just heard, like everyone else in town, that he was rich and young and handsome and that every other girl was setting her cap for him, including this friend she'd made named Lady Sylvia—"

"Oh, Lord," her brother interrupted, "you made Caroline think you could get her Rotherwood? I think that's beyond even your powers of cunning, Het. They're chalk and cheese."

"You think I don't know that? But you understand I had to make a little effort. If I told her straight off that it was unlikely, she would think I was trying to thwart her again. Which she did whenever I chanced to say a word to him. But now I fear she thinks she is making progress!" Briefly, Hetty recounted Mr. Rotherwood's call and Caroline's triumph afterward.

When he got done laughing about labeling the transverse axis, with Hetty hushing him again, he said, "She may not be the one for Rotherwood, but I'll admit she's pretty and cheerful enough. Why don't you push someone else on her? Clinker once said he admired her."

Hetty's eyes widened. "Do you think something could come of that? But how would I bring it about?"

Holding up his hands, Lionel backed away from her. "Oh, blast me for a big mouth. My friends and I are here to enjoy the vacation, not to participate in your schemes. I don't want to see the Sidneys, remember?"

"Well, can't you at least *ask* Clinker if he'd like to see her again?" Hetty coaxed. "I could manage it that we would run into you somewhere harmless, like Hyde Park or—"

"No."

"—Or the British Museum—"

"*No.*"

"—And I could swear her to secrecy about it."

"Secrecy? Caroline?" he snorted. "No. Pick someone else for her and have done."

Putting her hands on her hips, she scowled at him. "Lionel Hapgood, supposing your friend Clinker and our cousin would be blissfully happy together? It's most unkind of you to separate them."

"I'm not separating them, Het—I'm just not forcing them together. What's the rush? If you don't have any luck finding her someone this season, she must give you credit for effort. And it isn't as if she were in danger of turning spinster. No—let it be. Let *us* be. I don't mind seeing you, but one must draw the line somewhere."

Though she made a growling sound, it had no effect on her brother, and Hetty was forced to concede for the present. Especially as Clunker wandered over to them with a stack of books in his arms.

"Do you plan to let Mr. Rotherwood know you are in town?" she asked, once greetings were exchanged and Clunker's selections looked over. "I think he would be pleased to see more familiar faces."

"My sister is now the expert on Rotherwood," put in Lionel.

"I'm not!" she insisted. "It is just that I think he considers me a familiar face, and I am not nearly as familiar as you all."

"Faces dear, what have we here..." Clunker meditated. He shrugged and looked at Lionel. "He was your tutor, Lion, not mine."

Lionel pulled a face. "I don't think so. How awkward would that be? 'Mr. Rotherwood! We've come to call because my sister Harriet says you seem lonely and beyond your depth.'"

Hetty huffed a sigh. "Is your presence in London to be a secret from him as well, then? Will you be vexed if I happen to mention it? He, at least, can be trusted to keep a secret."

Her brother waved the question away. "Honestly, Het. Leave the man to find his own way. The last thing he needs is former pupils foisted on him. We'll be off now, my insides are wrung with hunger."

"Shall we accompany you home?" asked Clunker.

"No, we will not!" exclaimed Lionel. "Clunk, I just said I don't want my aunt to know I'm here. Besides, you brought a maid or somebody, didn't you, Het?"

"I did, you unchivalrous beast," she retorted, "so you needn't trouble yourself. Though thank you all the same, Edward. Good-bye."

Unruffled by her irritation, Lionel only called after her, "Let us know about Argyll."

CHAPTER FOURTEEN

Hop as light as bird from brier;
And this ditty, after me,
Sing, and dance it trippingly.
— Shakespeare, *A Midsummer Night's Dream,*
V.i.2241 (c.1594)

"A masquerade ball?" Lavinia Sidney repeated in incredulity. "Absolutely not!"

"Oh, Mama," pleaded Caroline. "Doesn't it sound fun? And you would be with us, of course, and many fashionable people attend them."

"And many *un*fashionable people," her mother declared. "Which is precisely the reason it would be unsuitable for young ladies in their first season like yourselves. Now, now—don't pout, my dear. Here we are, going to a genuine, appropriate ball, where any gentleman you meet will be certain to *be* a gentleman and known to the Finlays. Shall I send Reddy to dress your hair?"

Sagging in defeat, Caroline retreated to her bedchamber, trailed by Hetty, whose posture was suspiciously unbowed, if her aunt had not been too busy to notice. But Caroline's spirits soon recovered, for she was indeed eager to attend the Finlays' ball and knew she was looking her loveliest in ice-blue silk that made her eyes glow like sapphires.

"Do you suppose he will be there?" she asked her cousin for the tenth time. "We have not seen him since he called."

"I don't know," replied Hetty, also for the tenth time. "But what a pleasure it will be to dance with anyone—except perhaps Mr. Pickford." Her voice was calm, but secretly her heart was racing. Not only in excitement for her first London ball (and she too hoped Mr. Rotherwood would be there), but equally because her aunt's rejection of the masquerade ball meant that Hetty must resort to subterfuge to attend. What impenetrable disguise should she assume? Whatever it was, it must cover her hair, or she might as well wear no disguise at all. A maid in a mobcap? A shepherdess with a powdered wig?

And whether Hetty liked it or not, her aunt's apprehensions made her hesitant. Perhaps she should not don any disguise that might attract unwanted attention, if there would be disreputable persons present. Hetty fully planned to cling as close to Lionel as she could and to dance with no one besides her brother and his friends, but she would rather not be approached by strangers. Not only would it be awkward, but it would increase chances of her discovery.

Something shapeless and unattractive, she thought. *A withered crone, perhaps.* Yes! She could tie a pillow to her back to be a hump, wear a straggling grey wig and blacken several of her teeth. The picture made her giggle. Certainly then no one unknown would ask her to dance—she was not even certain Lionel or his friends could be brought to.

While it did not carry the cachet of Almack's vouchers, an invitation to the Finlays' ball was not to be despised. And this invitation the Sidneys owed to Mr. Sidney being a childhood schoolmate of Sir August Finlay, whose family's fortune came, it was whispered, from the previous baronet being an eager and lucky speculator. But any hope Hetty had of pairing her cousin with a young scion of the family was dashed when her aunt informed them the Finlay children were entirely female.

Caroline sighed at this. "How many of them are of marriageable age, Mama?"

"All, my love. All of them. Why do you think they are hosting a ball?"

While this was news to sink any girl's heart, upon their arrival in Mount Street, where the Finlay home occupied a space that would have held four of the Sidneys', Hetty was relieved to see that none of the Misses Finlay were as pretty as her cousin. In fact, the family resemblance of light brown hair, pale blue eyes and long nose was so strong that they reminded her of an optical illusion, where one single person was warped and reflected in different mirrors. If Mr. Rotherwood indeed came, and if he were able to resist one Miss Finlay, he would be able to resist them all.

And Mr. Rotherwood did come.

Hetty was standing up with Mr. Pickford (her worst fears realized) when she saw Sir August and Lady Finlay welcoming the Rotherwoods. Mrs. Rotherwood wore her customary dark blue, but gems flashed about her neck. Mr. Rotherwood, handsome and elegant in black and buff, made his exact bow to the four versions of Miss Finlay, and they curtsied and bridled as one.

"Miss Hapgood, permit me to say, you look lovely tonight," her partner forced himself into her thoughts.

"Thank you." She would have liked to tell Mr. Pickford that *he* put her in mind of a shark: sleek, dark, and predatory. And it vexed her that she should be dancing with him when Mr. Rotherwood arrived. But perhaps Mr. Rotherwood wouldn't notice.

Mr. Rotherwood noticed.

He had every intention of dancing with Miss Hapgood that evening, and nothing short of a refusal on her part would thwart him. She was halfway down the set when he caught the flash of her bright hair, curled on this occasion and wound with a gold bandeau. Amidst the other dancers, the simplicity of her ivory gown stood out for its plainness, but it was well-cut and flowed in graceful lines as she took her partner's hand and went in circle.

His eyes narrowed when he recognized Mr. Pickford, the overly handsome young man at whom Miss Hapgood had thrown herself at the Tower, and, unnoticed by him, Anne's gaze followed her son's. *Ah. That one again?* Before she could reclaim his attention, however, here was bald Lord Camberwell claiming her hand, and off they went to join the set.

"Mr. Rotherwood," cried Lady Finlay, "you are so new in town—may I introduce you to a partner?"

With her four daughters directly at hand the hint was too broad to be ignored, so he turned to the nearest Miss Finlay (Miss Felicity? Miss Fiona? Miss Flora? He could not remember which was which) and requested the honor, etc.

It was relatively early yet, so the dance lasted only twenty minutes, but the time seemed long enough to St. John. After determining that the Finlays named their daughters in alphabetical order, he decided the girl beside him must be Miss Flora Finlay, and by the grace of God he happened to compliment her on a diamond-studded brooch she wore in the shape of a cat. Miss Flora liked cats, it seemed, and between a summary of how each Mount Street servant felt toward Mr. Fluffkins and Piglet, and how Mr. Fluffkins and Piglet felt about being shut upstairs all day because of the ball, the dance was accomplished.

Trying to avoid the appearance of hurry, he rushed her back to her parents, his gaze sweeping the room until he saw where Pickford escorted Miss Hapgood back to her aunt's side. But before he could take a step their direction, the Stanleys materialized before him, Lord and Lady Stanley blocking his passage while their glorious daughter stood behind them like a stronghold to be taken.

"Mr. Rotherwood," beamed the countess, "what a pleasure to see you again. It has been over a week, has it not? Almack's is all very well, but I do appreciate the intimacy of a private ball."

"The young people dancing," put in Lord Stanley. "Fine sight."

Short of saying he did not intend to dance (which he could not say anyway, having just danced with Miss Flora), or of twisting his ankle, St. John had no choice. And if he could not manage a smile, he at least succeeded in not grimacing as he led Lady Sylvia to the floor. But he was resolute that he should have his way after this, and to this end he maneuvered them next to where Miss Hapgood and her cousin were forming up, having exchanged partners, Pickford for Elwood.

Miss Sidney's face lit up and she clapped her hands. "Oh, Mr. Rotherwood, Lady Sylvia, good evening!"

St. John was improving at reading Lady Sylvia's expressions, and the slight lift to one corner of her mouth indicated that her pleasure in seeing her friend was not unmixed with irritation. But he didn't care, frankly. He was too aware that only Miss Sidney and Mr. Pickford separated him from Miss Hapgood and Mr. Elwood. Miss Hapgood, naturally, was looking up the room and not at him, but he could see from this distance that her simple ivory gown was patterned with glossy dots.

Lord How's Jig in three-couple sets was called, and St. John made rapid calculations, finding that fortune favored him, and Miss Hapgood fell into his set. A genuine smile spread over his countenance then, and Miss Sidney glowed at him in return—why, being in the same set as Mr. Rotherwood was nearly as good as partnering him for the dance, for they would pass in hey and hold hands for the circles! Delightful.

As for Hetty, she was torn between delight and dismay. She loved to dance and had never thought herself deficient at it, but somehow having Mr. Rotherwood mere feet from her, winding through the figures with him, and lightly taking gloved hands in circle, made her pulse fly and her feet uncertain. When Mr. Elwood stamped upon her slippered foot with his heel, he politely apologized, but Hetty suspected it had been her own fault for pausing to think and not being where she was expected.

Mr. Rotherwood did not give any particular squeeze to her fingertips when he took her hand (as Mr. Pickford did on her other side), but a bolt of warmth shot through both layers of their gloves nevertheless, as if she had taken hold of the wrong end of the fireplace poker. She felt his eyes touch on her—how could one *feel* a gaze?—and she knew she blushed, but she prayed if anyone noticed they would assume it was the heat of exercise or of the ballroom.

"Good evening, Miss Hapgood," he murmured, the next time he wound past her. Hetty positively stumbled against Lady Sylvia, who showed more liveliness than she was wont and gave her a severe look.

Muttering an apology, Hetty recovered and was grateful she and Mr. Elwood arrived at the bottom of the figure and could take several measures to observe the others in circle. If her own feelings had not been involved, it would have been as good as a play for intrigue. There was Caroline, her attention all for Mr. Rotherwood and not her own partner. There was Mr. Pickford, resentful. There was Lady Sylvia, displeased and beautiful. And Mr. Rotherwood? Hetty only ventured the barest glance, but by that mysterious phenomenon, his eyes flicked to her in the same instant, making her insides revolve as if she had tumbled off the roof of the Patterton mail coach.

Then she and Mr. Elwood were in motion again, and there was Mr. Rotherwood again, and there was the jolt to her hand again, and this time his low voice said, "May I have the next dance?"

Helpless, Hetty nodded. Caroline would not be happy. Aunt Lavinia would not be happy. Lady Sylvia would not be happy. But what could she do?

No—it was clear what she must do: she must encourage Caroline to prefer some other gentleman. As soon as possible! For Mr. Rotherwood showed not the least sign of falling in with the Sidneys' wishes. But who should be the new man? Lionel did not seem to think throwing her at Clinker would yield much, even if Hetty could figure out how to do that. And if Clinker and Caroline couldn't be brought together, that likely ruled out Clunker and Bailey as well.

That left the three mutton-heads, she thought with repugnance. Sir Keane was rich and titled but too old, even if he didn't have that infantilizing speech impediment. Mr. Pickford was simply not to be thought of. Too oily and self-satisfied. Mr. Elwood, perhaps? One never really noticed Mr. Elwood, but—

Raising sharp eyes, Hetty scrutinized her partner. Of the three mutton-heads, he was undoubtedly the least mutton-headed. He was nice enough to look at—nothing like Mr. Rotherwood or Mr. Pickford, but nice enough. Medium height, neither stocky nor emaciated. Sandy hair and hazel eyes. A good chin, she thought. And he had been very nice about stepping on her foot. He could not be any older than thirty or two-and-thirty, and at least he didn't lisp. But nor did he put himself forward. Look at Caroline chattering away and Mr. Pickford leering and even Mr. Rotherwood saying things *sotto voce*—but Mr. Elwood was not doing a thing to further his aims, if he had any!

"How well you dance, Mr. Elwood," she blurted, determined to learn more of him.

If she caught him off guard, he succeeded in hiding it and replied, "As do you, Miss Hapgood."

"Did you grow up dancing with siblings in Warwickshire?" Frankly, she couldn't remember a thing about him, and Warwickshire was pure conjecture.

"Warwickshire?" he repeated. "Miss Hapgood, I hail from Surrey."

"That's right—there have been Elwoods in Surrey since before the Conquest," she recalled tardily.

"Since shortly *after* the Conquest," he corrected, his expression pained.

"Right. After. Sorry. In any case—did you dance with your siblings?"

"My two brothers are considerably younger than I am, so I did not, I'm afraid."

Good, good, she thought. *An oldest son.* "Ah. How do you like to pass the time in Surrey, then? Hunting? Other sport? Making improvements on the land?"

Mr. Elwood ran a finger under his neckcloth, Miss Hapgood's unwavering gaze and quick questions reminding him uncomfortably of oral examinations at university. "Er—all of the above, I suppose."

"So industrious! That must please your parents greatly."

"I cannot say, unfortunately. They are both gone."

Hm. He certainly does improve upon acquaintance, Hetty told herself wryly. She wondered if he liked Caroline already, or if he dangled after all suitable young ladies equally, as Mr. Pickford seemed to. It was a beginning, at any rate, if he included her cousin among the candidates. But how to make Caroline turn her thoughts to *him*? To judge by Caroline's attachments to Lionel and Mr. Rotherwood, she—she—what? She liked good looks, yes—what girl didn't? But what else had those two in common? It couldn't be the mathematics, since, as Lionel pointed out, Caroline could not be trusted to work out two plus two. Wealth? Another thing that didn't hurt. Humor? But Caroline liked Mr. Rotherwood before she knew the man had any humor.

She would just have to ask her cousin straight out, Hetty decided, and then enlighten Mr. Elwood accordingly. It was enough for now.

Satisfied with her plan, she smiled upon her partner as the music closed. Mr. Elwood took her hand to lead her back to Aunt Lavinia, from whence Mr. Rotherwood would fetch her, Hetty supposed.

"Oh, Hetty," cried Caroline, "wasn't that so enjoyable? I even felt kind toward Mr. Pickford and Lady Sylvia. I do hope Mr. Rotherwood will ask me to dance soon—he must, don't you think? Even though we were practically dancing with him already."

Hetty tried to look innocent and thought it best to divert her cousin. "I don't know. But I think Mr. Elwood improves upon acquaintance."

"Mr. Elwood? You always call him a mutton-head."

"Him? Nonsense. I was wrong. There are only two mutton-heads."

Caroline shrugged, but Hetty's aunt caught at the idea. "Indeed, I saw you speaking with him, Harriet. He is an acceptable young man. I am glad you made some effort to acquaint yourself with him."

Hetty could see right through that into her aunt's mind, and then she had the delicate task of praising Mr. Elwood while simultaneously stamping out her aunt's idea. "Yes, aunt. Were I seeking a husband, I think Mr. Elwood might be termed even better than acceptable. Because he is pleasant looking and gentlemanlike and comes of good family. But, alas, he will have been long caught up before I think of marriage."

Here her cousin gave a little shriek. "He's coming this way! Mr. Rotherwood! How do I look?" Furtively she pinched her cheeks and bit her lips for color, while Hetty wished she could skulk away unnoticed. Oh, dear, oh, dear! Was there any way to make it look like there was no previous understanding?

In her panic she almost hid behind her aunt while he made his bow, meeting his questioning look with a tiny jerk of her head at Caroline. Raising her eyebrows, she tried to communicate silently: Her! Ask *her!* We can dance later, if we must.

There was the merest hesitation on his part and a shake of his head even more imperceptible. He was not here to ask Miss Sidney to dance, confound it. But seeing Miss Hapgood's mutinous mouth he said smoothly, "Miss Sidney, I hope you are free for the supper dance?"

"Oh!" she breathed, sinking in a curtsey. "Oh, yes, Mr. Rother-wood. Thank you."

"Splendid," said St. John tightly. "Then, in the meantime...per-haps Miss Hapgood?"

This treatment of her as an afterthought pleased everyone, appar-ently, for Miss Hapgood glided to take his arm under the beneficent gaze of her family.

"Thank you *so* much for that, Mr. Rotherwood," she said, when they were out of earshot. "I cannot tell you what a favor you do me when you show my cousin a little attention."

"And I cannot tell you what dangers a gentleman runs, when he shows a young lady attentions which mean nothing," he answered.

"Oh, pooh," Hetty retorted, too relieved to be bothered. "They will just say you are a flirt. Look at Mr. Pickford: he shows all sorts of young ladies meaningless attention."

"I have no intention of modeling my conduct on Pickford."

"No, I don't suppose you do."

"Why were you determined that I ask Miss Sidney to dance?"

She gave him a pleading look. "I can't say, precisely. Only that I am here on sufferance, in a manner of speaking, and it makes my life easier if Caroline outshines me. It is very kind of you to befriend me, Mr. Rotherwood, but the greatest favor you could show me would be to favor my cousin."

The took their places for the cotillion, and Hetty was disappoint-ed that the frequent interchanges of partner and constant move-ment meant they would not have further opportunity to converse. But she would have to be content with the thrill of taking his hands every minute or so and being drawn near to him when they circled. If only he might have asked her for the supper dance! Caroline would get to talk to him (or at him, as the case might be) at length, whereas Hetty wasn't even sure of a partner for it. She dismissed this thought, however, as a later worry, choosing instead to devote her concentration to remembering the steps. It would never do to crush Mr. Rotherwood's foot or to collide with another dancer. Gradually she began to relax, and her dancing improved as a result. A smile overspread her face, making her every bit as pretty as her cousin, and unconsciously his own features softened in return.

Those who happened to be watching them—and there were many—did not especially like what they saw. Even Lavinia Sidney found herself wondering again. (Fortunately, Caroline had been asked to dance by Sir Keane and could not observe.)

One person in particular took especial notice. From across the ballroom, around the shoulder of whichever gentleman was attempting to ingratiate himself, Mrs. Anne Rotherwood watched and considered. Why, of all the glittering, exalted young ladies present, did St. John persist in noticing this nobody? This unfashionably red-headed, freckled (she could not be sure of this, but when was a redhead ever without freckles?) creature of no particular beauty or fortune? An ungraceful girl so awkward that she alternated between not meeting her son's eyes and then meeting them with too much...earnestness? Anne shook her head, not even hearing what the man who addressed her was saying. Were all their years of suffering and deprivation to be rewarded with no more than this? Her handsome son, grandson of the Holts of Glennard, rich as a prince—was his sense of his own worth still so low that he dared look no higher than this Hapgood chit? Unlike his mother, had he not yet begun to dream of returning to Glennard in glory as its rightful master, the bride beside him adding to his luster with her own?

She would send Mr. Pinckney a note the next morning, Anne decided. He could leave off preparing those little reports on all the men Anne had not the least intention of marrying and concentrate his time and powers on learning what he could of this Harriet Hapgood.

And in the meantime Anne would do what she could.

CHAPTER FIFTEEN

**I do confess heartily and openly, I wish it were in my
power to break the Match, by Heavens I wou'd.**
— William Wycherly, *The Country-Wife,* II.20 (1675)

When a carriage was heard in Devonshire Street, Caroline jumped up from the pianoforte and flew to the window, crying, "Could it be Mr. Rotherwood come to call again?" But before her aunt or cousin could respond, she drew back with a little gasp. "Why—it's his mother—Mrs. Rotherwood—and only Mrs. Rotherwood."

"Is she alighting?" asked her mother, leaping up to tidy the room.

"No, no—Carter has gone down, and she is speaking to him...here he comes!"

The footman entered the drawing room, his wig somewhat untidy from the blowing wind out of doors. "Madam," he bowed to

Lavinia, "a Mrs. Rotherwood requests you go for a drive with her, if you are free."

"A drive?" echoed Lavinia. "Oh! Oh—of course. Certainly."

From the mixture of awe and joy on her aunt's face Hetty would have thought the king had summoned her. Clearly Aunt Lavinia interpreted Mrs. Rotherwood's unusual request as a precursor to marriage between their children, and Hetty could not imagine what it could be, otherwise. Unless Mrs. Rotherwood had been struck by an inexplicable desire to cultivate Lavinia Sidney's friendship, which seemed unlikely.

Whatever the reason for it, Mrs. Sidney was willing enough and was gone in an instant, swathed in her cloak and wreathed with smiles.

Caroline turned from the window, coming to clutch Hetty's hands and emitting a long squeal. "Do you think this is it? Do you think she wants to know how I feel toward Mr. Rotherwood?"

A girl like Harriet Hapgood was rarely at a loss, but this was one of those times. She did not think Mr. Rotherwood had any intention of offering for her cousin, but she could think of no other reason for his mother to seek her aunt's company. For the barest instant she wondered if Mrs. Rotherwood sought Aunt Lavinia to speak to her about *her*, Hetty, because Hetty had no parent present. But—but—

"Caroline, listen to me: I don't know what Mrs. Rotherwood wants, but one thing I know—Mr. Rotherwood is a grown man, fully capable of speaking for himself. There is no earthly reason he need send his mother as an ambassador. Therefore, I think whatever the impetus for her visit this morning, she does it on her own initiative."

"But—then—if—" sputtered Caroline, "what else could she want to discuss, especially without her son's knowledge?"

"I don't know," Hetty repeated. "But we probably will not like it. In any event—with Aunt Lavinia out, there was something I wanted to say to you." She took her cousin's hand and drew her to the sofa. "Caro, it occurred to me at the ball that I was cruel and wrong to call Mr. Elwood one of the three mutton-heads. In truth, there are only two mutton-heads, and then there is Mr. Elwood."

Caroline made a puzzled face. "Yes. So you already told me. Whatever you like. I never called them that myself."

"Exactly. And you reproached me for doing so. I am often wrong, and I hope to continue to benefit from my time with you."

At this uncharacteristic humility, Caroline's skepticism deepened. "What is it, Hetty? What do you want to say?"

"Only that I think Mr. Elwood deserves consideration. He is an unexceptionable man. Not as rich or handsome as Mr. Rotherwood, to be sure, but unexceptionable. I enjoyed my dance with him and would welcome another."

"Are you saying you want to marry him?"

"Not *I*, but *you*. I am saying you would do well to consider him."

"You aren't saying that because you want Mr. Rotherwood for yourself, are you?"

"No—no. I only want to do Mr. Elwood justice. We cannot control who Mr. Rotherwood chooses, and he has all of London before him. But it would be foolish to disregard a gentleman so...unexceptionable as Mr. Elwood simply because we are blinded by Mr. Rotherwood."

"Why do you keep calling Mr. Elwood 'unexceptionable'?" Caroline asked suspiciously. "Does that mean dull? I am not sure I understand you."

"It means—" Hetty hesitated. She was not positive she would appreciate the word being applied to herself, so did that make it a bad word? "It means he is perfectly adequate for the situation—which is saying a great deal. It means his family, his person, his age, and his fortune meet your requirements! Really—how few men in London could that be said of?"

"It could be said of Mr. Rotherwood," said Caroline unhappily.

"Yes, well...but of so many others it could not! It could not at all be said of Sir Keane or Mr. Pickford, for example. Only promise me you will take a fresh look at Mr. Elwood, when next you meet him."

Caroline said nothing, but she did not say she wouldn't, and with that Hetty must be satisfied.

Whatever the unsatisfactoriness of their conversation, it must have gone off better than Lavinia Sidney's with Anne Rotherwood, for Lavinia returned within the hour, red-faced and at her most indignant.

The girls were still in the drawing room, Caroline sewing and Hetty trying to read, because they were too curious not to learn the purpose of Mrs. Rotherwood's call as soon as they might.

"What was it, Mama?" demanded Caroline, her sewing falling to the floor as she sprang up. "What did she want?"

Hetty was on her feet as well, her eyes searching her aunt's face, and Lavinia gave her a measuring look.

"Sit down, girls. You had better both hear this. The impudence of the woman! She might have been born a baronet's daughter, but she did not live the life of one for decades, and the sudden resumption of her station seems to have blown her full of conceit."

Breathlessly, Caroline and Hetty obeyed, waiting for Lavinia to peer into the passage and fasten the door behind her. Then she needed to regain her calm, stalking up and down the room several times until her pace slowed and her color diminished.

At last she said, "The meat of the matter is this: she came to warn me off. That is, she came to warn me that neither of you would do for her son." Seeing their wide eyes, she took a deep breath and gripped the back of the armchair nearest her.

"How—did she express this?" asked Hetty.

Her aunt grimaced. "Oh, at first it was all pleasantries and how were we liking our time here and such, but once we reached Park Lane she got on with it. She told me she had every hope that her son would marry well, and I said, of course, what mother would wish otherwise for her child?

"'Oh, indeed, every mother does,' she told me, 'and I hope you will not think me immodest if I say St. John has everything to recommend him.'"

"He does," murmured Caroline, her face screwing up in unhappiness. Her mother placed a bracing hand on her shoulder.

"Of course I agreed with this—he is a fine young man. And I thought she might be bringing herself to mention you, dear Caroline, at this juncture, but she went quite another direction! She told me it was her dearest wish that her son should make a match with Lady Sylvia.

"'His mother and I have come to our own little understanding,' was how she put it, '—without telling our children so much, you understand—and we trust that, with time and further acquaintance and our encouragement, they will see the advantages of the match themselves.'"

At this point in her mother's narrative, Caroline burst into tears and threw herself face downward on the sofa, crying, "I knew it! I knew Lady Sylvia would have him!"

There was a fuss as the other two attempted to comfort and restore her, but Caroline was still sobbing intermittently into her mother's bosom when Hetty could wait no longer and asked, "Did she say whether or not her son shared her fondness for the idea?"

Her aunt regarded her sharply. "I just said that she said they hadn't discussed it with their children."

"Yes, I know, aunt," Hetty said, trying to sound as humble as she could in her impatience. "But I must say, apart from admiring Lady Sylvia's beauty, which he did from the outset, time and further acquaintance and their mothers' encouragement do not seem to have added to that admiration. I am not saying he *dislikes* her, but I don't believe he is any more in love with her than when he met her at Lady Aurora's rout."

Caroline sat up again, blowing her nose in her handkerchief and then pointing at her cousin. "There you go again, Hetty, acting as if you know him better than the rest of us, only because you met him the one time in Oxford."

"I don't mean to—I can't help it. I'm not saying anything beyond my opinion that, despite Mrs. Rotherwood's and Lady Stanley's wishes, I don't see any evidence that a match will ever take place. And, while both Mr. Rotherwood and Lady Sylvia are respectful children, I am sure, I think they are both unlikely to marry someone just because their mothers propose the idea."

"Lady Sylvia would marry him, I'll warrant," Caroline put in sullenly.

"Say Mr. Rotherwood, then," Hetty conceded. "He might balk at it."

Her aunt's cheek worked as she studied her niece. "Harriet, my dear, if you have formed *notions* about Mr. Rotherwood, I must advise you that it would be better to abandon them."

"Notions?" Hetty felt color flood her.

"Yes. If you have begun to think you might like Mr. Rotherwood yourself, it behooves me as your aunt and as the person responsible for you here, to say again that you had better not set your heart on him."

"Aunt Lavinia," replied Hetty, her voice shaking only a little, "I promise you that I am not indulging in fantasies about Mr. Rotherwood. I like him very well—of course I do—he is clever and interesting and—and all that, but by no means do I entertain—I don't think he—that is, please don't worry about me."

Drawing herself up, her aunt smoothed Caroline's hair and put her aside with a pat. "I am glad to hear you say as much, Harriet, because it so happens Mrs. Rotherwood spoke in particular about you."

"About *me*?"

"I was inclined to resent it at first, my dear, because she was almost at pains to say that her son was an affable young man, and young ladies such as yourself must not mistake that affability for something more."

"Affable?" echoed Hetty, almost laughing. "While I believe at heart that is probably true, I do not think Mrs. Rotherwood could find ten people together in London who would apply such a word to him!" But her mockery hid something that felt very much like a blow to the ribs. Mrs. Rotherwood thought it necessary to give such a warning in particular to *her*?

"Tell me the truth, Hetty," commanded Lavinia. "Have you encouraged Mr. Rotherwood? Does his mother have any genuine reason to give me such a warning?"

Suddenly Hetty was spitting fire and on her feet, hands gathered in fists. "I have not encouraged him, aunt. And I most heartily protest both the accusation and the assumption that *I* am the one to be warned! Why must something be said to me, in particular? Even if—even if I did have—thoughts—about him—which I don't, I cannot very well propose to him, can I? If she is so desirous that there be no match between us, she would do better to warn her own son. To say such words to me implies both that she thinks me guilty of trying to—to—to entrap the man *and* that she thinks him in danger of being trapped! There is no truth in either. But even if there was, she has no right to say such things to me. She has no right to cast aspersions on my reputation simply because she fears her son will not marry as prudently as she hopes."

"Sh-h-h..." soothed her aunt, actually rising to put her arms around Hetty. "Calm yourself, my dear. I told you I too was inclined to resent her interference, and now that you have set my mind at ease, I feel that resentment was justified. You are right. If she would like her son to marry Lady Sylvia and nobody else, chasing off every other girl in the kingdom is hardly the means to bring it about."

"No," said Hetty, her anger melting away like wax in the face of her aunt's unexpected kindness. In fact, she all at once felt dangerously close to tears. Even if she did not think Mr. Rotherwood wanted to marry her—even if she did not have hopes of such a thing—it hurt to be rejected out of hand by his mother. Oh—what could it mean? Did it mean she had, somewhere deep down, nurtured such hopes?

Anger felt safer than hurt, and Hetty tried to fuel it. And just or unjust, Hetty thought Mr. Rotherwood must come in for his share. Extricating herself from her aunt's embrace, she fairly blazed. "Exalted Lady Sylvia is welcome to the baronet's grandson. They may marry, and hug their wealth and ranks to themselves, without fear that I will try to come between them. Perhaps the next time Mr. Rotherwood tries to speak to me, I will ask him if he has first begged his mother's permission."

"Hetty," breathed Caroline, "you wouldn't!"

"Wouldn't I? They may all marry to suit themselves, but I ask them to leave me out of it."

"Hetty, you must make some allowances for her affection," Caroline insisted. "Remember how he told us that he and his mother were so close? You would not want him to marry and estrange them, even as his mother and grandfather were estranged?"

"*I* don't want to do anything to them!" But Caroline's words struck her, and Hetty felt her rage ebbing once more. What a topsy-turvy day! Being accused of trying to seduce Mr. Rotherwood—Aunt Lavinia embracing her—Caroline speaking insight and reason.

"Then that is that," said Lavinia. "I have delivered her message as she requested; you have assured me that you have no designs on her son. She can ask no more of us, and we are not obligated to do any more for her. If she would like her son to marry Lady Sylvia, that is entirely up to them, and we have nothing whatsoever to do with it."

"Indeed!" agreed Caroline, her pretty little brow furrowed.

With a rueful smile, Hetty realized Mrs. Rotherwood's interference might accomplish one thing: it might cure Caroline of her infatuation with the man. If Hetty had her pride, the Sidneys did as well. First the insult of the Almack's vouchers, and now this—

The less exalted and more flattering Mr. Elwood might win her cousin yet.

More than anything, Hetty wanted to escape everyone's company. In solitude she might be able to make sense out of her feelings—after a good cry.

Which was ridiculous.

She never cried. What was coming over her?

And there the heavens must have taken pity on her, for her aunt Lavinia said something about taking Caroline for a fitting, and did Hetty want to come?

Hetty most certainly did not.

She had the ridiculous cry, she took a short nap, she wrote Edith a crackling account that ended with the passionate declaration that she would not marry Mr. Rotherwood if he were the last man on earth, no matter if she liked him a little.

And then she called for Trilby, and they went shopping for elements of Hetty's disguise. Because, oh, she had her fill of the 'gadding about with the swells'! Especially swells named Stanley or Rotherwood.

Yes, she would take a little holiday from earls and baronets and wealth and who-should-marry-whom. She would sneak away for a little fun with Lionel and his friends, and no one would be the wiser.

Chapter Sixteen

Or hail at once the patron and the pile
Of vice and folly, Greville and Argyle!
Where yon proud palace, Fashion's hallowed fane,
Spreads wide her portals for the motley train,
Behold the new Petronius of the day,
Our arbiter of pleasure and of play!
There the hired eunuch, the Hesperian choir,
The melting lute, the soft lascivious lyre,
The song from Italy, the step from France,
The midnight orgy, and the mazy dance,
The smile of beauty, and the flush of wine,
For fops, fools, gamesters, knaves, and Lords combine:
Each to his humour—Comus all allows;

**Champaign, dice, music, or your neighbour's spouse.
— Byron, *English Bards and Scotch Reviewers* (1809)**

I n the quiet along Devonshire Street, three low whistles sounded. After a moment, three chirps came in response. Then a figure rushed from where it had been concealed against the side of the house behind the drainpipe, to be met by another in a cloak, hat pulled low.

"Anyone home?" asked the cloaked one, taking the other by the arm.

"Just the servants," answered the first, "and they all went down to the kitchen to enjoy themselves after the family left. It's a good thing I'm not genuinely ill, or I suspect it would be hard to make my bell heard. As it is, I told Trilby I was going to sleep and wasn't to be disturbed on any account, not even when the Sidneys returned. Did you buy the things I asked?"

"Of course, of course. And Clunker has even hung a curtain in a corner, that you may uglify yourself in peace. Though I'm sure none of my friends are eager to be seen dancing with some hunched old crone."

"Then don't dance with me, you vain creatures," retorted Hetty as they turned into Portland Place. "What disguises have you all chosen, then?"

"You'll see when you see. They're better than yours, to say the least."

She laughed. "Keep your secret then. It's not as if I'm so eager to dance with the four of you either."

"Would you rather I take you to join the Sidneys, then? What were they up to tonight?"

"Some musical performance. Italian singing or something. No, I don't want to go with them at all, and I'd much rather do this, whether or not anyone dances with me. I'll be good now, Lionel, and nice to your friends. Promise."

Entering the concert hall with his mother on his arm, St. John spied the statuesque Lady Sylvia standing with her dumpling parents to one side, surrounded by a little court of admirers.

"Shall we?" beamed his mother, following his gaze and feeling her heart lift. How incomparably lovely the earl's daughter looked in her rose silk. Strings of pearls graced her neck and ornamented her hair, and Anne had again that sensation from the Robillard rout, where every eye present was fastened on the two parties.

Obligingly, St. John led them through the gathering crowd toward the Stanleys, his own eyes sweeping the space in what had become his usual search for Miss Hapgood. He was surprised to see the Sidneys keeping a distance from Lady Sylvia (and affecting to admire the wall hangings) and disappointed to note Miss Hapgood was not among them. Miss Sidney was there, yes. Her parents. Elwood and Sir Keane. But no Miss Hapgood.

"Lord Stanley, Lady Stanley, Lady Sylvia," Anne greeted her favored ones. "What a treat we have in store for us. I hear Mrs. Dickons' '*Ah, chi mi dice mai*' is unparalleled."

"Indeed," answered Lady Stanley, "and the quality of sound in this space ideal. We have been looking forward to this. Sylvia's music master adored *Don Giovanni.* In fact, my dear, did you not practice one of the arias in the program?"

"'*Mi tradì quell'alma ingrata,*'" murmured Lady Sylvia.

"Ahh, a favorite!" exclaimed Anne. "St. John, is it not one of yours, as well?"

"To be frank, madam, I'm not sure I know a hawk from a handsaw when it comes to music."

Lord and Lady Stanley chuckled at this, as if he had said something very amusing, and Lady Sylvia's cheeks lifted a fraction, but St. John felt a wave of impatience. "I see the Sidneys across the room. Shall we greet them?"

His mother gave a shrug. "It's growing crowded. By the time we made our way across, everyone will be finding their seats."

"You are right," he admitted. "It would be more easily done by one person. If you will excuse me..."

He knew he would have to make amends for his abrupt departure later, but he would cross that bridge when he came to it, and he wove his way through the gathering, pausing only to greet those he could not avoid acknowledging.

"Good evening, Mr. and Mrs. Sidney. Miss Sidney. Sir Keane. Elwood."

To his surprise, his appearance seemed to dismay the little group. Mrs. Sidney and Miss Sidney, in particular, straightened and gathered closer to each other, suddenly seized with Miss Hapgood's affliction of not being able to meet his eyes. But everyone made the proper gestures and greetings.

A little silence fell and, to his own rueful amusement, St. John heard himself offering Lady Stanley's remark: "I hear this soprano's '*Ah, chi mi dice mai*' is unparalleled."

"You have heard wight, Mr. Wotherwood," agreed Sir Keane amiably. "I have twice had the good fortune to hear Mrs. Dickons and welcome another opportunity."

St. John nodded at this and turned to Miss Sidney. "Er—does Miss Hapgood not share your enjoyment of Italian opera? I am become used to thinking of you and your cousin as nigh inseparable."

Miss Sidney colored and made reply to his topmost waistcoat button. "Hetty was feeling unwell, so she stayed home. I don't know what she thinks of opera, but I don't think it broke her heart to miss."

"Unwell? I am sorry to hear it. I hope it is nothing serious."

"She will be fine," was Mrs. Sidney's cool reply. "My niece has a hardy constitution, but she does tend to get overexcited at times. A little sleep and she will be good as new."

St. John wanted to say that he would certainly call the following day to see if Miss Hapgood improved, but their cold demeanor gave him pause. Had he done something to offend them? While he had often been exhausted in the past by Miss Sidney's fusillades of questions, he found he preferred it to Miss Sidney not speaking at all.

And she did not speak, except to answer lisping questions put to her by Sir Keane and the occasional remark by Elwood.

He would go, then, he decided. Return to the Stanleys, though the thought made him feel heavy and restless. He really didn't care a fig for opera, and if Miss Hapgood were not even there to be talked to or occasionally looked at, he thought he would as soon go himself.

Judging from his companions' discomfiture, *they* would make no objections to his departure. He wondered briefly at Sir Keane and Elwood hovering about Miss Sidney instead of Lady Sylvia. Was it because they assumed they had no chance against him? Or because they found her as dull as he did?

"Where's Pickford tonight?" he threw at Sir Keane.

The baronet chuckled. "Pickford? Am I my bwother's keeper?"

"Not a devotee of opera either, then?"

"Not compared to masquerade balls, in any event," interposed Mr. Elwood. "I believe he can be found in the Argyll Rooms this evening."

"Myself, I pwefer activities such as this," added Sir Keane. "More wefined. There can be some wather wough types at those masque-wade balls."

"So there can," answered St. John, though he had never been to one. With a bow, he took his leave of them to make his slow way back across the room.

Wheels were turning in his head.

A masquerade ball sounded refreshing. No one looking at him. No one knowing who he was or remarking who he talked to. No one placing bets and adjusting odds on his marital prospects. All that aside, it sounded more stimulating than an evening spent by his mother's side, listening to some screeching soprano. And if he were to investigate this masquerade ball, he could tell Miss Hapgood about it, when he called the next day.

By the time he reached the Stanleys, his mind was made up. He would excuse himself during the interval, and he had only to arrange for the earl's family to keep his mother company and drive her home. He knew she would be disappointed by his early departure, but in his reckless mood he didn't care.

Clinging to her brother, Hetty did her best to hide her excitement at the scene before her. Oh, wait till she described it to Edith! The Argyll Rooms were composed of a vast rectangular ballroom, glittering under chandeliers and arcaded by pointed arches, ground-floor alcoves and boxes on the upper storeys. Tilting her head back carefully, she took in the vaulted ceiling with its painted scenes and carved borders, but even the glories of the space could not distract long from the masqueraders filling it. For one thing, Aunt Lavinia was entirely right: there was a spectrum of attendees present, and not all of them would be termed respectable in the Sidney book. The disguises, for example, ranged from elaborate and expensive, to scanty and scandalous. Some wore full masks, completing the impenetrability of their masquerade; others wore or carried simple dominoes, and did not seem concerned about whether they would render the wearer incognito. Some people were decorous, dancing or speaking quietly; others were loud and showy and running about, weaving in and out of the gathering. There were kings and queens and harlequins and executioners and devils and angels; there was an

Ophelia (Hetty guessed) with wet hair and gown, tangled in water weeds; there was an Anne Boleyn with a scarlet ribbon tied about her neck to indicate her beheading. There was a Don Giovanni in black cloak and mask, a Louis XVI (again with the red ribbon), at least two Napoleons, and a young lady in breeches(!) dressed as the late Spencer Perceval, clothed all in black, with a little powdered wig and a fake wound on her chest.

"I needn't have feared anyone would notice me," Hetty whispered to Lionel, who was disguised as the front half of a horse. Bailey formed the rear half, but as the two halves didn't trouble themselves to stay together, and as Bailey was so much shorter than Lionel, they looked most peculiar. Clinker had painted a single eye in the center of his forehead above his mask and wore a club on a strap to be the Cyclops, while Clunker surpassed them all with long feathers pasted in perpendicular fashion the entire length of his body and head. He claimed to represent a quill pen, but Hetty thought he looked more like an ostrich flattened in a press.

She herself looked as hideous as a pretty young lady could look. Her bright hair was eclipsed under an unevenly powdered wig, its grey and white locks here pinned up and there dribbling down. She wore a shapeless coarse brown frock under which she had strapped a cushion to her back to form a hump, and she had painted lines upon her smooth hands and alongside her mouth to indicate age and hardship. Over the ensemble, including her mask and wig, she bound her jaw as if she had the toothache. Lionel's friends had nearly shrieked in horror when she emerged from behind the curtain, and the earlier promises they had made to dance with her and to keep constantly to her side now struck them as exacted under false pretenses.

"What *are* you?" demanded Lionel. "You spent money on such a costume?"

"I'm a withered crone, of course," she explained, coloring under her paint. "I'm already risking my life in going at all, for Aunt Lavinia would at best ship me back to Somerset and at worst have me locked up in the Tower if she knew I'd lied to her and sneaked out to come with you all. Much less to a masquerade which she already nixed! Therefore I must be entirely invisible. I go merely to partner each of you and to observe."

"Heaven help us," he groaned. "It's fortunate I already have someone willing to marry me, for you boys won't have any luck finding partners after they've seen you with Het here."

The Clinketts and Bailey were too well-mannered to agree with him aloud, but she could read their faces easily enough and wheedled, "Just one dance each, please! And I promise you I won't *dance* like a withered crone."

"There's a mercy," said Lionel.

Valiantly, and as a good brother should, he offered to partner her first, and they stood up for a reel, a more uninhibited one than Hetty had witnessed in other settings, but perfectly delightful. Soon she and Lionel were flying and romping as they swung and looped and stamped and circled. In their exertion and all her layers of disguise, Hetty's paint soon began to run into the cloth strapping her jaw, and Lionel told her frankly that she looked like a melted syllabub.

"If you don't clean up, even my friends won't partner you, without a large bribe on my part."

Hetty put out her tongue at him because no one would reprimand her for that in a place like this, but when the dance was over, she dragged him off to an alcove so she could put herself in order all the same. Her toothache bandage was irreparably stained, and she hadn't lines left on her face to speak of, but she comforted herself that she still had enough covering to remain unknown.

Crying, "Who's my next victim?" she laughingly took hold of Bailey. "If I have danced with the forepart of the horse, it had better be the hindquarters next."

Clinker succeeded Bailey ("Which eye would you prefer I look into, sir?"), and Clunker followed his brother, and by the time she coerced Lionel into standing up with her again, it must be admitted that Hetty was having such a very good time that she didn't even notice strands of red-gold hair were escaping beneath her unsightly wig, and she forgot herself enough to lift her mask briefly, that she might fan cooler air underneath.

As she had planned, when presented with far more beauteous partners, no one took any interest in a withered crone, even if that crone moved with surprising sprightliness despite her hump and occasionally was heard to give girlish peals of laughter. She thought Don Giovanni regarded her briefly, only to decide it was just a trick of the dark mask hiding his eyes. He might just as easily have been looking at Anne Boleyn next to her, whose ribbon of decapitation now drooped down like a necklace.

But when she was sitting beside Clunker on a carved and gilded bench against the wall, sipping lemonade and recovering her breath as she idly watched the dancers, she saw that same Don Giovanni lift his own mask to pluck a thread that was hanging down.

"Gracious heaven!" she gasped.

Clunker, whose quill disguise was half-plucked by this point, glanced at her, blowing a loose feather out of his mouth. "What?"

"I know that man," hissed Hetty. "That Don Giovanni over there. No one important, but I would rather not be seen by him."

"Fair enough. You had better put your wig in order, then."

Putting her back to the room, Hetty hastily felt at her neck and stuffed up the stray locks. Then she tugged her toothache bandage to its widest, covering nearly half her face. "How do I look?" she asked him.

"Worse than ever," Clunker replied obligingly. "If I didn't know you were Lion's sister, I would offer you a few farthings."

"Thank you."

"Hm. And I'd better tell you that Don Giovanni is headed our way."

"Oh! Oh! You mustn't go anywhere, Clunker. And you talk for me, please. Tell him whatever you like, but make him go away!"

Not often—or, indeed, *ever*—cast in the role of shining knight, Clunker swelled with importance, drawing in a deep breath that accidentally sucked a feather up his nose and resulted in him sneezing several times in succession, feathers flying off him with each explosion.

"Good evening," said Mr. Pickford (for it was he), bowing and regarding the quill pen and the hag with mocking amusement.

"E-e-evening!" sneezed Clunker.

"I wonder if you would do me the honor of introducing your...lovely companion here."

Clunker swallowed, his prominent Adam's apple bobbing. "Uh—er—Aggie," he fumbled, the name popping into his head because it rhymed with "hag." "That is, Miss Crone. Miss Agatha Crone."

"Your servant, Miss Crone," drawled Don Giovanni. "May I ask for your hand, for the next set?"

Miss Crone shook her head as hard as she dared, not wanting to disarrange her disguise.

"What a shame," interjected Clunker, "for you see, my—my aunt—Miss Crone here is my aunt—she has twisted her ankle."

"I am sorry to hear it. And you were so fleet and light of foot just moments ago, Miss Crone. I was all admiration. Such agility, for a woman of your years."

"Well, she's paying for it now," Clunker lied stoutly. "Probably won't be able to move tomorrow. Sometimes the—er—the rheumatism lets up, and then she doesn't—uh—practice moderation, and this is the sad result." Abruptly he rose, beckoning to the approaching two horse halves. "What do you know, fellows—my aunt Agatha has twisted her ankle."

The others made sounds of commiseration, while also coming to flank the bench, Lionel edging himself between his sister and Don Giovanni.

The latter held up his palms and retreated a step. "My loss, I'm afraid. I do wonder, though—Miss Crone, at your age, with your—sporadic—rheumatism and weak ankles—which part of your ensemble forms your disguise? This is a masquerade ball, after all."

"A ball, after all," whispered Clunker.

"It's the mask, naturally," Lionel interposed. "And the bandage. She hasn't got a toothache, have you, Miss Crone?"

Miss Crone nodded her head yes, putting a hand to her jaw and moaning.

Don Giovanni chuckled. "Never say—a toothache too. What a shame. Well, Miss Crone, I bow to your ability to rise above life's aches and pains. Alas for your twisted ankle. I will have to do without the pleasure of partnering you. Gentlemen..." With a bow, he took his leave, Hetty's protectors watching him go before turning back to her.

"Who was that, Het? Did he know you?"

She gave a genuine groan this time. "Argh! It's this self-satisfied man named Mr. Pickford, who is always hanging about Caroline and me. Thank you for driving him off. I hope he didn't recognize me. He always speaks in that insinuating manner, so it is hard to tell."

"Well, if he's a gentleman, he'll not refer to it, even if he did recognize you," Lionel mused. "But you'd better keep your distance all the same."

"That shouldn't be hard, since I don't dare dance now."

"I'm sorry about saying you twisted your ankle," said Clunker. "Inspiration failed me."

"You did just fine," Hetty replied, patting his sleeve and dislodging two more feathers. "And you and Bailey should go ask some ladies to partner you now—Lionel will sit with me a while."

"I could sit," offered Bailey. "Not many ladies seem eager to dance with a horse's a—horse's hind end, rather."

"Where's my brother, anyway?" Clunker asked.

"With the Ophelia, last I saw," answered Lionel, pointing with his thumb over his shoulder.

"What do you know!" exclaimed Bailey, trying to peer around him. "I tried to ask her, but then one of the Napoleons took offense at it—he'd already had a few drinks too many, I'm guessing, and he—"

A roar interrupted him, and every head turned in time to see the very Napoleon Bailey had been describing launch himself at Clinker, while the other dancers scattered and Ophelia screamed.

"Jerome! Jerome!" she shrieked, pulling on him and then climbing up his back.

"Clinkett!" hollered his friends, darting up to shove their way through the throng. Hetty scrambled atop the bench to see over all the heads, wringing her hands and praying Lionel wouldn't get in any trouble again. He mustn't!

The masqueraders, recovering from their surprise, began to rush back toward the scufflers like a wave sucked back into the depths.

"Oh, oh!" Hetty fretted. "I can't see what's happening."

"Allow me to assist you."

Before she could register that she was being addressed, an arm caught her behind the knees, and she tumbled backwards, landing in an untidy heap in the speaker's arms. Arms which tightened into iron bands.

In the uproar of Napoleon's scuffle with the Cyclops, not a single person noticed the withered crone being carried off, wriggling and protesting, her toothache bandage coming loose and sliding over the eye holes of her mask.

Chapter Seventeen

What can this hurly-burly, this helter-skelter mean?
Jove looks confounded surly!—Chaos is come again.
— Kane O'Hara, *Midas*, I.5 (1764)

"Put me down!" ordered Hetty, scrabbling at the bandage covering her eyes as she was spirited away from the ballroom tumult.

"But your ankle is twisted," returned Mr. Pickford amiably, tightening his grip as Hetty squirmed and kicked.

"Put me down this instant, sir!"

He carried her away from the flow of people through an alcove and passage into what appeared to be a cloakroom. Not until he kicked the door shut behind him and leaned against it did he set her down. "Given your injuries, aches and pains, I didn't want you to be caught up in that scuffle, Miss *Crone*," he smiled.

Under her toothache bandage, Hetty's jaw set, and the blue eyes that peered out from her mask were murderous. "Thank you," she replied coolly. "But my friends would not let anything happen to me. If you will excuse me..."

She waited for him to move aside, but instead he leaned back against the door, crossing his arms over his cloak.

"You remind me of someone...it's your voice."

She said nothing.

"Or perhaps it was the red hair I glimpsed beneath your wig."

"Let me out."

"When I saw it, I thought to myself, *there's more where that came from.*" Extending a hand, Don Giovanni plucked her wig from her head, yanking out pins and causing Hetty to squeal.

"How dare you!" she cried, leaping to retrieve it as he held it out of reach.

"Behold! Your ankle is miraculously healed," he went on, "not to mention your toothache. If I did not know better, I would guess you were not such a *Crone* after all, and actually more of a *Hapgood*."

Furious, Hetty ceased her jumping. Her lips pressed into a line, and her eyes narrowed to slits behind her mask. "What of it, Mr. Pickford?"

His eyes glinted. Handing her back the wig, he pulled off his own mask. "I little expected to find you in such circumstances. Hardly the proper setting for a young lady like yourself. Can the Sidneys possibly know about this escapade?"

She did not reply, only busying herself with pinning the wig back on and shoving her hair underneath.

"But I am glad of the opportunity to speak with you apart," he went on. "I had been intending to, you see."

Keeping her eyes lowered, she glanced about in the dimness. Should she run at him? Shove him aside? Pull his mask into his eyes? Tear a cloak from its hook and fling it over him?

"What could you possibly have to say that could not be said in front of my family?" she said icily.

"Well, before a man speaks to a young lady's family, he would like to know he has some chance of succeeding."

Hetty's bosom heaved underneath her shapeless gown. She hoped he did not mean what she thought he meant.

"You see, Miss Hapgood, I have not made many proposals, you may be surprised to learn. And I might have hesitated now, if not for the encouragement you've given me."

"Encouragement?" she cried. "I don't know what you mean; nor do I require explanations. If you will please excuse me—"

"I meant the encouragement of your conversation in general, but more particularly, the way you took hold of me at the Tower," he explained in the same pleasant voice that made her want to slap him.

"Mr. Pickford—I did not take hold of you at the Tower out of...fondness for you, but rather out of alarm, as I believe I mentioned." She broke off—was it possible to say to a man, *And, whatever you do, please never propose to me*, when he had not yet proposed? She might venture it, she thought. Mr. Pickford did not seem the sort who would be crushed by the blow. In fact, his confidence seemed singularly robust. Still, she hesitated. Because, whatever the robustness of his vanity, no one liked rejection.

This momentary sympathy for him was banished when he began to laugh silently, shaking his head. "Ah, Miss Hapgood, you need not bother with the coyness and appearance of modesty. Not when I find you in such a place as this."

Behind her mask she flushed scarlet, all too aware of the truth of his words. If she had listened to her aunt—if she had not lied and deceived and sneaked out—she would not now be in this situation, and Mr. Pickford would not think he could kidnap her, lock her in a closet, and say such things. But even if she was in the wrong toward her aunt, he was no gentleman if he saw it as an excuse to press an unwelcome advantage!

"Call it what you will, Mr. Pickford," Hetty said, her voice trembling more in rage and chagrin than fear, "but I ask you again to move aside and let me go."

"Patience, Miss Hapgood," he soothed. "I find that, discovering you in this setting makes me think I might first take a deposit on my earnings."

With that, he seized her arms with both hands and forced his mouth upon her own.

Hetty lost her mind.

The girl in his grip transformed into a wildcat, fiercer than any in the Tower menagerie. She scratched and screamed and kicked and shoved and *kneed*, and it must have been the kneeing that answered, because Mr. Pickford doubled over with an oath, and she fairly clambered over him to seize the door handle and fling open the door.

Then she was careering along the passage, mask askew and bandage streaming, head turned to glance over her shoulder, terrified lest she see him in pursuit.

Whoof!

Her frantic flight ended abruptly in a collision, her head whipping forward to smash sideways into a collarbone. Hetty would have fallen to the floor, but hands seized her again by the shoulders, and she screamed, thinking somehow Mr. Pickford had laid hold of her again.

Instantly she was released. Gasping, she looked up at a tall figure in a red domino, a domino which was then whisked off to reveal—Mr. Rotherwood.

"Hetty?—Miss Hapgood, that is—are you all right?"

She was panting. Her wig hung by two pins. And somehow the sight of him—the concern in his eyes, his solid presence, the safety he represented—made her want to burst into tears. Those tears—the threat of them—choked her, making speech impossible.

She should explain herself. Explain what she was doing in the Argyll Rooms at a masquerade. Explain why she was running as if a wolf pursued her. Explain why she screamed.

But her throat would not open, and the tears were hot behind her eyelids.

He waited, equally at a loss, even as he felt a rising drumbeat in his pulse. Something—some*one* had terrified her. What had happened?

He had arrived in Little Argyll Street as soon as he could excuse himself from the concert and call a hackney coach, only to learn that tickets to the ball were not sold at the door. With a shrug and a sigh he was turning away, when two fellows stumbled out of the Rooms, one dressed as Napoleon and the other wearing a red domino, which he ripped off and tossed aside. "What a row," the second said to Napoleon, who was clearly in his cups. "Bad form, hurling yourself at that boy."

"He shouldn't have—shouldn't have—Betsy—shouldn't have—" slurred the other.

"Uh-huh," agreed his companion. "Just so. Come on with you."

When the two men staggered away and turned the corner, St. John bent to pick up the discarded domino. A cardboard ticket fluttered to the ground.

He was going to the masquerade after all, it seemed.

The scene within looked like a hurricane had passed through. Instead of orderly rows or groups of dancers, people were disheveled and wandering hither and yon, arranging their costumes or discussing what had just passed in vehement knots. The musicians were taking their seats again and tuning their instruments, adding to the cacophony.

"Clinker, you madman! Didn't we have enough trouble this summer?" came a familiar voice behind him. "And now we've lost my sister."

Whirling, St. John saw a tall young man with bright auburn hair, a horse's head tucked under his arm, addressing three other familiar figures. The Cyclops, whom he recognized as James Clinkett, moaned. "How was I to know asking Ophelia to dance would make that Bonapartish madman take a swing at me? And then all those people piling on. What a scene! I still taste pomade and hair powder on my tongue. Bah!"

"Where can Miss Hapgood have gone?" asked Edward Clinkett, who appeared to be clothed all in white, with just a few stray feathers attached to him in random places. "She isn't on the bench where we left her."

"Do you think she went home?" suggested Bailey. St. John couldn't tell what his disguise had been either.

"Why would she have gone home by herself?" reasoned Lionel. "And I daresay she wouldn't choose the moment when something exciting was happening to leave."

"Maybe she went upstairs to escape the fray," Bailey tried again.

"Maybe. We better split up and look for her. We can meet back at the bench."

Without discovering himself, St. John decided to take part in the search. It was only after the others had gone each in a different direction that he realized he didn't know what he was looking for. She could be disguised as anything.

As it happened, Hetty found him first by hurtling into him, and now here they were.

"Your brother and his friends are looking for you," said St. John, when she didn't speak.

At this, her eyes grew enormous, and she began hastily straightening herself, thrusting her bright hair under her repulsive wig, smoothing her gown, tying a great bandage around her head. "Mr. Rotherwood," she breathed as she worked, "I must ask you a favor. A very great favor."

Distracted by the metamorphosis taking place before him, he asked, "What are you supposed to be, Miss Hapgood?"

"A crone. A withered old crone," she answered, as if pretty young ladies often chose to hide their lights under bushels thus. "Please—do say you will oblige me."

He bowed. "However I can, of course."

"Then please, I beg you—say nothing of how you encountered me. I mean, my unkemptness or my—my lack of composure."

"Lack of composure?" he murmured. "My dear Miss Hapgood, you put it rather mildly. I would call it distress. You were greatly distressed."

She glanced back once more and then gave him a pleading look. "Mr. Rotherwood—I *beseech* you! Call it whatever you like, but Lionel must not know about it, or he will—he will surely do something unwise. I am fine, as you see. Perfectly fine."

"Miss Hapgood," said St. John ominously, in the voice his former pupils would have known from when they had performed abysmally at collections or done something that would surely get them gated. "Miss Hapgood, before I make you any promises, you must tell me what I am concealing."

"Nothing!" she declared. "Nothing you need worry about. Nothing anyone need worry about." Seeing his jaw set into even greater sternness, panic spiraled through her midsection. Why must he be difficult? What had it to do with him?

"Very well," she conceded. "It is this: Mr. Pickford made advances to me, which I—I rejected."

It would require a chisel to chip that jaw now, she thought. And for the first time since Mr. Pickford chopped her behind the knees, she felt the beginnings of a smile. But clearly Mr. Rotherwood had yet to see the humor in it, for he said, "He took liberties with you?"

Hetty swallowed. Heaven knew she didn't want to defend the odious Mr. Pickford, but if she could not douse that little flame starting to burn in Mr. Rotherwood's eyes, it might flare into a blaze that enveloped her brother, and they did *not* need Lionel falling afoul of the law again. If Lionel and his friends heard Mr. Pickford had seized, kidnapped, closeted, and accosted her, that would be the end. Only see how mischief followed those boys! They could not attend a simple masquerade without Clinker getting in a brawl.

Taking a deep breath, she strove for an even, light tone. "He tried to take liberties. I say 'tried.' But I was having none of it. He seemed to think my presence here justified some...presumption, and I...let him know otherwise. But you see, Mr. Rotherwood, one cannot entirely blame him—I shouldn't be here, you know. I asked my aunt if Caroline and I might attend, and she forbade it outright, so I am expressly disobeying and deceiving her, you see."

"Miss Hapgood," he said slowly, "that may be, and you must be the judge of that. But a wrong on your part does not excuse a wrong on his."

Then Hetty did laugh, to his surprise. Laughed and laid a hand on his sleeve for a moment. "Oh, Mr. Rotherwood, how relentlessly logical you are! It must be the mathematician in you. I had better tell you my reason for making little of Mr. Pickford's naughtiness, if you will not leave it. I do not know if you know, but Lionel had rather a harrowing summer, and for a time we quite feared for him, because he attacked another gentleman over a matter of honor and had to answer to the law. It was a miracle he escaped the consequences, really. And his intended—my dear cousin Edith—would be *beside* herself if I let him squander that and get in another life-threatening scrape. You understand, don't you? Please—please say you will say nothing of the matter to him."

"Hetty!" cried a voice behind him, and Lionel was upon them, becoming the third person that night to take her by the shoulders. But he added a ruthless shake, vexed as he was, and she had to wrench out of his grip. "Where did you go?"

"I—was here in the passage. Where I ran into Mr. Rotherwood."

The unexpected encounter with his former tutor succeeded in distracting her brother and sweeping Hetty's disappearance under the rug, to her vast relief. And Mr. Rotherwood, after one last look at her—a look that clearly said, *This matter is not yet finished*—did as she asked and kept her earlier distress to himself.

They were soon joined by the Clinketts and Bailey and spent some minutes in greetings and polite questions and answers. Hetty could see it was not easy for the boys to forget the former tutor's role in their lives, and she was at first amused by their restrained deference. Then, as the shock of her experience with Mr. Pickford receded and her equilibrium returned, she began to remember all she had forgotten of Mr. Rotherwood in the joy and relief of seeing him. That is, she remembered his mother's disapproval of her and Caroline as possible matches for him, and Hetty thanked God Mrs. Rotherwood had not witnessed the past few minutes. Only imagine what the woman would have thought, to see one of those same objectionable girls at a masquerade ball, fleeing one suitor and throwing herself at St. John!

She would have thought it a ploy, Hetty thought. *A scheme to put myself forward. To force myself upon him.* As if she could not think of a better way to catch someone's attention than hurling herself at him physically!

In the meantime, the Argyll Rooms recovered from the earlier upheaval, and the music and dancing resumed.

"We'd better get you home, Het," said Lionel reluctantly. "It'll never do to show up at the same time as the Sidneys returning."

"I was at the same musical performance as they earlier," spoke up Mr. Rotherwood, "though I left at the interval. I think Miss Hapgood would have time for one last dance, if she would do me the honor. Then I could call a coach and see you all safely home."

"Er—I'll let Het answer for the dance, but I'd better see her home, sir."

"Thank you, Mr. Rotherwood," she told his shoulder, "but I think I'll ask my brother to take me now. I would hate it to be a near thing."

"Then I'll call the coach this minute," amended St. John, aware of his disappointment.

It was just a dance. They could dance another time. But why was she addressing his shoulder once again?

Hetty read Lionel's wavering, but she was determined now. Her pride was up. "Thank you again. Better not. When a girl goes lying and sneaking out of her aunt's house, she can't come clattering up to the door."

Lionel's eyes widened at this honesty, but St. John's brow furrowed. "I hope, Miss Hapgood, you will give me some credit for sense. We could let you out at the corner, and one of us could see you the rest of the way."

Standing around arguing the point wouldn't help matters, so she yielded with poor grace. "Oh, very well. Thank you, sir."

"Thank you, sir," echoed Lionel and his friends. "We're sorry to be troublesome, aren't we, Het?"

Hetty nodded. "Yes. Sorry. Thank you."

Their expressions of gratitude only seemed to annoy him. "Do you not think you all could call me St. John now? Or at least 'Rotherwood'? You make me feel a century old."

"I don't know, sir," admitted Lionel, "you're one of fortune's high flyers now."

"Confound your 'high flyer'!" uttered St. John. "My Oxford days have more charm for me now than you can realize."

Clinker grinned at this. "You don't say. Why, then—Rotherwood is rather good in our book. It's a deal, s—Rotherwood, I mean. If you'll drop the 'misters' from our names."

They all shook on this and clapped each other's shoulders, with the exception of Hetty. She sighed behind her toothache bandage and wondered why it was that boys got to have all the fun. They would all be "Rotherwood" and "Hapgood" and "Bailiwick" and "Clinker" and "Clunker" now; but she, who had found inexpressible comfort and safety in the man's presence, and who cared for him more than any of them did, she suspected, must go on calling him "Mr. Rotherwood" and be addressed as "Miss Hapgood" to the end of time.

Chapter Eighteen

**No, monster! First over my dead body thou shalt tread.
— Coleridge, tr. from Schiller, *The Death of Wallen-
stein,* V.v.147 (1800)**

That she need not answer too many questions, and that she might put her mind in order, Hetty continued her feigned illness the next day.

"That Mr. Rotherwood called," reported Caroline, as she sat at her cousin's bedside, sewing. "We told him at the concert that you were unwell, and so he came today. What do you think of that?"

Hetty gave a listless shrug and rolled onto her back, that she might stare up at the bed canopy and avoid her cousin's eyes.

"I suppose it's more to the point to ask, what does Mrs. Rother-wood think of that?" Caroline went on. "For here she is, telling us that we are not good enough for them; yet here he is, calling."

Hetty thought there could be two reasons: either he was just being polite, or he wanted to talk more about what happened in the Argyll Rooms with Mr. Pickford. And if it was the latter, as she suspected, there could be two reasons for that, as well: either he was just being polite, or he truly cared what had happened with Mr. Pickford. And if the latter case again, there were two further possibilities: either chivalry motivated him, or affection did. And if it was affection, was it affection for the sister of a former pupil, or was it *affection* affection, such as Mrs. Rotherwood feared?

This branching tree of possibilities really did make her head and heart ache because she wanted it to be the latter and the latter and the latter and the latter. She wanted him to care for her as she cared for him. Her heart could not help but thrill as she remembered fleeing the detestable Mr. Pickford and his detestable kiss—fleeing him in fear and panic and running straight into the arms—well, straight into the chest—of Mr. Rotherwood.

Beloved Mr. Rotherwood.

She must not call him that.

Not even in her mind.

For even if he came to care for her, what sort of marriage could it be, if his mother rejected her? If Mrs. Rotherwood disapproved the match, she and her son would become estranged, even as mother and son had been completely alienated from their Holt relations.

Every part of Hetty—or nearly every part of her—revolted at the possibility. He had said himself how, for most of his life, he and Mrs. Rotherwood only had each other. How his cruel grandfather's greatest gift had been to give him this closeness of duty and affection with the only real family he could claim. Hetty was not the sort of girl who would blithely slice through such bonds in the blind selfishness of her own happiness. Was it not plain that she disliked being at odds with family? Why, here she was, trying to make amends for how she had favored her Hapgood relations over her Sidney relations!

But maybe it was her fate to cause dissension among those she should love best.

"He had better not call again," said Hetty. "Whatever his reason. Because I don't suppose Mrs. Rotherwood unbent any, when you saw her at the concert?"

"No. She only nodded from a distance. And we did not approach the Stanleys, and the Stanleys did not approach us. To think I ever thought Lady Sylvia was my friend! I should have known it from the moment she sat upon my fan and broke it that she would do me no good."

"Maybe she will be friendly again when she feels secure of Mr. Rotherwood," suggested Hetty dismally.

"Maybe." Smiling a little, Caroline rose from her chair and pulled it closer to the bed. "It was just as well they didn't talk to us be-cause—because someone else did." She prodded Hetty's hip and gave a little squeal. "Don't you want to know who?"

"Let me guess," said Hetty, perking up. She rolled up on her elbow. "Did he tell you your cheeks are like woses?"

Caroline gave an unladylike bark of laughter that made Hetty feel a surge of novel fondness for her. "No, he didn't! I do not refer to Sir Keane. I meant Mr. Elwood, of course. Mr. Elwood talked to me and sat beside me (so did Sir Keane, but never mind him). It's as if all of us have given up on either Lady Sylvia or Mr. Rotherwood and have settled for each other. Well—not all of us. Mr. Pickford wasn't there, so I can't speak for him. What? Why do you look like that?"

"No reason," Hetty returned. But she covered her face with a pillow nonetheless. "It's just that I think I hate Mr. Pickford. Let's not talk about him. Tell me more about Mr. Elwood and what he said."

"He's rather a nice man. Nice to look at—not so handsome as Mr. Rotherwood or Mr. Pickford, of course—but nice to look at, and not so very old as Sir Keane. And he asked me all sorts of things about myself, and we found we both like the color blue and summer better than winter and music better than cards. And he asked me how I felt about dogs because his younger brothers have two little dogs, and I said I like little dogs very much, and he asked if I liked white dogs in particular, and I told him white dogs were my favorite, and that is exactly the color dogs his brothers have!"

"What are the odds?" Hetty said with a grin, but she was genuinely pleased. Might Caroline actually warm to this plan? She had no fear Mr. Elwood would fail to come up to scratch. If no Lady Sylvia had ever been seen, Caroline Sidney would have dazzled.

"He said I seemed to enjoy visiting the Tower, and perhaps he might invite you and me to see another sight," her cousin went on.

"I would love that!" cried Hetty, sitting up at this and thinking she might make a rapid recovery after all. "Did you say yes?"

"I did, but I said I would talk to you about it because we could only go when you were well. But really I wanted you to choose because you know it's all the same to me. Although I did very much like animals and the crown jewels. Oh, but Hetty—it's nice to talk to someone who doesn't fill me with doubt and panic like Mr. Rotherwood does. And nice that Mr. Elwood never mentions such things as Benjamin Franklin and the Royal Society."

"Nor does he lisp or leer," sighed Hetty, delighted. "He is altogether unexceptionable." She hugged a pillow to her chest. And wouldn't that just show the Stanleys, if Caroline were to catch Mr. Elwood, and Lady Sylvia never succeeded in winning Mr. Rotherwood?

"Let me see...why do we not go see the Banqueting House in Whitehall? The rest of the palace is gone, but I've heard it's very fine." She saw no cause to mention that it was the Rubens ceiling which drew her—no need to bring up Edith when the two of them were getting along so well. "And then we might visit the Adelphi rooms south of the Strand, since they are nearby. The Barry paintings are supposed to contain all sorts of historical figures."

"Very well," said Caroline, not particularly caring, as Hetty expected she would not. "When I next see him, I will suggest it. I do not suppose we need invite Sir Keane or—anyone else—but if anyone else hovers about, we may not be able to avoid it."

Hetty agreed to this and, after a few more minutes decided she would get up after all. Lying in bed pretending to recuperate was a bore, and if Mr. Rotherwood had already been and gone, the danger was past. She would just have to remember to cough periodically if Aunt Lavinia was present.

She might have avoided Mr. Rotherwood with her ruse, but Hetty neglected to take into account Mr. Pickford, and no sooner did she breakfast and join her aunt and cousin in the drawing room than that gentleman was announced.

A genuine coughing fit racked her because, in her alarm, she swallowed wrong, and the horrid man entered to find Hetty burying her face in her shawl while Mrs. and Miss Sidney greeted him and pretended not to notice.

"Mr. Pickford," began Lavinia. "How nice of you to call. We hear you attended the masquerade ball in the Argyll Rooms last night."

His habitually half-mast, supposedly-seductive eyelids opened entirely at this, and he glanced at Hetty, who peered at him through eyes now watering with her hacking.

"Indeed I was. How...well-informed you are."

"Mr. Elwood told us," said Caroline demurely.

"Ah." He glanced at Hetty again, whose recovery had succeeded to the point where she was merely clearing her throat repeatedly.

"Mrs. Sidney," he resumed, his eyelids drooping again in the way that made Hetty want to kick him, "I wonder if Mr. Sidney be at home?"

"Mr. Sidney! Why—I suppose he is in his library." Lavinia put a hand to her bosom. "Did—you want to speak with him?"

"If I may."

There was nothing for it but to call a servant and send word to the master of the house. The group sat, immobile and silent until Carter returned. "He asks you to come back and see him, sir."

When the door shut behind them, Caroline gasped and Lavinia leapt up to pace before the fireplace. "What can it mean? He must be here to ask Mr. Sidney's permission to pay his addresses. But to whom? Girls—has he said anything to either of you?"

"No! Not a thing," declared her daughter.

Hetty was drained of color, and she thought she might genuinely faint. *Was* Mr. Pickford there to pay his addresses to her? He had said as much at the Argyll Rooms, but surely after what happened there he had abandoned the idea! He had not come to expose her misdoings, had he?

Neither possibility made sense. He could not possibly imagine she wanted to marry him, but what would be the use of telling tales on her to her uncle?

"Harriet." Aunt Lavinia's voice cut through her mental tumult. "Has Mr. Pickford given *you* reason to believe he cares?"

"I—I—I—oh, aunt," she stumbled. "I do not know."

"Your uncle will take the measure of him," Lavinia continued, not sounding as confident as she might. "We expect. But I must tell you, my dear, that I am not sure his fortune and reputation are all that may be desired. Of course, your father has assured me you will have a respectable competence, but one must also choose a husband who will steward your portion wisely."

"Aunt," croaked Hetty. "I thank you for your advice, but I assure you, if Mr. Pickford has any intentions toward me, I have none toward him."

Her aunt gave a grim smile. "I am relieved, Harriet. Quite relieved. Very well, if anything is afoot, it must be got through. If—my husband is not sufficiently discouraging to the man, you may trust that I will back you up."

"Ooh," breathed Caroline, making little fists of excitement. "How I envy you, Hetty! Not Mr. Pickford, so much, but the fact that you will have your first proposal."

To Hetty's mind, it was rather like Caroline telling her she envied her a stomach-ache, and she wished she had not used up her excuse of unwellness, that she could call upon it now.

An agonizingly long time seemed to pass. The Sidneys sewed; Hetty held a book. Finally, voices and steps were heard in the passage, and the door opened to admit her uncle and Mr. Pickford.

"Harriet, my dear," said Wellington Sidney, "Mr. Pickford would like a word with you. Lavinia, Caroline, if you would come with me, I should like to consult you on the invitations we have received."

Obediently his wife and daughter followed him, Caroline throwing her cousin a last look, and Hetty wished and wished she might accompany them, or that she could crawl under the sofa or climb out the window. How could the man have to gall the face her, after his behavior at the Argyll Rooms?

As if he read her thoughts, he leaned insolently against the mantel and regarded her. "Well, Miss Hapgood, are you surprised to see me?"

"I am. I cannot think what we may have to say to each other, sir."

"I judge you managed to keep your little secret, then? The Sidneys have no idea where you were last night?"

She burned a bright red and that was answer enough.

"Come, come," he said, one side of his mouth lifting and his aggravating eyelids lowering in his most lady-killing fashion. "I too can keep a secret, when it suits me. And it just might suit me. You see, Miss Hapgood, we have known each other just a brief time, but it has been more than long enough to convince me that you are a charming young woman of good family, and I—"

"Mr. Pickford," breathed Hetty, on her feet and a hand upheld, palm outward. "Forgive me—I must stop you right there. I think there is—there is no need to say what you are in—in the process of saying."

"Oh? And what am I in the process of saying?"

If it were possible for her to redden further, she did so. But this wave of color rose from indignation. Wretched man. She was trying to spare him—why should she have to be explicit?

Seeing her jaw set, he grinned. "Was that unfair of me? If it was, you will have to forgive me in turn. I appreciate your show of maidenly modesty, but I assure you I will not think the less of you for abandoning the pretense."

"Pretense!"

"Miss Hapgood—a young lady who would attend a masquerade ball without the knowledge of her family, and indeed without any chaperone whatsoever—such a young lady need not make a show of guilelessness."

"I was not unchaperoned!" blurted Hetty, her eyes almost shooting sparks.

He affected mild surprise. "You were not? Ah—I suppose you refer to those young men: the one seated beside you and the other two who came along. I know you are new to town, Miss Hapgood, but I must inform you that employing young men as chaperones is most unusual and possibly worse than no chaperones at all."

She found she was light-headed from breathing so rapidly, and she sank with a bump onto the settee. Should she confess that one of the young men was her brother? *I must*, she thought. *I know I promised Lionel I would keep his presence in London to myself, but who could have foreseen this turn of events?*

But what would happen if she did make the disclosure? Two things, she imagined. Firstly, she would break her word to her brother and get him in hot water with their Sidney relations. Hot, hot water. The secrecy, the sneaking, the masquerade—! And secondly, Lionel would want to know why Hetty opened her big mouth, and she would have to tell him about Mr. Pickford. And Lionel would be furious at the man's impudence, and then would come all the trouble she had tried to avoid in the first place.

No.

No, no, no.

It would be better to let him make his insolent remarks and to bear them as a not-unjust consequence of her foolish actions.

"You are right," she rejoined after some time, folding her hands in her lap so that he would not see them tremble. "I was unchaperoned. It was wrong of me, but I was...curious. Those—young men—were nobody in particular."

There was a gleam in his lazy gaze. "Hmm. I rather like your sense of daring. So many young ladies are downright dull, if one is honest

They are timid; they are conventional; they never venture outside the strictures of propriety."

Hetty gritted her teeth, determined to let him say his piece, that she might be done. And after going on for another minute in the same vein, he finally exhausted this line of wit. Then, taking a deep breath, he left the window to saunter over and drop to one knee.

"Miss Hapgood, you are perhaps displeased with me for the advantage I took last night, though, again, I will say an unchaperoned young lady must expect to pay the piper for her lack of restraint. You might not have known that, but I daresay you learned. Do not allow your momentary vexation to prevent you from hearing me."

She said nothing, only clenching her jaw harder.

Just possibly, Mr. Pickford experienced a twinge of doubt. He was handsome, to be sure, and many young ladies deemed him irresistible, but this Miss Hapgood was not many young ladies. In fact, there was an intensity in her blue eyes that could almost be described as chilling. With a slight shudder he remembered the knee she had aimed at a sensitive part of his anatomy. But there were his debts and his creditors to think of, and Miss Hapgood would be an easier target than her cousin or that Lady Sylvia Stanley. Miss Hapgood's portion was not so outsize, and she had no hovering parents to interfere.

"From the first moment of our acquaintance," he resumed, "I thought you beautiful and winsome. Your playful nature, your sparkling conversation—" (From the corner of his eye, he saw her shift restlessly.) "And when you took hold of me at the menagerie, I allowed myself to hope. So now I ask you: Miss Hapgood, would you make me the happiest of men? Would you honor me by saying you will one day become Mrs. Pickford?"

For a long space there was no sound but the ticking of the mantel clock and, somewhere below in the kitchen, the rattle of a pot and the bang of the back door closing.

Hetty was struggling inwardly. She was young, after all, and inexperienced, and angry at herself and at him. She would cringe later for how she answered Mr. Pickford, but in the moment she could not help it, she was so incensed. "Mr. Pickford," she said in a voice of stone, "I will not do you that honor. I will never, I may fairly say. Even though I was at fault for being at the Argyll Rooms yesterday, a true gentleman would not have taken advantage of my foolishness. Not then and not now. Therefore, I pray you will say no more. Please excuse my baldness of speech, but I did try to prevent you from making your offer."

Slowly, he rose to his feet again. "Am I to understand you are refusing me?"

"Yes."

"Because I kissed you at the masquerade ball?"

"Not just kissed me!" she flashed. "You—you fairly kidnapped me from the scene. And when I protested and asked to be let out of that—closet—you did not let me by until I compelled you." Just the recollection of it made her begin to tremble with remembered panic and fury. "Mr. Pickford, after such conduct on your part, not only will I not marry you, but I would prefer never to spend another minute in your company ever, ever again."

As she spoke, her would-be suitor grew scarlet. The effrontery of this girl! She took this high-handed tone with him, after her own deeds? Charles Pickford was not the sort of man who would let some scrap of a person have the last word, and he did not do so now.

"I will certainly spare you my company in future, Miss Hapgood, but before I go, allow me to proffer you some advice. You are young and not used to town ways, but you had better learn now that a girl who is found in such places unaccompanied may expect far worse than what happened to you." He made a scoffing sound, his eyes narrow and scornful. "Worse? Why, I think on reflection you will find little to complain of. If I had meant to insult you, would I then have offered for you?" He shook his head regretfully, maddeningly. "No, no, Miss Hapgood. You have nothing to reproach me with. Nothing to justify the aspersions you have cast at me today. If you were a man—well, let that rest."

"If I were a man, sir, I would make you answer for your actions!" cried Hetty, springing up. If the man would not go, she must flee him again. Flee him, or—heaven help her—she would be the next Hapgood hauled to the watch-house by a constable!

CHAPTER NINETEEN

Do I stand here to hear stories? Sir tell me the truth, the whole truth and nothing but the truth.
— **Thomas Thomsen,** *The English Rogue,* **II.iii.12 (1688)**

Four days passed. St. John Rotherwood called two more times at the Sidneys', each time to be told that the family was not at home. On the last occasion, he left a card on the salver and embarked on a lengthy walk, turning down Portland Street to look in at Booth's (no Miss Hapgood), and then following Oxford Street, glancing in at each shop as he passed (again, no Miss Hapgood). Nor had he seen her brother or his friends anywhere after having dropped them in Fitzroy Square the night of the masquerade. As Lionel leapt down, he put a finger to his lips and grinned at his former tutor. "If you don't mind, Rotherwood—not a word of this to my Sidney relations. They don't know I'm here, and I'd like to keep it that way." St. John nodded agreement at the time, but now he wished he had asked where they were lodging.

When at last his walk returned him to North Audley Street, he found his mother closeted with her solicitor Mr. Pinckney.

"Do come join us, St. John," she called. "Mr. Pinckney has gossip to share." Reading his expression, she added, "Truly—it might interest you, for it concerns some of our acquaintance."

Biting back a sigh, he complied, tossing his hat on a side table and taking a seat with them. "How are the betting books faring, Pinckney?" he asked. "Whom do the odds favor now?"

The agent smiled wryly. "I believe the latest numbers favor *you*, sir, because Mrs. Rotherwood has been so discouraging to the gentlemen who have tried their luck with her."

"Ah. And, in regard to myself, with whom am I being paired?"

He caught a glance between the two of them, and then Mr. Pinckney said, "It seems Lady Sylvia Stanley is considered the favorite." As he spoke, both he and Anne watched St. John carefully.

His face was blank.

"That makes sense," he said.

"Naturally," agreed Mr. Pinckney, brightening. "When two people are equals in rank and situation, and when a match between them would be deemed fitting by any reasonable person—"

"Yes." St. John rubbed at a smudge on the gloss of his boot and then added idly, "But, of course, when two people are as wealthy as Lady Sylvia and I, we have the freedom to marry a greater range of people, do we not? Including those whose rank or fortune falls somewhat shorter." His eyes flicked up abruptly to meet Mr. Pinckney's. "What other names have you heard?"

The agent cleared his throat. "To be sure." He drummed his fingers on his knee as if recalling the list in his mind. "The Honorable Miss Kempshott, Lady Julia Crawley, Miss Beatrice Ellsworth…"

St. John could summon only the vaguest impressions of these young ladies, but he looked up sharply when the agent concluded, "and, of course, Miss Sidney and her cousin Miss Hapgood."

Seeing the movement, Anne hastened to add, "It is the latter two whom gossip swirls around, unfortunately."

"What sort of gossip?" St. John asked ominously.

Mr. Pinckney tented his fingertips together as he leaned forward. "Mr. Rotherwood, I make it my business to stay abreast of my client's affairs, as you know. Which means that, any parties that show interest in either of you are of interest to me, and I find out what I can about them."

"You spy, you mean."

The solicitor lifted a deprecating hand. "For those of spotless reputation, there is nothing to be concerned about. Most of my inquiries are general knowledge. The Stanleys' estates, for example, can be found in any Peerage. One word to their man of business, and I discover the health of their financial holdings."

"Yes, yes," St. John interrupted. "So much for the Stanleys. What have you heard of Miss Sidney and Miss Hapgood?"

Still the man hesitated. "For one thing, I learned Miss Sidney's cousin and Miss Hapgood's brother, one Lionel Hapgood, had an action brought against him for assault this last summer."

"*That* I knew already. And I know further that the action was dropped. It happens that I was Lionel Hapgood's mathematics tutor at Magdalen. Is that all?"

Mr. Pinckney took a long breath. "Well. I regret to say—indeed, I would regret to say of any young woman—that there are rumors Miss Hapgood has on occasion been seen where a young lady ought not, and all unchaperoned."

"What sorts of places?" wondered Anne with feigned alarm (for her agent had already told her this before her son came home).

"Madam, I am sorry to say, she was seen in the Argyll Rooms at a masquerade ball. Yes—you know those can sometimes be rough. A mixture of persons and levels. Certain people will use the excuse of anonymity to engage in behavior frowned upon in more genteel settings. I would be leery enough of a young lady attending such an event even accompanied by a chaperone, and indeed I learned there was an altercation there which resulted in the removal of one drunken man and his friends."

"How dreadful!"

St. John said nothing. He was too upset. His brow thunderous and his jaw hard, he looked every inch the man of marble. Who exposed her? It had to be Pickford, didn't it? Why, the next time he saw that man, he would take him by the lapels and shake him so hard his bones would rattle and his teeth clack!

Although—if that man succeeded in recognizing Miss Hapgood through her crone's disguise, there was every chance others did too. Multiple others. Her hair had only to escape the hideous wig to give her away, and she had been dancing. Most likely speaking, too, with her brother and friends. Had she not collided with St. John himself, he might have made the same discovery shortly after.

But he would not have spoken of it! He would never have spoken of it, to anyone but her!

"As a result," the solicitor continued, gaining courage from Rotherwood's silence, "there has been a growing coolness toward the family in social gatherings. I have heard at least one hostess intends on withdrawing an invitation sent earlier, and the lady patronesses of Almack's mean to refuse the Sidneys and Miss Hapgood admittance."

"They had no vouchers in the first place," snapped St. John, "therefore how can they be refused?" He rose impatiently, tugging at his neckcloth as if it offended him. "This is ridiculous. Have you any more tattling to do here, Pinckney?"

"St. John!" reproved his mother.

Her agent shrugged. "It seems enough..."

"Indeed it is," rejoined Anne. "For what can be more precious and fragile than a young lady's reputation?"

"I consider those young ladies to be friends," her son declared.

"Oh, St. John—"

"And indeed we were first introduced to them as friends of Lady Sylvia Stanley. I recall it, if you and she do not."

"I recall it."

Turning, he regarded the solicitor steadily. "Thank you for your...services, Mr. Pinckney. If you would excuse us, I'd like a private word with my mother."

"Certainly." The agent bowed, his mouth thinning at this dismissal. But he lifted a conciliatory hand when Anne began to apologize and took his leave.

She dropped her head in her hands.

"I'm sorry to have made your solicitor angry, Mama."

"He is *our* solicitor, St. John," she corrected. "If he tells us things that do not please us, he means them to be for our own good. Our own, mutual, ultimate good. That is why I—why we—pay him."

"That may be, but are all of his services truly necessary? Need we pay him to poke and pry into other people's affairs?"

"My dear, you still do not understand the great responsibility laid upon us," protested Anne. "We have a positive duty to steward both our fortune and our position now."

Shaking his head, his mouth twisted wryly. "Do you hear yourself? Do you remind yourself of anyone?"

Fondly as this was said, she reddened. "Perhaps my father was wiser than I thought, St. John."

"Perhaps. If you had it to do over, would you not have married my father?"

"I would have married him," she replied, her voice soft. "I only mean to say that—if—if hearts are not yet involved, would it not be better to be prudent than otherwise?"

Ah, but there was the rub. St. John suspected his heart was already involved.

He wondered—if he were so fortunate as to win Miss Hapgood, would his mother be able to see past her newfound prudence?

Would she be able to lay aside all the prejudices she held in Lady Sylvia's favor, in order to love the girl of her son's choosing?

She must be given the chance.

These feelings growing daily with St. John were so new to him that he could be forgiven thinking that anyone who spent time with Miss Hapgood must begin to love her. His mother only needed more time.

Taking a seat beside her, he took her hands in his.

"Madam—how long now have we been grand people with these positive duties you speak of? A month?"

She pouted, not liking the question.

"Let us call it a month. A month since we were nobodies, who, if not crushed beneath Fortune's wheel, were at least nowhere near the top. We had no friends but each other, no money but my fellowship. Have you forgotten?"

"Of course I have not."

"Nor have I. And therefore I cannot hear of...new friends...similarly isolated and unchampioned without wishing to assist them. It would please me if you could share my feelings."

Anne loved her son far too well to defy him. Indeed, her heart's insistence on Lady Sylvia as the only young woman worthy to partner him stemmed as much from her ambition for him as her devotion to him.

"What would you like me to do?" she murmured.

"Shall we have that supper for the Stanleys you've brought up several times?"

"Oh, yes!"

"And will we invite the Sidneys and Miss Hapgood as well? It would do much to rehabilitate them in society and might help them reconcile with the Stanleys."

Her eagerness dashed, her lips opened to protest, but then she heaved a sigh and nodded, resignedly. "As you wish, St. John. I will say no more about—what Mr. Pinckney discovered—except to say—to warn you, my darling, that it does not take much, on a gentleman's part, to be misconstrued. That is, any interest you take in defending those young ladies might be attributed to—tenderer feelings."

There was a pause, and then he said, "If I am clear with them, there can be no misunderstanding."

"Yes, yes." She lifted his hands and pressed her cheek to them. "You will be clear with them, won't you, St. John? You won't let yourself be trapped by your good intentions?"

In answer he dropped a kiss on her hair and gently extricated himself. "Shall we say Friday?"

The first indication the Sidneys had that something was wrong was that their parade of callers ceased. The Stanleys had vanished some time before, but now others went missing. The salver in the foyer held fewer and fewer cards and then none at all.

"What can it mean?" Lavinia asked her husband.

Then came a note from Lady Barstow expressing deepest regrets, but an arrival of family members from the country meant that she must perforce rescind her supper invitation for the time being...

"Is it a coincidence?" Lavinia demanded.

Wellington had no answer to either. At his club he spoke to no one, but that was his usual custom and could not be helpful in reading the signs of the times.

The following evening at the opera, the Sidneys bowed to Lady Aurora Robillard, and that lady fumbled with her opera glass and peered right over them.

It could not be a mistake.

Hetty shrank smaller and smaller, figuratively speaking, and grew quieter and quieter, literally speaking. If people were drawing back from them, was it because of her? Had that man said something—that horrid Mr. Pickford? Had he bruited it about that Miss Hapgood attended masquerades unchaperoned, with the approval of her relations? Why had she been so brutal in her rejection of him? She could never accept him, of course, but she should have been gentler. She should have pretended gratitude. She should have known what danger he posed.

Her aunt had not complained when Hetty reported her refusal, only saying, "I am not surprised, my dear. Nor is he one I would have chosen for Caroline—a something slippery about the eyes."

To find Aunt Lavinia so understanding, it was a hundred times on the tip of Hetty's tongue to confess all: the lying, the sneaking, the regrettable choice. But how could she, without also incriminating Lionel? And if she made half a confession—leaving Lionel out altogether—Aunt Lavinia might die of apoplexy, imagining her disobedient niece *alone* at a masquerade ball, amidst drunken ruffians and the-lord-knew-what-all.

Hetty did write to Edith at length, however, admitting every-thing, even as uncharacteristic tears blotted the page. But Edith was so far away that Hetty thought this must be how King Midas felt, when he dug a hole in the ground and whispered his secret into it.

She thought next of asking her stepmother's counsel, but she could not put pen to paper. There lay her stepmother's most recent letter, full of her brother Norman's marriage and Rosie's progress—all innocent joy that would be spoiled, blasted, by Hetty's confession. How shocked—how horrified her parents would be! How ashamed of her behavior and how apologetic to the Sidneys! And again there would be the dilemma of either incriminating Lionel or making matters sound ten times worse by leaving him out of the story.

At last, at last she decided to consult her brother. In the days since the Incident, he had sent one note via a messenger boy, who knocked at the back door for Trilby, in which he asked if she felt like "falling ill" again and seeing an exhibit of a talking pig. She declined. But the note reassured her because it meant that, whatever gossip was abroad, it had not reached him, nor had he been silent from indifference or because he was locked up in Newgate for ambushing Mr. Pickford.

But as Hetty sat at her desk, fiddling with her pen knife and accomplishing nothing, she heard voices and steps below. Unusual enough, in these days when everyone seemed to draw back from them. (Even Mr. Elwood had vanished, and Hetty had taken inwardly to calling him a mutton-head again.) Emerging from her room to peek over the stairs, she saw figures pass beneath and then heard Carter announce, "Mr. Rotherwood."

Hetty's pulse sped, and she gripped the newel post till the carving bit into her palms. Oh! Of everyone in the entire world, he was the person she most longed to see. The only one who knew her secret. The one she loved.

Like a sleepwalker she descended, trying to even out her breathing and pressing hands to her heated face.

He rose when she entered, his eyes fixed on hers. Hetty's mouth made a convulsive movement instead of the smile she had been attempting.

"I was just asking Mrs. and Miss Sidney if you were entirely recovered, Miss Hapgood."

"Yes. Thank you, sir." Gracelessly she dropped into a chair beside her cousin, who looked confused. Actually so did Aunt Lavinia. It was only when her aunt said, "We hope your mother is in good health," that Hetty remembered. Of course. The Sidneys were still aggrieved by Mrs. Rotherwood's high words. Hetty had been so absorbed in her own concerns that she quite forgot that injury.

"She is, I thank you," he replied, either unaware of their discomfiture or choosing not to acknowledge it. "And she requested that I pass along an invitation from her."

"An invitation!" Lavinia could not refrain from repeating. "From Mrs. Rotherwood?"

"Yes." He paused, bewildered by their patent astonishment. But when no one chose to enlighten him, he went on. "An invitation to supper at our home in North Audley Street. We have also invited the Stanleys."

So wide were Caroline's eyes that he might as well have said they invited the Prince Regent.

For the first time in days, Hetty felt the urge to smile. To giggle, even.

"And we would be happy to issue more invitations to the dinner, if it would give you pleasure. That is, if you would like other friends to be there. Sir Keane Montridge...Mr. Elwood—"

"Mr. Elwood—his presence won't be necessary," declared Caroline with uncharacteristic haughtiness. The mention of Mr. Elwood apparently riled her; his failure to call had not gone unnoticed. Hetty didn't know whether to be triumphant, that her cousin had begun to like the man, or disgusted, that he proved unworthy and it was all too late.

Mr. Rotherwood bowed in acknowledgement. "Very well. Yes to Sir Keane and No to Mr. Elwood." His eyes slid to Hetty. "What about the third of that trio? Mr. Charles Pickford, is it not?"

Then Caroline laughed. "Absolutely not, to Mr. Pickford! Not that he would come, I imagine, if he knew Hetty would be there, because she refused him the other day."

"My love," remonstrated her mother.

"No to Mr. Pickford as well," said Mr. Rotherwood coolly. He was fighting his own incredulity and anger. That villain—offering for Miss Hapgood, after making unwelcome advances to her? Where some might see it as proof of the man's honor and devotion, that he would propose after finding her in disgraceful circumstances,

St. John thought otherwise. No—that man estimated her character by his own. Just as Pickford thought forcing his attentions on her when she was defenseless was perfectly acceptable, he also believed she would still entertain the idea of marrying him. That her own apparent unscrupulousness would match his.

By heaven! If Miss Hapgood ever gave him permission to throw Pickford's conduct in his face, St. John would leap at the chance. He was now certain that scoundrel lay behind the circulating rumors. It likely salved his wounds, to tear at her reputation.

Hetty saw the emotions flitting across his countenance (how had she ever thought it marble and blank?), and she clutched her hands together so tightly her knuckles cracked. Heaven only knew what he thought of her, or of Mr. Pickford, for that matter. But whatever he thought, he must not say anything to anyone!

Raising pleading eyes, she mouthed, *Please.*

A wave of something washed over St. John. And like a literal wave, it swallowed him and stole his breath. His gaze fell to those coral lips. Please? Please what?

Shifting in his seat, he dug a finger under his neckcloth, feeling suddenly warm. Something about the vulnerability in her gaze brought suddenly to mind the moment when she collided with him in the Argyll Rooms. Her eyes had been desperate then, and her entire body tense. The body that ran against his chest.

Please.

He needed to speak with her alone, he decided. He needed to know what she was asking.

Abruptly he stood, running a hand through his gold-shot curling hair. "Shall we say Friday, then?" he suggested.

"That would be delightful," agreed Lavinia Sidney quickly. Was he leaving so soon? She stood as well, giving her daughter and niece a tiny nod, and they scrambled up.

But he did not go. He took three strides, whipped around, took one stride back, halted.

"Is that—is that a Tompion clock?" St. John blurted in desperation, pointing a finger at the timepiece on the mantel. "How often must you wind it?"

As he hoped, the three ladies turned as one to look at the clock, and he lunged at Mrs. Sidney's workbasket, snatching up her scissors.

"I couldn't say," Mrs. Sidney replied, bemused. "Carter the footman winds it."

"No, Mama," said Caroline, "I think it is Bevins' duty."

"Bevins, then. Shall I...call him and ask, Mr. Rotherwood?"

"Mr. Rotherwood!" cried Hetty. "You're bleeding!"

"Bleeding?" shrieked Caroline.

And indeed, their guest held one hand in the other, that he might not drip on the carpet. "It is nothing," he said. "I merely picked up some scissors from the floor and did it carelessly. Mrs. Sidney, if I might beg you for a piece of court plaster?"

"Certainly. They should have some in the kitchen. Hetty, girl," she added, as she swept to the doorway, "get my salts. Caroline is going to faint."

For the second time in her life, Hetty had to catch her cousin before she sank to the ground. Mr. Rotherwood lunged to help her, but she exclaimed, "No—stay right there. You'll get blood on her. I'll just lay her down here…"

"Miss Hapgood." He had ignored her command and was directly beside her, so close his breath stirred her hair, and it was fortunate Hetty had wrestled her cousin's limp body to the settee or else she might have dropped her. "Miss Hapgood, what did you want to say to me?"

"Oh!" When she turned their mouths nearly brushed, and Hetty thought she might faint right across Caroline. Stumbling back a step and blushing crimson, she muttered, "I only wanted to ask you not to mention—all the—everything—you know—Mr. Pickford—the ball—my brother. One day I may confess but—but not to them just yet. Please."

He nodded gravely. "Very well. You have my word." His voice was so low it was just a rumble. A rumble that made her every nerve tingle. "I would not have spoken without your permission in any case."

"Oh. Thank you for that. For your assurance."

Then Mrs. Sidney's steps were heard rushing up from the kitchen, and he retreated from Hetty's side to the mantel, feigning interest in the clock again.

"Court plaster!" she announced, waving the pale pink square. "And a rag to dry the cut first." Catching sight of her daughter, she thrust the items at Hetty. "Can you help him, my dear, while I tend to your cousin?"

Trying to hide his pleasure, St. John held out his hand, palm up. Hetty did not dare meet his eyes as she supported it with her own and pressed it gently with the rag. "I think it has stopped bleeding," she said.

"It certainly feels better now," he replied. "Just a scratch, after all." He nodded at the square of court plaster. "You must dampen it. Or it won't stick."

Helplessly, she looked about, but there was nothing to moisten the silk with.

Caroline gave a groan as her mother helped her to a sitting position.

"You might, perhaps, lick it," came Mr. Rotherwood's low voice. Then he flushed. "Never mind. I—never mind."

Hetty's heart thumped so emphatically in response to this that she feared Mr. Rotherwood would have heard, if her aunt had not spoken: "It was just a little blood, sweeting. Are you still dizzy? Here, now—take it slowly."

Lick it?

Like a kitten's, the pink tip of Hetty's tongue darted out along the edges of the plaster, and then she placed the square over his cut and hastily patted it down. "There. Is it all right?"

He didn't trust himself to speak. Not in words. What his eyes said was another matter.

And then Mrs. Sidney said, "Is it working, Mr. Rotherwood?"

He held up the bandaged hand. "Good as new. Better than new. Let us hope it does not leave a scar."

"I am glad to hear it," she smiled upon him. "Oh, and Bevins was down in the kitchen, and he reports that it is indeed a Tompion clock, and that he winds it every three weeks."

He bowed. "Astonishing machinery. Thank you, madam. I am sorry to have been the cause of any trouble. No—indeed—I have stayed long enough. But we will see you all the day after tomorrow, will we not? And I hope I might prevail upon those present for a little music."

Eagerly the Sidneys repeated their assurances, and he was seen to the door with the enthusiasm usually reserved for conquering heroes.

And why not? thought Hetty. To the victor go the spoils.

And her heart felt positively plundered.

CHAPTER TWENTY

Nuns fret not at their Convent's narrow room;
And Hermits are contented with their Cells;
And Students with their pensive Citadels:
Maids at the Wheel, the Weaver at his Loom,
Sit blithe and happy.
— Wordsworth, *Poems in Two Volumes* (1807)

As Trilby was dressing Hetty's hair, there came a firm knock at the door and Aunt Lavinia entered. "You look very nice, my dear. And Trilby, I daresay you have potential to become quite a capable lady's maid." While Hetty was beginning gradually to trust her aunt's new warmth, Trilby was taken wholly by surprise and promptly dropped both the hairbrush and a handful of pins.

Shutting her eyes, Lavinia sighed but let it alone. "I wanted a word with you before we go to the Rotherwoods' because I believe we owe this invitation to you."

"Oh, aunt," said Hetty.

"Let us be frank, Harriet. I am not saying that I expect him to offer for you. Indeed, I would be sorry to hear your heart was set on it—"

"Please, Aunt Lavinia—I assure you I have no such expectations," Hetty interrupted, scarlet with embarrassment. "I know he is the catch of the season and rich as Croesus, while I am—plain Harriet Hapgood. He is only friendly to me because of knowing Lionel. Truly. Besides, I know his mother wouldn't like it at all—"

But then it was Lavinia's turn to interrupt. Her hand came firmly down on the dressing table, her rings clinking. "Now you listen to me, Harriet: any objections I have do *not* include Mrs. Rotherwood's personal likes and dislikes. She doesn't even know you to dislike you! You may not be an earl's daughter, but you're a perfectly...unexceptionable girl." (This word choice drew a wide grin from her niece.) "I only mean to caution you. To urge you to guard your heart. For your own sake, and not for anyone else's."

In answer, Hetty reached an impulsive arm around her aunt's waist and hugged her. "Thank you, aunt," she murmured into the folds of her gown. Who knew that her aunt could be so kind, so generous? Lionel would never believe it. Hetty barely could. And yet she did.

She intended, moreover, to be more worthy of it. As she embraced her aunt, Hetty made a vow in her heart of hearts: no matter the temptation, she would not lie to nor deceive her Sidney relations again.

"I hope everyone will like us again after this," confided Caroline, taking Hetty's hand in the carriage as it rolled toward North Audley Street. "Though I cannot think why people grew cold in the first place."

"Perhaps—perhaps my refusal of Mr. Pickford had something to do with it," suggested Hetty. "I think he is generally well-liked."

But her aunt was too clever for that. "No, it began before he proposed. I can only surmise the Stanleys might have said something. They are influential, naturally."

Hetty grimaced a little, to have her own sins pinned on the Stanleys, but it was certainly true that the Stanleys had not been friends enough to counter any rumors flying about. No, that wasn't fair either. If they were willing to meet the Sidneys socially, that was worth something. *But they would not have met us if the Rotherwoods were not the hosts*, her cynical side insisted.

It was all too muddled. All Hetty knew was she had sent her note via Trilby to Lionel asking him to meet her at Booth's again the following day. Whether he liked it or not, she had a plan.

Just one more day, she promised herself. One more day, and she would make a clean breast of it all.

The Sidney carriage arrived in North Audley Street at the same time as the Stanleys' and had perforce to wait its turn. But then the footmen were letting down the steps and handing them out, and they were following the earl and family up to the door of Number 28.

Hetty could not but be conscious of a pathetic desire to please Mrs. Rotherwood. To prove that, though she was not a *Lady* Harriet, she was nevertheless an unexceptionable girl with whom many reasonable families would welcome a connection. She was conscious moreover that her growing affection for Mr. Rotherwood must be hidden at all costs, both from him and from his mother. The combination of these factors was sufficient to tie her in knots, with the result that she tripped on the topmost step and nearly tumbled into the entrance, knocking against her cousin, who then ran into Mrs. Sidney, who then stumbled forward and stepped on Mrs. Rotherwood's slippered foot.

"Heyday, Lord bless you," exclaimed Wellington Sidney, putting out an arm to brace his womenfolk.

Mrs. Rotherwood gave a tight smile and her son looked amused, but the proper greetings and salutes were given, and they passed into the drawing room where Sir Keane stood with his back to the crackling fire, beaming and bowing. Two other gentlemen were there whom Hetty didn't recognize, but the elderly one was introduced as Mr. Winston and the bald one as Lord Camberwell. Invited to make the numbers even, she supposed.

It was a beautiful room, she observed, hanging behind Caroline and trying to steal unobtrusive looks. Elegant Hepplewhite furniture complemented the burnt-umber painted walls and sand-colored window hangings. A gleaming pianoforte anchored one corner, and along the front wall tables had been set with fresh packs of cards and little boxes of mother-of-pearl fish.

"How we spend our evening will depend on you young ladies," Mr. Rotherwood addressed them, having to sweep his gaze from where Caroline and Hetty stood to where Lady Sylvia held herself gracefully aloof some yards distant. "After the meal, we can have music or cards or roll the carpet back for dancing."

"What if we each choose something different?" asked Caroline.

"Then we must do a little of each. We are at your service."

"Lady Sylvia must choose first, of course," Caroline said diffidently.

The earl's daughter drifted two steps closer to them. "Music."

"That's what I was going to choose!" declared Caroline, with a glow. She lowered her voice and added, "Because we only have enough people for four couples, if someone has to play the pianoforte, and that gentleman Mr. Winston—his age might not permit…"

A grin flitted across St. John's face, and he shifted for a better view of the lurking Miss Hapgood. "That's two for music, Miss Hapgood. What do you say? Will it be all music, or would you like to insist on a hand of cards or a quadrille for the more agile?"

Hetty would have loved to play whist with Mr. Rotherwood. She suspected he would be a good partner. But the odds of her being paired with him were slim, so she said, "Music, to be sure."

Now that the company was gathered, Mrs. Rotherwood nodded toward her son. He extended an arm to Lady Stanley, and they led the way to the dining room, followed by Mrs. Rotherwood and Lord Stanley. Lord Camberwell then bowed to Lady Sylvia, who barely touched his arm with two fingertips. Hetty had been working out the pairings in her head and repressed a sigh when she saw Sir Keane would take Aunt Lavinia and her uncle Wellington his daughter. That left her on the arm of the aged and hunched Mr. Winston, but he gave her such a friendly smile that she smiled back—if only she had worn her withered crone disguise! They might then have made quite an amiable couple.

However humbling her entrance to the dining room, Hetty found herself seated between her aunt and uncle and nearer to Mr. Rotherwood than either Caroline or Lady Sylvia. If not for Lady Stanley and Sir Keane across from her, she might have been altogether happy. As it was, Lady Stanley had many compliments for Mr. Rotherwood's carving and Sir Keane many compliments for the Rotherwoods' cellars. Mrs. Rotherwood seemed determined that conversation should be general, though it entailed those at her end to raise their voices slightly. Neither Hetty nor the Sidneys put themselves forward, but after a week of virtual isolation, they listened with pleasure even to the exhaustive discussion of the weather, the progress of the war with the Americans, and the news of a ship run aground in Cadiz. Moreover, the food was delicious, and when Hetty helped herself to another serving of the savory pudding, Mr. Rotherwood teased her with, "That is one of my favorites as well, Miss Hapgood. I had better move it farther from you if I hope to have more." Before she could reply, Lady Stanley on his right hand requested another slice of the roast, and the moment passed.

"How did you like Miss O'Neill in *The Gamester* last night?" Mrs. Rotherwood asked the company.

"Deeply affecting," Lady Stanley declared. "Her solicitude for Mr. Beverley brought me almost to tears."

"Indeed, but I found her less successful in expwessing scorn or howwor," said Sir Keane.

"Oh, decidedly," Lord Camberwell agreed, "but there she was crippled by Terry's performance. Too overdone for my taste."

"He has been better in other roles," agreed Lord Stanley.

"What do you think, Lady Sylvia?" Mrs. Rotherwood prompted.

Lady Sylvia set down her spoon. "Very engaging."

At first it appeared that was all that would be got from her, and a cloud settled over Mrs. Rotherwood's brow, but then the earl's daughter uttered one of her rare monologues: "Did you see it, Miss Sidney? Or have you not been much about in recent days?"

Hetty drew a sharp breath, and a little silence fell over the table. The Sidneys had not been at the Covent Garden Theatre for the performance, of course. They had not ventured out much at all since the Great Snubbing at the opera and the withdrawn dinner invitation. As if by common agreement, they remained in Devonshire Street, or the girls walked in Regent's Park, avoiding society as if they shared Lionel's aversion to gadding about with the swells. Hetty had caught murmured discussions between her aunt and uncle in her uncle's library and suspected they were debating whether they ought to leave town and return to Crawley, but after Mr. Rotherwood's visit and invitation, she assumed this plan was put aside. They must wait and see if matters improved.

Caroline was seated too far away for Hetty to press her foot under the table, but she was proud of her cousin's response to this aggression. "We haven't seen the play," she answered, her chin lifted. "We have been keeping rather quiet this week."

"Fancy that!" Lady Stanley marveled. "Why, I envy you your repose. Sometimes the London season makes one feel like a shuttlecock batted from invitation to invitation and entertainment to entertainment."

Peeking at Mr. Rotherwood, Hetty saw he was at his most lofty, his narrowed eyes sweeping from the offending Stanleys to his mother. Flustered, Mrs. Rotherwood signaled for the course to be removed, oblivious to poor Mr. Winston trying to catch the footman's eye, that he might try the fish at the other end of the table.

"You know, of course, that I am wholly unused to the battledore-and-shuttlecock nature of London social obligations" began Mr. Rotherwood, with a nod at Lady Stanley, "—and a very apt analogy you chose, madam. Therefore I confess I have often missed the solitude and relative quiet I enjoyed at Oxford, when I did not 'feel the weight of too much liberty.'"

The footmen swept in with the fruit tarts and nuts and custards of the second course and laid them out in silent efficiency. When they were gone again, he went on. "Not every person has the disposition and qualities to be content in seclusion. If you do, Lady Stanley, you and I must be kindred spirits."

The countess hardly knew what to make of this. Was the man mocking her, or was he sincere?

"Well, I don't like solitude and quiet one bit," spoke up Caroline frankly. "I get bored. If it weren't for my cousin's company, I don't know what I should do."

"I wejoice that you pwefer company," Sir Keane beamed at her. "Lest we be depwived."

Hetty could not refrain from a faint grimace. Sir Keane had certainly tolerated being 'depwived' of their company the previous week, for he had not called once.

"And you, Miss Hapgood?" Mr. Rotherwood asked. "What do you prefer?"

"That poem you referred to," Hetty responded, not directly answering his question, "does it not begin with saying how happy certain people are in their narrow circumstances? Nuns and hermits and such? I think therein lies the answer: if your seclusion is chosen, you can easily be content. But if it be forced upon you—just as I suppose having the world 'too much with you' can be forced upon you—why, then it is very hard to be happy."

"Hmm," murmured Lady Stanley. "But surely your family's retirement this past sennight was chosen, was it not?"

This had gone far enough, in Lavinia Sidney's opinion, and she resented Lady Stanley probing the matter. "We were not entirely well, Lady Stanley. Therefore, while not being chosen, per se, our seclusion was necessary and not altogether unpleasant. Mrs. Rotherwood, pray, what do you call this particular custard? It is so light and creamy."

When the time came to leave the gentlemen to their port, Anne Rotherwood led her female guests back to the drawing room, her heart rather depressed. It was clear that her plans for St. John to marry the glorious Lady Sylvia were failing. Lady Sylvia had no more life to her than a bowl of porridge, and Lady Stanley's barbs at the table only made St. John angry. (It hardly mattered that Anne herself sympathized with Lady Stanley's views—the Sidneys and Miss Hapgood should not be restored to society's good graces without first being made aware that it came at a cost.)

Even as she gestured at seats for the ladies, placing the Stanleys closest to the fire, Anne was running through other possible candidates. Who had Mr. Pinckney said was still considered in contention? She had been so set on Lady Sylvia that she hardly listened. With a mother's heart she suspected St. John liked this dreadful Miss Hapgood with the bad reputation, and it only added to her sunken spirits. Even the pretty, vapid Miss Sidney would be better than Miss Hapgood, Anne thought. Pretty, vapid girls did not get into trouble like less-pretty, overly-clever girls.

And pretty, vapid Miss Sidney hadn't the pride of the other one. Only look at how Miss Sidney approached Lady Sylvia, asking, "Would you like to look over the music first?"

The gentlemen were not long in joining them, St. John having no particular attachment to any of them and guessing the ladies would not be enjoying themselves. He found Lady Sylvia at the instrument, Miss Sidney obligingly turning the pages for her, while Lady Stanley sat beside the fire. Mrs. Sidney was reading a book that had been lying on a table, and Miss Hapgood was at a card table where she had laid out the little mother-of-pearl fish counters in rows.

His mother looked up from her embroidery when they entered. "Ah, darling. I confess we began our musical evening without you, only because Lady Sylvia has been practicing. Shall we all gather?

Gentlemen, please be seated. We will hear the young ladies and then have some tea."

Hetty thought she would sit beside her aunt, but Caroline took one side and her uncle the other. Then she thought she might take a chair and place it beside their sofa, but that was precisely what Sir Keane did. Nor did Hetty want to move her chair to the far side of the sofa, because that would put her right beside Mrs. Rotherwood! In the end, she merely turned her seat away from the card table and remained where she was. Mr. Rotherwood, she noticed, remained standing, leaning in the doorway.

Lady Sylvia began again to play the piece she had been practicing, and Hetty felt some satisfaction to note that her performance was correct but undistinguished. It would have been too tiresome all around if, in addition to being beautiful and rich and titled, Lady Sylvia were also a virtuosa. When she concluded there was loud applause, and bald Lord Camberwell drew near the pianoforte crying, "Brava! Brava! Please, Lady Sylvia, indulge us with another. And would it be too much to ask that we might have the pleasure of hearing your voice?"

Hetty almost giggled at Lady Sylvia's expression, for heaven knew her voice was one thing the earl's daughter usually kept to herself. But it turned out to be only a ploy on Camberwell's part, for it became clear he was eager to sing himself and wanted only some polite urging to hold forth in a booming bass.

By this point Hetty had edged her chair halfway back toward the card table and was unobtrusively rearranging the fish, even as Mr.

Rotherwood made his way across the room. He pulled out the chair on her right and set it next to hers.

Hetty's fingers trembled, and she tried to replace the counters in their dish. Oh! He mustn't sit with her—not when every eye in the room took note! Not when she had promised her aunt that she would guard her heart. And yet every fiber of her thrilled in response.

Bending to retrieve a fish that had fallen to the carpet he murmured, "I apologize for Lady Stanley's...hostility. I do not know if the evening has served the purpose I intended."

She folded her hands in her lap and regarded them. "I know you meant to help us. It's my fault, is it not, that people avoid us? They have—heard—about my escapade."

"I fear so. And I suspect Pickford lies behind it."

She nodded once. "I am sure you are right. Mr. Rotherwood—I have not made my full confession to my family yet, but I intend to. As soon as I can speak to Lionel."

Lord Camberwell reached a stirring passage in his solo and thumped his chest, eyes cast to the ceiling. Lady Sylvia, however, continued to play with no variation in volume or intensity.

"I thought you did not want Lionel to know of Pickford's doings," Mr. Rotherwood resumed.

"I don't. But I do want him to show himself to my Sidney relations. They—have not been pleased with him, which is one reason he has been secretive about being in town—I can't say more than that, but I think they would forgive him now." Hetty began to fan herself, both because her confession made her warm and also to muffle the sound of her whisper. "And if Lionel will only let them know he is here, then I will be free to admit I deceived them and went to the Argyll Rooms. Which I know was wrong, and doubly so because my aunt said it was not a proper place to be—but I can also deserve a little less opprobrium because I did not go there alone, you see?"

He made a sound of agreement, tapping his fingertips on his knee. "But will not the Sidneys be even less pleased with your brother, when they learn he not only hid his presence from them, but also encouraged you to go—and I suspect he did encourage you—to the masquerade in the first place?"

It was a weakness in her plan, and her face fell a little. "I know. I do. But I hope I can persuade him—if I beg him and tell him how our actions are hurting our Sidney relations, who are perfectly innocent in the matter."

"And what of Pickford...?"

Then she glanced at him. It was the pleading look again. "I will not tell my brother that part. I *cannot*. And I ask you again, Mr. Rotherwood, to keep my secret. The worst is over. You have helped us recover socially tonight—I am sure of it. Therefore Lionel need never know what Mr. Pickford did. No one need ever know."

Mr. Rotherwood was silent and grim, and her heart misgave her that she could not convince him.

Meanwhile, Lord Camberwell caterwauled up to a tenor note for the finale, and Lady Stanley made haste to begin applauding, wanting to rescue her daughter from further accompanist duties.

Rising to resume his role as host, for the barest instant Mr. Rotherwood rested his hand on the back of Hetty's chair. Then came the words to relieve her:

"You have my word."

Chapter Twenty-One

Again her name appeared in the newspaper—again her face was at every print-shop.
— Harriet Lee, *Canterbury tales; or, the year 1797* (1797)

Yes, they were definitely looking at her.

Hetty shut the book she was holding with precision and replaced it on the counter at Booth's, her face burning, as one of the gentlemen muttered something in the ear of the other and they doubled over laughing, the first gripping the second by the shoulder.

"Would you like this one, miss?" asked the clerk, his mouth smirking.

"No, thank you."

She was being silly, she told herself. Overfearful. Even if a few people were taking note of her or whispering about her, word would soon get about that the vaunted Rotherwoods accepted her socially, and that would be that. Nevertheless, she decided, she would wait for Lionel by the entrance.

Gathering her dignity, she straightened and prepared to march, head high, only to find Lionel himself blocking her path, face red and eyes blazing.

"Good heavens," she gasped. "Whatever is the matter?"

"Come with me." He took hold of her elbow none too gently, and steered her through the various shelves and displays of the circulating library into the less crowded corner they had visited before. There Lionel put his back to the window, whipped something from his pocket and spread it on the table beside them. "Look."

Hetty looked.

And felt all the blood drain from her body.

It was a lampoon. A rather beautiful watercolor print entitled "Desire Unmasked." The scene was clearly the masquerade ball at the Argyll Rooms because there were the arcaded alcoves, the pointed arches. And there, tangled in a mingled, writhing mass, were the dancing masqueraders. The Napoleons. Anne Boleyn. The dripping Ophelia—hardly clad at all in this depiction. Ladies of the night. Rogues in slipping dominoes, their arms clasped around their partners and hands reaching.

But the worst part was the couple in the foreground. Leering through his black mask, a man was pinioned by an eager and decidedly redheaded young lady, whose grey wig was dangling by a single pin, and whose brown dress hardly deserved the name of clothing. She pressed swollen lips to the man's face, even as a balloon above him declared, "Miss H________, will you not wear even the *disguise* of modesty?" Beneath this shameful illustration the caption read, "No Good Happens when Somerset sirens shirk chaperonage and disdain Devonshire Street devoirs."

Hetty swayed on her feet.

"Who is responsible for this?" demanded her brother *sotto voce*. "I was at Fores' Gallery in Piccadilly where everyone was gathered around, snickering, and I managed to lay hold of this last copy, while they were rushing to print more. Explain this to me!"

"Lionel"—she took hold of the capes of his greatcoat—"you must come back with me to the Sidneys' and tell them you are in town. Please. You see how it has got about that I was there that night. But no one knows that you were there with me—that I was not wholly alone and unchaperoned. I knew there were rumors, but I did not know—I did not know it would reach this point. You *must* come tell the Sidneys! Please!"

He said nothing, only taking her arm. His felt like iron. He led her from Booth's, his expression belligerent and challenging to anyone whose eye met his own.

Trilby startled, to see her mistress emerge pale and shaking from the library, accompanied by a stranger. But when Lionel said, "I am Miss Hapgood's brother. Give us a little space," she nodded, wide-eyed, and trailed them without remark some yards behind.

He said nothing until they reached the corner of Portland and Devonshire Streets. Then: "I will of course tell my aunt and uncle Sidney of my presence, both here in town for the past fortnight and at the masquerade. I will also tell them I urged you to attend. That I insisted upon it."

"No. No, I insisted," Hetty protested feebly, a tear tracing its way down her cheek. "You invited me, Lionel, but I was the one who chose to go, even after Aunt Lavinia said it wouldn't be a proper place for young ladies. And I was the one who lied and sneaked. I won't let you claim my share."

She wasn't even certain he heard her. He was scowling and growling, "But who dared to expose you? It wasn't Rotherwood. It couldn't be. He wouldn't. So who was it? Do you know, Het?"

There was murder in his eye, and Hetty wouldn't have told him if her life depended on it, much less her reputation. She shook her head, and the lie came easily. "I can't imagine. I suppose it would have been easy enough to recognize me—my hair, you know. And my wig did come loose when we were dancing. And maybe someone overheard me talking with you or the Clinketts or Bailey."

"But why would—anyone—slander you like this? You are pictured *pawing* this person—you are singled out and—and named! Why would they do it? Why would they dare to say you were throwing yourself at someone—kissing someone?"

Hetty gulped, shaking her head. She refused to give way to sobs. Not out of doors, in the streets of London, where every person would add to their budget of gossip that they saw the disgraced Miss Hapgood weeping. But it was a battle.

A battle she almost lost when they passed Portland Place and Number 68 loomed ahead. Someone was leaning against the railing. Someone who straightened when he caught sight of them.

"Rotherwood?" muttered Lionel.

He was with them in a few strides, his eyes boring into her. "Are you all right, Miss Hapgood?"

She couldn't speak. She knew if she did she would cry, but she tried to nod.

He turned to Lionel. "You have seen it." It wasn't a question. When her brother gave a jerk of his head, Rotherwood said, "Let us discuss this within."

"Oh, Mr. Rotherwood, you've returned," Lavinia Sidney said, rising. She and Caroline must have been in deep discussion because Caroline blushed and folded something up quickly, stowing it in her pocket.

Their preoccupation prevented them at first from seeing Lionel and Hetty, but when Caroline looked up she gasped and colored even more deeply. "Why, Lionel!"

"Greetings, Aunt Lavinia, Cousin Caroline."

There was an awkward pause where no one knew quite what to address first, but then Lavinia glided over to her nephew and gave him a brief salute on his cheek. "Welcome, my dear boy. We did not know to expect you."

"Indeed. I gave you no warning." Lionel's color was high, and Hetty knew he was screwing up his courage. He glanced once at Rotherwood, who had gone expressionless and merely raised one eyebrow.

"Madam, there is much to tell you, but first I must make a confession."

"A confession!" Lavinia fluttered. "Yes, well, perhaps after Mr. Rotherwood has gone…?"

"Mr. Rotherwood already knows everything," choked Hetty. "Because—because—well—you will understand why, shortly."

What this could all mean was beyond the Sidneys, and Lavinia helplessly submitted to Mr. Rotherwood's presence. "If you say so. Er—please do be seated, Mr. Rotherwood. I am sure this cannot be made clear too soon."

Lionel reached for Hetty's hand and guided her to a seat. "Aunt, my confession is that I have been in town this fortnight. Yes. But…knowing that you were not pleased with me after the events of the summer, I thought it fit that I…not burden you with my presence during my visit."

Caroline's eyes were enormous, and Lavinia colored, perhaps in recognition that Lionel was not mistaken in his assumptions. She folded her hands together carefully. "Did Harriet know you were here?"

"I did," Hetty whispered. "Madam, I—"

"I asked her to keep it to herself, Aunt Lavinia," her brother interrupted. "It was not by her own choice. Therefore you must not blame her for it. But that is not all of my confession. There is more. You see, I lured her to meet me—"

"Oh, Lionel, not *lured*," Hetty objected.

"—One afternoon, and when she did come, I told her my friends and I—for they are in town as well—planned on attending a masquerade ball at the Argyll Rooms, and would she keep us company?"

His aunt sucked in a sharp breath. "Harriet—you didn't! After I told you—"

"Madam, I—I did. It was very wrong of me. It was the night I said I was too ill to go to the musical concert."

"You weren't unwell, then?" cried Caroline. "It was a very nice concert, though I would have preferred a ball myself."

"I was not. I pretended. And then I sneaked out."

Aunt Lavinia began flapping her handkerchief before her face as she sank onto the sofa. "Oh! Oh, child. And this is why? This is why. This is why we have been whispered about and ostracized?"

Hetty pushed Lionel to the side and threw herself to her knees. "Yes, it is, aunt. Everything is entirely my fault. I own it. And how badly I feel now! How badly I *have* felt when I saw the consequences. When I saw people drawing back and being cold to us. To you. I wanted to tell you everything then, but I could not without first speaking to Lionel."

Caroline looked from her mother to her cousin. "But I don't understand. Do you mean to say we stopped being invited to things because somebody found out Hetty was at the masquerade ball, and they disapproved, just as you did, Mama?"

"That is exactly what I mean," sighed Lavinia. "As I told you girls, it would have been inadvisable for you to be there even under my wing, but for Hetty to go—only in the company of some young men—" The handkerchief began flapping even more rapidly. "One almost hopes whoever recognized you there understood you were with your brother."

"It gets worse," Hetty squeaked. She pressed her heated face against the folds of her aunt's frock.

"What can you mean, child? Worse? It was very bad. Very wrong. And there were indeed consequences. We have Mr. Rotherwood's kindness to us that the damages may be contained— may be limited—in future. I will have to explain that you are young and heedless and have promised me you will never do such a thing again. Oh, Harriet, did you not think of your cousin's reputation, when you risked your own?"

"I did not." She was scarcely audible. How could she tell her aunt about the lampoon now? How could she tell her that it was even more dire than she supposed? And yet, if she did not make a clean breast of the entire matter, the Sidneys would learn of it the moment they stepped out of doors.

Lionel must have made the same calculation, for he stepped forward again. With a sigh, he lay the scandalous print beside Lavinia. "Aunt."

Then there was a to-do! Lavinia took one look at the scurrilous satire and shrieked, bringing Caroline flying across the room to peer over her shoulder. "Oh! Oh! What does it mean?" Caroline gasped as her mother fainted, and Hetty scrambled up to fetch her aunt's smelling salts.

"Mama never faints! Oh! Oh! What can it all mean?" Ignored by her cousins as they tended to her mother, Caroline plucked up the print in desperation and held it out to Mr. Rotherwood. "I don't understand   why is Mama so upset by this picture? Is it because it's the Argyll Rooms?"

Taking pity on the girl, St. John said gently, "Yes, it's the Argyll Rooms. But Mrs. Sidney is distressed because the figure in the foreground is meant to be Miss Hapgood."

"Her?" Caroline pointed in incredulity. "Because of the hair? Otherwise it doesn't look a thing like, and I don't see why anyone would assume it was Hetty. There is the 'Miss H__________,' I suppose, but there must be any number of young ladies whose surnames begin with H."

"It's the caption," explained Lionel, with some impatience, as he attempted to heave his aunt to a sitting position.

"You mean the Somerset part?"

"That, and the 'No Good Happens,'" said St. John. "No Good Happens. Good Happens. Hap-good."

"Oh-h-h-h-h-h," breathed Caroline, comprehension dawning. "Oh-h-h...it does mean Hetty."

"Yes."

"Oh, my."

"Indeed."

Caroline studied the picture anew, so forgetting herself that her little mouth hung open. "But Hetty—why should someone draw you kissing someone? You surely didn't kiss anyone, did you?"

"Of course she didn't," snapped Lavinia, her eyes still shut. She put the back of her hand to her forehead and gave a little groan. "It's these wretched satirists. What do they care for a young lady's reputation? As if it were not bad enough that she was there in the first place. No, they portray her as indecently dressed and throwing herself at some man, that they might sell more copies."

But Caroline had been watching her cousin, and her amazement grew when she saw Hetty go so red she might as well have been a hothouse tomato. "Hetty—*did* you?"

"Of course she didn't!" Lionel echoed his aunt. "Whyever would she? This is the figment of some blackguard's imagination, from having seen her dance with me or the Clinketts or Bailey, for she was never with anyone else!"

Hetty swallowed repeatedly. She had no intention of bringing up Mr. Pickford or his insults, but she could not control the blood rushing beneath her skin, and some infernal lump had risen in her throat that could not be choked down. She wondered if she was going to faint or—worse—vomit. *Lie!* she screeched inwardly. *Just tell the stupid lie. No one will know it's a lie but Mr. Rotherwood, and he will not expose you.*

"I—I—" Furtively she held her aunt's smelling salts nearer her own nose, but that only made her wince and gag.

"Of course she did not kiss anyone," blurted Mr. Rotherwood, coming to stand beside her. "But someone kissed her."

Hetty inhaled so sharply she coughed, and she would have flown to cover his mouth with both her hands, if she thought her legs would support her. What was he thinking? He would get Lionel killed!

"No one—that is—nobody—" she sputtered.

He met her gaze for one long moment, trying to communicate with her wordlessly. Then he turned to Mrs. Sidney. "She did not kiss anyone, but someone kissed her," he repeated.

"How would you know, Mr. Rotherwood?" asked Caroline wonderingly.

"Because I was the one who kissed her."

Gasps and squeaks and "What the deuce?" greeted this utterance. Hetty dropped the bottle of smelling salts altogether.

"I intended to offer for her," he went on, as if this were all quite usual, "and perhaps anticipated myself, for I took a liberty, and someone must have seen." His gaze flicked back to the dumbfounded Hetty. "I was unable to propose that evening because Lionel and his friends soon joined us, and I have not had the opportunity since, but it is still my purpose."

If he had announced that he was Napoleon escaped from Elba, he could hardly have astonished them more. Not a person present besides himself seemed capable of stringing words together. Therefore St. John found himself going on.

"Miss Hapgood, I hope you will forgive me for introducing the subject in this unconventional manner, just as I hope you have forgiven me for my actions in the Argyll Rooms, but you see that my intentions have been, and continue to be, entirely honorable. I only wait to speak with your uncle when he is home. Or perhaps to write to your father, if you think that would be better."

Everything else was forgotten.

Lionel's and Hetty's egregious behavior. The family's subsequent shunning. Very nearly the lampoon itself and the storm it would provoke. All eclipsed in the wonder of Mr. Rotherwood offering for Hetty. Or signaling his intention to offer.

Lionel was the first to break the ice, lunging at him to clasp him by the hand and shoulder and shake both vigorously. "Rotherwood! Never say! Hetty? You're certain? Well, it's your neck."

And then the Sidneys collected themselves enough to offer bewildered congratulations, Lavinia murmuring, "What is Mrs. Rotherwood's opinion?"

"I have not yet discussed it with her, madam, but I trust she will be delighted."

His trust did not appear to be shared by anyone else present, but of course that could not be expressed.

"Won't the Stanleys be surprised!" was Caroline's ingenuous comment, which also could not be taken up.

Lavinia's mind began to operate at its customary speed once more. "There must be a dinner. An engagement dinner. A very large one. Both to celebrate and to—to—"

"To quash the gossip," supplied Lionel, grinning. "An engagement will turn ignominy into triumph. You may even want to reprint the lampoon on your invitation cards."

The only person with nothing to say was the young lady applied to.

It was all very well, Hetty thought, to make jokes and felicitate each other. No one seemed to assume she had any say in the matter, or that, if she did, she would ever refuse the man. She had disgraced herself catastrophically, only to have rescue and elation appear in the form of Mr. Rotherwood. She would be a fool to gainsay it, of course. Especially since she loved him.

And yet.

Chapter Twenty-Two

If you were upon your trial for life or death...you could not look more resolutely guarded.
— Maria Edgeworth, *Moral Tales for Young People* (1801)

Upon Wellington Sidney's return home to Devonshire Street, he was dispatched instantly by his wife to his library, that Mr. Rotherwood might be sent after him.

Lionel had gone, with an assurance that both he and his friends would be seen at the engagement dinner and quite often besides, an injunction received with good grace when he considered how easily he had got off on the whole.

Left alone with her aunt and cousin, the drained Hetty could only say once more, "Aunt Lavinia, I do apologize most sincerely..."

"Harriet, were it not for the almost miraculous way we have been saved, this would be a very different conversation," replied Lavinia, restored enough to have taken up her sewing.

"I, for one, am hurt," Caroline pouted. "That you neither invited nor confided in me."

Her mother rounded on her in amazement. "After all you have heard and seen? Sweeting, your presence would have compounded the injury to our family, and if Harriet confided in you, it would have put you in the awkward position of either betraying that confidence or condoning something very, very wrong."

"All the same," her daughter sighed, "I do hate being left out. And though you don't deserve it, Hetty, I will not respond in kind. I will share my confidence with you. You see, it happens that Mr. Elwood was not among all those who deserted our family in time of need." She plucked the note from her pocket and waved it. "He has been out of town tending to business matters in Surrey and writes to Mama to ask if he may see us as soon as ever he returns."

"I am glad to hear it," Hetty replied, sincere. "I did not like to think he was unworthy of our newfound fondness for him."

Lavinia shook her head. "I do not know if his absence qualifies as bravery, but we will see soon enough. In the meantime, let us return to the matter at hand. Harriet, I admit I had no idea Mr. Rotherwood nurtured such feelings for you—that he would—why—" She trailed off, making a clicking sound with her tongue, and then a most un-Aunt-Lavinia-like smile spread over her face. "What I wouldn't give to be present when Mr. Rotherwood tells his mother the news!"

"She won't like it," said Hetty.

"Of course she won't like it," agreed her aunt. "But what is that to us?"

"Aunt—what if, instead of marrying Mr. Rotherwood, I were just to go home to Somerset?"

"Whatever for?" asked Caroline, bouncing over to sit beside her. (Apparently her cousin had completely forgiven her.) "You wouldn't leave me, would you?"

Her niece's suggestion banished Lavinia Sidney's smile. "You would not be so foolish, Harriet, as to refuse Mr. Rotherwood."

Hetty said nothing, but at the set of her mouth, her aunt took genuine alarm. "You must not. You may not. Unless you positively despise the man, Harriet, you must accept him. Here he is, in his kindness, saving you from the momentous consequences of your actions! *Saving* you. Do you not understand?"

"I understand," Hetty allowed.

"Do you not like the man, then?"

"Of course I like him," said Hetty desperately, "and I do appreciate his kindness. But must this be the result? Could I not disappear until everything blew over?"

"An engagement to the man is the only wind strong enough to blow this scandal away," Lavinia said with decision.

"But aunt—"

But so quick was Mr. Rotherwood's interview with her uncle that the ladies all heard the door opening in the passage and two pairs of footsteps returning.

Wellington appeared in the drawing room doorway, a bemused look on his face. "My dear Lavinia, Caroline, it seems we must withdraw again. This time, I hope, to better purpose." He gave a wink to his niece as his womenfolk hurried to join him, each throwing Hetty a last glance, her cousin's excited and her aunt's *meaningful*.

And then she was alone with Mr. Rotherwood.

Hetty repressed a sigh. Ah—he was so kind and clever and handsome and good—if he had come to her under other circumstances—under almost *any* other circumstances, she would be overwhelmed with joy. She would fly to him and let her whole heart shine through her eyes and speak through her words. But this—this was unbearable.

He seemed no more at ease than she was, and she thought she was beginning to recognize the way his hand ran through his curling, gold-shot hair and his finger dug under his neckcloth. He paced the room as if he were measuring it, from the doorway to the opposite wall, past the windows, to the fireplace, and then once more in the circuit; finally, he returned to the near window to stare into Devonshire Street.

And then he looked at her.

"Miss Hapgood, I realize that, in the urgency of the crisis, I took matters into my own hands today without consulting you. You have been silent in return. I ask you now to interpret that silence. My own feelings supply reasons for it that make me almost frantic."

Frantic? Why should he be frantic? Was it because he had driven himself into a corner, or rather both of them into a corner? She hardly knew what response to make, but one must be made.

"Mr. Rotherwood, I am in a state of such puzzlement, I don't know what to say or where to begin. Except perhaps to tell you that you have done a very rash thing. Something I think you will soon regret."

"No." His shoulders squared, as did his jaw. She recognized this as well: his marble look.

For lack of anything better to hold, lest he notice her trembling, she picked up her aunt's sewing and nervously rolled it into a ball. "I know you are a kind man. You were kind already, when you invited us to dinner and tried to repair matters with the Stanleys, and by extension with all of London society. Therefore, I cannot say I am entirely surprised that you would go one step further and engage yourself to me, the case having become that much more desperate. But there are limits to what can be asked of a friend, Mr. Rotherwood, and you have passed that limit."

During her speech he had returned his gaze to the street, running one finger along the uneven surface of a mullioned pane. "Miss Hapgood. I concede that restoring your family to the good graces of society was one motivation in asking you all to dinner. Not that I particularly care whom society smiles or frowns upon—"

"That is easily said," she interrupted, "when one inhabits the very pinnacle. When it is one's own smiles and frowns which matter most and from whom others take their cue. Which is not to say I am ungrateful," she added with an apologetic face. "On the contrary. I mean only to say it is those least in need of society's approval who can regard it with indifference."

"True. Perhaps, then, my indifference cheapens what I hoped to accomplish."

But at that Hetty almost *wailed*, and she flung aside her aunt's needlework, to join him at the window. "Only see what a wicked creature I am! I try to say you are too kind, and I end in saying you are not kind at all. Please forgive me, Mr. Rotherwood. Again."

There were her pleading blue eyes once more, and there once more was his sudden desire to take hold of her and comfort her. Feeling his chest tighten, St. John retreated a step. He meant to regain mastery of himself, but she read disapproval in the movement.

"Yes—you see how it is," she said. "This is what I am trying to express, in my fitful, clumsy way. I am afraid one can go too far in being kind. When I make mistakes—when I get myself into scrapes, sir—it is not your responsibility to rescue me. You have done enough. You should not be allowed to do more. You will not be allowed."

"Are you saying you will not marry me? I know I failed to ask you first. That is what I am trying to mend now."

"I am saying you should not even be allowed to ask me. I forbid it."

Ruefully, one corner of his mouth lifted. "But even that villain Pickford was allowed to ask."

"Only because I could not stop him and because he was not gentleman enough to refrain when I told him to," she insisted. "But you are—gentleman enough, I mean."

The day was cold outside. He could feel it through the panes of glass. "Then, Miss Hapgood, I am sorry to disappoint you. Because I fear, like Pickford, I mean to urge my point."

She was afraid of this. Both afraid and...admiring. She might rail and snip at the odious Mr. Pickford, but she did not dare do so to Mr. Rotherwood.

"The unfortunate situation in which you find yourself," he began, "might have had the effect of...speeding matters along, but I assure you, Miss Hapgood, the idea of offering for you did not spring into my head fully formed because I saw the lampoon at Fores'. No, indeed. I have been thinking for some time that we are good companions, are we not? We find it easy to speak to each other, to be in each other's company."

Her face was lowered. She did not want him to read there that she agreed with him—oh, so wholeheartedly!

Whatever his declaration, St. John was not finding it particularly easy to speak to her or to be in her company at the moment, but that was because he had never spoken words of love to any young woman in all his life. Indeed, in all his life he had spoken few enough words on *any* subject to any young woman. He had imagined talking to young ladies would be trying, difficult, and so it had in fact proven—apart from when he talked with Miss Hapgood. But even to this young woman the words of love would not come. He did not fear she would mock him or repeat what he said to her intimates later, for humorous effect (in which he was mistaken, for, had Hetty not been in love with him, she very well might have). Rather he feared his awkwardness and inexperience would leave her unmoved, apart from pity. Pity and its appurtenant embarrassment.

Therefore he sought sanctuary in reason and logic.

He cleared his throat. "Consider this, Miss Hapgood. You have indeed got yourself in a wretched scrape from which I flatter myself that I can deliver you. Not only you, but your Sidney relations as well, who, as you witnessed, were also held accountable for your...mischief. I like you. I like your family. You seem familiar to me, in a time when much is unfamiliar and therefore uncomfortable to a creature of habit like myself. Can we not help each other? I have a good name and—heaven knows—a good fortune to offer you, and you are just the sort of young lady I think will suit me."

In this approach, luck was against him. Where tender confessions might have succeeded in persuading Hetty that he did not offer himself from gallantry alone, this businesslike manner only made firm her resolutions. If he could be cool and reasonable, as if she were a knotty mathematics problem to solve, so could she.

"Sir, I understand your motivations," she said softly, "and I do see the sense in your arguments. My respect for your kindness and generosity only increases, but I fear accepting your offer is impossible."

He paled, feeling the dreaded pity and embarrassment threaten, and grew more stiff and solemn than ever. But she saw at once how she had offended him. And hating it, she could not forbear trying to make things better. She laid a light hand on his sleeve and almost twinkled at him. "I feel I had an unfair advantage over all the other young ladies, sir, just because we met in Oxford and because you were my brother's tutor. Small wonder that I should be more comfortable to address."

He wanted to say that that was not all that made her comfortable, but she went on before he got his words in order. "I will always count you my friend, Mr. Rotherwood, and would be honored if you would do the same for me. But I would be no friend to you if I let you surrender the rest of your life in a moment of chivalry!"

"It would not be a surrender," he succeeded in saying. "Miss Hapgood, indeed, I like you very well. We might come to feel affection for each other. I am certain I would, in any case."

Lukewarm words never won fair lady, however. Hetty had her pride, after all. It was bad enough he felt he must cover her social infirmities with the spotless cape of his wealth and eligibility—but he thought he might come to "feel affection" for her, given enough time? As if she were a puppy or a naughty child, whom one came to love as much for the trouble they caused as for themselves?

But that was not the only obstacle.

Hardly less repugnant was the idea of being presented to Mrs. Rotherwood as her exalted son's intended. Even before any scandal attached to Hetty, the woman had disliked her enough to warn her off. What her response would be now, after Hetty's name had been dragged through the mud, did not bear thinking of. That Hetty would be deemed unworthy was a given—she had been that already. But now she would likely be considered the worst possible choice he could have made!

She will think me deceitful. Unscrupulous. Wanton. She will think I took advantage of past acquaintance to play upon his noble nature.

All these unpleasant reflections raced through Hetty's mind and spurred her answer. "Mr. Rotherwood. While you may believe you could eventually learn to care for me, I do not share your certainty," she said with a frostiness she would later marvel at. "I believe, rather, that a bad beginning will lead only to a bad middle and a worse end. I would rather keep your friendship and strive to deserve your respect. To accept your offer would accomplish neither."

St. John was silent, his countenance unreadable. In truth, he was cursing himself. Cursing himself for a wooden, blundering block. However, as cursing oneself seldom results in instantaneous improvement, he felt at an impasse.

He knew in some part of his mind that he could have asked any other woman in London to marry him and received a different answer than Miss Hapgood gave, yet he did not fault her for refusing. Miss Hapgood was not, in fact, any other woman in London. She was wholly herself, and he rather respected her the more for not holding herself cheaply, in spite of everything.

But it was equally apparent to him that her refusal of him would be disastrous, and he thought that, if he could not convince her with clumsy attempts at wooing, reason might serve.

"Miss Hapgood, if you would hear me out—I understand you feel you might never care for me—"

Hetty almost writhed, to hear her lie repeated back to her, but she managed to clamp her lips together.

"—And I would certainly not want to force you to give your hand where you cannot love, but before you reject my proposal altogether, I beg you to consider several factors."

He waited for her to respond, and, after another moment, she gave a short nod.

"Firstly, it would be possible for us to become engaged without proceeding any further. I mean to say, you might—we might—receive all the benefits of the engagement without having ultimately to marry. There is no need to set a date. You are young—that is excuse enough for a long engagement. But if we did indeed become engaged, it would do much to remedy matters, as you know. You are right in saying you could return to Somerset until scandal-mongers had new scandal to 'mong,' but that would still leave your Sidney relations in a difficult place and possibly compromise Miss Sidney's marriage prospects."

Stricken, Hetty looked up at him. He was right about Caroline's prospects. She thought of Mr. Elwood's reappearance. Would the man disappear for good, if an immoveable cloud of opprobrium settled over the Sidneys? And if he did slink away, would anyone dare take his place? Was Hetty's own plan to remove herself to Somerset not an act of penitence but one of cowardice? She meant to help Caroline to a new husband, but her flight might only ensure Caroline would never get any husband at all.

Yes—if she left the Sidneys to bear the brunt of her misdeeds, it could not be otherwise.

"I—I—what you say makes some sense, Mr. Rotherwood," Hetty rejoined faintly.

He gave her the shadow of a smile. "You might always jilt me later, Miss Hapgood, when the situation has improved."

"Yes," she breathed. "What a sorry return that would be for your kindness."

A gleam of genuine humor lit his eye. "Or you could marry me after all, if you thought you could stomach it."

"But...supposing—supposing you should want to marry someone else, while you were engaged to me?"

"You would be the first to know. I promise. And should *you* want to marry someone else, well then jilt away! It would be no more than we planned for."

For the first time that day, Hetty smiled, but it was a watery one. And she came close to telling him the truth when she said, "Oh, Mr. Rotherwood, if I cannot bring myself to feel affection for a man so kind and generous as you, I suspect I shan't be likely to for any other gentleman I meet this season."

He was relying upon it.

"Come, Miss Hapgood," he urged her. "This will be an adventure. A benevolent trick we play on a credulous public for their own betterment. I like you to call me kind and generous, but I think this may yet be the best use I have found for my newfound fame and fortune. Perhaps after you have jilted me, I will make it my business to rescue other maidens who jeopardize their good names. I will engage myself to one after another, until all London has not a soul to gossip about."

Then Hetty did laugh. "There is only one flaw in your plan, sir: I don't suppose the next young lady will be so cooperative as to jilt you, so you had better like her well enough to see it through."

"Sound advice," he agreed. "I fear everyone may not be as likeable as you, Miss Hapgood, but I will bear it in mind. In the meantime, shall we call your family back and confirm the news? And hadn't I better write to your father?"

Her father!

Forgetting all about the pleasure that flooded her when he called her likeable, she laid a panicked hand on his sleeve. "I did not think of that! Oh—Mr. Rotherwood, would it be all right if I wrote to him instead and told him the truth? That we are engaged, but not really engaged, I mean. I dare not tell the Sidneys it isn't real because I think Aunt Lavinia would wear me down and Caroline would not be able to keep the secret, but my father I could tell. *Please.*"

It was probably just as well she hadn't consented to marry him, St. John thought, because he was discovering he could refuse her nothing when she asked in such a way. Especially with her hand upon him, which he was careful not to look at or even affect to notice.

This particular request of hers was not easy to yield to, however.

Because St. John hated for Mr. Hapgood to think he offered for his daughter only as a ruse, a painless ploy. Would she tell her father that his initial offer had been genuine? Probably not. Unlike himself, Miss Hapgood was not eagerly plotting what use might be made of even a temporary engagement, where each day it lasted was an opportunity to try again.

Reluctantly, St. John gave one brief nod and was surprised to see her anxious look remained.

"What is it?" he asked gently.

Her hand tightened on his arm, and then she did realize it and released him, trying to smooth out the crease her clutch had made. "Mr. Rotherwood—what will you tell Mrs. Rotherwood?" Her eyes rose no further than the top button of his waistcoat. "The truth or—or not the truth?"

"For simplicity's sake, Miss Hapgood, I am afraid I had better not say the engagement is a sham. For her own reasons, I am sure my mother would be as tempted to share that secret as Miss Sidney."

It was Hetty's turn for the brief nod. She didn't need to guess what Mrs. Rotherwood's reasons would be. The woman would be relieved and *elated* to learn the engagement was a hoax. And if Mrs. Rotherwood began to bruit it about that her son was still available, well, then there was no point in the scheme at all.

"I understand," she said, her chin lifting. "And I thank you again, Mr. Rotherwood. I will never forget your friendship. Will you shake hands with me on our bargain?"

He would. He took her bare hand in both his. One press—a jolt of warmth and concurrence—and the matter was settled.

CHAPTER
TWENTY-THREE

**It is permitted to counter-plot
what is plotted against us.
— Gabriel Naudé (tr. Wm King), *Political considerations upon refin'd politicks* (1711)**

As the conspirators had foreseen, no sooner did the thunder-bolt of the lampoon strike Mayfair, than its potential damage was neutralized entirely by news of the engagement. Mothers raged and cried; daughters raged and cried. Every betting book in London registered an unprecedented swing of the odds from son to mother, and Mrs. Rotherwood found herself more courted than ever.

"The bettors know you don't approve of the match," her agent Mr. Pinckney explained. Anne surmised he must not approve either, for he was looking somewhat pale and careworn.

"How could I approve?" she demanded, barely above a whisper, even though her son was from home. "I tell you in profound confidence, Mr. Pinckney, that I grieve the engagement. St. John could have had anyone. Anyone! And he chooses this—this shameless, deceitful, forward, unladylike—oh! My heart breaks within me. I put on a brave face for him, but my heart is truly broken. I do not know how I will survive this wretched engagement dinner, for I don't even want to set eyes on that creature. I blame my father. Because he told St. John to take care of me, now my son believes he must be every distressed woman's shining knight. What can be done, Mr. Pinckney? Can anything be done to prevent the marriage? St. John says there is no day named yet, but I am positive she will hound him for fear he will escape."

The solicitor sighed and passed a hand over his eyes. "Madam, there are things that can be done, but these things might damage your relationship with Mr. Rotherwood."

"Tell me."

"Well, you might curtail his allowance severely, for example. Or you might specify that only a certain amount of his allowance may go toward his wife or his wife's relations, but that would be complicated and lead to much wrangling over what constitutes an expense that is solely her own."

Anne was already shaking her head and groaning. "I cannot. I cannot. St. John would be so angry! Suppose he took her part? And he would take her part if he believed I was being unjust. He is proud enough that he would cut himself off from the money altogether before he accepted it on any of those terms."

"There are...other possibilities," Mr. Pinckney said slowly.

"Yes? Such as?"

Mr. Pinckney hesitated. It was an unusually clear day, and in the slanting sunlight Anne saw blotches of color mark his face. "Well...you might rewrite your will to create a trust. One which benefitted only your bloodline and was managed by a trustee whom you appointed. After your death, that trustee would then dole out funds to the beneficiaries—your son and his children, but not the wife—according to terms you had set. This is assuming, of course, that you do not want to do as your father did, and disown your son entirely?"

She dismissed this last option with a wave and sat forward in her chair. "You mean I might appoint you as my trustee and keep the money and Glennard from that girl? Would St. John need to know?"

"He need not, unless you told him. And if you chose not to, he would not know of it until you were gone."

Then her reply was scarcely audible. "He would know then. And curse me then."

Another pause. "God willing, we are discussing a time far in the future, madam. A point by which he might even have become disenchanted himself with this unfortunate alliance. If this Miss Hapgood is truly as bad as you say, by the time of your death he might praise your foresight and be glad of the excuse to tell his wife he knew nothing of the matter."

A sparkle returned to her eyes. "Why, Mr. Pinckney—how very dastardly you are! How cunning. But, when I am gone, would you not be afraid that St. John's wrath—if there is any—would light upon you?"

If anything, the blotches on his face grew brighter. "I would not take it personally. A trustee must not. It is not the trustee, after all, who sets the conditions of the will. And as a man of business, Mrs. Rotherwood, my instinctive loyalty will always lie with the best use of the money."

"Indeed. So it must. If there is no money, there is no business, after all. Ah, Mr. Pinckney, you are a treasure to me." She rose and gave him her hand. "Let us alter my will. In profoundest confidence. You have comforted me and given me the courage to bear this dreaded supper. Our little secret will keep my spirits up."

While Anne Rotherwood plotted her next move, her son was also at work. He had sent a note around to Cleveland Street and offered what he knew would be irresistible to a university student: a free meal.

"If you're approaching satiation, Hapgood," St. John said, as Lionel fell to his fourth chop, "I wanted to consult you."

With an effort, Lionel swallowed his mouthful. "I figured this wasn't all about catching up on Magdalen news. Happy to help, sir."

"I want to buy your sister an engagement gift. As the one who has known her longest, I thought you could advise me. And what did I tell you about the 'sir' and 'Mr. Rotherwood' business?"

"Right. Rotherwood." Lionel grinned and set down his knife and fork. "The person you ought to ask is my betrothed, Edith, or my stepmother, but as one is in Rome and the other in Somerset, I suppose I must do. Can't say I've favored Het with too many gifts myself. But you saw—she likes books. She likes art. She likes music. Less keen on fripperies and gewgaws."

"An engagement gift had better be jewelry, I'm afraid. But expensive enough that I hope she wouldn't consider it a gewgaw. Do you think she would prefer earrings or a necklace?"

Lionel tried to picture his sister wearing jewelry and nothing came to mind. "Does—er—does she even wear jewelry?"

St. John rolled his eyes. "She does. I have seen a silver-and-peridot cross—"

"That's right!" Lionel snapped his fingers. "My father and stepmother gave her that."

"—And some pearl earrings. Also silver."

"My parents again. I guess you look at my sister more than I do," he added wryly.

"Never mind. I will choose the jewelry, then. You would advise an informal gift as well? A book or print or sheet music?"

Lionel was grinning again, and he sawed another bite from his chop. "I'd say keep that lampoon, sir—Rotherwood, I mean. In a few years she'll laugh at it as hard as everyone else in town."

One eyebrow rose, and St. John was beginning to look somewhat tutorial. "Look, Hapgood. I've a mind to leave you with the bill, if you can't make yourself more useful than this—"

"Sorry, sorry," Lionel said, still chuckling. "Though I still recommend you pocket one for later. I do have one word of indispensable advice, Rotherwood: you'll let me tell Hetty that you plan on giving her something. She won't like at all to be caught out, with nothing to give in return."

In Devonshire Street, Hetty had not emerged since the lampoon was published, trusting that the invitations her aunt soon sent hurtling hither and yon would do their work, and she need only appear at the dinner on St. John's arm, accepting congratulations as best she could.

There was no avoiding her father's letter, however, which arrived the morning of the dinner, and Hetty sought the privacy of her room to read it, pulse speeding and palms damp.

Patterton
20 December 1814

My dear daughter,
I trust you are alone as you read this. Your stepmother and I were deeply grieved by your letter. By the choices both you and Lionel made and equally by the attendant consequences. We would summon you home, but you are right in thinking your departure from the Sidneys' house would likely compound the injuries done to them.

Nor will we join you in London for Christmas, we have decided. We understand the need for your ruse with Mr. Rotherwood but feel it would be too difficult to play our role in the deception of others. You may tell whom

*you like, however, that your parents are "pleased." For
so we would be, were it a genuine engagement. Indeed,
Mr. Rotherwood already held our admiration even
before his determination to help our family.*

*If you would make our excuses, you may say in all
truth that your stepmother is quite occupied with the
preparations for her brother Norman's wedding, and
we regret we will have to postpone our planned visit.*

*We wish you a happy Christmas, my dear girl, and
much wisdom in the New Year.*

Your loving father

Hetty was simultaneously relieved by what she read and ashamed
of her relief. To be glad, when she knew they had been looking
forward to coming and seeing Lionel and herself again! But it would
be far, far easier to pretend she and Mr. Rotherwood were happily
engaged if she did not have to do so under her parents' gaze.

I can do this, she told herself, as Trilby dressed her hair. For
one thing, how hard could it be to sit beside Mr. Rotherwood
and speak to him and give the impression that she enjoyed it? The
greater danger would be overdoing matters. She had had to choose
his engagement gift (an engagement gift! Whatever for? What was
he thinking?) carefully, lest it be too thoughtful or meaningful. It
would never do to appear she had agonized over it, though she had.

He and his mother arrived on the heels of Lionel and his friends, whose laughing and bantering presence bolstered Hetty's courage. A glance at her aunt revealed that Lavinia Sidney was relishing the moment of welcoming Mrs. Rotherwood as her niece's future mother-in-law; she could only have appreciated it more if it were her own daughter putting Anne Rotherwood in her place.

"Mrs. Rotherwood, Mr. Rotherwood, you are very welcome."

Anne had paid special attention to her toilette that evening. She was in her customary blue-black, her faded blonde hair piled high, curled and enclosed in a gold-and-onyx circlet, a matching gold-and-onyx pendant hanging about her neck. She intended to look every inch a baronet's daughter and to cow this nobody of a Miss Hapgood. But Hetty had prepared herself for rock and ice and was therefore able to meet it with calm. She would have preferred Mrs. Rotherwood to like her, naturally, but if the woman chose not to, there was at least the cold comfort that Hetty would not be around very long to hate.

Whatever poise she mustered for the mother, however, vanished with the son. He bowed to her, handsome, intense, stern, and she felt her heart do a funny little hitch, like a horse asked to canter before it was trotting quickly enough.

"Miss Hapgood."

"Mr. Rotherwood."

"I have something for you."

"And—I for you."

Everyone was watching them. He pulled from his pocket a small velvet box, which he placed in her unsteady hands.

"Oh," breathed Hetty. Her eyes rose to his, and he gave her the smallest nod. Taking a deep breath, she opened the box to reveal a pair of earrings: silver filigree with peridots cut in a teardrop shape. "Oh! They match my cross."

"So they do," said Lionel over her shoulder. "Well done, Rotherwood."

"Do you like them?" Mr. Rotherwood asked.

Her shining eyes were answer enough, but there was distress there as well. *What was he thinking, giving her such things?* Biting her lip, she snapped the box shut. "I will put them on in a moment, sir. Thank you. My gift to you is not nearly so—so—so nice," she finished lamely.

And yet it was, in his eyes. Lacking inspiration, Hetty had sent Trilby out to buy him a snuffbox, though she had never seen him take snuff. And then, at the last minute, she threw the snuffbox in her trunk, took a napkin, and wrapped this up instead.

"Your Wingate's *Arithmetic*," he marveled, fanning the pages. "I am astonished you would part with it."

"I've—mastered the contents," she declared airily. "And I thought you might like a...nostalgic reminder of the past."

"I would." He opened it again to the inside cover. "You've added your name, as you promised. It will be doubly precious then, when Harriet Hapgood is no more and only Harriet Rotherwood remains."

Frowning and going pink, she gave him a questioning look, but then the other guests were being announced, and the room was filled with chatter and motion.

Mr. Rotherwood came to stand beside her, drawing her hand through his arm. He had a lovely, solid, steady arm, and the warmth and firmness of it reassured her, as if he were a stone rampart she leaned against on a sunny day.

She would never remember what people said to her that night. There were just impressions of knowing glances and sly asides and grudging congratulations and, through it all, the strength of his arm. She began to lean against it and he against her, as if they were the two sides of a collapsing arch finding a new point of equilibrium.

"How are you?" he asked in a low voice, when they had greeted the Stanleys. "Are you ready for this?"

"I am not sure anyone could be ready for this. Oh, Mr. Rotherwood, I cannot think why you would get me such an expensive gift when you know—yes, good evening, Mr. Elwood—what a pleasure to see you again. I hope your family are all well—when you *know…*"

"If we are to be convincing, I could hardly give you some worthless trinket. Good evening, Lady Aurora. Thank you. Yes. Thank you."

And at the next opportunity: "Have you written your parents?"

"Yes. They have—decided they will not come up at Christmas after all."

"Ah." He nodded, and she thought the expression which flitted over his face was chagrin. "I am sorry for it."

She was too. "How did—what did Mrs. Rotherwood think of it all?"

Another fleeting grimace. "My mother has old-fashioned notions of like marrying like, but as you become better acquainted, I know she will rejoice in it."

Hetty made her own skeptical face before she could avoid it, but then the arrival of more guests made further response unnecessary.

"Thank you."

"Thank you very much."

"No, we have not yet set a date."

"Our families are very happy."

"Thank you."

"Thank you very much."

They were seated beside each other at dinner. Hetty's face began to ache from the constant smile she wore. Mr. Rotherwood was fortunate for his reputation of speaking little and smiling less. He might be as silent and block-like as he pleased, and no one thought it amiss. There were enough present that Hetty need not speak either; she need only smile and smile as if this were exactly how she planned her life, to bury herself in scandal and then soar above it into the social ether.

The Sidneys' delight was unfeigned. They might have achieved their newfound ascendancy by an unconventional route, but they meant to revel in it all the same. And Mr. Elwood's reappearance lifted Caroline's spirits several more notches. Hetty thought the man looked sheepish, having played no heroic role in standing by his would-be lady through her difficulties and only returning when there was no danger. Yes, he claimed family troubles with his younger brothers had detained him in the country, but Hetty could only think that Mr. Rotherwood's steadfastness shone in comparison.

There was one thorny moment: Lady Stanley called down the table to her, "Miss Hapgood, we know gossips and scandal-mongers and satirists are not to be relied upon, but I would give much to know if you truly attended the masquerade ball at the Argyll Rooms and what your costume was."

"She was with me," both Lionel and St. John blurted.

"Well, you showed up there later, Rotherwood," Lionel amended, "but it was I who invited my sister and kept to her side all evening."

"I was disguised as a withered old crone," Hetty replied clearly, her blush brilliant. "My brother and I were always wont to get into mischief, and I have been roundly upbraided by my wiser relations for this latest and last escapade."

Mr. Rotherwood's hand moved to cover hers, just for an instant, but it was long enough for that reassurance to flow between them again. "Small wonder she was recognized," he said to the table at large. "Even a tangly grey wig and shapeless gown could not contrive to hide her beauty."

This declaration only made Hetty redden further and James Clinkett erupt in a coughing fit, but it got them through the worst of it, and the subject was not raised again.

When the women left the gentlemen to their port, Hetty found Mrs. Rotherwood by her side, steering her to a sofa in a farther corner. "Will you sit with me, Miss Hapgood?"

Her engagement might be a farce, but Hetty was human enough to wish Mrs. Rotherwood would begin to like her. The woman's *a priori* rejection dealt a blow to her pride and her self-love, whether Hetty wanted it to or not. Therefore she followed her with a heart both sinking and defiant.

The two women sat in silence a minute, each gathering her thoughts. Anne wished to express as much disapprobation for the match as she could manage without angering St. John, and Hetty wished to comport herself as respectably as she could, fully believing that, if she had genuinely agreed to marry Mr. Rotherwood, she would not have been any more unworthy of him than the wooden Lady Sylvia.

"Ah, Miss Hapgood, my son is very dear to me, as you might imagine."

Already Hetty encountered a difficulty, for should she not respond in kind? Should she not say he was very dear to her as well? It would be odd if she did not. And she did love him, in any case—though that was her secret and for no one else. (Besides Edith, who at any rate was too far away to count.)

She compromised: "Yes, he is an admirable man."

"Indeed, thank you. St. John is everything that is admirable," Mrs. Rotherwood took this up. "If a fond mother may say so, he is clever and affectionate and handsome and virtuous. Every mother might say as much of her son, but in no instance would she be more justified in such a boast than I am."

"Yes," said Hetty. She was aware of a stubborn inclination rising in her, both to defend herself and to forestall any more of Mrs. Rotherwood's attack. "Yes," she said again, half-turning in her seat to meet her companion's gaze squarely. "He is all those things. I would add that, not only might a mother take pride in his person and character, but a wife would as well. And I am aware that you feel he has stooped in looking to me to fill that role. I am further aware you would wish any wife of his to be beautiful and titled and wealthy and accomplished and free of—scandal—and that you do not think I meet these requirements. You made yourself clear to my aunt on the matter, and I very well know my conduct in attending the masquerade only bore out your fears. I can only beg your pardon for my presence there, as I have begged pardon of my family. Such a thing will never happen again. They have all forgiven me, as I hope you will. But as for the rest—" she held up her palms— "as for the money and title and so on and so forth, I can only be who I am. I can only believe that, if Mr. Rotherwood has no objections and sees fit to—love me—it must be enough. Indeed, madam, the primary reservation I have in the entire affair is that I dread to be the object of your scorn. Family is dear to me, you see."

To her surprise, Anne felt a flicker of admiration for the girl's dignity. And seated this close to her, she could see she was almost pretty—that is, Anne could understand why many would deem her pretty—and not unintelligent. Knowing her son as she did, she admitted finally that stolid Lady Sylvia could not compete. Beauty could open a door, but it could not push the young lady through, where a discerning man like St. John was in question. If only this particular girl weren't so...ordinary in so many respects! She would make a fine wife for some little banker or solicitor or very minor landowner. How unfortunate it was altogether that she had crossed

St. John's path and that he knew her brother. The dangers of proximity!

"Every positive characteristic of my son has its concomitant drawback," Anne replied at last. "He is brave and loyal; therefore he feels it incumbent on himself to protect his family and friends, even at great personal cost—"

Yes, yes, yes. It was not as if Hetty hadn't realized all this herself. She could not bear to have it presented to her as a fresh discovery. Therefore she was goaded to interrupt. "Of course, madam. I understand that about him, and that was why I refused him at first. I saw it was a martyrdom of sorts."

"Refused him!" cried Anne.

"For his own sake."

"But then why did you change your mind...?"

Hetty felt her face flaming. Argh! How had they ever thought this scheme would work? Why had she let her pride provoke her to burst out? It only forced her to tell more lies.

"He was insistent," she bit out. "And—our affections for each other—overpowered other considerations."

"Mm."

To Hetty's immense relief, the gentlemen entered the drawing room—they must have been as eager to join the ladies as the ladies were to welcome them. Avoiding Mr. Rotherwood's eye and catching her brother's, she gave Lionel a look that meant, *Get over here and save me.* Had he not still felt guilty for his part in the Argyll Rooms Debacle, Lionel would have teased her by ignoring this nonverbal summons, but as it was, he came with alacrity. "Het, what would you say to giving us some music? Clunker warbles a pretty tune."

"I am happy to," she agreed, springing up. "And perhaps we can also prevail upon Caroline and Lady Sylvia."

Opening the pianoforte, she spread some of their favorite sheet music out, that Edward might choose. He did indeed have a lovely tenor and was soon joined by Caroline's soprano and his brother James' comic bass.

After Hetty had played several songs through and joined once in a duet with Lionel, she yielded her place to Lady Sylvia and retired to a seat at the back to enjoy not being stared at. The earl's daughter was more than pleasant to rest one's eyes upon, with her graceful, perfect posture and tapering white fingers. Nor did it detract from Hetty's gratification that Lady Sylvia performed with her usual accuracy and soullessness.

"What are you smiling about?" It was Mr. Rotherwood at her elbow.

Hetty had the grace to look embarrassed. "Nothing. Something spiteful, I'm afraid. I'm quite a wicked creature, you know."

"I know your opinion on the ubiquity of wickedness, at least," he said with a grin. He pulled a chair nearer hers and took a seat. "But would you say yours has Lady-Macbeth-ish potential?"

"Oh, sir—I hope not, but who can say? I had better not be tempted."

"Ah. But what would tempt you, Miss Hapgood? For I know wealth would not, rank would not."

You might, she thought, looking at him. Mr. Rotherwood might not tempt her to wickedness, but he operated on her in other ways. Suppose she were to swallow her pride and tell him she would like to marry him after all, despite him not loving her and despite his mother's contempt? If she had a lifetime, might she not try to win him—to win both of them?

She shook this off. "I think power might tempt me," she murmured. "I do not mean power over others, but rather the power to live my own life. Determine my own course. Only see what lengths everyone has gone to, to rescue me from my own actions."

"I do see," he answered, under cover of applause for Lady Sylvia's piece. He waited for Bailey and Clinker to coax her into playing another before continuing, "Without the power to determine your own course, you are subject to the strictures and whims of the world."

"Yes." Those eyes of her turned on him again, glowing to be understood, the peridots at her ears and throat winking. "No one seems particularly concerned, for example, that *you* were at the Argyll Rooms, or Lionel, or his friends. No one whispered about any of you, or drew satiric pictures of you, but I—"

He was silent a minute, considering this, his gaze on Lady Sylvia as she plied the keys mechanically.

"You are right," Mr. Rotherwood rejoined at last. "Fair or not fair, so it is. Miss Hapgood—perhaps I ought to beg your pardon. When I...managed matters...I meant to help you, and yet it must have seemed as if I were just another *thing,* another inexorable tyrant, exerting my power at the expense of your own."

"Oh, Mr. Rotherwood." To her dismay, she felt her eyes fill, and she hastily looked away, fiddling with her gloves. She did not know why his sympathy should hurt, but it did. "You needn't beg my pardon, but I thank you all the same."

"May I...call again after the holiday?" he asked. "We might see another sight in town, with your cousin or anyone you like."

The low gentleness of his voice did curious things to her. A flutter in her stomach. Shallowness in her breathing. Keeping her gaze averted, she gave a nod of agreement.

I will get used to him, Hetty told herself, watching Lady Sylvia play as if her own life depended on it. *The more I am around him, the easier it will become to take things as a matter of course.*

She was not ordinarily a girl who told herself untruths, but in this case it was a matter of self-preservation. Because what would become of her otherwise?

What would become of her if, instead of growing more and more inured to him, the only thing that grew was her love?

Chapter Twenty-Four

You thinke twice before you speake, and may be demanded twice before you answer.
— Richard Brathwait, *Ar't Asleepe Husband?* (1640)

Christmas in North Audley Street was a quiet affair. St. John had requested that no guests be invited, that he and his mother might dine alone.

"It was kind of you to give the servants the holiday," Anne beamed upon him. "And I treasure these times that remain, with just the two of us."

"It might be just the two of us more frequently, if we were not always accepting invitations and attending functions."

"You know what I mean, my heart." She swirled her wine in its glass, admiring the rich color. "I suppose you will be married by Whitsuntide."

St. John took a deep breath. "We have not yet set a date."

"There is no hurry, of course. I did ask Miss Hapgood about it at your engagement dinner, and she did not seem overeager either."

No, she wouldn't.

"How do you like her, madam? I have been wanting to have this conversation with you these past several days, but you seemed determined to avoid it."

Anne gave a light laugh. "Oh, but the Christmas season is so busy! What a whirl. And we had accepted all those invitations before you became engaged—when Miss Hapgood and her relations were still deemed *outré.*"

"Well, let us talk now," he insisted. "With no interruption. Madam, I know you were uneasy even when I suggested I would like you to be a friend to Miss Hapgood and the Sidneys, so I can only imagine you are that much more uneasy to consider Miss Hapgood in light of a daughter."

"If you read my thoughts, what need is there of putting things into words?" his mother murmured.

His brow knit. "I had hoped, as you grew accustomed to the idea, and after having spoken to Miss Hapgood herself at the dinner, you might have warmed to her."

"Now, St. John..."

"Her visit to the Argyll Rooms was regrettable," he continued. "No one argues that with you. But it is done, and she has repented of it and been forgiven by all—"

"Only because your championship of her forced everyone to *appear* to forgive her!" Anne objected, goaded. "Do you think forgiveness would have come so easily had you not salvaged her ruined reputation with your own sterling character?"

"The deeper question is, why did Miss Hapgood require forgiving, when she was not the only one at the Argyll Rooms?" he demanded, remembering again her look when she put the question to him. "I was there, her brother was there, her brothers' friends were there. If all of us were there, why is it only Miss Hapgood who is criticized for it?"

"Because she is a young lady!" cried Anne, eyes flashing. "And young ladies are held to higher standards."

"Or young men are held to lower ones."

"Do you not want a bride of spotless repute? Would you have a girl who has been—insulted—by other gentlemen?"

Now it was her son's eyes with the dangerous glint. "If an insult is forced upon a young woman, it is an insult only to the one who did the forcing."

"St. John, in the lampoon, she was throwing herself at somebody—"

"Madam." The chill of his voice sent a shiver through her. "I would expect you to be wiser than to credit what you see in a satiric print, something created solely to mock and ruin a fellow human being, in order to make money."

He had never spoken to her thus, and when Anne burst into tears, it was provoked as much by outrage as distress.

"Mother—Mama—please calm yourself," he urged, on his feet and beside her chair in an instant. "You must pardon my temper, but

I cannot hear Miss Hapgood maligned and overlook it. You would be as quick to resent any slight to her if you knew her better."

"If I knew her better?" sobbed Anne. "How well do *you* know her? Are you so certain she is as innocent as you say? How could she be? Why, every girl in London has hoped to capture you—only this Miss Hapgood was cleverer. She played upon your kindness, your nobility—"

At this, St. John threw up his hands. How ridiculous was it, that both his mother and his supposed betrothed raised the same objections? Both Miss Hapgood and his mother protested the need for and the offer of his rescue, Miss Hapgood because she chafed at the bonds society placed on her, and his mother because she thought Miss Hapgood used those bonds to her own advantage. Further contributing to the farce, all this conflict arose over an engagement that did not even truly exist!

But I mean it to. And if that is ever to happen, I will need every means of persuasion in my power.

It was not a successful Christmas.

When they finished their meal and were sitting beside the fire, Anne sewing and St. John pretending to read, an entire hour passed without a word spoken.

At last, he shut his volume and looked over at her. "I go with Miss Hapgood and her cousin to the Banqueting House in Whitehall tomorrow. I trust that your belief in my 'sterling character' will eventually convince you that I am both old enough and wise enough to choose a wife for myself. May I give Miss Hapgood your wishes for a Happy New Year?"

Anne's lips tightened as she gave a short nod. She almost hated that girl. Of course he would remain steadfast in his commitment to that interloper—Anne hardly expected otherwise of him. But she hated Miss Hapgood for it all the same.

Where the Rotherwoods' Christmas week was full and busy, the Sidneys and Hetty continued to stay close to home. They ventured once to church and once to the British Museum in Montagu House (at Hetty's insistence); they shopped, although not in Oxford or Bond Street. Mr. Elwood called twice. Lionel and his friends came for Christmas dinner.

"I think matters have improved, have they not?" Caroline asked. In the salver lay her proof: two invitations which she hugged to her.

"I hope so," said Hetty. If Mr. Elwood felt confident enough to show his face twice, that seemed promising.

From Mr. Rotherwood came a note with a basket of hothouse fruit, wishing them a happy Christmas, and another card followed, offering to accompany Hetty and Caroline and "anyone else you choose" to the Banqueting House. While this was another sight Caroline didn't care for especially, she did like the idea of Mr. Rotherwood sponsoring an outing, and the girls invited Mr. Elwood, along with Lionel and company, of whom only Clunker showed interest.

"Should we invite Lady Sylvia?" wondered Caroline. "I think she and I might be friends again."

"Were you friends in the first place?" Hetty asked wryly. But she made no objection, and, to her surprise, Lady Sylvia accepted.

Therefore, the day after Boxing Day, the grand old Holt coach rattled up to the house in Devonshire Street, and their party of six climbed in. Having not seen Mr. Rotherwood for nearly a week, Hetty found she had to get used to him all over again. Used to his height and his solid presence and his handsomeness and his stern demeanor. Being seated beside him addled her completely. She dropped her reticule and, when she bent for it, accidentally kicked him. And then long-limbed Clunker sat on the other side of her, taking up a great deal of space and forcing her to move so near Mr. Rotherwood that she could feel his warmth, though she tried to lock her legs together and keep her arms glued to her sides so she would not brush against him. It did not help matters that Clunker dug out his tiny notebook and pencil, jostling her and jabbing her with his elbow until she had to creep another inch toward Mr. Rotherwood. When she threw him an apologetic glance, he met it with a mischievous twitch of his mouth.

Caroline and Mr. Elwood kept up a steady chatter all down the New Road to Edgeware Road. Lady Sylvia contributed nothing, naturally, and Hetty could hear Clunker muttering something about "tawny hue, eyes of blue" as he stared at the earl's daughter and scribbled.

"How was your holiday?" Mr. Rotherwood murmured.

"Quiet. Yours?"

"Quiet."

"Did you not go out?"

"We were out every day except Christmas. Therefore, on that day I wanted nothing more than to remain home after church."

No more was said, though Hetty was yearning to know if he and his mother discussed the engagement. How could they not? They must have. The Sidneys must have asked her ten times when she thought the happy event would take place.

The coach descended Park Lane, drawing Caroline's attention to the riders and drivers in the park, before veering at Hyde Park Corner into Piccadilly. Clunker fell against Hetty, who then fell against Mr. Rotherwood, like so many dominoes. Almost in the man's lap, Hetty muttered apologies while his gloved hand took hold of her elbow and hoisted her upright. She jerked it from his grasp as soon as she was able, only making the moment more awkward.

At last, they alit in Parliament Street before the stately Banqueting House, admiring the Inigo Jones design, its pinkish and tan façade partially refaced in Portland Stone. Hetty turned to Clunker, giving him a folded piece of paper. "We must each make a sketch of the ceiling for my cousin Edith—Lionel's Edith. And whoever's sketch is less ugly I will send her."

Clunker nodded in agreement, but Mr. Rotherwood's chuckle surprised her. "Why not buy her a print of the ceiling?"

"Because Edith has no need of a print," returned Hetty. "She would be far more amused by our depictions. In fact, I will send her both of them and ask her to guess whose is whose."

After pausing below the spot where Charles I was executed ("Heavens!" shivered Caroline), they entered the Banqueting House. The vast interior soon swallowed the small group, which drifted apart to explore. Lady Sylvia's hold over Clunker gave place to his passion for art, and he forgot all about her as he wandered with head tilted back, fanning himself with the paper Hetty had given him. Because the space was just one long room, it was no affront to propriety for Hetty to seat herself on a bench and for Mr. Rotherwood to join her, observing as she set pencil to paper.

"Honestly," said Hetty, roughing out what looked like a pile of rocks but was meant to be the *Apotheosis of James I*. "I can barely see the Rubens paintings away up there. I wish I had opera glasses with me. Edith will think my skills sadly deteriorated, and they weren't impressive to begin with."

"Have you heard from her, since she departed for Rome?"

"Just once. One letter to me and one to Lionel, but I wasn't allowed to read Lionel's. It's almost as if she has gone to live on the moon. At this rate, I might get one more letter from Rome and one from Paris before she comes back herself."

"She does not know of your time in London, then."

"No." Hetty colored, not because of the scandal she had been involved in, but rather because she remembered writing to Edith about her growing attraction to the man beside her. Only imagine what Edith would think, when she learned that Hetty and Mr. Rotherwood were supposedly engaged!

"Mr. Rotherwood." She tapped her pencil anxiously against her knee. "I must seize upon this chance to speak with you alone."

"Certainly." He braced for it, but when she turned her blue eyes directly upon him, he still felt his breath catch. It was odd, how he had once thought Lady Sylvia and Miss Sidney her superiors in beauty. They were lovely, of course, but what could match Miss

Hapgood's particular glow? Her intensity when she was fascinated or delighted or wretched or amused or indignant? She was so *alive*.

"At our—dinner—last week, Mrs. Rotherwood and I spoke briefly. Your mother was not—pleased to think us engaged, and I cannot help but feel, for your own family peace, that you ought to tell her the truth, after all, as I have told my parents. Tell her that we are not really, truly engaged. Unless she has warmed to the idea...?" Hetty added on a hopeful note.

His hesitation and the darkening of his brow were answer enough.

Her face fell. "That must be very difficult for you both. I am sorry for it."

"As am I." His hand rose to hover over her forearm, but then it balled in a fist and he withdrew it. "But you must not let it trouble you, Miss Hapgood."

"How can it not? I know, sir, how dear you are to each other, having only each other. I hate to think this comes between you. Especially since it need not." In her anxiety, she crinkled the *Apotheosis* under her hand, her thumb smudging James I's face. "Why not simply tell her the truth? If you assure her it is only for another week or two—a month at the uttermost—she will take such comfort."

"A week or two?" he echoed, distracted. "Nonsense."

"Why, nonsense?" Leaning toward him, she hissed, "We have already begun to receive invitations again! And look—here is Lady Sylvia willing to join us on an outing. You have done your part. Our mock engagement has served its purpose. I think I may be able to jilt you shortly."

"And what would happen to your newly restored reputation, if you jilted me so soon?" he countered, feeling his own color rise. "You would be right back where you started, with gossip flying about your head and the Sidneys again. Think on it, Miss Hapgood."

She made a fretful motion. "Oh—I don't know what to do. Very well—if you think it too soon. But if I cannot jilt you until the spring, say, that is a very long time to be at odds with your mother, and a very long time for her to show me her displeasure."

Gently, he plucked the crushed sketch from her grasp and smoothed it upon the bench between them.

"What would you have done, Miss Hapgood, if our engagement were real?" He tried to sound offhand, but it was a failure to his own ears. "There are, I wager, many matches made where one parent or another disapproves, and yet the couple marries all the same."

"Indeed there are. Mr. Rotherwood, you need only recall your own family's history! I would think you would be the last person on earth to make a match in direct opposition to your family's—to your mother's—will. Was one estrangement not enough for a lifetime?" she pressed. "Would you cause another? Would you be without her—and her without you—for the rest of your lives?"

"She would grow to love you," he insisted, "for my sake, if not your own."

Hetty made a face. "As your grandfather grew to love your father?"

At this, Mr. Rotherwood sprang to his feet, removing his hat to run agitated fingers through his hair. "It would not be the same."

"No—for it would be worse," Hetty rejoined, gaining confidence now. "Because you would have done this even after all the pain and sorrow and poverty that the two of you experienced. Your choice would wound all the more deeply because of your history. Don't you see?"

He stared unseeingly at Clunker in the distance, hunched over his drawing. Caroline and Mr. Elwood and Lady Sylvia were at the far end but starting back their way, Mr. Elwood pointing at something out a window.

At last Mr. Rotherwood spoke again. "What you say is indeed persuasive, Miss Hapgood. A mock engagement is certainly not worth an estrangement." His mouth twisted. "What do you suppose Mr. Edward Clinkett would make of that rhyme?"

She only shook her head ruefully.

"But a real engagement," he went on, "one that led to a real marriage—well—it would grieve me, and I would not soon give up trying to remedy matters, but for a real engagement, I would pay that price."

Her throat felt tight. She shook her head again. Why could she not make him understand? "I suppose—it is fortunate this is merely a theoretical discussion, then."

"Miss Hapgood—what if it were not? What if I were to tell you that—" His face felt on fire and his heart began to hammer. He felt unsteady on his feet. *Speak, you idiot! Speak now!*

"Miss Hapgood, what if I were to tell you that I have—begun to care for you—and that I would—would—would genuinely like to make you my wife?"

It was her turn to stare, her lips parting. Their minds were in two such different places at the moment that Hetty could hardly comprehend him. "I—I—Mr. Rotherwood!"

He dropped down beside her on the bench again, his gaze intent, urgent. "Had none of this happened—the masquerade, the gossip, the lampoon—I would eventually have asked you anyway, I am certain."

Certain? How could he be certain? Only a week prior, he said he thought they might eventually come to feel affection for each other. And now he was "certain" he already did?

She would love to believe him. She would. She felt in danger of believing him just to please herself.

But while giving in to this delusion of his would bring immediate happiness—she had no doubt of that—would it not also bring ultimate *un*happiness?

Who cares? a contrary part of her mind whispered. *Who cares about the consequences? You might have him now and his affection for however long it lasts, and let tomorrow bring what trouble it may!*

And Hetty might have listened to this voice, had she not just been through what she had been through. Had she not just learned and experienced what she had learned and experienced, and had it not thus scored into her very being the consequences of living to please only herself.

For better or worse, Harriet Hapgood was a scarred, more cautious girl now. And it was this girl who remembered what Mrs. Rotherwood had said. About her son being brave and loyal and casting himself as the rescuer of his friends and family. Yes—such a man might convince himself that, where he once only ventured to say he might learn to feel affection, he now believed he had felt it all along. Was Hetty's chief charm in his eyes her role as damsel in distress, a role his own mother had played his life long?

Even if it was, I would have time to win him, she thought stubbornly. *He likes me well enough. If I had time, I could win him.*

One thing was certain, however: the break with his mother would come. Either literally, in that mother and son would become estranged, or—perhaps worse—figuratively: Hetty and Mr. Rotherwood would marry, and there would remain Mrs. Rotherwood, under their own roof or very near it, scorning and despising her daughter-in-law.

It would be dreadful, whether literal or figurative. It was not to be contemplated. Only consider the contrast Hetty found in living with an Aunt Lavinia who was angry with her, versus living with an Aunt Lavinia who embraced and forgave her! A mother-in-law who did not love her would be ten times worse than an aunt who did not; and a mother-in-law would have a hundred times the power to wound Hetty, because Hetty would want her love that much more.

No.

She must resist this temptation.

St. John felt his spirits sink even before she answered. He could see the answer in her clear blue eyes, as incredulity gave way to hope(?), which yielded in turn to thoughtfulness and determination. Many a young man had been daunted by what he found in Miss Harriet Hapgood's eyes, and St. John found himself joining that sorry band.

"Mr. Rotherwood," she began hurriedly, seeing the rest of their party now halfway back to them, "yet once more I thank you for the goodness of your offer. And this time I add what an honor I feel it, for you to—confess to such flattering feelings for me. But I think we had better keep matters exactly as they are."

"Because you persist in thinking you could never return my feelings?" He was stiff again. Awkward. Crushed.

For the merest instant she debated this. And then the finest hairline crack developed in her resolve, and the truth slipped out. She might never, never have a chance to say as much again—could she not enjoy the relief of it, just this one time?

"No," she murmured. "It's rather likely I could. Might. Would." (She just managed to shut her mouth before "Do" emerged.)

"Then *why*," he persisted, turning his back on the approaching others and ducking his head to try to get her to look at him again. "Why, if you think so, do you still refuse?"

"I have already told you!" she hissed. "If you refuse to look at matters plainly, I must! I never want to marry a man whose mother disapproves and disdains the match. Family is dear to me, as it has been to you, Mr. Rotherwood, only you are forgetting it at the moment."

"Then you will not marry me unless my mother gives it her blessing?"

"No," said Hetty with decision. "I never will. And you will thank me later for saying so."

"And if she does give it her blessing?"

Her chest heaved—the stubborn, marble man! Why must he press her? Did he not know she was on the point of weeping and throwing herself at him? But she raised defiant eyes to his.

"I do not trust you. You might come and tell me that she has blessed it, and I may yet find that she has not. Not in her heart."

"Then what would convince you?" he demanded.

Hetty's chin rose. She would ask for the impossible. Because if it ever did happen, she would take it as a sign from heaven, no more, no less.

"She must come and tell me herself," she said. "Then I would know if she meant it. She must come and tell me that she would like me for a daughter."

Again his hand dragged through his hair, and she could tell from his countenance that he shared her thoughts. The proud Mrs. Rotherwood might submit to the match because she loved her son, but she would never bend her knee. She would never say to the scandalous nobody Miss Hapgood that she would like her for a daughter. And to ask her to do so with conviction added impossibility upon impossibility.

St. John could not bring himself to reply, but he gave one short, curt nod before the others were upon them, and everyone but Hetty was left to wonder the rest of the afternoon what ailed the man.

CHAPTER TWENTY-FIVE

1815 arrived in a round of parties, and the Sidneys were delighted to find themselves once more in the thick of things.

"Why, we are more popular even than before," crowed Caroline, very early one morning as they returned from the Featherwicks' ball. "Mama, I believe Hetty's disaster was all for the best. If Mr. Elwood does not watch himself, he will find me stolen away by any number of other gentlemen who seem to have noticed me for the first time."

Hetty yawned, leaning her head against the side of the carriage and shutting her eyes. She was trying not to remember how her eye caught Mrs. Rotherwood's as she was standing up with her son, and how Mrs. Rotherwood pointedly looked away.

"I would never wish another such calamity to befall us, no matter how well things might turn out afterward," Lavinia replied quellingly, "but I agree that the worst seems to be over. And as for Mr. Elwood, I think it more important, Caroline, that you know whether *you* prefer any other gentleman to him. You must prepare your answer, if he offers for you."

Caroline only sighed, inspecting a leaf of her fan which was coming free of its rib. "If he were to offer tomorrow—or would it be called today now?—I would say I didn't know yet. Or maybe I might say yes and then not set a date, like Hetty and Mr. Rotherwood. If I changed my mind later, I could choose someone else."

"Caroline!" scolded her mother.

"Is that why don't you set a date, Hetty?" her cousin prodded her. "You think someone better might appear? Though who could be richer or handsomer?"

"What is the rush?" Hetty complained. "My papa hardly knows him yet—just that one dinner in Oxford."

"Then why doesn't Uncle Hugh come to London? I suppose Mrs. Hapgood's brother's wedding is over and done with by now."

"Lionel has gone back to school," Hetty hedged.

"And you and your intended are not important enough to visit?"

Hetty shut her eyes again and waved her off. "I don't know. I can't answer that now. I'm too tired. Do leave me alone."

Rescue from her cousin's curiosity came in an unexpected form, when Hetty rose again in the early afternoon. Going downstairs she found two letters for her on the tray, one from Edith and one from her father. The rest of the family being still abed, Hetty had the luxury of the drawing room to herself, and she curled up in her favorite armchair to indulge.

Naturally she opened Edith's first, to find that the second sheet of paper was the promised sketch of Bernini's *David,* done from several angles, with more writing on the reverse. Hetty held the drawing up to the faint winter sunshine, the joke they shared seeming very long ago. Even knowing Mr. Rotherwood as she did now, however, she thought the likeness still held. The stern face, the noble person, the curling hair. *Is this what he would look like, if he wore nothing more than a length of fabric in a particular place?* she wondered, blushing. In her imagination she tried without success to clothe Bernini's *David* in a frock coat, neckcloth, and breeches.

Setting the picture aside, she plunged into Edith's long account of her daily life in Rome. What they saw, where they went, acquaintances they made. As ever in Edith's letters, it was full of more art than Hetty cared for, but when she finally turned over the Bernini sketch to continue reading, Edith seized her attention.

> *Hetty! I have just received your last letter, and what could be more appropriate than I continue this one on the reverse of Mr. R? I could hardly credit what I was reading, when you told me you thought you might care for him! But I confess I gave a loud screech and leapt up and ran about my little room (my aunt and uncle had fortunately gone for the evening passegiata, so there were no witnesses). Hetty in love? How I wish I were Caroline and right there beside you to witness every-*

thing. If you love him, he must not only be a handsome man but also a clever one and—dare I say—amusing? I cannot imagine this stern face marked by levity, but nor can I imagine you loving someone who cannot laugh at a joke. Oh, Hetty, you must write again immediately and tell me more. Tell me all, in fact! Does he return your feelings? What efforts have you made to win him? Because you have tried to win him, have you not?

Send your next letter to the Poste Restante in Paris. I think we will leave Rome within the fortnight and then be another fortnight traveling. Aunt Eliza thought we should remain in Rome until the weather warms somewhat, lest it be too difficult to cross the Alps again, but Uncle Alwyn is all optimism, as you might expect, and he says there will be no difference between January or February for travel, so it may as well be January, and that he is tired of meeting the same English people everywhere we go and would like to be introduced to a "new batch." Therefore, Paris.

But write, Hetty. This instant. I must know what is happening. It almost makes me want to skip Paris and just return to England, but of course I do not mention this, when my dear aunt and uncle have been so kind. Besides—it would only distract Lionel, and he is nearly done with his studies. You would laugh to see the letter he wrote to me. Sincere and heart-warming but, as you might guess, so very, very brief! That boy.

Your frantic cousin,
Edith

Hetty sighed, wishing every bit as strongly as Edith that they were not separated by a thousand miles. She would love a confidante her own age. If only Edith had received Hetty's later missive with its account of the scandal and its makeshift remedy! What would she have said then?

She had only her parents for (disapproving) confidants, and it was to her father's letter that Hetty turned next. But she no sooner unfolded the scrawled page than she sat forward suddenly, her breath held.

My dear daughter,
You have much on your mind and heart of late, but I write in haste to ask you home again. Your stepmother and sister have fallen ill, and your care in nursing them would do much to ease my distress. It is some sort of fatigue and aching and intermittent fever, and they are not the only ones in our neighborhood who have succumbed.

I must beg your uncle to accompany you back to Somerset, inconvenient as it is. I know your presence has been necessary there, that the Sidneys' reputation and yours might be bandaged up, and I promise I will return you to town when the danger is past. Only do come, my dear.

Your loving father

Absolutely she would go. Hetty was on her feet the second she read his request, taking the stairs an unladylike two at a time, that she might begin packing her trunk.

When Caroline heard she was in tears. "Oh, but Hetty, you will come back, won't you? And you won't get sick yourself? I cannot think why Uncle Hugh cannot hire a nurse for them—"

"He says many people have caught this, so I suppose nurses are in short supply."

Even her aunt was sorrowful. "If you must go, you must, Harriet, though it is terribly inconvenient of them to fall ill just now. We will have to do without Mr. Sidney's company as well for a few days, just when I had got him to agree to the Paulsons' card party. It is too bad you and Mr. Rotherwood are not married already. Then he might accompany you into Somerset."

"Yes, well…"

It took several attempts, but Hetty wrote a note that would have to do:

Dear Mr. Rotherwood,

My father writes that my stepmother and sister have fallen ill with the grippe or some other sickness, and he requests that I return home for a time to help care for

*them. It must be rather serious, or he would not ask.
When they are better, I have promised the Sidneys to
return to town.*

Please give my compliments to Mrs. Rotherwood.

*Your servant,
Harriet Hapgood*

The man himself appeared not an hour afterward, while Hetty was packing her trunk. Because her aunt and cousin were shopping for little treats they could send their relations, Hetty was obliged to go down and receive him alone.

"Miss Hapgood."

"Mr. Rotherwood."

She did not know whether she should offer him a seat. Perhaps he was only calling in passing? To be sure, he appeared rather agitated, if a man of marble could appear agitated. The crease in his brow was there and the tension in his shoulders.

"May I sit down, Miss Hapgood?"

"Oh! Of course. Please." She chose a chair and folded her hands in her lap.

But he did not sit after all. He went to lean against the mantel, running an abstracted hand over the Tompion clock.

"I am sorry to hear your family is unwell," he said, glancing at her.

"Yes. I hope it is not very bad. Rosie has always been on the frailer side. She will be glad to have me home. And I know it will ease my stepmother's mind."

He nodded at this, returning his gaze to the clock.

"It has been wound recently," Hetty couldn't help but add, half smiling.

He did not acknowledge her teasing, instead turning to face her. "You will come back, then."

"Yes," she answered, clasping her hands more tightly. "Yes, of course. As I said in my note. I promised the Sidneys."

"Then this is not some...stratagem on your part?"

"Stratagem? What do you mean, Mr. Rotherwood?"

In two strides he was before her, looming over her. "I mean, is this a scheme? Are you fleeing to Somerset in order to escape our engagement prematurely?"

Again she had that feeling that she was standing at the base of a tower, and she made haste to scramble up from her chair, so that he was not so very tall.

"Surely you cannot be in earnest with such an accusation!"

"Answer the question, Miss Hapgood."

"How dare you!" Hetty retorted with an indignant frown. "Mr. Rotherwood, when I end our engagement, I will have no need for stratagems or schemes or escapes. I will tell you first, and I will tell you plainly. I am perfectly capable of being straightforward and decent in my dealings, my visit to the Argyll Rooms notwithstanding."

The doubt she read in his face provoked her, and she added snappishly, "Or do you think you're the only one who can behave nobly?"

"The only one—whatever makes you say that?" he demanded, provoked in return. "When have I ever claimed to be noble, much less boasted of it?"

It was unjust of her, she knew. If anyone had boasted of his nobility it was her own conscience—and his mother's pride. Not him—never him.

But she didn't care about that at the moment. He accused her of resorting to stratagems—simply because his spotless character never required them? He did not say so explicitly, but that was the implication. If she was being unjust to him now, had not the use of a word like "stratagems" merited it? No—at the moment she did not care about justice. She only knew she was angry: angry at him for being such a stubbornly good man; angry at his mother for her haughtiness; and angry at herself for falling in love with someone who—if he loved her at all—loved her the more because it required sacrifice. Noble sacrifice. Oh—could any girl bear it?

She couldn't.

Not one second longer.

One got very tired of having always to receive and feel grateful.

"Noble, noble, noble," Hetty very nearly jeered at him, feeling a naughty thrill to know she was going to behave badly. She dropped a mocking curtsey. "Of course you've never insisted on your nobility or boasted of it. It wouldn't be the noble thing to do, would it, your nobleness?"

"What the devil has got into you? Stop calling me that!" he snapped.

"Why? You *are* noble, are you not?"

"Stop this instant!"

She made a clicking sound with her tongue and wagged a finger in his face. "My, my. Is barking at me in keeping with your perfect, flawless virtue, Mr. Noble MacNobleness? Mr. Noblety Noblekins?"

She had gone too far.

"I'll show you noble," he roared, seizing her by the arms and crushing her to him. His mouth came down so hard on hers that Hetty felt her tooth cut her lip, but she hadn't any thought to spare for it because it was as if one of the great big lions at the Tower menagerie swept her up in velvet paws to break and devour her. Mr. Rotherwood was even growling like a beast, and Hetty might have been making sounds of her own if only the pressure of his arms and chest had allowed her breath.

Good heavens—this was nothing like Mr. Pickford's attack! For one thing, though Mr. Rotherwood was going to snap every bone in her body if he continued squeezing her like this, Hetty had not the least wish to be released. For another, she found she was kissing him back, as hard as he was kissing her, despite the blood she could taste from where she bit herself. She strained and wriggled to work one arm out of its bonds, that she could wind a hand in his gold-shot curls, just as his fingers were tangling in her own bright hair. And, unlike with Mr. Pickford in the Argyll Rooms, it never even occurred to Hetty to raise a knee in self-defense. No—she wanted to melt with him. Melt into him.

How long this all might have gone on and where it might have led was not a mystery to be solved that day, for somehow, over their furious urgency, they heard Trilby and Reddy in the passage:

Reddy scolding Trilby for not folding some linens properly for Miss Hapgood's trunk and Trilby stammering her defense.

Mr. Rotherwood's arms fell back to his sides, and without their support (or any of the blood flow those arms had cut off), Hetty promptly collapsed back into her chair.

There was a firm knock at the door, and Reddy entered. If she noticed the dishevelment and rapid breathing of either, she was too good a servant to let it show. "Miss, will you be wanting your woolen cloak laundered before you go?"

"I—I can't imagine why," Hetty said, trying not to pant and hoping her mouth was not noticeably swollen. "It'll just get dirty again on the road."

Reddy bobbed in response and went out, shutting the door behind her.

It was a tiny interruption, but enough to break the spell—the madness which had overtaken them.

Mr. Rotherwood stared down at her. With an effort he unclenched his fists and flexed his fingers.

"Miss Hapgood, surely my behavior just now is enough to convince you that I do not offer for you out of an excess of nobility. Indeed, an impartial witness to what passed would be excused for thinking nobility had nothing to do with it."

She cleared her throat. "Your—point—ahem—is well taken, sir."

"Look at me, Hetty."

He waited for her to comply. Slowly, she raised her head, her face bright as a sunset.

"For the third time—is it the third?—I ask you to be my wife. Not because you compromised yourself. Not because I am noble. But because I am in love with you." A tentative smile spread over his countenance. "I said it," he said. "I did it. I have been trying to say that to you since—well—for a while now. I—love you. Will you be my wife?"

If this was love born out of a sacrificial impulse, she thought, it was indistinguishable from the genuine article.

She knew what she wanted. She wanted to hurl herself back into his arms and say Yes, *Yes,* she would marry him, because she loved him every bit as much as he loved her. *He loved her!*

Pressing hands to her feverish eyes, Hetty struggled to slow her pulse and to make her mind engage again. Think. She must think. Not feel. Think. She should do an arithmetic problem. What could be more ordinary? More mundane? What, say, was 124 times 19? Well, 124 times 20 would be...would be 2480, and then one would subtract 124 for a total of—of—subtract the 4—2476—then the 20—2456—and lastly the 100—2356. 124 times 19 was 2356.

"Hetty." He broke into her calculations. "Answer me. What are you thinking?"

She lowered her hands. "I was thinking of arithmetic. I was making a calculation." But it had worked. She could think again. Although it helped if she didn't look right at him.

He was probably the only man on earth who would not blink at such a response. "And what were you calculating?"

"Nothing of any importance," she dismissed this. "Mr. Rotherwood—and you really oughtn't to call me Hetty—how are things with your mother?"

He shifted restlessly. Marched away from her and then returned. Took a seat across from her. "Listen to me, Het—Miss Hapgood, rather. My mother—will learn—to love—this match."

Sorrow shadowed Hetty's face. "Then she has not yet begun to change her opinion? I thought as much. The few times I have seen her since the engagement dinner, she and I have not spoken. And because our engagement was not a true engagement, I did not think it appropriate to approach her or try to make it better. But if *she* believes it a true engagement and still does not...does not want to..."

St. John said nothing. The atmosphere in North Audley Street had been strained for the past week, as both mother and son avoided what occupied each of them ceaselessly. St. John hoped that his mother would come to accept his decision, while Anne hoped that her son's resolve would waver. Which of these hopes was the more foolish remained to be seen, but neither one seemed in immediate danger of giving ground. They talked of anything but the engagement when they did talk, but topics were dwindling that did not touch at some point on the sensitive subject. Anne once jokingly mentioned Mr. Pinckney's latest suitor reports, only to have St. John bristle, and she could tell by the set of his jaw that he had not forgiven the solicitor. Another time she said with a laugh, "We really ought to attend Almack's again, my love. After all, we paid for our vouchers and have used them only once," to which he quietly replied, "As I am an engaged man, and as you have no wish to remarry, there seems little point in showing our faces anymore at the Marriage Mart. Therefore we must consider the vouchers as a loss." Anne never raised the matter again.

In Mr. Rotherwood's silence, Hetty read the truth of the situation, and it helped to shore up her battered resolve.

"Mr. Rotherwood," she began, addressing his left shoulder as she had often done in the early days, "now more than ever I can honestly say I am moved and honored and flattered by your willingness to marry me—"

"Not 'willingness,'" he interrupted in a hard voice, already guessing that she was going to be obstinate. "Say my desire to marry you. My fervent desire."

"Yes. Very well, then. Your desire," she amended primly. "I admit that—kissing you—was quite—er—pleasant. Quite pleasant. And—and—and—if marriage were nothing but kissing, I suppose we would do nicely. But it is not."

"Harriet Hapgood," he broke in again sternly, in his most tutor-ish manner, "before you reject me again, answer me this: do you return my feelings?"

Groaning, she clapped her hands to her face again. "I told you not to call me by my Christian name!"

"I deserve an answer," he persisted. "And I will have one. Do you return my feelings?"

"Do not ask me that!"

"Do you, you wretched girl?"

"I—I—"

"Because if you can say you do not, after what has passed between us," he resumed, "I will accept my defeat. I will go my way and trust to time and effort to...conquer this. But if you do return my feelings—if you can give me hope that you already, or might one day, love me as I love you, then I refuse to give way to your fears."

"They're not my *fears*," she insisted, meeting his gaze once again with fire in her own. "*Fears* refer to—to imagined perils—to phantasms—to threats that have life only in the mind. I do not *fear* that your mother will hate me and that any marriage will cause a painful break of some sort, I *know* it! She already hates me. You cannot deny it. She disliked me even before the Argyll Rooms, but that sorry episode of mine was the nail in the coffin. Oh, Mr. Rotherwood—if you and I were to marry, what would our life be like? It's easy enough to say love conquers all, but I have seen situations where the victory proves hollow. Don't you see? As water wears away a stone, happiness can be eroded, can be undermined, by persistent, determined opposition. This is what I wish to avoid.

"And I will not lie to you and say I don't care for you, Mr. Rotherwood," she went on. "What would be the use in that? If I had responded to Mr. Pickford's kiss as I did to yours, how differently everything would have turned out!

"It is just as well that I am retiring to Somerset for a while. We must not allow—this—to happen again, or I will end up marrying you in spite of myself. Let me go away for a time."

St. John replaced his beaver hat upon his head and rose. For a man who had been rejected a third time, he did not appear unduly discouraged, and it had everything to do with Hetty's admission. Which he could not resist wanting to hear again.

"Allow me to clarify two things, Miss Hapgood, and then I will leave you in peace. Firstly, I am to understand that you do, in fact, care for me...?"

In response she only scowled, which drew a grin from him. "Thank you. And secondly, does the offer still stand that, if my mother comes to you herself, and if she tells you herself that she would like you for a daughter and that she blesses the match, then you will relent?"

The utter unlikeliness of this made her eyes narrow further in suspicion. But after a pause, she gave him a grudging nod.

"Then I bid you good day and a safe journey," he said cheerfully. Darting at her before she could react, he planted another kiss on her lips, this one gentle.

"My own Hetty."

CHAPTER TWENTY-SIX

Soon after this period, her anxiety was awakened by the indisposition of her father, who was attacked with a fever; which, though not thought to be of a dangerous kind, gave a severe shock to his constitution.
— Ann Radcliffe, *The Mysteries of Udolpho* (1794)

When Hetty left for Somerset, she imagined a visit of perhaps a fortnight—a month at the longest. But it was the beginning of March before circumstances improved to the point where the clamor from London began to outweigh the demands of home.

When her uncle deposited her in Patterton, carefully passing the night at the Swan, lest he catch something from his Hapgood relations, Hetty found her family's cozy lodgings in an alarming state: her stepmother and younger sister bedridden, the servants either ill themselves or harried, and her father sleepless and wan.

"Oh, Papa!" she cried, dismayed to find him aged and afraid his poor looks were not solely attributable to the influenza in circulation. "I am here. Let me help."

There was much to be done. While both her stepmother and Rosie were just as her father had described and not in ultimate danger, according to Mr. Lewis the doctor, they were both greatly weakened and helpless. Mrs. Hapgood suffered headaches and only longed to lie quietly, a dampened cloth over her eyes and forehead, but Rosie was fretful, and Hetty knew her discomfort must be extreme to make her so. Caroline Sidney's recommendation to hire a nurse would have been a good one, had the grippe not swept through the county. Over at Bramleigh the squire, the housekeeper, and the cook were all laid low, with Mrs. Hapgood—the one who ordinarily complained of ill health—ironically spared. "Though she has taken to her bed in any case," Hugh said, "out of distress for the others." At the vicarage the Benfields all had it and one of their pupils, and Mr. Lewis was of the opinion that this sickness would likely carry off the vicar's aged mother.

Just when Rosemary Hapgood and little Rosie grew strong enough by the end of January to sit up and speak and take broth and bread, Hugh Hapgood finally gave way, and he was in danger for a period. Hetty took to falling asleep at the table or whenever she happened to sit down for longer than a minute. She had too much time altogether to think about Mr. Rotherwood, but this was counterbalanced by too little energy to work herself into a fit about him.

He did not write, but Hetty heard of him regularly and indirectly through Caroline. "Mr. Elwood says he ran into Mr. Rotherwood at the stationer's in Pall Mall, and Mr. R asked again after your family's health." "Today we saw Mr. Rotherwood in Kensington Gardens, and he is very sorry to hear that your father is now ailing." "Driving in Hyde Park today and saw Mr. R riding. He asks me to send his wishes for your continued strength and health and hopes you will take care." "At the Stanleys' supper, Mr. Rotherwood asked if there were any books he might send you. He would like to send fruit, but he suspects that, through either thievery or rough handling, it would not survive the journey." "When we saw him at the theatre, Mr. Rotherwood said he was sorry Mr. Hapgood's health would not allow him to receive visitors, or he would have liked to go down to Somerset himself."

For several weeks Hetty was too weary even to feel envy of all these meetings and occasions for amusement. Her time in London seemed eons ago. But as the women in her family recuperated, they began sharing the care of Hugh; and as the demands on her diminished, Hetty's longing to see Mr. Rotherwood and the Sidneys again grew in proportion.

Caroline's letters came less frequently now, mostly because Hetty had been too careworn to be a satisfying correspondent, but as she re-read the earlier missives, she now felt pangs for all the things she was missing. How busy they all were, and how the fashionable world continued to bowl along, with or without her! She was disappointed that Mr. Rotherwood did not write and then angry with herself for being disappointed.

How could he not write? Single gentlemen and single young ladies did not correspond, of course, but they were allowed if they were engaged, and were not she and Mr. Rotherwood supposedly engaged? Should he not have written, if only to keep up the pretense that they were so? Unless it was a pretense he had lost interest in maintaining.

But Hetty could not make sense of that either, after what had passed at their last meeting. Mr. Rotherwood was no Mr. Pickford, to grab a girl and kiss her senseless and have it mean nothing. Then why, why, why? Was it because of Mrs. Rotherwood? He had been so…confident almost, that his mother could be persuaded in the end. Perhaps he was finding it as impossible as Hetty predicted, and he had not the heart to tell her.

Gradually Hugh Hapgood gathered strength, but it fretted his family to see how slowly. Even the squire was up and about again, despite the fitful state of his heart, and baskets of food were sent from Bramleigh: roast duck, broth and bread and preserves.

"He will recover completely, will he not?" Hetty asked Mr. Lewis after he came down from seeing the patient. "I can never remember a time when he was ill before."

"He is older now, Miss Hapgood," answered the doctor. "And he was worn down from tending Mrs. Hapgood and Miss Rosalie."

"But he will recover?" she pressed, a hand at her heart. Imagine if, after years of everyone thinking of her father as the heir to Bramleigh, the squire were to outlive him!

"I believe he will. Truly. But it will be slow. And you must take more rest yourself, Miss Hapgood. You are pale and thinner than when you came. I would not like to see you fall ill as well."

"Yes, sir," she agreed absently. "How are your other patients? I am sorry Mrs. Benfield has died, but Mr. and Miss Benfield are much better, I hear."

"They are. But I am afraid Mr. Thomas pushed himself too hard in caring for his parishioners. He is not a young man, you know. I do not think he will last much longer."

"Not Father Thomas?" breathed Hetty. "Oh, dear. He has been the curate at Bramleigh for ages. Ages and ages! That will be a sad loss for them."

"Indeed. I do what I can to keep him comfortable," the doctor sighed. "It will be an unwelcome shock to the rector of Bramleigh. I do not believe that man has set foot in the parish these twenty years. He will have to now—at least until another overworked and underpaid curate can be found to relieve him again."

Altogether it was a grim season. It was left to Hetty to call on the Benfields and condole them on the loss of their mother and to Hetty to venture to Bramleigh and thank them for the baskets. Another letter from Edith, forwarded by Lavinia Sidney, brightened one day with its descriptions of the journey to Paris, Paris itself, and more art art art. But Hetty could not hand the letter around to be read because of one particular passage:

When I read your account of the masquerade in the
Argyll Rooms and its aftermath, you may imagine

I did not recover quickly! Oh, Hetty, what enormous consequences attend our little acts of mischief, now that we are grown older. That wretched Mr. Pickford! I wanted to kick him myself for his conduct to you. That, and I wanted to kiss Mr. Rotherwood in thankfulness for coming to your rescue. No wonder you love him, and I know I will love him too. I know this is not how you would have liked an engagement to come about—in any way—but need that be a reason to reject it? And, yes, Mr. Rotherwood is being noble, but need that be a reason to reject him? Because I do not believe many noble gentlemen would offer for a woman they disliked. He may not express it, but I am sure he must care for you. I do understand the problem with his mother, however. I am fortunate in Mrs. Hugh Hapgood as a future mother-in-law, for a more kind and just woman does not exist. I may say honestly that I do not think I would be able to bear it either, if I knew my husband's mother hated me.

Oh, dear. I seem to have talked myself out of supporting the match. But that is me, Hetty. You know how timid I am. It would make me miserable to be despised by someone I wanted to love, but I daresay you could ignore it. You are so much bolder and more confident than I!

*I must stop now, for we are going out, but do write soon
and tell me where things stand...*

Edith might call Hetty "bolder and more confident" than she, and
just a few short months ago Hetty would have agreed, but now...?
Now, in those intervening months Hetty had encountered things
altogether new to her and learned some sharp lessons. As in, it was
easy to approve of oneself, until one felt the overwhelming weight
of social disapproval, including the disapproval of perfect strangers!
It was easy to approve of oneself, until the yardstick one always
used was snatched away and replaced with a new one—one which
might appear nonsensical, but which nevertheless was the accepted
standard.

If in this new world, Hetty was become as timid as Edith, then at
least she had Edith's agreement that marriage was unthinkable, if it
brought that disapproval into the circle of one's closest intimates.

Yes, Edith's agreement was a comfort, Hetty thought. But it was
a cold one.

Anne Rotherwood rejoiced when she learned Miss Hapgood was
absenting herself for an indeterminate period. How could it harm
matters, for both St. John and Miss Hapgood to have a space for reflection? Anne was careful, however, to hide all signs of satisfaction
and even went so far as to say, "How admirable of Miss Hapgood to
answer her father's summons. Few young ladies would be willing to
abandon London mid-season, in order to sit beside family sickbeds."

St. John regarded her as if he would read her motivations, but
she bore it steadily, and then he replied, "Yes. Family is very dear to

her. Those fortunate enough to be connected with Miss Hapgood would never have cause to complain."

This was a jab too near the bone, and Anne would have dropped the subject, but her son chose to take this as a sign that they must have the matter out again. They had rubbed along well enough for some weeks by avoiding all mention of Miss Hapgood, St. John because he hoped for time and better acquaintance to operate on his mother, and Anne because she never wished to hear the girl's name again. But all good things must come to an end, she supposed, even unspoken armistices.

"Madam, you have had some weeks now to accustom yourself to the idea of my marrying Miss Hapgood," he began, "and I would gladly hear how you fare."

They were driving in Hyde Park where the road was hard with frost and few riders braved the cold. Temperatures were low, yes, but there would be no frost fair as there was a year ago. St. John smiled fleetingly, remembering accosting Miss Hapgood on the subject at Lady Aurora's rout.

Anne saw the smile and took heart. This need not drive a wedge between them. He was still her devoted son who might eventually be brought round to understand his new position in society. She must tread softly, in the meantime. She must give as much ground as she could, without giving up the object itself.

"I have indeed given it much thought," she answered. "And, as I just said, I admire her affection for her family. Moreover, I believe your generosity to her has done much to rehabilitate her reputation." Hearing his impatient breath, she hastened to add,

"And—and I think she has gained in wisdom from the whole affair and would not find herself in such a scrape again."

"Therefore...?" he prompted.

Anne adjusted her gloves and then affected to catch sight of an acquaintance. She lifted two fingers in a wave, but when this charade was finished and she sat back, he was still watching her and waiting.

"My dear St. John, remember how you told Mr. Pinckney that you wanted to explore the life of a man of fashion and rank?"

"And so I have."

"Hardly!" she laughed. "Can a mere few months satisfy this desire? Supposing—supposing you were to wait another year to marry? Why, there would be another bevy of young ladies to consider—some of them might even vie with Lady Sylvia for beauty. It is a sad fact that nursing her relations has likely exacted a toll on Miss Hapgood's fresh looks, and every day she risks catching the illness herself."

He was silent, partly because he shared this anxiety that Miss Hapgood would fall ill and partly because he was absorbing the disappointment of his mother's unmoved position.

"Tempting as these hypothetical young ladies might be," he said dryly, "the fact remains that I am already engaged to the woman of my choosing."

"And...you think you might prefer her to any others?"

"I know so. And I persist in believing that you will share my admiration for Miss Hapgood, if you would only permit yourself."

"Oh, I do admire her!" Anne seized upon this. "She is, as you say, quite clever, and she is pretty enough—or she was, when last I saw her—but—but—"

"But what, madam? You still cannot bring yourself to give your blessing?"

"Oh, St. John!" cried his mother, cornered. "If you only understood! If you only fathomed who you are now—it is my fault. Had I married whom my father wished, you would have grown up with a full awareness of what was due to you."

"Had you married whom your father wished, I would not exist," he returned. "For I am a product of both my parents."

"You know what I mean. Had I not displeased my father, you would have known all your life what it was to be a baronet's grandson and wealthy and landed, and you would have—hardly noticed a girl like this Miss Hapgood. Who is, indeed, a very good sort of girl for her station."

He straightened, and there was fire in his eye. Anne felt all a-flutter at this. Her good, good son, who had never shown her an unkindness! Only see how she would lose him, when once they had been each other's all in all!

"Mother," he began again in a steely voice, "you must listen to me. Our shared experience has yielded different outcomes. You wish you might return to your youth and make a different choice, that you might never have been estranged from your family, nor experienced the privations you found so humiliating. I, on the other hand, having known only those privations, am discovering that the 'life of a man of fashion and rank' holds little charm for me, if it means I cannot marry the woman I would choose no matter my station in life."

"Oh, St. John!"

"When Miss Hapgood returns from Somerset," he continued inexorably, "I ask you to go to her and tell her you will receive her as your daughter-in-law. Surely you would not like to repeat your father's treatment of you?"

"You cannot compel me to love her!" she protested.

"I cannot," he admitted. "But you must understand that I have made my choice. I will tell you frankly that the reason a date for the wedding has not been set is that Miss Hapgood desires your blessing. To marry without it would grieve me as well, but my mind is made up. If I did not know, in my heart of hearts, that Miss Hapgood is worthy of your love, I would be a cruel son to ask this of you. But I do know it. And you, who are always so quick to praise my character and judgment, must trust to those things once again, until you find—and I believe you ultimately will find—that you can love her."

With that, he rapped on the roof of the coach. "I will walk home, that we may each have time to think."

Poor Anne waited until she was alone, after St. John had waved away assistance and sprung down himself. When the coach was in motion again she twitched down the brocade window coverings, her mind too full to acknowledge passersby.

It was come to this?

It was come to this.

Miss Hapgood's weeks of absence had not availed in weakening the hold she had on St. John, and Anne knew her son well enough to recognize when he was immoveable. When he was stone. He had decided upon this insignificant, scandalous girl, when he might have had anyone, and Anne must either yield to it or lose him.

How many times in her life had she bewailed her father's iron coldness and his rejection of her own marriage? How many times had she wished Sir Gordon would soften enough to recognize the qualities of her chosen husband? Qualities which, she now admitted, he had passed on to his son. If overweening pride came from the Holts, kindness and humility were the gift of the Rotherwoods.

She and St. John had come to the fork in the road at last, and she could no longer put off her choice or deceive herself that there was any other direction to be taken. It was either follow where he led or strike out alone on the other road away from him.

It did not take Anne long to decide.

She could never, never lose St. John. Cost what it might to grovel to this nobody Miss Hapgood, Anne would do it. She could never bear to cast off her son as her father had her. In the end, what had he gained by it? Through his stubbornness, Sir Gordon had lost the chance to love and be loved by a very good son-in-law; he had lost his daughter, who had once been the apple of his eye; and he had foregone any relationship whatever with the best of grandsons. Only see how St. John felt nothing for the Holts! If one day he and this Miss Hapgood were to have children, Anne could not bear for them not to know her and love her. And if she were to pass the rest of her life apart from the only one who was dear to her—

No. Her hands took hold of the edge of the carriage seat, as if to brace herself for the revelation unfolding in her mind.

It was worth anything, submission to this.

Worth any price.

She would do it. She would do as her son asked. She would go to this Miss Hapgood.

A little pain sliced through her heart as she made up her mind, but, like the lancing of a painful swelling, it was not without its accompanying, sweet relief.

Chapter Twenty-Seven

It seemed too much trouble to ask her Uncle Sidney to come down again and take her back to London, but equally unappealing was to press her father to do it. By the end of February, everyone was recovered, but Hugh moved more slowly than he had used to and required more rest. Hetty would have to beg her uncle to come when least inconvenient, she decided, and she counted on Caroline to apply pressure from the other side.

Before final arrangements could be made, however, history intervened.

"'I regret to say,'" Hugh read aloud at the breakfast table one morning, "'that plans to retrieve Harriet from Somerset must be postponed. We ourselves will be leaving town for Crawley shortly because the rumors of unrest grow daily. Crowds have gathered around Parliament and the houses of several MPs and lords while the Corn Bill is debated, and its passage will surely mean rioting. While Devonshire Street seems a safe distance from any gathering points, we elect to take no chances. Please express our regrets to Hetty, and we hope to hear again, etc., etc.'"

"I don't understand. What is happening?"

He sighed. "It's a bill to protect corn prices. With the peace, grain from the Continent becomes available again, and prices go down. If farmers make less money, they may not be able to pay their rents. But if you maintain the high, wartime price of corn, the poor are understandably angry."

"Will there really be riots, Papa?"

"I would not be surprised. Your uncle is wise to retreat to Sussex, but I am sorry your amusement must be put off after you have already made such a sacrifice of time."

"Oh, Papa!" Reaching across the table, she pressed his hand. "Please don't fret about something so silly as my 'amusement.' I already enjoyed my share. Nor would I have been able to go to balls and card parties and such, knowing you all needed me. It's no sacrifice when I would not have been happy otherwise."

No sooner did she say the words than she thought, as she often did, of Mr. Rotherwood. Maybe he was right. If you loved, sacrifice became less a noble thing and more a matter of course. You did it because you would not be happy otherwise. And because you would not be happy otherwise, the sacrifice was no sacrifice!

What would she have felt, if her father and stepmother and Rosie all jeered at her for being "noble" in returning to Somerset, when the truth was simply that she loved them?

Ah, she thought. *I have been misguided and even cruel.*

No, the only thing she regretted in not returning to London, was that she would not see Mr. Rotherwood. What were he and his mother going to do? Did any members of Parliament or famous lords live in North Audley Street? The Rotherwoods could not escape to their estate of Glennard for it had been let, had it not?

"Papa," she said, when she had taken her seat again, "do you think it would be improper of me to write to Mr. Rotherwood—or to his mother Mrs. Rotherwood—just to ask if they are well?"

Hugh set down his cup of tea to mull this over. "Have you changed your mind about marrying him?"

She knew she was turning scarlet, and she crumbled the toast on her plate. "I think—I have always liked him, you know. And I—like him—even more now." She did not add that her liking seemed to be growing minute by minute as she understood him and the human heart better. "But I have told him that we could not really marry as long as Mrs. Rotherwood was so opposed. She doesn't like me at all, Papa. I am not rich enough or beautiful enough or exalted enough for her. She wanted Mr. Rotherwood to marry an earl's daughter named Lady Sylvia—you remember her—you met her when you first brought me to London. Lady Sylvia is all those things Mrs. Rotherwood likes, but..."

"But that is neither here nor there, if her son doesn't want her," finished Hugh.

"Do you think I should marry him, Papa, even without her approval?" Mr. Rotherwood would have recognized (and been melted by) the pleading eyes Hetty turned on her father, and Hugh did not fall far short of this. She half wanted her father to persuade her, but her honest nature required her to lay out all the facts.

"Mr. Rotherwood says she would come to love me, but she does not show the least hint of it, Papa. And I would hate, hate, hate to cause a rift between them, after all the early hardships they underwent, precisely because Mrs. Rotherwood's father disapproved of her marriage. Would it not be dreadful for history to repeat itself, sir?"

His mouth set in grim lines, and Hugh had to swallow the first few responses that rose to his lips. Who was this tiresome proud woman who would disdain so fine a young lady as his Harriet? She might go farther and fare worse, where daughters-in-law were concerned. And what use would a title be, in such tumultuous days, except to get a rock thrown through your window for protecting your wealthy interests?

But after he mastered himself he said only, "If he truly does care for you, Mrs. Rotherwood may find history repeating itself even if she succeeds In keeping you apart. He seemed a rational, intelligent, thoughtful young man, and he will surely resent his mother judging for him in this matter, as if he were a child."

That only made Hetty feel worse. Was the damage done, then? Should she then give in and tell Mr. Rotherwood she would marry him, and hope the happiness they found in each other would outweigh the unhappiness of family division?

"If Mrs. Rotherwood feels so strongly about this," she whispered, "it must mean she came to regret marrying Mr. Rotherwood's father. And if—if Mr. Rotherwood ever came to regret marrying me—oh, Papa! It would break my heart!"

She did cry then, and her stepmother came rushing in, and there was much fussing and explaining and sniffling and embarrassment, but it ended in Hugh saying, "You need not decide today, Hetty. You are tired and disappointed. Let it rest a few days, and then we will discuss it again."

Hetty did not write. She waited, and, as the days went by, the reports from town worsened. The riots and violence and property destruction continued, and soldiers were called in. But soon enough even the turbulent passing of the Corn Bill was eclipsed by the news from the Continent: Napoleon had escaped Elba, landed in France, and was marching on Paris with a swelling army!

Her first thoughts were for Edith, and she hastened to Bramleigh to find the squire and Mrs. Hapgood panicked, the squire stamping and blustering and threatening to join his majesty's army and his wife wailing and fainting, while the dogs cowered and the housekeeper Macready managed as best she could.

"But have you heard from Edith or Mr. Arbuthnot?" Hetty asked insistently.

"Nothing, nothing," growled the squire.

"Alwyn! Edith! Oh, my dears!" Mrs. Hapgood shrieked, flapping her handkerchief and collapsing against the back of the sofa.

"Now, madam," said Macready waving the *sal volatile* beneath her mistress' nose. "What did Mr. Lewis say about keeping calm?"

"Mr. Lewis does not have a daughter and a brother in France! Oh! Heaven have mercy! Richard, why did we ever let her go?"

"I'll show Boney what exile is!" bellowed her husband. "Hanging's too good for him! Where's my rifle?"

"Richard, you cannot go," his wife protested, sitting up. "If we were to lose you too, whatever would become of us?"

The squire gave the carpet a kick. "That'll be Hugh's problem. Wellington will need every Englishman with two arms, if we are ever to be rid of this tyrant."

"Well, if it comes to that, then he'll need Papa too," Hetty pointed out.

"What? Nonsense. Your father can barely walk for two minutes together after his recent illness."

"And *you* have a weakened heart," she retorted. Clearly she must take charge and talk sense, if she wanted Edith to have anyone to come home to. "Come now, Mr. Hapgood. You cannot join his majesty's army at your age and in your health, and I will not be responsible for something happening to you, when everybody already has so much on his mind. And who would read the order for the burial of the dead for you, now that poor Mr. Thomas has died?"

"That worthless rector will have to," said the squire, nothing daunted. "You should have seen the man when he dragged himself away from his idleness in town to read our service. What a picture of woe! He will have to part with more of his tithes if he wants to lure a new curate to Bramleigh."

But the alarming redness of his face was receding, and Mrs. Hapgood appeared decidedly more cheerful. "Oh, Hetty," she said, "you were a troublesome child, but you have grown into a helpful young lady."

"Thank you, madam," Hetty grinned.

"You should come to see us more often. We have been quite lonely without any of our girls about, haven't we, Richard?" (He grunted assent.) "How glad we will be when Edith returns and marries Lionel. We have been refurbishing a set of rooms for them—did Mrs. Hugh Hapgood tell you?"

"She did. And you both could not be more anxious than I am to have her safely home again," Hetty answered. "I suppose Lionel will be down upon us all next, for you know he will think it easier to come all the way from Oxford than to write to us for news."

"Well, when he arrives, you must all be sure to come for supper."

From the first-floor bedroom she shared with her sister in Patterton, Hetty had a good view of the mail coach arriving at the Swan, and she took care to peek from the window the next morning to see if Lionel descended. When he did not, there was nothing for it but to see if the next day brought him.

That afternoon, as she sat in the parlor reading, a carriage clattered up. Lionel! Had he come with the Clinketts? Leaping up to fetch her father and stepmother, a knock at the door checked her. Her brother would never knock.

Hetty slipped back into the parlor to let Olcott answer it, and she felt her stomach plummet when she heard a voice say, "Mrs. Rotherwood here to see Miss Hapgood, if she is at home."

Mrs. Rotherwood? This, she had not been prepared for.

Was the woman come to announce that she blessed her son's match with Harriet Hapgood? It seemed impossible, and yet what other earthly reason could she have to come down to Somerset and present herself?

Hetty had a childish urge to run upstairs and hide, but then there was Olcott looking in, eyebrows raised in question.

After two attempts to voice her assent, Hetty gave up and nodded. Then she retreated to the chair she had lately occupied and took up her book. The next moment she cast it aside as "too frivolous" and scrambled for her neglected and disorganized workbasket.

"Mrs. Anne Rotherwood," announced Olcott.

It was the same Mrs. Rotherwood—clothed in blue-black, faded blonde hair, impeccably dressed—and yet not the same. For one, her color was high and the usual cool hauteur was absent from her gaze.

She and Hetty made their curtseys and then stood regarding each other until Hetty remembered herself and gestured at the sofa. Ought she to call her parents? Should she send Olcott for refreshment from the Swan?

"I—hope your journey was pleasant," Hetty began at last, nervously twisting her sewing into a rope.

Anne Rotherwood was no more at ease. She hardly knew how to begin, and yet she must begin. She too saw that Miss Hapgood was not quite as she remembered. In the weeks of her absence, she had grown paler and thinner. The brightness of her hair imparted a false sense of bloom. But her eyes were still clear and direct, if wary.

Anne wished she could take Miss Hapgood's hand—it would be a comfort to have something to hang onto—but an unbridgeable chasm seemed to divide them. And yet she must build the bridge herself, if she could.

"Thank you," she murmured. "The roads were hard and dry. Please tell me how your family is. I was sorry to hear they were unwell."

Hetty's own color rose, knowing one of Mrs. Rotherwood's chief objections to her was the comparative anonymity and humbleness of the Hugh Hapgoods. "They are recovered. I thank you."

"How glad I am. And...were you not planning on returning to town?"

"I was, madam, but the late unrest has chased my Sidney relations back to Sussex for the present, and even if it had not, my own father would hesitate to send me there. Did the—violence—come near North Audley Street?"

"It came as near as Berkeley Square," Mrs. Rotherwood answered with a shudder, and the two women exchanged their first sympathetic look. "We were not much out of doors those several days. Things grew more settled when they brought the soldiers in, and then—with the news from France—"

Another silence fell. Anne bit her lip. She must bring the conversation back to the matter at hand.

"I know, my dear Miss Hapgood, that we—stumbled at the very threshold of our acquaintanceship. I was...cold and—and harsher with you than—I was harsh with you," she finished. "When we spoke at the engagement dinner—you recall? You resented my treatment, I know."

Hetty began to tremble. She could hardly fail to remember their earlier conversation, and yet she wondered now how she had mustered the courage to be pert with this woman. There was no pertness in her now. Now, on the brink of having her every wish granted, Hetty thought the moment might incapacitate her.

"You know of our history, St. John's and mine," Mrs. Rotherwood went on, when Hetty said nothing. "You know he is all I have in the whole world. Surely, Miss Hapgood, you can understand a mother in my situation being a thousand times more cautious and protective than a mother with twenty sons."

Hetty managed to make a vague sound in her throat.

"And such a son as he is," Mrs. Rotherwood went on, her voice tightening. "A good, good man. Noble—" (Hetty smothered a squeak here) "—gentle, faithful. He has been the best son I could ever have asked for, and—and—and—I know he will be just such a husband."

Hetty could not speak; the tears which threatened choked any possible reply.

"Miss Hapgood, you may have guessed why I have come." And then Anne did reach hesitantly for Hetty's hand, unwinding it from her strangled sewing. "I have come to say that it would…give me great joy to see you married to my son. I offer my blessing, if it would matter to you."

"It matters," whispered Hetty.

Anne's grip on her tightened. "I know I have been proud and disagreeable. You don't like me, I suppose. I haven't deserved for you to like me. But—but I hope you can grow to, Miss Hapgood. Hetty. Grow to love me. As I—like you and—fully expect to love you. St. John assures me I will love you more and more, the more I know you, and I trust no one's judgment as I do his."

Hetty's face was turned away through this speech, and Anne had one crippling instant of thinking that she was going to refuse. That this girl would not marry St. John, even with Anne's approval, and perhaps her refusal stemmed from Anne's own obstinacy and pride being carried on past bearing, and St. John would be heartbroken, and then he would blame his mother, and the dreaded estrangement would come, and all would end in wretched alienation and abandonment and loneliness—

"Will you not have him, Hetty?"

Hetty gulped. She was getting a pain in her temple from trying not to cry, and then the battle was lost in any event because one single tear overflowed, the precursor to the utter collapse of the dam.

And then the two women were in each other's arms, weeping, and Anne was thanking God repeatedly, thinking she was doing it in her mind but actually muttering it aloud, and Hetty didn't hear her because she was sobbing herself, "Oh, Mrs. Rotherwood! Oh! Mrs. Rotherwood!"

It was some time before calm was restored. Before the two of them could release each other, smiling ruefully, to restore order with their handkerchiefs. Hetty hopped up to find her parents, and then there were introductions to be made and an invitation to tea and supper, and her family did not need to ask her the significance of Mrs. Rotherwood's visit because the glow of Hetty's face told the story.

"Will you come back with me to London tomorrow, my dearest girl?" Anne asked at the end of the evening. "I know your Sidney relations are not in Devonshire Street at present, but you might stay with us now."

Hetty shrunk, trying to imagine bursting from the coach in North Audley Street and announcing to Mr. Rotherwood that, not only was she willing to marry him now, but she was come to stay!

"Madam, your offer is too kind and hospitable. But perhaps you might tell him how our time together went first."

Anne laughed at this. "Very well, my suddenly modest mouse. Though you have nothing to fear. I know all too well my St. John is not the sort of man to change his mind."

Chapter Twenty-Eight

I entirely release you from any engagement. No contract can be binding between parties who have not a full power to make it at the time, nor ever afterwards acquire the power of fulfilling it.
— Henry Fielding, *Tom Jones* (1749)

Mrs. Rotherwood took her fond leave the following morning, eager to return to town with the good news, and no sooner had the Holt coach rattled off than the mail coach rattled in, bearing Lionel, who bounded down from his outside seat almost before they were come to a halt.

"What are you so happy about?" he demanded. "Have you heard from Edith?"

Guiltily, she shook her head. "Not a thing. But surely they are headed back to England. They must have heard of Napoleon's return even sooner than we did, in Paris. And heaven knows Aunt Eliza does not lack for funds. Any horse and carriage money can secure will be theirs."

"All the same..."

He had half a mind to travel to Dover, and thence to Calais, but his father succeeded in pointing out the futility of such a plan. "All will be chaos, and you will only add to it, and the odds of you missing each other are great. To ease their minds at Bramleigh, I have already sent a letter to the inn in Dover from which the Arbuthnots and Edith departed, instructing them to send an express to us as soon as ever they land. If anything, you might go to London, for they will have news from the Continent before it makes its way out to Somerset."

"Miss." It was Olcott. She deposited a letter beside Hetty's plate.

"Edith?" cried Lionel, reaching for it.

Hetty slapped his hand away and studied the direction. "I don't know this hand."

"I do," said her brother, peering over. "That's Rotherwood's. Has he never written you a note yet? Why, I've written Edith four times."

Ignoring him, she excused herself and fled to the parlor. She slid her finger under the seal, aware of her racing heart. Mrs. Rotherwood could not have given him the good news yet, but he must have anticipated it, knowing that the mere fact of his mother going down to Somerset signaled victory for him.

In fact, Hetty found her first letter from Mr. Rotherwood nothing that she expected.

28 North Audley Street
London

16 March 1815

My dear Miss Hapgood,
We have not spoken since you left London in January, as you know. Though I did not write, I was glad to hear through the Sidneys of your family's recuperation and hope you have continued in health, despite what must have been a wearing time.

It is with the utmost respect for you and the promise of my enduring regard that I now take up pen to say I am releasing you from even the semblance of an engagement we agreed to. It has served its purpose, for which I am grateful, and I wish you every happiness in the future.

If my mother has not yet left Somerset, I request that you say nothing of this to her. I would prefer to explain matters myself when I see her again, if the truth can be kept from her that long.

Your obedient servant,

St. John Rotherwood

Hetty had no words. She could hardly make sense of what she read.

He was ending their pseudo-engagement on the very cusp of it becoming a genuine engagement? He knew his mother had come down to see her, and yet he "released" her?

She felt dizzy and tried to take deeper breaths. Had he tried to dissuade his mother from seeing her at all? Had they somehow exchanged places, with Mrs. Rotherwood now in favor of the match and her son opposed?

But how could that be? How could he write this, after their last interview? When he kissed her and claimed to love her? When he seemed so elated by the confession he had wrung from her?

He cannot have fallen in love with somebody else, she argued with herself. *Not this quickly.* It was not that she thought herself unforgettable; it was that it was not in his nature. Lightness was not. Inconstancy was not.

She read the letter again, her mind slowly beginning to recover from its initial shock. There was some mystery here. Something which he did not want Hetty to tell Mrs. Rotherwood—as if Hetty even guessed at what it was! He could not be referring to the breaking of the engagement. About that—something which would embarrass Hetty equally—he would trust her to keep her mouth shut.

Oh, how she wished now that she had accepted Mrs. Rotherwood's offer to return to London! Then she might have descended from the carriage, marched straight up to him, and dared him to say such things to her face. What right had he to end their *faux* engagement with no explanation?

The door opened, and there was her brother. "Well? What does Rotherwood have to say for himself, or is it too sentimental to share?"

"Too sentimental," said Hetty, folding the letter up with resolution. She was finding anger a convenient substitute for puzzlement and hurt. "What have you decided? Are you going to town?"

"I am. I've got a little time before Trinity Term because I convinced Bagley to give me my exam early."

"Then take me with you, Lionel. The Sidneys have gone to shelter in Sussex, so I must stay with you. Are you thinking Cleveland Street again?"

"I hadn't thought that far ahead. I say, Het, you can't come with me," he protested. "Our last lodgings were fine enough for university students accustomed to squalor, but they were no place for a girl—"

"Nonsense," she interrupted. "They will do very well. I only need a place to stay and a—a chaperone—until the Sidneys return."

He grinned. "And we all know what a model chaperone I proved last time."

Hetty huffed. "You did just fine, and no one would have been the wiser, if not for Mr.—" Abruptly she broke off. Good heavens. She must keep her wits about her and erase Mr. Pickford entirely from her memory.

She began again, tacking slightly. "Despite everything that happened, I still chafe at the thought that I need a chaperone. That only girls do. I can't travel by myself, I can't stay in London by myself—"

"Now, now, Het," Lionel soothed. "I see Rotherwood's rescue of you has not diminished your willfulness. He managed to quash the Argyll Rooms crisis, but if London catches you misbehaving again, Rotherwood can hardly engage himself to you twice."

To his surprise, Hetty's shoulders sagged, and the fire left her. "That's just it, Lionel—I must see Mr. Rotherwood. About that first engagement. And if you won't take me, I don't know what I will do."

"I'll take you, I'll take you," he said, more alarmed by Hetty's uncharacteristic wilting than by her demands. "Though I hope you don't plan to jilt him. I'll take you as soon as you can pack your trunk."

She had been absent from town two months, and it was a changed place. It had always been noisy and lively and dirty, but now as they rumbled in on the Great Western Road, past Hyde Park and along Piccadilly, she could see clusters of soldiers who had come to keep order after the riots, and there was a general air of tension, whether from the riots or Napoleon's return or both, she knew not.

Lionel bought three newspapers as soon as the weary pair got down in Fleet Street, handing one to Hetty, which she rushed to peruse. "It's more of the terrible news," she frowned, as she scanned the column. "'The extraordinary Bonaparte...has burst the bonds of his seclusion at Elba, and at the head of a hostile force, has landed at the department of La Var, in France.' So so so....oh, Lionel! It says he has 1000 men, and his former Marshal Massena goes to meet him with 27,000 men! So so so... The French funds fell 6 per cent and nothing was permitted to be said in the Paris journals. But surely they *know* in Paris! They must, for it says here King Louis has declared him a traitor."

He wasn't listening, but rather reading much the same information in another paper. It seemed everything was either the Corn Bill or Napoleon, so it was only much, much later, after they had gulped down a spartan meal in their modest lodging, when Hetty was tearing one of the papers into spills for the fire, that her eye chanced upon an advertisement:

DORSETSHIRE.
TO BE SOLD BY AUCTION

AT THE RED LION INN, IN SHAFTSBURY, IN THE COUNTY OF DORSET ON FRIDAY, THE 14TH DAY OF APRIL, 1815, AT ONE O'CLOCK IN TWELVE LOTS, THE CAPITAL AND VERY IMPROVABLE FREEHOLD MANOR OF GLENNARD, WITH THE RIGHTS, ROYALTIES, AND APPURTENANCES THERETO BELONGING; ADVANTAGEOUSLY SITUATED IN THE PARISHES OF MELBURY COMPTON, FONTMELL AND WEST ORCHARD, NEAR SHAFTSBURY, A COUNTRY ABOUNDING WITH FIELD-SPORTS, AND WITHIN AN EASY DISTANCE OF THE CHACE; COMPRISING DESIRABLE FARMS IN

DEMESNE, AND THE REVERSION IN FEE OF MANY CAPITAL ESTATES AND TENEMENTS, HELD FOR ONE, TWO, AND THREE LIVES UNDER NOMINAL RENTS.

PRINTED PARTICULARS MAY BE HAD AT THE GRECIAN COFFEE-HOUSE LONDON; AT THE PLACE OF SALE; AND AT THE PRINCIPAL TENANTS, WHO WILL SHOW THE MANORS AND ESTATES; AND FOR FURTHER PARTICULARS, APPLICATION MAY BE MADE TO MR. BLAKE, LAND SURVEYOR, AXMINSTER, WHERE PLANS OF THE MANORS MAY BE SEEN.

"Lionel." It came out as a croak.

"Mm?" He was hunched over the desk, composing a note to Edith, to be sent to the same inn in Dover his father had written to.

"Mr. Rotherwood is selling Glennard."

"What's Glennard?"

"His estate. Or, I suppose, his mother's estate, in Dorset."

"They must like London, I suppose. It might have been nice if he consulted you first."

Hetty shook her head. "That's not it, Lionel. Put your pen down and listen to me for a moment. Something is wrong. That letter he sent me—it wasn't sentiment, like I told you. He was releasing me from our engagement."

"He *what*? He can't do that!" protested her brother, thumping a fist on the desk and dotting his page with ink. "What reason did he give?"

"He didn't give a reason, but this must be it. Don't you see? We must go over to North Audley Street at once."

"It's ten o'clock, Het. We couldn't possibly. Ten to one he isn't even at home. How often were you at home at that hour? He'll be at the theatre or a ball or a play or a card party."

"Then we can leave a note," she insisted, "saying we will call again tomorrow morning. Please, Lionel! It's no use going to bed. I won't be able to sleep for wondering."

"Won't you? After that wretched inn last night, I could sleep through the world ending."

"Then sleep as we go. Come—we will get a coach in Golden Square."

Though she had urged him, Hetty felt her bravado leaking away as they neared North Audley Street. The streets were unusually quiet, apart from the soldiers patrolling particular corners where she supposed violence had taken place. She had prepared herself for the Rotherwoods being from home, but what if they were not? What if the London social scene was paused because of the Corn Bill unrest? Too late now!

When they arrived they found the house dark, but for a few lights on the first floor.

Lionel paid the fare. He looked at Hetty. She looked at him.

"Well?" he asked. "Have you lost heart?"

She squirmed, her arms wrapped around her midsection. "I have, I'm afraid. But give me a minute."

Whistling softly, he put his hands in his pockets and leaned his back against the iron railing. She thought it was "Oh, whistle, and I'll come to ye, my lad."

When he reached the bit about coming "down the back stairs" to court her, Hetty straightened and lowered her arms. "All right, then. I'm ready now."

Without answering her or ceasing to whistle, her brother spun on his heels, and in two bounds he was at the door, lifting the knocker. And then there was nothing for her to do but follow him.

CHAPTER TWENTY-NINE

We well remembered that in the revolutions of Fortune's restless wheel,...“some raised aloft come tumbling down amain.”
— The Sun (London), *11 March 1815*

A knock at the door interrupted St. John's brooding.

His head lifted, but he made no other motion. No one had knocked at their door since the news. Of course, all things social had been suspended with the disorder rocking the town, but this isolation had a different flavor. It was as if they had become a house of lepers. Or just one leper, since Mrs. Rotherwood was away in Somerset.

Away in Somerset! Ah, how the thought had pained him, the contrast between the fulfillment of his all his hopes and the dashing of them being so sudden, so stark.

When Mrs. Rotherwood returned, climbing the steps with face aglow, he met her at the door that she might know instantly. He also met her at the door because there were no servants left to open it. Even the very footman who handed her down and the coachman who drove her must be told the truth when they returned from stabling the coach and horses.

"St. John, my love, what is the matter? You look so pale. Have you been anxious? There was no need to fear, no need at all. If it might make any amends for my former coldness to her, we are fully reconciled. My darling, you were right—she is a dear girl, and she has forgiven me, and I intend to make up for lost time—to more than make up for lost time—in my kindness to her—" All the time she spoke, Anne was allowing him to assist her in removing her cloak and unwinding her wraps, and only when they were in his little library in the back of the house did she ask, "But where are all the servants? Have you given them the night off?"

"I have been forced to dismiss them, Mother."

"*Dismiss* them? What can they all have done, St. John?"

"Not them, madam," he answered heavily. "I am afraid the wrong lies with us."

"With us?"

"Yes. You see, we could no longer afford them."

It had taken a long time, a very long time, to make her understand. He was still not certain she did fully comprehend what had befallen them, and he wondered if, added to everything else, this calamity would deprive him of the only person left to him.

This was the cause of his brooding two days onward, the night the knock came. His mother was upstairs in her room, having cried herself to sleep again. And St. John sat in his library at his mahogany desk, his untouched plate pushed to the corner, staring into the embers of the fire.

Well, there was no one to answer the door but he himself, and when the knocking continued, he rose slowly, as if he had not moved in hours (he had not), to see what it was about. Perhaps the rioting had erupted anew, and a mob was headed this direction.

St. John hardly cared.

The door opened to reveal his former pupil Lionel Hapgood on the step.

"So you are at home!" the young man declared. "Don't be alarmed, Rotherwood, but you look like you haven't slept in days. Which makes me hope I didn't just wake you."

"I was awake," said St. John. His heart began to pound. Lionel Hapgood was quite possibly the last person in the world he expected to find there, and yet, instead of feeling curiosity, St. John only cared to look past him to see if—

She was with him.

For a long moment, he and his erstwhile pseudo-intended stared at each other. She had been his genuine intended for the space of a day, he supposed, before his note released her. Why on earth had he released her?

Because it would not be right to hold her.

But what did it mean, that she was here? Against his will—against his better judgment—hope rose in his breast, and he tried his best to tamp it down.

"What—are you doing here?" St. John managed.

"May we come in?" asked Lionel cheerfully. "We'd rather not be shouting in the streets. It sounds like there's been enough of that to go around." Without waiting for an answer, he nudged St. John back into the entry and then turned to reach for his sister's hand. "Come on, you. It's like the two of you have turned to statues."

Without the light from the street, the passage was dark and cold.

"Better keep your cloak on for now, Het," advised Lionel. "I say, Rotherwood, we saw some light, or we wouldn't have knocked. You have got a fire lit somewhere, haven't you?"

Wordlessly, St. John led them to the library where he had been sitting.

"Are you out of firewood or out of servants?" Lionel mocked. "Here, let me fix this." Kneeling down, he began poking the embers and inspecting the logs in the scrolled iron rack for the most promising.

St. John turned then, having gathered himself sufficiently, to regard Miss Hapgood. She too withdrew her gaze from her brother and faced him. He saw, with a little pain to his heart, that she had grown thinner and lost color. Her eyes looked enormous in the low light.

"Miss Hapgood. Won't you sit down?" The library held only the chair before his desk and a small sofa, on which papers and books were piled. He made to shift the stacks off the side nearest the fire, and they cascaded onto the rug. She said nothing, only stepping over the litter to seat herself in the small space he cleared. Her cloak billowed about her, and she smoothed it down.

He was staring, he knew, and he gave himself a shake. "What—brings you here?"

Hetty fumbled with her reticule. She had thought of nothing but what she would say to him, the entire journey to London, and now every word, every speech was flown. With trembling fingers, she drew out the letter he had written her and held it out to him. "I—I have come to ask the meaning of this," she said hoarsely.

"Miss Hapgood—"

"I would be the last person to thrust myself on anyone, as I hope you know," she went on, in the same quiet voice, gathering courage, "but I do not think it too much to ask for an explanation. *Any* explanation."

"Miss Hapgood—"

He glanced Lionel's direction and then plucked the chair from before his desk to set it opposite the sofa, that he might not loom over Miss Hapgood like a crumbling cliff.

Feeling the glance, Lionel stood up, brushing off his hands and taking up the wood basket. "I'll just refill this," he announced, to no one in particular.

Hetty didn't even look her brother's direction when he left the room. "Sir, I received this note the same day your mother departed Somerset. Which was, as it happened, the very day after she came and told me she had relented and was pleased to bless our marriage after all."

"Yes."

"Therefore I cannot suppose that she changed her mind. She would not have had the time to communicate it to you."

"No. She did not change her mind."

"Have you then changed *your* mind, Mr. Rotherwood?" she pressed, her voice unsteady, to her vexation.

What could he answer to that? As she sat there, more beautiful than ever to his eyes after so long an absence, the firelight playing on her bright hair and reflected in her clear gaze. His lips parted, but no ready reply came to them.

Her gaze faltered. "Do—do you wish to be released because you have come to prefer someone else?"

"No!" That was simple enough to address. "*No.*"

A faint smile passed over her face. "I am—relieved to hear it. Though we agreed that, if either one of us did come to prefer another, the other might be freed without hindrance. Still, I thought it...unlikely."

And then, because he could not help himself—it would be the last time he indulged himself, he swore— "I love only you, Miss Hapgood."

Her smile became genuine, and she raised her eyes to his again. To his delight—though a guilty pang followed hard upon the delight—there was a playful light in them. "How glad I am to hear it, sir. But then, it seems, we have a problem. Because what reason will you give me, then, for 'releasing me' from our engagement? If I recall, Mr. Rotherwood, fondness for someone else was the only loop-hole we specified."

If she continued to look at him like that, his self-control might fail him. As it did the last time he saw her.

Feeling his breathing grow rough, he rose abruptly and strode away from her, gazing blindly at his bookshelves, where his old textbooks ranged in a neat row. With his fingertip he brushed the spine of Wingate's *Arithmetic.* "The reason I must give you, Miss Hapgood, goes deeper than—than an infatuation with somebody new. It is, in fact, a point of honor that I let you go."

But she had seen the flame in his eyes. Rising herself, she removed her cloak and crossed the room to him. She hesitated. Considered. And then laid a tentative hand on his sleeve.

"Mr. Rotherwood," she murmured, "I hate to contradict you, but I do believe only a lady may break an engagement. Whatever 'point of honor' you claim in jilting me, I'm afraid it must yield to that ironclad law."

He was staring at her hand, at the tapered fingertips whose touch was just perceptible through the layers of his frock coat and shirt. Spellbound, almost without volition, his own hand rose to cover hers. "Hetty—my own—"

"St. John—"

And then she was in his arms again, as if two months had never passed. He was saying her name over and over until his mouth found hers, and she had that squeezed-breathless sensation once more as they clutched each other, the buttons of his waistcoat digging into her bodice. It seemed to Hetty that they could never be close enough, and she was pressing against him as hard as she could, only he was doing the same and was considerably stronger. In their urgency they knocked into the bookcase, toppling several volumes, and an empty inkpot on the top shelf tipped over and rolled off, hitting St. John squarely on the crown of his head.

It had its salutary effect.

He uttered a groan and, with a prodigious effort, wrenched himself away from her, holding her at arm's length. "I am sorry for that. I—I—I apologize for that."

She looked forlorn, and retreated a step, pulling free from his grasp to lean against the desk for support. "Please don't be sorry. I'm not. Only—I wish you would tell me what has happened, St. John. Please. Tell me."

He took a long breath, waiting for his heart to slow. His hands drew in fists. "I will."

But first he needed to put some space between them, or he would never be able to maintain his resolve. Lord—he was as bad as Pickford.

Circling to the opposite side of the desk, he placed his hands flat upon its surface.

"It is this. When my mother was gone into Somerset—directly after she left, our agent Mr. Pinckney called. He came to say—to confess—that he had...speculated with our funds."

Hetty inhaled sharply, her mind leaping ahead. It was no more than she had thought when she saw the auction advertisement.

"He claimed he had never done such a thing in his professional life before," St. John went on, "but that he—fell in love with my mother and wanted to be worthy of addressing her. He thought if he came and told her he had not only stewarded her money well, but had even succeeded in *doubling* it, she might recognize him as more than a mere solicitor." St. John gave a rueful grimace. "But his speculation failed. On a monumental scale. You see, Pinckney invested in a Parisian bank. With the peace and the rebuilding, he thought he had a sure card. What could go wrong? But then he received word the bank director had vanished, having embezzled millions and leaving only trumped-up balance sheets behind. And then, when the news came from France, Pinckney understood where it all went: the director had been secretly financing Napoleon's return, as well as the army that grows daily around him."

Hetty was shaking her head in horror, a hand to her mouth.

"That is not all. When at least two other families were lured to invest where the Rotherwoods' agent invested…well—we were all of us—"

"Ruined," breathed Hetty.

"Ruined," he agreed. "So you see, I am not only penniless now, I am more than penniless. For I feel a moral obligation to make what reparations I can to those two other unfortunate families."

She nodded. Yes. She knew. She understood. It was that noble side of him again. For which she loved him.

"I saw the advertisement in the newspaper," she said, "for the sale of Glennard."

His head came up swiftly. "Yes. The Rotherwood fortune is no more, but I hope, with the sale of the estate, we might recover some of the money lost by the other families."

"Oh, St. John."

"And that, my dear Miss Hapgood, is the reason I released you."

"Because of your pennilessness."

"Because of my pennilessness."

She hoisted herself to sit on the corner of the desk at this juncture, swinging her legs and thinking hard. Her marble ex-millionaire was a sensitive man underneath his stone façade, and she must be careful in the application of her chisel.

"I am sorry for you," Hetty began carelessly. "Did you very much like being a man of fashion? Having handsome clothing and a dozen servants and an estate in Dorset and everyone in love with you?"

In spite of himself, he felt himself begin to smile. "I did, if it made *you* in love with me."

Hetty made a wry face at him. "I ought to disavow such a sentiment, sir, if you think I loved you for those reasons. Or those reasons alone, perhaps I should say, for it would be unreasonable in you to think they had absolutely no effect on me. But supposing I did love you, or that I might love you still and in spite of all—you cannot expect me to admit it, when you have just jilted me. Or tried to jilt me, I should say."

"Have I not succeeded, then?" He could not help it—his voice lifted a little. She made him hope.

"Oh, you haven't succeeded at all," she said roundly. "How many times must I repeat myself? Gentlemen don't have the power to break an engagement. Young ladies haven't many powers in this world, as I have discovered in the last few months; therefore you cannot be surprised if I insist on clinging to the few given to me. Such as the power to accept or refuse an offer of marriage and the power to end—or refuse to end—an existing engagement. In fact,

Mr. Rotherwood, I do believe if you insist on jilting me in earnest, I will be forced to sue you for breach of promise."

He was grinning now. "But I'm more than penniless."

"Yes, there's that. I suppose I would have to loan you the money to pay the damages, and you would then have to repay that loan over many, many years. But I would give you good terms."

He didn't know if he wanted to cry or kiss her, so he kissed her. Gently, above her ear. "Are you saying you still want to marry me?"

"Mm." Turning her head, she gave him a kiss of her own. "I am, if *you* still want to marry me."

"I can't think of anything in all the world I want more," was his simple reply. "I didn't care a straw for the fortune—or not as big a straw as one might expect. But it cost me dearly to relinquish you. I wrote that note to you in my heart's blood."

"Oh, St. John." Reaching for his hand, she kissed the back of it and hugged it to her.

"But Harriet—Hetty—could you bear to be a poor man's wife? I might find employment at a school, or in a household as a tutor."

"Mm," she said again dreamily. "You might. But St. John, you are in orders, are you not? What would you say to being a curate?"

He straightened. "What do you mean? Where?"

Taking both his hands, the words rushed from her now. "When everyone at home got sick, not everyone got better. Poor Mr. Thomas, the old curate over at Bramleigh, died. And according to the squire, my father's cousin, the rector Mr. Fotheringay is miserable because now he must come down from town and give the sermon on Sundays, and he really would rather not be bothered.

He was quite stingy in what he paid Mr. Thomas, and Mr. Hapgood—the squire—says Mr. Fotheringay will surely have to pay a little more, if he hopes to attract anyone to the post. Why shouldn't you have it, St. John? There is a charming little rectory—it would need some work, I'm afraid, before it was quite livable—I do believe old Mr. Thomas shut up half of it while he lived there. But if it were fixed up, there would be room for some pupils to board there, as Lionel did with Mr. Benfield in Patterton. And *eventually* Mr. Fotheringay would die, and then the squire could give you the living altogether! Isn't it a marvelous plan? Providential, I would say. But only if you think you could bear the country and giving a sermon on Sundays and living in the bosom of my family."

And then St. John really did feel like crying. "I—would love to have a family, in whose bosom I might live." He shook his head in incredulity. "Can this be true? I think your plan truly is a marvel. Such a marvel that I hesitate to trust in it."

She raised a hand as if she were in court. "I swear it, St. John. Everything I tell you is the truth."

"But—hadn't I better see this Mr. Fotheringay and the squire first?" he asked. "Even if it is all true, the curacy is certainly not yours to give."

"No," she conceded. "It is not. But St. John, even if Mr. Fotheringay takes a dislike to you, for whatever reason, mightn't we still marry? You could surely get a curacy *somewhere* or a job teaching *somewhere*—any position with a place to live would do—and we might live off my portion until Mr. Fotheringay dies. The Bramleigh living would be yours then, I am certain, because it would be in the squire's power to bestow."

He grinned at her. "My dear Miss Hapgood, are you proposing to me?"

"I am making a proposal, at least, and all my family will tell you that my proposals are generally good. But I do hope Mr. Fotheringay likes you, because the rectory would easily accommodate Mrs. Rotherwood as well. And I have an additional confession, St. John: when I joined the Sidneys in London for the season, my father deliberately told them my portion would be smaller than it actually is, in order to make them feel better."

"Careful, my love, or I will marry you for your money."

"My dearest St. John, I wish you would."

When Lionel Hapgood cracked the library door some time later, he saw his former tutor and his sister had come to an amicable agreement, to judge by how they sprung apart with embarrassed smiles, their fingers still intertwined and Hetty's hair hanging all about her shoulders.

"What will it be, Rotherwood?" Lionel demanded. "Am I to congratulate you or call you out?"

In answer, St. John crossed the room in two strides, taking Lionel's hand and giving it a wringing shake. "Watch yourself, Hapgood. You are speaking not only to your older brother but possibly also to your future spiritual father."

"Oh, Lord," laughed Lionel. "What has Hetty done now?"

Epilogue

But this is not the only wedding we are to have—
Mistriss is resolved to have the same frolick,
in the naam of God!"
— Tobias Smollett, *The Expedition of Humphrey
Clinker* (1771)

The Bramleigh church bells were ringing again. They had rung out the day before to mark the victory at Waterloo, and this morning they pealed merrily for an event scarcely less anticipated in this corner of Somerset.

The bride and groom emerged from the dank, ancient church to cheers and flying grains of wheat, and one small boy turned to his father, tugging on his hand to ask, "Why do we throw things at them, Papa? You will never let me throw things at my sister Gussie."

"When your sister Augusta marries," answered his handsome golden-haired father, picking him up, "you may pelt her with all the corn you please, Freddie, and she'll like it."

Little Frederick puzzled at this, but then decided his Aunt Edith did not seem to mind the wheat, though she ducked her head, laughing and holding up her veil in defense.

To a young boy's eyes, seeing the entire Hapgood clan gathered for the first time, it seemed a great many people. Far more than his Tierney relations. There was his grandfather the squire, bluff and red-faced and loud and happy, standing beside Grandmother's chair as she fluttered a handkerchief and asked to be wheeled further back into the shade. There was Mama, the most beautiful of anyone present, Freddie thought, and Papa, and little sister Augusta, who was just old enough to be troublesome to him. Beside his parents were his aunt and uncle Tierney, Aunt Alice pointing out a passing butterfly to Freddie's baby cousin Charlotte. And across the way were Freddie's aunt Margaret and uncle Dashiell. His uncle Waite had fought in the war and knew the great hero Wellington, which, along with Uncle Dashiell's gold-headed cane, invested him with a dashing glow in Freddie's eyes.

His youngest aunt Edith made a beautiful bride, with her black hair and smiling eyes. She made pictures, and his mama said she had once painted her cousin and new husband Lionel, and it had hung in a gallery in London. Freddie would have liked to see it because he liked his new uncle and distant cousin who, even in the midst of all the wedding preparations, had shown Freddie how to bowl on the Bramleigh lawn the day before. But even more impressive in Freddie's opinion was the fact that Aunt Edith had fled the Continent, pursued by Napoleon, or something like that.

"Don't forget to pay the clergyman, Lionel," teased a young lady with bright red-gold hair. She looped her arm through the curate's and everybody laughed.

"Who is that one again, Papa?" Freddie asked.

"'That one' is also your mama's cousin. Miss Harriet Hapgood. Sister to the groom. She is going to marry Mr. Rotherwood the curate, as soon as his house is ready, and they will be poor little happy church mice together."

Freddie did not see what church had to do with mice, but he said, "Papa, I like the look of that church man."

Frederick glanced at his son. "Do you? Well, when you're older, you may come to live in Somerset and study with the parson. Should you like that?"

In answer, Freddie only shook his head, pushing off his father to reach for his mother.

"A wise choice," grinned Frederick, giving his wife a decorous pinch that made her squeak.

The wedding breakfast was a grand affair that taxed the utmost efforts of Bramleigh's cook Button, the catering services of the Swan, and the planning skills of Mrs. Hugh Hapgood. Three long tables were placed in a u-shape on the lawn, with the happy couple in the center and their many friends and relations seated to either side. Hapgoods, Sidneys, Arbuthnots, Rotherwoods, and schoolmates toasted Lionel and Edith, Clunker read the epithalamium he had composed, and slices of wedding cake followed the meat and eggs, bread and butter, chocolate and wine.

"I hope you'll give Mr. Elwood an answer soon," Lavinia Sidney leaned to say to her daughter Caroline, but Caroline only giggled, glancing again at James Clinkett. "Oh, perhaps. But I'm having far too much fun. If he grows tired of waiting, he can always have Lady Sylvia."

Across the table, Rosemary Hapgood patted the hand of Anne Rotherwood. "Soon this will be your St. John and our Hetty."

Anne's gaze swept the gathering, and when she looked at Rosemary, her eyes were full. "When I think of how little we had a year ago, and how little I thought we would have again, I never supposed our life would hold such riches."

And St. John and Hetty themselves?

The company was admiring the bride's favors Edith had made: miniatures of some of the works of art she had seen in her recent travels. To St. John she gave a tiny *Mona Lisa* with mathematical golden rectangles traced on its surface, and Hetty was not the least bit surprised when she unwrapped her favor and found a diminutive Bernini's *David*. She kissed it and Edith, too.

"You think this looks like me?" St. John murmured, examining it in bemusement.

"More than ever," returned Hetty. "Only see his noble brow, so like your own! And his marble perfection. You again. He is nothing daunted by the giant he faces or the challenges of life."

"Because he has all he needs. His secret weapon. With it, what worlds can he not conquer?"

"You mean his sling and the five smooth stones?"

"In his case, yes. But in my own—" he gave her a mischievous smile "—my secret weapon will be my bride, armed with her wits and her beauty."

"Ah!" Blushing, she squeezed his hand.

"And her money," he added. "Let's not forget that. That's worth two stones, at least."

"You!"

"Then there's the living she has as good as promised me..."

Laughing, Hetty pelted him with some of the wheat sprinkled over the tablecloth. "You had better watch yourself! I haven't married you yet, and there's many a slip, 'twixt cup and lip."

But when the renovation of the rectory was completed that autumn, poor put-upon Mr. Fotheringay was obliged to leave his house in town once more and come down to Somerset, where, before much the same gathering, he joined Mr. St. John Gordon Holt Rotherwood to Miss Harriet Morrow Hapgood in holy, and wholly-happy, matrimony.

As we bid good-bye to the Hapgoods, come meet my next family! How will poor Florence Ellsworth be able to prevent her father making another disastrous marriage? Perhaps the handsome new family lawyer might be of service…

THE HAPGOODS OF BRAMLEIGH

The Naturalist
A Very Plain Young Man
School for Love
Matchless Margaret
The Purloined Portrait
A Fickle Fortune

THE ELLSWORTH ASSORTMENT

Tempted by Folly
The Belle of Winchester
Minta in Spite of Herself
A Scholarly Pursuit
Miranda at Heart
A Capital Arrangement

PRIDE AND PRESTON LIN

www.christinadudley.com